RANDOM HOUSE
LARGE PRINT

ALSO BY ALEX BERENSON
AVAILABLE FROM RANDOM HOUSE LARGE PRINT

The Prisoner

THE
DECEIVERS

A JOHN WELLS NOVEL

ALEX BERENSON

RANDOM HOUSE
LARGE PRINT

Published in the United States of America by Random House Large Print in association with Putnam, an imprint of Penguin Random House LLC, New York.

Cover design by Eric Fuentecilla; Cover art: Washington D.C. © Petrovic Igor / Shutterstock; Kremlin © Awl Images Ltd / Shutterstock

The Library of Congress has established a Cataloging-in-Publication record for this title.

ISBN: 978-0-5255-8929-7

www.penguinrandomhouse.com/large-print-format-books

FIRST LARGE PRINT EDITION

Printed in the United States of America

10 9 8 7 6 5 4 3 2 1

This Large Print edition published in accord with the standards of the N.A.V.H.

FOR NEIL NYREN, THE BOSS

For the worst of all deceptions is self-deception.
—Socrates, as quoted in Plato's **Cratylus**

THE DECEIVERS

PROLOGUE

DALLAS, TEXAS

Ahmed Shakir should have gone with his gut. He'd met the guy at the Dirt Hole in East Dallas. Despite its name, the place was a decent enough bar. It had thirty-cent wings at happy hour, a pool table that needed new felt.

And a bartender named Dale. For two hundred bucks a month, Dale looked the other way when Shakir sold coke out of the bathroom. Shakir wasn't Pablo Escobar, but he dealt more than casually. Fifteen regular buyers, thirty or so occasionals. Enough to keep him busy.

Shakir's customers were nice white people. They called him Adam. They didn't seem to mind that he'd been born in Cairo. He had mastered the secrets to success for drug dealers. He didn't use his own product, didn't sell on credit, didn't get greedy. He was small, with wiry black hair and dark eyes. A forgettable face, which suited him fine.

But everything went sideways after that Thursday night, cool for Dallas in the fall. The Bengals and Falcons played on the flat-screen behind the long wooden bar. Katy Perry sang about teenage dreams on the satellite radio. Shakir was in his usual spot, the booth by the bathrooms. Dale nodded him over.

"Somebody wants to say hi."

The guy sat alone on a stool in front of the taps. He wore cowboy boots and a black sweater with sleeves pulled up to reveal a steel watch. Shakir hadn't seen him before. The Dirt Hole attracted cable technicians, UPS supervisors. This guy was fancier.

He caught Shakir looking, tipped his Heineken.

Up close the guy's skin was pockmarked. The watch was a Rolex. "I'm Jake." His fingers twirled on the bar. Antsy hands. Cocaine hands.

"Adam."

"That so?" The guy gave Shakir a sly sideways look that stuck in Shakir's throat. "Bartender says you're the man with the plan."

Shakir didn't recognize his accent. It wasn't Texas. "I don't know you."

"My guy's not answering. A girl I know said she hooked up here—"

"Name?"

"Katrina. Tall. Pretty. Short blond hair."

And cold blue eyes. Shakir remembered her. She'd come to the Dirt Hole with a squinty little guy named Jimmy who owned a steak house. Katrina was taller than Jimmy and in a different time zone looks-wise. Shakir saw plenty of those pairs. You couldn't be a coke whore if you didn't like cocaine. Hearing Jake mention her made Shakir feel better. She was no narc. She'd practically marched Jimmy to the bathroom to start the party.

"Says your stuff is primo. She would know."

Word of mouth, the best marketing. "What are you looking for?"

Jake nodded at the pool table. An eight-ball, then. An eighth of an ounce of cocaine, or three and a half grams. Also known as a party ball. Enough for a few friends to have a late night or one dedicated user to go on a bloody-nose rockstar bender. Shakir charged his regulars two hundred dollars for an eight-ball and everyone else two-fifty. A lot of coke to want on a first buy, enough to make Shakir nervous.

Though Jake's Rolex suggested money wasn't a problem.

"You drive here?"

"Flew on my broom."

"Keys." Shakir held out his hand. Jake seemed to understand that if he wanted his Bolivian marching powder, he would need to play nice. He handed Shakir an Audi key fob.

"Drive carefully. That's my baby."

Shakir found the A4 at the end of the parking lot, its midnight blue paint glowing under the lights. Standard black-and-white Texas plates. Shakir walked around it, seeing nothing unusual, nothing that suggested the car belonged to the cops or the Drug Enforcement Administration. The lot was mostly empty tonight. No weird dry-cleaning company vans or guys in trucker caps keeping a too-casual eye on him. Not that he rated that kind of attention.

Shakir slipped on gloves, slid inside. The A4 was so new that the leather still smelled fresh. Whoever he was, Jake kept his car immaculate. No candy wrappers or fast-food bags. The glove box held only the slim owner's manual, no registration or insurance. Or pistol.

Shakir drove southwest toward Deep Ellum, slowed for a yellow light. As it turned red, he gunned the engine and swung left. A few turns later, he was on Highway 75. Then east on I-30 among the big rigs. Nice car. He was no expert, but as far as he could tell, no one was on him.

He was going to a lot of trouble to sell one eight-ball. But Shakir didn't know what to make of this guy. Jake was too slick for his taste. Yet Shakir also sensed he might turn into a good customer, a fish who wouldn't care about price. Shakir hadn't had one of those in a year, since he'd lost a cardiologist at Presbyterian to rehab.

Shakir drove another five miles east before doubling back to the Dirt Hole. He parked the Audi where he'd found it, tucked a plastic bag holding three and a half grams of cocaine under the driver's seat, stepped out.

—————

Jake stood outside the front door, arms folded over his chest. "I was about to call the cops." Shakir stepped past. Inside, they settled into Shakir's booth. The Mavs game was winding down, the Mavs up twenty on the ridiculous Brooklyn Nets.

"See why you like that car. How do you pay for it?"

"I'm a lawyer."

"Have a card?"

"You're not the only one taking a chance. I

don't care if your stuff is straight from the jungle, gimme my keys—"

Shakir slid them over. "Before you go, bet you the Mavs win."

"Now you're a bookie?"

"Two-fifty. I got the Mavs. You got the Nets."

Jake looked at the screen. Understanding dawned, and he extended a hand. "Two-fifty, sure."

Thirty seconds later, the game ended. Jake slid five fifty-dollar bills to Shakir. "Last time I bet basketball. So? We just do it here?"

Shakir kept a straight face. "Go home."

"My money—"

"Make sure you adjust your seat."

Jake's head swiveled to the door. "If I have to come back—" he said, and trotted out.

In three minutes, Jake **did** come back, and Shakir felt a flutter of anxiety. He had protected himself from a typical buy-and-bust. His fingerprints weren't on the bag or the Audi. The bet gave him at least a little cover for Jake's money. But if they were after him, if they'd wired the car . . . Why, though? Shakir couldn't see anyone going to that much trouble for a three-gram bust. Not when South Dallas was an open-air drug market.

"My man," Jake muttered in his ear. "Katrina was right. I mean, that is tippy-toppy. You feel me?"

Shakir wondered why cocaine made lawyers talk like rappers.

"Gimme your number."

Shakir wasn't ready to be on intimate terms with this guy. "I'm here Thursdays and Sundays."

———

On Sunday, Jake picked up another eight-ball. The next week, too. But he didn't show up the week after that. Too bad. Guys who dropped five hundred a week weren't easy to come by.

Then Jake was back. A Thursday, early, barely 9 p.m. Wearing a white shirt lined with sequins. Yeah, sequins. Two women with him, blond and brunette, stuffed into dresses that barely covered their asses. "My man. Meet Amber and Lacey." He was slurring a bit.

"**Riley**," the blonde said. "Not Lacey." She smiled like she didn't care.

Jake pulled out a money clip thick with hundreds and tossed one out. Actually tossed it. They all watched it flutter down. "Ladies, have a drink." He wrapped an arm around Shakir's shoulder. "You, walk with me."

Outside, sirens blared to the west. Shakir tried to shrug off the crawling sense they were meant for him.

"Need a little more tonight. Two ounces." The words fast and low.

Two ounces would last even the most serious cokehead for weeks, and the party might end with a heart attack. Shakir was also well aware that under Texas law, selling fewer than four grams of cocaine was a third-degree felony. More moved the crime to second-degree.

An eight-ball fell conveniently just under the four-gram line. Two ounces—fifty-six grams—did not. In four years of dealing, Shakir had sold that much only once before, to the cardiologist. The guy said he was going on vacation for five weeks. **Hate to run out in the middle of the Grand Canyon.** He rubbed his runny nose. By then, Shakir knew the doc was headed for rehab. Or worse. Problem with coke, your best customers eventually went south.

"Who's it for?"

"These girls **party**. And their friends. Figured I'd pick up what I needed for the weekend all at once. Maybe a volume discount, know what I'm saying?"

"No."

"Help a brother out. Party with us, if you want—"

"Forget it."

"An ounce? Don't make me beg, Adam."

Suddenly Shakir changed his mind. An ounce or two ounces made no difference; either way, he was deep in second-degree felony territory. He either cut Jake loose or took his money. And he wasn't ready to cut Jake loose. "Two ounces. Fine. But no discount. Four thousand flat." The price of sixteen eight-balls. He'd cut it more than usual, too. Make two grand—plus for a few minutes' work.

"Should be like twenty-two, twenty-four hundred."

"Call your old dealer, then."

"Thirty-five. But it's gotta be now. Like, right now."

By the dumpster behind the bar, Jake counted thirty-five hundred-dollar bills from his clip.

"Give me your keys. I'll be back." Shakir wasn't sure why he was still pushing Jake's buttons, except that he didn't like the guy.

"Take your own car. Don't be a peasant."

Peasant. An odd word. At the end—the **very** end—Shakir would remember it. But at the time, in the lot, with the bar garbage perfuming the night air, it merely annoyed him. "Keys or no deal."

—————

Shakir lived with a purebred Persian cat whom he'd cheekily named Base—as in **freebase**—in a one-story ranch in East Dallas. He paid the mortgage every month with money orders. He kept his scales in the kitchen—nothing illegal about scales—and his stash in a wall safe. Now Base whined for milk as Shakir weighed out forty-nine grams of cocaine and seven grams of mannitol. A seven-eighths cut was plenty fair. He covered his mouth with a surgical mask, blended the powders, poured the whitish mix into a plastic sandwich bag.

His pulse thumped as he tucked the baggie into the Audi's glove compartment. He was taking a risk for no good reason. Maybe he was tired of selling cocaine by the gram to sniffling electricians. Tired of living small.

He didn't even get back to the bar. Three blocks out, a big black SUV loomed behind him and flicked on the red-and-blues in its grille. He thought about putting pedal to floor. Then a second SUV appeared beside the first. Chevy Tahoes, brand-new and mean-looking. Everything about this operation was expensive and new. Shakir wondered why he rated the attention.

He pulled over, lowered the windows. He curled his fingers around the steering wheel like he was already chained to it. The traffic rolled by, drivers gawking. Normals, living boring normal lives. Could he make a deal, talk himself back into their world? But the thought of wearing a wire on his next buy from the Downside D Homeboys, his suppliers, scared him more than prison.

The second Tahoe parked in front, bumper-to-bumper, boxing in the Audi. Two men stepped out of the one behind. They wore black T-shirts and jeans and pistols snug on their hips. Their badges swung on neck chains. Shakir wondered if they were local. No, probably DEA. From what he'd seen, the Dallas cops liked to show off during their arrests. They never used a patrol car when a SWAT team would do. These guys seemed relaxed.

The narc on the driver's side strutted up. He was white, with a brush cut, and the same bad skin as Jake. They could have been brothers.

"Mr. Shakir. I'm Agent Emery Reed of the Federal Bureau of Investigation." He even sounded like Jake, the accent unrecognizable to Shakir but not Texan. He flipped open his wallet to show Shakir his identification.

FBI? Not DEA?

"I know this is not your car. You can tell me where the stuff is. Or we can get a dog, impound it, add grand theft auto to the narcotics charges."

Shakir sensed this wasn't the moment to stand on his constitutional rights. "Glove compartment."

The other agent, a mountain of a man, reached inside with a gloved hand, came out with the baggie.

"Next question. Any firearms?"

Shakir shook his head.

"Good. Let's take a ride."

"Am I under arrest?"

The agent pulled a phone from his pocket, tilted the screen: a long-lens shot of Jake handing Shakir money, the dumpster completing the perfect ugliness of the image. "If you don't come, you will be."

===

They frisked him and put him in the back of their Tahoe behind a thick wire screen, but they didn't cuff him. He assumed they'd take him to the main Dallas FBI offices, west of downtown. Instead, the Tahoe went south. The streets turned mostly poor and black, brightly lit chicken joints and car lots, their NO MONEY DOWN pennants limp in the night air, flags for a losing team. The driver seemed to know exactly where he was going, no GPS necessary.

After fifteen minutes the SUV turned into a corrugated steel garage. Inside, the agents led Shakir into a windowless room, empty except for steel chairs and a table, surveillance cameras high in the corners. Reed put Shakir's wallet and keys and phone and the hundred-dollar bills in a plastic bag. The second agent took it and disappeared.

"Ahmed Shakir," Reed said. "You may not believe it, but this is your lucky day. Probably wondering why we picked you up, not the DEA. Why you're here and not at our office. Thinking we want to flip you."

Shakir held his tongue. He was in enough trouble already.

"We couldn't care less about the cocaine. As far as we're concerned, the war on drugs . . . Well, drugs won. We don't even work out of Dallas. We're based in Houston and we're in CT. **Counterterror.** We're interested in your cousin. Second cousin, to be precise."

Now Shakir understood. "Gamal."

"The one and only Gamal el-Masry."

Shakir and el-Masry had come to the United States as kids in the nineties, before September 11, when middle-class Arabs still had a shot at getting American visas. Their families wound up in Dallas. The North Texas heat agreed with Cairenes. As children, they'd been close, the eldest sons of ill-tempered fathers. They'd compared bruises more than once.

But they'd grown apart. While Shakir dealt eight-balls, el-Masry drove for Uber. He had a wife, who never left home without a headscarf, and three little girls. He was a regular at the Masjid al-Sunni, a mosque in Cedar Crest. Its Saudi-trained imam preached that Allah wouldn't be satisfied until the world lived under the laws of the Quran. El-Masry asked Shakir to pray with him every so often. Shakir found excuses to turn him down. Given his profession, he preferred to stay off Allah's radar. He did fast for Ramadan every year, mainly to prove he could.

Despite their differences, Shakir saw el-Masry and his family a few times a year. They were Facebook friends, too. El-Masry often posted news stories about American bombs that killed civilians in Syria. ALLAH WILLING, THE KAFFIRS WILL PAY FOR THIS!!!

The second agent returned, holding a manila folder.

"When was the last time you saw Gamal?" Reed said.

"Maybe two months."

"You know how he feels about the United States?"

"I've seen his Facebook page."

"What about terrorism? Has he talked about committing an attack himself? Think carefully, now."

"No." But the possibility shocked Shakir less

than he would have expected. El-Masry had a temper. Shakir had once seen his wife with a black eye. **I fell**, she said. **Clumsy.**

"Seen his Twitter feed? That's the nasty one."

"I've never even been on Twitter."

"Good for you." Reed smirked. Shakir already knew he would grow to hate that smirk.

The second agent slid photographs from the folder to Shakir. A pair of handsome Egyptian men, tall and skinny. "I've seen them at Gamal's. Brothers, right?"

"Rashid and Nassir Fardous. We're very concerned about your cousin and his friends. They've reached out online to dangerous people. Raised money for Islamic charities tied to terrorist groups. That mosque—at least one guy from there wound up in Syria."

Reed stared at Shakir until Shakir couldn't stand the silence. The silence and Reed's pockmarked face. Shakir had always thought FBI agents were supposed to be pretty. "Has Gamal done anything? Besides the online stuff."

Reed's smile revealed a mouthful of capped teeth. "Not yet. That's about to change."

Slowly his meaning sunk in.

"You want me to entrap my cousin."

"Just help him do what he wants. Now I'm gonna talk, and you're gonna listen. Save your questions." For the next half hour, Reed outlined the FBI's plan.

You go to Gamal, tell him you've seen the light. Guys beat you up in a Walmart parking lot, called you a dirty Arab, broke a couple ribs. You are seriously pissed . . . Or you had a dream that convinced you to change your ways so you don't spend eternity in the fire. The Prophet was big on dreams, right? Either way, you're ready to roll. You know he is, too . . . And, lucky you, the business you're in, you know people who know people. Your buddies will be happy to hook you up. AKs, Kevlar vests, so you guys can last a while once the cops show up . . .

You and Gamal and Rashid and Nassir pick a target, nice and juicy, New Year's Eve down-town, whatever he likes, and you practice, you scout it . . . We'll wire you, nothing cheap, nothing he's gonna catch, and we'll even set you up at an old gun range we bought east of town, it's wired, too . . . We don't need a ton of tape, just enough that it's clear that everyone was more than willing . . . You make suicide videos, go right to the edge, like it's really gonna hap-pen . . . We're watching all along, just in time we show up and make the bust . . .

Presto! Ahmed Shakir, American hero. They'll

make a movie about you, my friend. The Muslim Who Came in From the Hot. **Now, questions?**

"I'm setting up my own cousin?"

"So he doesn't kill innocent people."

"That's not Gamal."

"Then he's got nothing to worry about."

"He won't believe I'm into this."

"He will. Same reason you trusted Jake, even though you never even saw him do a line, did you?"

Reed was right. What a fool Shakir had been. "It's entrapment."

"It's not. Leave the law to the lawyers. Why we take it to the end, prove everyone was ready to go. Nobody gets entrapped into driving around with AKs and boxes of ammunition."

"I still don't get why it has to go that far. Unless—" And then Shakir understood what Reed wasn't telling him. "You want to make a show of it. How close it was. Show all those people watching on CNN what a good job the FBI did."

"I'd advise you to stay focused on your own role in this, Ahmed."

"Will I have to testify?"

"No way around it. But here's the best part. This little incident tonight, it goes away. I mean, a hundred percent. No charges, no plea bargain, it never happened."

Shakir saw why the agents hadn't officially arrested him or taken him into custody. "You want me clean. So the defense can't cross-examine me, ask me what I'm getting out of this."

"You're a concerned citizen who came to us when you saw your cousin's Facebook posts. We took it from there. But you will have to stop dealing while we put this together. Can't have the Dallas cops stumbling onto you. Your buyers know where you live?"

Shakir shook his head. He didn't want desperate cokeheads showing up on his door.

"Then just stop answering your phone. They'll get the hint." Reed paused. "And you have a girlfriend, right? Jeanelle."

A question that made Shakir wonder how long they'd been watching him. He hadn't seen Jeanelle in two weeks. "Not my girlfriend, but, yes."

"Get rid of her. Can't risk her either."

"How do I pay my bills?"

"We'll give you three thousand a month. Cash. You can even keep the money from tonight."

"And at the end it goes away."

"It goes away."

"What happens if you're wrong? Gamal won't play?"

"If it comes to that, we'll talk, but we're not wrong."

"Can I talk to a lawyer?"

"Talk to whoever you like, but this is a take-it-or-leave-it offer. One time only. Tonight."

"If I say no?"

"You're gonna make me say it, Ahmed." Suddenly Reed seemed tired. He rubbed his knuckles across his pockmarked cheeks. "Two ounces isn't the crime of the century, but you have the bad luck to be in Texas. Which doesn't like cocaine. And you made it so easy. Didn't even hide the cash. We have pictures, marked bills, a bag in the car with your prints. We'll hand it to the DPD narc detectives. One call, you're right in the middle of that two-to-ten band. Realistically, four or five years. We want to be nasty, we'll make sure they hit your house, too. Don't know how big a stash you have back there, but I'll bet it takes you closer to eight. No gang looking out for you, that's eight **long** years wherever the Texas Department of Criminal Justice sees fit to send you—"

Shakir didn't like any part of this offer. He didn't want to get his cousin in trouble. He wasn't sure he could trust this man across the table. In fact, he was sure he couldn't. But he didn't see any other way. He raised his hands in surrender. "You win."

"Good man. You're doing the right thing. Keeping America safe." Reed slid a blank white card to Shakir, a number handwritten on the back. "That's my cell. Emergencies only. We'll be in touch."

The other agent, who had never introduced himself, disappeared. He returned in a minute with the plastic bag of Shakir's stuff.

"By the way, you can assume we've copied your house keys and put trackers on your phone and car. Don't make us look for you." Reed slid the bag across to Shakir. The second agent whispered in Reed's ear and Reed grinned.

"Ahmed, Agent Mercer thinks a beatdown would give you the perfect excuse for a change of heart."

"No."

"You don't have to. But if you can't get Gamal interested—"

They left him with a black eye, a fat lip, and a bloody nose. Then they dumped him a block from the bus station downtown.

═══

"You need to go to the hospital," el-Masry said.

"Forget it."

"What happened?"

Shakir spat blood into an empty Gatorade bottle that smelled of piss. "You were right."

"About what."

"About them." He refused to say more, knowing his silence would drive el-Masry to imagine the worst.

———

A week later, the bruises still mottling his face, he knocked on el-Masry's door. "Cousin, I want to talk." He was surprised how quickly el-Masry bought in. He'd expected he'd have to speak in the coded language of drug deals. But when he mentioned punishing his attackers, el-Masry nodded.

"I knew Allah would give you a chance to save yourself from Hell. Staying out late, drinking alcohol, fornicating with their women. You think I don't know."

If only.

"You want to find these men, Ahmed?"

"I told you, after they hit me, they drove off. I barely saw them."

"What, then?"

"The Americans see us all the same way. Dirty Muslims. It's only fair we do the same to them."

El-Masry patted Shakir's hand. "Not just fair. Allah's will."

"I've wasted my life, cousin. I'm ashamed."

"Not anymore."

======

Shakir quickly realized that for all their fury at the United States, his cousin and Rashid and Nassir suffered from a certain naïveté about their adopted homeland. They all worked alone as drivers, so they didn't have American coworkers. They spent their free time with other devout Muslim men. Their understanding of American society came mostly from the imam's sermons and television. They didn't question Shakir's breezy assurance that he could buy assault rifles from a gang of Hells Angels he had met at the Dirt Hole, like motorcycle gangs regularly sold AK-47s to random Egyptian immigrants. They barely raised their eyebrows when he told them that the Angels would let them train at an old gun range east of Dallas.

Do they know what we're doing?

I told them we're robbing a bank, Shakir said. **They like that idea. They don't like the police either.**

How much will all of this cost?

Twenty thousand. Twenty-one, to be exact. You have that much?

All my money, Shakir said. **I was saving it to get married, but I'd rather use it for this.**

The most annoying part of being undercover was el-Masry's insistence that Shakir pray at the mosque once every couple weeks. El-Masry wanted him to come even more frequently, but Shakir said that too much sudden devotion might look odd. The brothers at the mosque were briefly suspicious, but they welcomed him after el-Masry told them what had happened to him.

━━━━━

He saw Reed and Mercer once a week. Reed, really. Mercer never spoke. They usually met at Burger Kings. Shakir didn't know if Reed had a weakness for Whoppers or liked the restaurants because they tended to be empty. Shakir never saw the other agents, but he noticed a white Chevy pickup and a black Tahoe following him. The vehicles came and went almost randomly, and he realized Reed had told the truth about the trackers on his car and phone.

After six weeks, he told Reed he was ready for the AKs.

"You were right." Shakir was almost embarrassed how enthusiastically his cousin had taken to the scheme. El-Masry liked to guess how many people they would kill. **Each of us should do as many as Mateen**—Omar Mateen, the shooter at Pulse, the Orlando gay nightclub, who had killed forty-nine. **Times four. Two hundred.**

"For the guns, we need paperwork," Reed said. He murmured in Mercer's ear and Mercer left.

"Nice to have an errand boy."

"Say it to him."

They sat in silence. Shakir wondered sometimes what Reed and Mercer did when they weren't with him, if they went home to Houston or stayed up here, if they had families. Neither wore a wedding ring, but maybe FBI counterterror agents didn't advertise they were married. But Shakir knew Reed enough now to know those questions would just annoy him.

Mercer returned with a manila folder. Reed leafed through it, made notes on the pages inside. "This says we're giving you five AKs, five thousand rounds of ammunition. Also five pistols. Glocks."

"Five?"

"If anyone else joins up." Reed slid two pieces of paper over, identical, both on official FBI letterhead, the figures inked in. Shakir skimmed, signed them, pushed one back. Reed wagged his fingers for the other.

"This is for our protection, Mr. Shakir. Not yours."

Of course. "When do I get the guns?"

"Park by the Sears at Southwest Center Mall at noon tomorrow. Shop inside for an hour. When you come back, they'll be in your trunk. It should go without saying but I'll say it anyway. Don't leave them with your cousin or Rashid. Tell them you don't want them in a house with kids—tell them whatever—but keep them yourself."

═══

In truth, playing with the AKs was fun. The firing range where they practiced was on the edge of Grand Saline, a one-stoplight town seventy miles east of Dallas. Even with the GPS, Shakir barely spotted the building the first time. It was low, concrete-walled, set back from the road. Faded signs nailed to the front door read HARLEY PARKING ONLY and SUPPORT 81, the number a barely disguised code for **Hells Angels**.

Inside, the range had ten shooting stalls that faced a thick sand berm. The odors of gunpowder and stale beer lingered faintly. Tattered targets hung at the far end. Posters warned, in black capital letters, FACE FORWARD! POINT WEAPONS DOWNRANGE! IF YOUR WEAPON JAMS, STAY IN

YOUR STALL! And, more pithily, DON'T BE A DUMBASS, DUMBASS!

They shot on semiautomatic. The AKs that the FBI had provided weren't set for full auto, and Reed had warned Shakir not to try to modify them. **You'll just mess them up.** After the first trip, Shakir downloaded manuals and online videos about how to attack for maximum civilian carnage. They were surprisingly common. **Three-shot bursts. Carry magazines on your chest, where you can easily swap them out. Cover one another during reloading so that your targets can't swarm you.** They set up obstacles in the middle of the range and worked on their tactical skills. Their accuracy improved, though Shakir was under no illusions about their chances against a trained police team.

They talked only once about the morality of what they were planning, or the fact it would surely result in their deaths. "You're not worried, cousin? About hurting women and children?" Shakir said, as they were finishing the third session.

"How many of us die every week in Syria? We're the lucky ones. Attacking the enemy."

"Won't you miss your daughters?"

"I'll see them in Heaven. Come on, cousin, don't tell me you're having second thoughts." El-

Masry swung his AK on Shakir. He smiled, but Shakir didn't think he was joking.

Shakir knew he wouldn't mention his doubts again. For the first time, he was glad the FBI had found him. Even after el-Masry's ready agreement, Shakir had feared he might be entrapping his cousin. And he still doubted el-Masry could have pulled this attack off without Shakir's help. El-Masry and the Fardous brothers weren't sophisticated enough to buy assault rifles without being noticed. But Shakir could imagine them bringing knives to a mall and stabbing strangers until they were shot. Maybe they wouldn't have killed hundreds of people, but they could have killed a dozen.

He was nervous when he drove back that afternoon. He made a mistake. On Highway 19, the two-lane state road that led to the interstate, he missed a speed trap. Suddenly he was driving 67 in a 45 zone. Even as he hit his brakes he saw the white Chevy Suburban tucked behind a stand of trees. The Chevy had steel ramming bars mounted to its grille, a five-pointed black-and-red sheriff's star on its driver's-side door. It pulled out as he passed, flipped on its lights.

El-Masry cursed in Arabic.

"It'll be fine." **As long as they don't search the trunk and find five unregistered assault rifles.**

"This isn't Dallas, Ahmed," Rashid said. "They don't like people like us here."

"If he tries to take us in—" El-Masry reached under the seat, where he had insisted on stowing a Glock.

Shakir signaled, pulled over as far as he could. To the left and right, hay bales lay gold on close-mown fields. Fresh asphalt stretched to the horizon. Another lonely Texas highway. "Don't be stupid."

The sheriff's deputy wore a cowboy hat, a long-sleeved khaki shirt, wraparound sunglasses. "Howdy, gentlemen. Where you headed?"

"Dallas."

"Where you coming from?"

Shakir saw too late he should have had a cover story. "Dallas," he mumbled.

The deputy tilted his head in mock puzzlement. "What brings you to Van Zandt County, then?"

"Just out for a drive."

In the passenger seat, el-Masry muttered in Arabic, **Looking for infidel pigs to slaughter.**

The cop's hand went to his pistol. "Excuse me, sir?"

Shakir's heart clenched. They were a sentence or two from **shots fired**. "He's saying how beautiful it is here."

"Yeah. Got Walmarts and everything. So you gentlemen are all Arabs."

"Egyptian, yes."

"Home of the Pyramids, am I right?"

Shakir wasn't sure if the deputy was joking or wanted an answer. "Yes, sir," he finally said.

"Mighty impressive, those Pyramids. Saw a **Nat Geo** special on them. You got papers?"

"We're legal." Though Shakir wasn't sure about Rashid and Nassir.

"Carrying anything in this vehicle I should know about? Narcotics? Weapons?"

"Of course not."

"You don't mind if I search it, then?"

I'll blow his head off, el-Masry muttered.

"Sir, I'm going to have to ask you to speak English and step out of the vehicle—"

Behind him an engine roared.

And a black Nissan 370Z with tinted windows blew past, at least a hundred miles an hour, clearing the deputy's ample backside by no more than a foot. The deputy's head swiveled as the Nissan disappeared south.

"Your lucky day, boys. Not even going to bother to tell you to wait." He lumbered back to his Suburban and kicked on the sirens. Shakir didn't think he had a chance. The Nissan was flying, and the Interstate 20 interchange was only a couple miles south.

"Allah is with us today," el-Masry said, as Shakir eased his Hyundai onto the blacktop.

Yeah, Allah and the FBI. Apparently, Agent Reed didn't want anyone searching Shakir's trunk either.

———

They took a break from the range and Van Zandt County to scout targets. They spent a day looking over Dallas/Fort Worth Airport, checking the terminal entrances and the check-in counters. The airport's great advantage was that they could park close, hide the AKs in bags, walk to the terminals and come out shooting. Rashid suggested that they could cook up homemade explosive and pack it in luggage. But, ultimately, they decided against DFW. Police and Transportation Security Administration officers were everywhere. Each terminal had dozens of doors and emergency exits. Lots of ways to escape. Mateen, the Orlando shooter, had been able to cause so much carnage by herding his victims into corners.

The Cowboys were another possibility, a symbolically important target, playing in front of a hundred thousand people. "America's Team," el-Masry said. "At AT&T Stadium. Everyone knows

AT&T spies on Muslims." The security checks at gates created choke points, long lines of ticket holders waiting to be screened. But after scouting a home game, they decided against AT&T. Driving close to the stadium was near impossible on game days. They'd have to park hundreds of meters away and try to approach without being noticed. Their rifle bags would stand out. And security was nearly as heavy as at the airport.

So they turned to the American Airlines Center, where the Mavericks played. The Mavs weren't the Cowboys, but the arena's name would resonate. More important, security there was notably lighter than at the airport or stadium. Instead of hundreds of police officers, the arena had a couple dozen. Even better, they could drive almost to the gates on the west side of the arena, which offered the same security checks as at AT&T Stadium and created the same choke points.

Best of all, if they could get inside, they could create panic. The arena's corridors were relatively narrow and encircled the seats that surrounded the floor. Two shooters could move in opposite directions and stampede victims toward one another. Meanwhile, the other two could mow down people inside the main seating area. With each minute, they would kill dozens more. Five times they went to games, scouting the screeners, walking the arena's halls to look for hidden security posts, checking sight lines.

They saw no obvious hurdles, nothing to dissuade them.

The American Airlines Center it would be.

The body armor was legal and easy to come by. To avoid arousing suspicion, Shakir ordered online from four different companies. The plates were military-grade, capable of stopping assault rifle rounds. Standard subsonic pistol ammunition would barely dent them. The armor made the plot feel more real to Shakir than the AKs had. The AKs were toys, somehow. The armor wasn't. When Shakir slipped it over his shoulders, its weight shocked him.

They wore the armor for their suicide videos. They made those at the range, in front of a black cloth emblazoned with the **Shahada**, the Muslim profession of faith. El-Masry spoke first. In English, and then again in Arabic, he explained that he was a soldier carrying out this attack as revenge for the way the United States treated Muslims. **The Americans kill innocent women and children. It's only right that people here feel the same pain. We are the proud soldiers of Islam** . . . Rashid and Nassir followed.

Then Shakir's turn came. As he stared at the camera, he wanted to laugh. **Thank God, this isn't real.** He knew the United States better than these men. This attack would backfire, making Americans even angrier. Anyway, he didn't see his cousin running to Raqqa to live under the caliph.

"Ready?" el-Masry said.

"I'd rather let you speak for me." But el-Masry pressed him. Finally, Shakir choked out a few sentences.

—————

Two days later, Shakir passed Reed and Mercer a copy of the videos.

"We're close. We've picked a date." He told them. They already knew the location.

"We'll step up the surveillance. Though you may not see us. The day of, we'll have helicopters and drones besides the on-the-ground stuff."

"Can't you make the arrests now?"

"It's America. Anybody can make a video. The lawyers will say they were puffing their chests, supporting the jihad symbolically—"

"We spent all this time scouting sites."

"You went to a few basketball games."

"Practicing with AKs."

"Which **you** provided, Ahmed."

"I'll testify."

"They'll say you're a liar. Hint at the drugs, even if we try to keep them out. Say you have a hero complex. I want these guys to spend fifty years in prison, and that only happens if we nail them right before they start shooting." Reed leaned in. "Your job is to keep them calm until we snap them up. No more getting pulled over, no dumb mistakes."

"What about when they see you? They'll start shooting."

"You tell them you're keeping the guns in the trunk when you drive to the arena. Easy enough to get them out when you get there. Eleven a.m., day of the attack, leave your car at Southwest Center Mall again, give us a couple hours. We'll pull the firing pins. The AKs will look exactly the same. Just be sure no one tests them after the switch."

"I'll tell them that I'll pick them up at Gamal's house, we'll go straight to the arena."

"And checkmate. Very good, Ahmed."

———

They went twice more to the range, examined maps, watched one final game at the arena. The day came. Dallas Mavericks versus Oklahoma City Thunder, 7:30 p.m. A full house expected. Eighteen thousand five hundred fans.

Shakir left his Hyundai at the mall as Reed had instructed. When he came back, he found a note on his seat. **See you tonight. Almost done.**

The weight of what Shakir was doing to his cousin descended on him. **Fifty years in prison,** Reed said. A life sentence, really. El-Masry would emerge stooped and old, if he came out at all. He would never touch his wife again, hardly see his daughters. All along, he would know that his plan had failed, that the enemy he'd hated had won.

Thanks to his own cousin.

Shakir wondered if he ought to tell el-Masry the truth, let him run. But he didn't need to guess at the FBI's reaction. Reed would be furious. Shakir would face the original drug charges, along with new ones, for compromising the investigation.

Anyway, the FBI had been right. His cousin wanted to shoot up a basketball game. He **should** be in prison. No, Shakir had to see the plan through.

As he drove home, el-Masry called. "Come over, Ahmed. Pray with us this afternoon. **A mouth that prays, and a hand that slays.**" An old Arab saying. "Make sure we're ready for Allah."

Shakir couldn't face spending hours with men who were about to go to prison because of him. "You get ready for Allah however you like, Gamal. I'll see you tonight."

The afternoon passed excruciatingly slowly, but at 6:20 Shakir strapped on his vest, pulled on a sweatshirt to hide its bulk, headed for el-Masry's house. Along the way, he saw a Tahoe following. Reassuring. He pulled up to el-Masry's house at 6:35, five minutes late. His cousin and the others stood outside, fidgeting.

On the drive over, they hardly spoke. Shakir wondered if the others were having second thoughts. He drove carefully, wanting to make sure the FBI stayed close.

The arena lay west of the downtown skyscrapers and north of Dealey Plaza, where Oswald had shot Kennedy. At 7:03, Shakir turned north on I-35E. He spotted the Tahoe once more in his rearview mirror. It seemed to be a long way back. The others murmured prayers in Arabic. Shakir wished silently for a quick, clean arrest.

At Exit 429, Shakir turned onto Victory Avenue. The arena stood close, a handsome building with a redbrick façade and a white shed roof. The pregame traffic was heavy but moving.

Then they were there.

Shakir stopped beside the bollards that protected the emergency entrance to All Star Way, a few feet from the line for the security checkpoint. He killed the engine, popped the trunk, flipped on his hazards. The others opened their doors.

"Coming, cousin?"

Shakir stepped out, looking for unmarked SUVs. For Reed and other men wearing FBI jackets. He saw only the usual security guards. The nearest Dallas police officers were a hundred feet away and paying no attention to the Hyundai.

"Can't park there," a security guard shouted.

"Ahmed!" el-Masry yelled. Shakir came to the open trunk. The other men grabbed for AKs. He reached down but didn't touch his. He didn't want to be holding an assault rifle, even if it couldn't really be fired. If the cops didn't know about the sting, they might start shooting.

But why wouldn't the cops know? The cops **had** to know, even if they weren't taking part in the arrests.

Something was wrong.

No.

Everything was wrong.

"Now." El-Masry and the other two lifted their AKs—

"GUNS!" yelled the security guard—

The AK came alive in el-Masry's hand. The guard's head exploded.

The pins . . . The firing pins—

The two cops turned, but even before they could pull their pistols, Rashid dropped them both. **"Allahu akbar!"** he shouted.

"Please—" a woman screamed.

An AK burst from el-Masry silenced her. The security line dissolved. The ticket holders ran along the arena's outer wall or forced their way through the checkpoint. El-Masry and the Fardous brothers stepped forward and strafed the crowd, moving with purpose and precision toward the gate.

Shakir watched in bewilderment. Then, too late, remembered what Jake had said the night they'd arrested him. **Don't be a peasant.**

In all his years in the United States, he'd never heard an American use that word. Never.

He'd been so happy at the get-out-of-jail-free card that he'd ignored all the warning signs. **Why hadn't they brought him to the main FBI office and given him a written cooperator's agreement? Why had he only met two of them? Most of all: Why hadn't they made the arrests in a controlled setting?**

Bursts of rifle fire. Shrill screams of the dying. Thumps of bodies falling.

Shakir knew, couldn't avoid the answer. Because they weren't FBI agents. Whoever they were, they'd set this up. They'd found him. Then tricked him into leading his cousin into a fake terrorist attack that wasn't fake at all. And far deadlier than anything el-Masry could have pulled off on his own. Shakir tried to scream, found he couldn't move. What to do? Shoot his cousin? Run—

He'd never escape. But maybe he could surrender, explain the truth. He didn't have much to back his story. But he had a little. He could take the real FBI to the shooting range. Dale had seen Jake at the Dirt Hole. The mall must have security cameras.

A beeping from the trunk. Shakir looked down. The AKs had been wrapped in blankets. With them gone, Shakir saw that someone had moved the mat that covered the Sonata's spare tire. He lifted it—

The tire was gone.

In its place, whitish gray blocks in clear plastic, shaped to fill the hole. Three detonators were stuck in the blocks, connected with red and yellow leg wire that ended in a black box the size of an iPhone.

"No." A wish. Shakir reached down—

A light on the box flashed red.

The world went white. He felt everything. And then nothing.

═══════

The explosive was C-4, rarely seen outside military arsenals. Bombmakers prized the stuff for its power and stability. It wouldn't blow up if it were dropped. It required a sizable priming charge that itself had to be triggered by an initiator. C-4 was a professional's weapon.

But the team that had set Ahmed Shakir up was as professional as any in the world. It had made no mistakes with the four-hundred-pound bomb in the Sonata's trunk. The explosion vaporized Shakir so completely that investigators couldn't find enough of him for a DNA sample. Its overpressure wave and shrapnel created a kill zone that stretched a hundred fifty feet. Two hundred ninety people were in that space, hiding against the arena's walls or running for safety. Most of them died, along with others farther out.

El-Masry and the Fardous brothers just missed their goal. They killed one hundred forty-five people before SWAT teams pinned them down. Even then they didn't stop shooting. Police snipers had to kill all three of them. In all, the C-4 and the bullets killed three hundred eighty-five civilians and thirteen police officers in twenty-eight minutes, more than any terrorist attack since September 11.

Even before the suicide videos went online, no one doubted Muslim terrorists had committed this atrocity.

ONE

1

COLUMBUS, GEORGIA

The Waffle House lay on Victory Drive, close by Commando Military Supply and the gates to Fort Benning, the two-hundred-eighty-square-mile base where the Army made soldiers into Rangers. John Wells remembered the restaurant from his own training, more than two decades before.

Back then, he'd still basically been a Montana boy. He'd come to Dartmouth for college, been shocked by the superior attitude so many East Coast kids put on. But Georgia had held its own surprises. At least Montana and New Hampshire both had mountains, even if the Bitterroots were bigger. Down here, the land was slap flat and swamp-cut.

Anyway, as far as Wells could tell, the Waffle House hadn't changed. Not the waitresses, not the plastic booths, maybe not the fryer grease.

The Ranger instructors eating one booth over looked the same, too. Square-jawed and narrow-eyed. Mostly white. Maybe a few more tattoos. They shoveled scrambled eggs in their mouths like they were machines for the ingestion of food. Cut, chew, swallow. Cut, chew, swallow. Wash it all down with the black liquid that Waffle House called coffee. They were almost too tired to speak, Wells saw.

Though not as tired as the soldiers they were training. Nothing in peacetime replicated combat, but Ranger School tried. **Rangers lead the way,** the unit's motto went. The training program was meant to weed out any soldier who couldn't. It was famously tough, especially at the beginning. Candidates were deprived of sleep and food while facing timed marches and the Darby Queen, a barbed-wire-studded obstacle course. Soldiers qualified through airborne training and a four-week starter course before they even had a chance at Fort Benning. Still, about sixty percent failed. Many who did pass had to repeat at least one part of the three-phase program.

Not Wells. He'd gone through in the minimum sixty-two days. He was made for soldiering. Not just because he was strong and lean and quick. Because he knew intuitively how to survive, to narrow his focus. Not to think ahead, not to promise himself that he'd get through this day or week but simply to **get through**.

A most un-Buddhist form of mindfulness.

So Wells went from Dartmouth to the Rangers, the Rangers to the Central Intelligence Agency, Langley to the Hindu Kush, the Kush back to the United States. Only the start of his travels. Two decades of spying and fighting, killing and not quite dying. He'd resigned from the agency but discovered he needed it as much as it seemed to need him. He'd become a Muslim, too, finding comfort, of sorts, in a faith not his own. And why not? All faiths were foreign in the end, walks through dark woods.

Had he changed? He supposed he must have. From the start, he'd been unafraid to kill, to take what he could never give back. Yet his dreams troubled him more than they once had—

"Need anything?" The waitress's smoke-roughened voice. Meaning: **You've been sitting in this booth a while, time to order more or move on.** Hungry soldiers waited by the door. Wells hadn't woolgathered this way twenty years ago, that he knew.

"Scrambled eggs with cheese. Triple order hash browns."

"Triple? Coming up." She offered him a brokedown smile and turned away. The United States had two thousand Waffle Houses, not one in the Northeast or on the West Coast. Places for working people who needed quick food cheap and cheap food quick. The eggs were iffy, but the hash browns were delicious, as long as Wells didn't think about what they were doing to his arteries.

He was waiting for his son. Evan. Though Evan didn't think of Wells as his father. Another man had raised the boy while Wells snaked the world's drains. Yet Evan, a grown man now, had decided to become a Ranger. Wells wasn't quite sure why. He was proud, but he feared Evan didn't understand the choice he'd made.

Evan had been one of the first-week Fort Benning failures. Not his fault. He'd blown his Achilles tendon eleven miles into the twelve-mile road march, the week's concluding exercise. Twelve miles didn't sound like much, except the candidates carried close to a hundred pounds of gear. Because Evan had failed for medical reasons, he could rehab here while he waited for another chance. If he wanted.

He'd called Wells the day before, two days after the injury, asked him to come to Georgia.

"Pep talk?"

"Something like that."

All his life, Evan had carried a golden ticket.

Now defeat hung in his voice. Wells caught a dawn flight from Boston to Atlanta, rented a car for the easy hundred-mile drive to Columbus, on the Georgia–Alabama border. Eleven a.m., and here he was.

He watched Evan park his gray Toyota Highlander—the SUV too new, too nice, for a young soldier, a vehicle that would earn Evan scorn rather than respect. The door swung open, and Evan hobbled out, a heavy white boot on his ankle. Like Wells, he was tall, with brown hair and cool-brown eyes. Though Evan was slimmer than Wells, more lithe. He was a superb basketball player, just a half step slow for the NBA. He'd started at shooting guard for San Diego State's nationally ranked team.

Wells met him at the door, gave him a hug that would have been awkward even if Evan hadn't been wearing the boot.

"John." Evan rarely called him Dad. "Couldn't take me somewhere classy like Denny's?"

"You don't know what you're missing."

"That's what she said." Evan banged his foot into the edge of a booth and grimaced.

"Maybe focus on walking."

The hash browns beat them to the booth.

"If this is what getting old is like, I'll skip it," Evan said.

"You may reconsider." Wells helped him sit.

"How's Anne? You're living together, right?"

So they were, in the farmhouse in New Hampshire that had become as much of a home as Wells expected to find. Anne was Wells's **girlfriend**, **partner**—whatever term of art the kids used these days. Not **wife**, though. Wells had proposed and been refused twice now. She'd told him she didn't want a ring, she wanted his heart, and she'd know when his heart was ready. Left unsaid were the words **And it's never gonna be.** Though his unready heart hadn't stopped them from having a daughter together. And now—

"Anne's pregnant." The first time he'd spoken the words aloud. He felt a swell of masculine pride despite the foolishness of having another child out of wedlock. But why not? He and Anne were good parents. And, truth, if anything happened to him, he'd put enough money aside to make sure the kids would have their educations paid for. Beyond that . . . Anne was smart and steady and he supposed he trusted she would find someone else. Evan had done all right without him.

"Seriously? Another half sister?"

"Sonogram says **brother**."

"You know there are these things called condoms, John—" Evan grinned in genuine pleasure. "Why didn't you tell me before?"

"I'm telling you now." What he wasn't telling, and wouldn't: Anne had miscarried three times since Emmie, their daughter. Wells hadn't wanted to say anything until they were sure. But she was sixteen weeks along, and the sonogram and every genetic test ever invented said the baby was healthy.

"Congratulations."

"Thank you."

"Glad one of us has good news, anyway."

"What happened?"

Evan grimaced, reliving the injury. "I felt the tendon getting super-tight, which used to happen at the end of games sometimes. Then **Snap!** I heard it even before I FELT it. Then I was on my ass, like someone took a blowtorch to my leg. The other guys tried to help me. I knew I wasn't going anywhere. I told them, **Don't stop, don't mess up your march.** Just waited for the NCOs. Man, it hurt. But that's not the part that's messed up."

Wells waited.

"Felt like I'd gotten a get-out-of-jail-free card." Evan mumbled now as if the words burned his mouth. "I can't stand these rules. Sergeants yelling at me. **Surfer boy! Pretty boy! College boy!**

And the other soldiers, they're barely eighteen, they all think it's a big gym class. Jackasses."

"If I recall, you engaged in a bit of jackassery in San Diego."

"I don't want to sound like a snob, but—"

"But you are, and you didn't even know until you got here."

"We barely get any sleep, anyway, and they won't shut up all night. Talking about how much ass they'll get when they tell girls they're Rangers. And when are they gonna blow claymores and try the 249."

"You're telling me you don't want to shoot a machine gun?"

"Worst part is, all this crap about how they can't wait to get deployed so they can start killing Arabs. **Make them pay for what happened last week.**" The funerals were still happening in Dallas, the flags still at half-staff. "**Nuke Syria.** They don't even know the difference between Sunni and Shia. Remember a few years ago, in Missoula—"

At the time, Evan had accused Wells of being a psychopath, a contract killer whose sole client was the United States government.

"And you grew up."

"I saw it was more complicated. But this takes me back to that, because that's all these guys want. Was it like that when you were here?"

Wells nodded. Though, back then, the imagined targets had been the Russians and the Chinese. **Chink-chonk-cho, I shoot you, ah-so.** Fortunately, that guy had washed out. "They're nervous. Trying to hide it."

"They don't sound nervous. They sound **amped.** If that's what it takes to kill people, I don't have it."

The real reason Evan had called him. Wells let him eat for a minute and then leaned close.

"I don't know if you have it. Or any of those other guys. Nobody knows. All those obstacle courses and live-fire exercises, they just tell you who **can't** do it. You flinch here, then you're probably gonna be no good in the real thing. But it doesn't work the other way. Guys can roll through the Darby Queen because in the back of their minds they know it's training. Combat's different. It's only when you're up against people who want to kill you that you can be sure how you'll react."

"Kinda late by then."

"You know what's more like combat than anything else? Football."

"Because of the hitting."

"Because, in the moment, it's you or them. And basketball's not the same in terms of the physicality, but it takes that focus. If I had to bet, I'd bet on you."

They were quiet for a minute.

"Say you're right. What am I looking at? Months of rehab. Then years of taking orders from guys who barely got through high school."

"On the bright side, by the time you're done you'll be a killing machine who can't live normal civilian life."

"You make it sound so appealing."

"Know where we could have used a couple Rangers last week."

Words that snapped up Evan's head.

"I haven't told you what to do this whole time. But I'm telling you now. Don't quit. Not this way. It'll feel good for a month and then it'll haunt you."

"And the knuckleheads?"

"Keep your mouth shut. If you can soldier, they'll respect you soon enough. Maybe dump that forty-thousand-dollar station wagon outside, too, so it's not so obvious you don't fit in."

"Mom's gonna kill you. She told me not to call." Heather, Wells's ex-wife and Evan's mom, hadn't wanted Evan to sign up. To say the least. Evan had told Wells that she'd threatened to cut off his hands.

"Least you won't be living in the basement like all the other millennials." The waitress was coming their way. Wells fished for his wallet. "Come on. We stay much longer she'll make us sign a lease."

———

Wells called Anne as the Highlander swung out.

"Babe." She'd started calling him that recently. "How's Evan? What I thought?"

"Yeah. I told him not to."

Silence. Anne told Wells not to argue if Evan wanted to quit. **You need to let him find his own way.**

"He wanted me to change his mind, Anne. Why he asked me to come."

"Hope so," she said, as his phone beeped with an incoming number, a 202 area code. Wells wanted to be surprised, but some part of him had expected this call since the first bulletins from Dallas.

"Call you back." He clicked through.

"Mr. Wells?" A man. "President Duto would like you to come in. Are you in New Hampshire?"

"Fort Benning."

A pause. Wells realized the man at the White House had never heard of Fort Benning. And civilians wondered why soldiers didn't respect them. "Military base in Georgia. Has an airport."

"I'll call you back."

The voice was gone. **President Duto would like you to come in.** Not a question. Wells called Anne.

"I have to stop in D.C."

I'm pregnant, John. Or have you forgotten? Words she'd never say. "Tell the gang I said hi."

———

Five hours later, Wells walked into the Oval Office to find Vinny Duto flipping through a briefing book in a black binder. Even when Wells had first met Duto a decade before, the bags under his eyes had been prominent. Now they sagged into his cheeks. He looked like he hadn't slept in days. He probably hadn't.

"John. Thanks for coming."

Duto had been been justifiably proud of his record, Wells knew. Proud the country hadn't suffered a major terrorist attack while he was director of the CIA or president. Until now. Four killers, three hundred dead, the Islamic State claiming credit.

Duto flipped through the binder. Wells glimpsed photos, pools of blood. He waited for Duto to explain what the agency and FBI knew and what they didn't, what the next moves would be.

"Want a drink?" Duto said abruptly.

Wells didn't. And it was barely 5 p.m. And

Islam forbade alcohol, anyway. But he couldn't make the President of the United States drink alone in the Oval Office. "Sure."

Duto closed the binder and gave a low, grateful sigh, the sound of a dog kenneling itself under a porch on a hot day. He'd installed a chrome-and-leather bar cart by the Oval Office's second door, the one that led to the bathroom and points beyond. He plucked a bottle, thick glass and a cork stopper, labeled with a hand-drawn cowboy sitting on a white horse. **High West, yippee ki-yay.** He poured himself half a highball glass. For Wells, barely a finger.

"To those pricks. May they rot in Hell." Duto raised his glass, took a pull. Wells gave himself a mouthful. The stuff wasn't bad, a little sweetness to hide the fire underneath. Duto's face loosened as the liquor hit him.

"Whiskey?"

"If the river was whiskey, and I was a diving duck . . ." Duto took another sip, wiped his mouth with the back of his hand. "Rye. You think I drink too much, John?"

People who weren't worried about their drinking rarely asked that question. "I think you're the president, and if you want a predinner cocktail, nobody's telling you no."

"Promised I'd keep us safe."

"Can't stop everything."

"I don't mind being divorced—as a rule, I enjoy it—but this last week I wished I had someone to talk to."

Wells and Duto had never liked each other. Duto loved power, for its own sake and for the rewards it brought. He'd used Wells a dozen different ways on his march from Langley to the Senate to the White House. But he'd been a case officer and then a station chief, too. At least he understood the field, unlike most of the men and women in this town. So Wells wanted to feel sympathy. Heavy is the head. But he couldn't start thinking of Duto as human. Not now.

"No one made you take the job, Vinny. Tell me you didn't call because you need a shoulder to cry on."

Duto raised both middle fingers, and Wells glimpsed the man he remembered, the one who had a quotation from Stalin for every occasion: **The people who cast the votes decide nothing. The people who count the votes decide everything.**

"Don't flatter yourself. I talk to you because you keep your mouth shut. Not that anyone would listen. You're like a dog that somehow learned to shoot."

"It's all on my blog."

Duto took another sip, settled back on the

sofa. **Good. I'm glad we got our feelings out of the way.** He pushed the briefing book at Wells.

"Don't ask me where they got the C-4 or figured out how to wire it. We don't know. Gamal and the brothers were in FBI databases for some online posts, and that mosque was on a watchlist, but it wasn't a priority. No alarms at all for the presumed fourth bomber, the lovely and talented Ahmed Shakir. I say **presumed** because despite a scraping of human remains that would make an Orthodox rabbi proud, the techs haven't found any of his bits. At least we can be sure about the other three, because we blew their heads off. We don't know where they trained or who supplied the rifles. If they were real Islamic State operatives or fellow travelers. Long list of things we don't know."

"What **do** we know?"

"Can't prove it yet, but we think Shakir was the leader."

"Because he blew the bomb?"

"And it was his car, and he was driving, and he was the most successful. The others didn't even get through high school. He's interesting, though. A few people told the FBI he dealt drugs. Then he stopped a few months ago and vanished. But— you guessed it—we don't know why."

"Other cells?"

"We can't find any. But there was no chatter. Came out of nowhere, like Orlando. Only this is worse. Three hundred people out to watch Russell Westbrook. Men, women, kids. And this one was so professional. It feels different somehow. If this is where they're going . . ."

Wells understood. The trend was frightening. The San Bernardino attackers had killed fourteen. Mateen had killed forty-nine. Now this. September 11 had come with its own solutions. Reinforce cockpit doors. Tighten passenger screening. Destroy al-Qaeda. Not this time. These sorts of attacks were nearly impossible to stop if the jihadis kept their mouths shut.

"What are we going to do, cancel the NBA?" Duto, reading Wells's mind. "And it just fuels the Paul Birmans of the world. You know he's giving a speech tonight in Nashville?"

"Why would I know that?"

Paul Birman, Republican of Tennessee, chaired the Senate Select Committee on Intelligence. He had spent Duto's presidency warning about Islamist terror groups. **Muslim terrorists want to destroy our way of life. They will attack the United States whenever they can. I thought our President understood the threat we faced from radical Islam. Now I fear he doesn't.**

Birman's popularity had risen with his aggressiveness. Two years ago, he had been an obscure senator best known for having married a former Miss America. Now he was a hero of the right. CRUZ CONTROLLED: HERE COMES BIRMAN, the **National Review** had headlined. He was hinting at a presidential run.

And he'd made those gains **before** the Dallas attacks.

"Never thought anyone would say I wasn't tough enough," Duto said. "Who knows what he'll propose today? Probably that we should nuke the Dome of the Rock. I'm guessing he doesn't know it's in Jerusalem." Birman wasn't known for his command of detail. **Big-picture thinker,** his supporters said. **He'll have a whole government to sweat the small stuff.**

"He can say what he likes. You're still president."

"People are listening. My pollsters—"

"You'll have to excuse me, but I couldn't care less about your approval rating."

"If that idiot gets in here, you will."

Strange that Evan, at the very bottom of the million-person American military pyramid, and Duto faced the same challenge, the same noisy saber-rattling. But Wells knew better than anyone that a lot of Americans were sick of the War on Terror and Islam. He had never talked much about his conversion to Islam. Now he avoided mentioning it at all. More than once, it had provoked outright disapproval. **You know Muhammad was a false prophet, and a pedophile, too, right?**

He wanted to be home with his hand on Anne's belly. The wars would go on without him.

"Vinny, why am I here? Half the FBI is working Dallas, and we agree I'm not your therapist."

Duto flipped open the briefing book to photos of charred corpses still wearing their Dirk Nowitzki jerseys. Reminding Wells of the stakes.

"Enrique Martinez. Ricky. Hickory Dickory Dock. Colombian intel officer. I knew him back in the day in Bogotá—" where Duto had been chief of station. "Rich family, good guy. He retired five, six years ago. He was running all their South American ops. Called me yesterday. Wants a meet."

"Another Colombian." Years before, Duto had asked Wells to meet a Colombian army officer turned drug lord named Juan Montoya. Wells had wound up with a cracked skull for his trouble.

"Look, that worked out, did it not? Anyway, Ricky's not dirty. If anything, he was too honest. He lives in the highlands now, got a ranch."

"Unless I'm mistaken, we still have a station in Bogotá."

"He wants an X meeting." Meaning no regular agency officers.

"Tell him to come to Miami."

"John, I know this guy, he's weird, but he's not the type to jerk my chain. I told him he had to give me something or I couldn't make it happen, and he said it's about Dallas."

The magic word. "Doesn't make sense."

"We both know you're going, so let's stop talking about it."

Wells looked at the briefing book. Nodded.

Duto raised his glass. "One more thing. You need help from the agency, leave Shafer out." Ellis Shafer, Wells's oldest friend at Langley. His **only** friend at Langley.

"Forget it, then."

"Hear me out. It's not just that he's old"—Shafer was well past the agency's mandatory retirement age—"it's that people don't want him around, he's this weird guy coming down the halls poking his nose in everything. No one's gonna say no because they know he knows me, but you don't want that guy asking for a favor you need fast. You want his advice, fine. But if you need help in the field, I want you to call Julie Tarnes."

"Who?"

"You really are out of touch. She's in the DO. Assistant deputy director for ops for the Counterterror Center." A big job. "Was in Pakistan for three years, Egypt—the real thing. Just meet her before you go, give her a chance."

"Okay." Even that much felt like a betrayal.

Duto slid a piece of paper to Wells, two numbers. "Top is hers. Bottom, Ricky's."

Wells tucked the paper away, left Duto in the Oval Office, with his briefing book and his bottle.

2

NASHVILLE, TENNESSEE

He'd warned them, hadn't he? Political correctness be damned, he'd told the truth. Muslims were a problem. Not all of them, but too many. They didn't want to play by American rules, follow American values? They wanted to live under **Sharia** law? Cut off thieves' hands?

Fine. Let them do whatever they liked.

But not **here**. People forgot—the media wanted them to forget—that fifty years ago the American population had been five percent foreign-born. Not even ten million immigrants. Most Americans had barely even heard of a mosque. Now the country was fifteen percent foreign. Forty-five million immigrants. Forty-five million! Almost as many people as Texas and New York combined.

A whole lot of those were Muslims. Anyone

with any sense could see the country needed a break. Time to stop the Muslim–Mexican overload. Enough prayer calls. Enough taco trucks.

Look at China. The Chinese, they didn't pretend to care about a bunch of Arabs. They didn't let anybody in. They didn't waste time worrying whether they were being mean to terrorists. They just worked their little Chinese butts off and put the rest of the world out of business.

As far as Paul Birman was concerned, the United States of America ought to act more like the People's Republic of China.

Hit pause. Probably his biggest applause line. Not saying we need to rewind, but it's time to hit pause. While we take care of our own. Not just for us. For them, too. Give everybody time to get straightened out, hear what I'm saying?

They did. He was popular now, more popular by the day. Not just in Tennessee, all over the country. Certainly the South and the Midwest, the real country, the states that nobody in California or New York noticed. Where Walmart was a place people picked up groceries, not a punch line for rich comedians. **Flyover country.** Two years ago, Birman was lucky to draw three hundred at a rally. Now he pulled three thousand easy. Three thousand people coming to hear him speak.

What the people who criticized him didn't understand was that he didn't say things to be popular. He said them because he believed them.

Because they were **true**.

As last week had proven. What had happened in Dallas was terrible. But all those voters who thought he was exaggerating, they knew better now.

Birman was no evangelical. He'd seen too many holier-than-thou types caught with their pants down. He understood folks weren't perfect. They gambled, drank, broke their vows. Sometimes they came back to God, and sometimes they didn't. He tried not to judge. He'd been faithful to Gloria since the day they met; he knew she wouldn't put up with a wandering eye. But growing up he'd done some stuff he'd wished he hadn't. So, no, he didn't believe in the Bible as the Revealed Word. But he believed in God, and he knew God had blessed him. With a beautiful wife, four great kids, all the money he could hope to spend.

Now he was beginning to believe God had anointed him to lead the United States.

He'd never say those words aloud. He knew **The New York Times** would mock him. He wasn't stupid, even if they thought he was. He wasn't an **intellectual**, sure. Didn't want to be. But he'd graduated from the University of Tennessee. He'd run his family's malls, in Memphis and Nashville and Birmingham, until the time came to sell them. His family was Tennessee royalty, political and business. During the post-Depression boom, the Birmans built hospitals and apartment complexes and factories. Then they went to Washington and made sure the state got its fair share of federal money, maybe a little more.

If the Birmans were royalty, Paul's branch of the family were the kings. His dad, Henry, had been the first Birman to reach the Senate, the real prize. Henry saw early that white Tennessee voters were tired of Democrats. He turned Republican, won five terms, then passed the seat to Paul. Good timing, because the family had just sold its malls for seven hundred seventy-five million dollars, cashing out at the peak of the pre-2008 real estate bubble. Paul took home two hundred ninety million. Enough money to sit around and do nothing for the rest of his life. He didn't want to sit around and do nothing.

Everyone in the state knew his name. People liked him, his pretty wife, his cute kids. He was a natural retail politician, a handshaker. No secret to it, he liked people. He didn't promise too much, just looked them in the eye, said he'd do his best. He looked the part, too: tall, blue-eyed, straight-backed, high-shouldered, and handsome. **Birman Does Right by Tennessee.** The only slogan he needed. He won the primary by twenty points and the general by thirty. He even took a quarter of the black vote, more than his father ever had.

In the Senate, Birman put up his hand for only one job, the Intelligence Committee. Most senators avoided the SSCI. It meant background checks and secrecy agreements. Members couldn't disclose much of what they learned. And the committee didn't have pork to dole. But Birman sensed it would give him a platform. He took the work seriously. Six years after Birman joined, the committee chairman lost his seat. The other members chose Birman to take his place.

As chairman, he had access to a surprising amount of information. He didn't get the morning updates the President received in the famous Presidential Daily Brief. Nor was he given what the agencies called **sources and methods,** specific information about the CIA's operatives or technical details about how the NSA gathered its electronic intelligence. But congressional committees could make the lives of officials at Langley and Fort Meade difficult. The agencies preferred to keep him happy. They would answer any reasonable question. **What kind of cooperation are the**

French giving us in North Africa? How good is our human intelligence on the Chinese Politburo? Do we have electronic coverage of the Kremlin? How seriously should we take these hacks?

More than anything else, Birman wanted to know about the Muslims. In his heart, he couldn't help thinking of them that way, a brown-skinned muddle that stretched across Africa and Asia. From Morocco to Indonesia, fifty countries he had no interest in visiting. More than a billion people, and they couldn't decide whether they loved the United States or hated it. He kept the CIA and the NSA and the FBI's Counterterror Division busy with questions. **How many fully radicalized Muslims live in the United States? How many are actively plotting jihad? Are any under the command and control of the Islamic State?**

The answers disappointed him. Mostly because they weren't answers at all. The agencies actively monitored a couple thousand people. They had tens of thousands more in their databases. But they couldn't tell Birman how many were serious threats and how many were just spouting off. They couldn't tell him what drove a potential terrorist from anger to planning, from planning to action. Even in retrospect, for example, they couldn't figure out what pushed Omar Mateen over the edge in Orlando.

"It's a balance, Senator," the FBI's counterterror director said. "We can't arrest everyone who doesn't like the United States or gay nightclubs. People have the right to say nasty things in this country. Most of 'em have the right to bear arms, too."

People tended to talk to him like he was an idiot. Mostly, he let them. "But Mateen, you were alerted about stuff he'd said, why not watch him?"

"We talked to him. We had to prioritize. Can't watch everyone."

Right, Birman wanted to say. Because there are too many of them. So you play Whack-A-Muslim. Hope you're on the right ones. Hope the NSA scans the right words. Hope somebody calls the police when they hear the guy telling his friends, **Don't be downtown tomorrow.** If all else fails, hope the gun jams, the bomb doesn't blow, the homeless guy sees the pressure cooker and tells the cops. In other words, hope the enemy is incompetent.

When he's not? San Bernardino. Orlando. More to come.

The math was simple, even if no one wanted to admit it. More Muslims in the United States meant more radical Muslims. More radical Muslims meant more terrorists. If the FBI couldn't adequately track the Muslims who already lived here, what would it do with twice as many? Or five times?

Birman started to speak out. Obviously, the United States couldn't deport American citizens or green card holders. But it ought to keep more Muslims from entering, he said. **Hit pause.** When the Washington gasbags said he was creating a "climate of intolerance" or "frightening law-abiding American Muslims," he said, **You know what? I don't care. I want American Muslims to be a little frightened. So they'll pick up the phone when they see something.**

The first time he'd said those words was on **Face the Nation**. Afterward, he flew back to Tennessee on his private jet. The Birmans lived in a famous Nashville mansion, built after the Civil War but in plantation style. A big white portico that framed tall windows, twelve thousand square feet, two kitchens. It was the kind of house that had a name, the Henrietta.

When his chauffeured Escalade pulled into the driveway, he was surprised to see his father Henry's prized Shelby Mustang there, a 1967 GT500, white with blue stripes. Henry was eighty-five now and couldn't drive. But he still rode in the Shelby now and again, his nurse at the wheel. He lived a couple miles away, in the house where Paul had grown up. A mansion, too, though not as big as this one.

Henry waited in the sitting room. The name hardly did justice to the space, forty feet long, thirty wide. It had as its centerpiece a first edition of **Gone with the Wind**, signed by Margaret Mitchell. Even Birman found this level of Southern self-love silly. But his wife traced her Alabama ancestry back six generations. He joked that he'd barely convinced her to move to Nashville. She thought the city was too far north.

Henry nodded for him to sit, like the house belonged to father and not son. Birman did so without complaint. Henry had always been his greatest hero. Birman's kids liked him fine. But he'd never deluded himself into thinking they revered him the way he revered his daddy.

"Paul." Henry was dressed in powder blue nylon pants and a loose sweatshirt with a faded University of Tennessee logo. Like an old man. Even into his seventies, and even on the hottest summer days, Henry had never gone out without a perfectly knotted tie and a crisp white shirt. Birman's heart broke a little.

A bottle of Wild Turkey sat on a spindly cherry side table between their chairs. Birman wasn't sure why. Henry hardly drank anymore. Birman tried not to wince as Henry poured two glasses, the golden liquor splashing onto the table.

Suddenly he knew his father wasn't just old but dying, that he wouldn't see the end of the year.

"No fun being old," Henry said. "One consolation: Seeing your sons grow up into men." Birman's younger brother Bobby lived in Los Angeles and made movies, sort of. His second marriage was ending. He still didn't have any kids. "Half-men, in Bobby's case."

"He'll get it together."

"Don't know about that. Can't do much about it now." Henry went silent, like he'd forgotten what he wanted to say next. Maybe he had.

"Didn't come here to talk about Bobby, anyways."

"The Shelby looks great."

"Yes, it does . . . Paul, you believe all that stuff you were saying today?"

For a moment, Birman thought his dad had hallucinated an earlier conversation between them. Then he remembered **Face the Nation.** "On TV? Yes."

"How we've got to make these Muslims behave? Even if it means treating them tough? You know, America's always been a place people can come if they have trouble at home."

For the first time, Birman wondered if he might be wrong. He didn't care what the liberals said, but his dad was no liberal.

"These people aren't like the others. A lot of 'em, anyway."

"All right." Henry Birman patted his son's arm. "Then you keep saying it, boy. And don't let anybody scare you when they get nasty." He lifted his glass, somehow keeping it steady. "Raise your glass."

"Sure you should be drinking, Dad?"

"Don't be a ninny. We both know my time's almost done."

Paul wiped his face to hide the tears that had popped. "What are we drinking to, then?" Expecting: **My grandkids** or **Tennessee** or **America . . .**

"That Ford in the driveway. It's yours now."

Now Birman couldn't hide his tears, they were a hurricane.

"Promise me you'll take it to the White House. You're gonna be president, Paul."

The old man had always known how to make an exit. He died three weeks later.

═══════

Henry's benediction meant so much to Birman that he never used it for political purposes, though he knew audiences would have loved the story.

Birman didn't suffer much doubt. But on those rare occasions when he wondered if he'd taken the right path, he went out to his eight-car garage, nicer than most houses, and sat in the Shelby. He cranked the engine once a month, drove it down the driveway so the gas line wouldn't seize. But he'd never driven it off the property. He didn't tell anyone, not even Gloria, but he was waiting for Inauguration Day. He saw himself driving the Shelby up Pennsylvania Avenue, the big engine rumbling, the heater on against the cold January air, Secret Service agents walking on both sides.

He started to believe the old man wanted it, too, and from Heaven was helping guide him. The only possible explanation for his sudden string of triumphs.

=====

Tonight's speech had been on the calendar for months, an address to the annual convention of the National Federation of Independent Business, conveniently in Nashville this year. The federation was a powerful force in the Republican Party. Birman had planned to give his standard business speech on the hidden costs of regulation. He understood these men and women. Dry cleaners who shut down rather than deal with new environmental rules. Restaurant owners held up in discrimination lawsuits. Used-car dealers who had to fill out twenty pages of forms every time they wrote a note. They were just getting by. Guess what? The government didn't help 'em a bit.

Then Dallas happened.

The NFIB had put most of its speakers at the Ryman Auditorium, which had almost twenty-four hundred seats. Even before the attacks, the federation had scheduled Birman for the Grand Ole Opry House, twice as large. Now it had moved him to the Bridgestone Arena, where the stars played when they came to town. It sat eighteen thousand. **Eighteen thousand people.** Birman worried he'd be looking at an arena of empty seats, but the federation president told him not to worry. **Our guys want to hear what you have to say.**

True enough. When Birman stepped onstage that night, he didn't see an empty seat. The crowd whooped for him, a deep, masculine sound, the roar of a spinning turbine. The lights dimmed, and a spotlight bathed him. As though he were a prophet come to bring the Word.

The crowd was restless. He waited for it to still. He'd had a speech ready, of course, a revved-up version of his standard. As he watched it unfurl on the teleprompter, he knew it wouldn't do. Not tonight.

"They don't stand for our values." No introduction. No **Hello, NFIB.** What he had to say was too important. "And we're not going to stand for them. Not anymore. Time to stop them." The crowd rumbled, the applause building.

Birman spread his arms, waved them down. "No cheers. Not now. Not while Americans are dying." The arena quieted then. The watchful restless quiet of an attack dog made to heel. "Safety is the government's first duty. And it is **failing!**"

His voice rose now, the fury building, surprising him with its power. "We need to show these jihadis they will have no safe havens, not abroad and not at home. Our politicians tell us, **Don't overreact. Don't be angry.** I'm **tired** of being told not to be angry. I **am** angry. And our President, he's not acting. We have to change that. I am ready to encourage my party to pass a war resolution. But all the resolutions in the world won't matter unless the President listens."

He paused, felt the crowd waiting with him, straining. Eighteen thousand people, desperate to be let off the leash. "It's time for them to understand. Not abroad. And not at home." And more loudly. "Not at home." Birman had never felt so connected to anything, not even making love to his wife. He raised his hands. "Not at home. Not—at—"

Until the voices rose and carried him away.

=====

Afterward, he had too much electricity in his veins to go straight back to the mansion. He headed to his office. Inevitably, Birman occupied the top floor of the AT&T Building, the tallest tower in all of Tennessee. The Cumberland River sparkled in the night below him. The city's lights stretched into the hills.

He called Gloria to tell her he'd see her by midnight. "Gotta catch up on email."

"Paul? You were great tonight. I love you."

"Love you, too." He sat back on his recliner and poured himself a small glass of Wild Turkey, just a taste, and watched his speech. He was half-way through when a knock rattled his office door.

His cousin Eric. Birman's bodyguard would have stopped anyone else. Birman paused the video. "Come on in."

Eric Birman stepped inside. Eric was four inches shorter, and a hundredth as rich, as Paul. He'd served in the Special Forces most of his adult life, quitting a few years before as a full bird colonel. He still had a soldier's bearing, ramrod straight and trim. Now he served as Birman's chief of staff and advisor on national security issues. An unusual arrangement, but Birman wanted someone he trusted. Eric was good on the details, the stuff that Birman hated. Truth, he was closer to Eric than his brother, Bobby. He saw Bobby only once or twice a year. He talked to Eric a dozen times a day.

"Jimmy tell you I was here?" Jimmy Sanders, Birman's bodyguard, a retired New York City cop who'd worked on the Joint Terrorism Task Force for a decade. He was still connected to the NYPD and FBI. He was also barely forty and drawing a full pension. No matter. Wasn't Birman's money.

"No one told me. I know you're watching yourself. Better than porn."

"You watch that stuff?"

"You don't?" Eric poured himself a glass of whiskey. "Guess you don't need to. You got this."

Birman started the video again. They watched in silence until the moment the crowd began to roar.

"I go too far?"

"I don't think so. You owned those folks to-night. They would have elected you Emperor of the Universe." Eric reached for a legal pad and a pencil. Birman felt his spirits sag. Whenever Eric grabbed the pad, playtime was over.

"**Not at home.** How'd you find that? Even better than **Hit pause.** Because it's the attacks **and** the attackers, right? **Send them home** would be too obvious. This way, everybody knows but you don't say it."

"I guess." In truth, Birman hadn't thought through what he meant. He'd just known **not at home** would work.

"You guess." A superior little smile snuck onto Eric's face for just half a second before he batted it down. "People are going to ask you tomorrow what it means. And we're going to need a coherent answer. Maybe even a policy. Case you forgot, you even threw in the war resolution."

Eric thought he was the brains? Fine. Let him work out the details. "You handle it." Birman pushed himself up. Gloria always rewarded him on these nights. He saluted Eric, made for the door.

"Paul—"

"I trust you, cousin. Let me know what I'm thinking in the morning."

3

WASHINGTON, D.C.

The capital placed strict height restrictions on its buildings, a way to keep the primacy of the Washington Monument on its skyline—and make sure no sniper could gain a shooting angle over the White House. The rule meant that the downtown streets were heavy with fifteen-story office buildings, concrete-and-glass boxes, each more boring than the next. With their marble lobbies and power-washed exteriors, they captured the city's character. Bureaucracy with a shiny coat.

Wells walked down K Street, head bent. Washington left him wanting a concealed carry holster. The lobbyists and lawyers descended from their lairs as the afternoon fled. They brushed past Wells, slipped into their black cars to ride to their Georgetown town houses. They strolled to fifteen-dollar-martini bars to invent new tax loopholes.

They weren't all white. And they weren't all men, not anymore. But they all looked prosperous and confident. Too bad they devoted so much drive and intelligence to scalping the other three hundred twenty million Americans.

Wells tried to stay out of politics. Strange to think, considering he'd just spent an hour at the White House. But he wondered if the whole system needed to be turned upside down. Though he had no idea how to fix it. Until the robots took over, governments would need people to run them. Call them courtiers, bureaucrats—whatever—those folks would find ways to take advantage of their position.

He had to call Shafer. He called Anne first.

"How's the big man?" she asked.

"Almost had me feeling sorry for him."

"Really?" She knew how Wells felt about Duto.

"He's taking Dallas hard."

"Maybe he's just worried about his approval rating."

"You're even more cynical than I am. Anyway, he has an errand for me."

"Of course he does." She didn't have to ask if Wells had said yes. "Days, weeks, months?"

"Not months. South America. How are you?"

"They still call it morning sickness if you have it all day?"

"I'll ask my OB," Wells said. "The little lady?" Emmie, his daughter. Now insisting she was three and a half. She wasn't even three. Why three and a half and not four? Or ten? Or a million? Only she knew. Maybe three and a half seemed achievable.

"She asked me where you were, and I said Washington. Asked me why, and I said changing into your cape. Mistake. Now she's obsessed. She asked me what color. I said pink with yellow dots. So you can look forward to that when you get home—"

She yelped.

"Anne?"

"Don't get killed. Your son wants to meet you. He just kicked me." Another yelp. "Hey there, buddy— I gotta go, John." She hung up. The fact she hadn't shown more concern about where Duto was sending him nettled Wells. But he could only blame himself. He'd proven too many times that his loyalties lay in the field, **to** the field. No matter that he might stay home for years. If the call came, he'd answer.

———

Wells reached the more modest streets around Logan Circle. On Sixteenth, he settled on a bench, called the Colombia number Duto had given him.

"Ricky?"

"Who is this?" **Who ees thees?** The accent moderate, understandable.

"My name's John. We have a mutual friend. A **muy** important friend. When can I see you?"

A pause. "It's not me. Someone I know."

Wells wondered if Martinez had told Duto he didn't have any information himself and was only arranging the meet. Duto rarely revealed all his cards, but Wells couldn't see why he'd hide that one. Unless the **someone** was particularly unsavory.

"This person have a name?"

"I promised him I wouldn't say."

Martinez was already irritating Wells. "But he's ready to meet?"

"You come down here?"

"Say the word." Wells realized Martinez didn't understand the expression. "Yes. Whenever."

"Come as soon as you can. Call me when you're here."

"Enrique."

"Sí."

Wells had plenty of questions. **Why not go through the CIA station? Did your contact insist, or did you come up with this plan all by yourself? And: What are you getting out of this?** He doubted he could sweat Martinez from three thousand miles away, but he had to try.

"You know what this guy has? Now would be a good time to tell me."

"Have a safe flight, señor."

━━━━

The second number from Duto was picked up after one ring.

"Tarnes here."

"This is John Wells."

"Hello there, John Wells." Her voice brightening. Wells wondered what she knew about him. "I'm working late tonight. Can we have coffee in the morning? I live in Shaw—"

Shaw was a D.C. neighborhood north of the Convention Center. East of there. It was gentrifying, like everything else in Washington, but it still had rough patches. The choice surprised Wells. As a rule, CIA employees lived in suburban Virginia. "Sure."

"Seventh, between P and Q. Compass Coffee. Seven forty-five."

Then she was gone, and Wells was out of excuses. He called Shafer.

"John. An unexpected pleasure." A slight ironic weight on **unexpected**. Wells supposed Shafer had figured this call would come after Dallas. "You down here to see the big man?"

"How'd you know?"

"Tracker on your phone."

"I hope you're joking."

"Me too. We having a drink? Usual spot?" Shafer chortled.

"No way, Ellis." The usual spot was Shirley's. The worst bar in D.C. Shafer dragged Wells there whenever he could. The bottles were watered, the bartender was eighty and grumpy, and the hamburgers were . . . the less said about the hamburgers, the better.

"What do you care? You don't drink. See you at nine-thirty."

"Why so late?"

But Shafer was gone. Apparently, no one said good-bye anymore.

———

Wells arrived at 9:15 to find Shafer sitting by himself at the bar. The only other people in the room were the bartender and four oldsters at a table littered with empty Bud Light bottles. The jukebox was for some reason playing Cyndi Lauper. **When the working day is done . . .**

"Place went downhill." Shafer's face was pouchy as a crumpled topographical map. Sprigs of white hair curled off his skull. An old-school Baltimore Bullets T-shirt hung limp off his scrawny shoulders. Seeing him immediately made Wells feel better.

"If Purgatory has a bar, it looks like this." Wells picked Shafer off the stool. "Gimme a hug, old man."

Shafer struggled like a raccoon in a trap, and about as effectively. "When did you start hugging?"

When I had a daughter. "So cute and cuddly. A Jewish koala."

"Anti-Semite."

"I'm anti-**everything**."

The bartender lurched over. "What you want?"

"Coke."

The bartender mumbled his disapproval but thumbed a spray of Coke into a smudged glass with two sad pieces of ice. "Four dollars."

"For a Coke?"

"What's the sign say, man?"

Wells instantly regretted talking back. "Shirley's?"

"It says **bar**. I don't trust anyone who comes in here and doesn't drink. And now it's five."

Wells fished in his wallet for a five.

"You don't tip?"

"Sorry about my friend," Shafer said. "He was dropped on his head as an adult." To Wells: "No, no, allow me. Please." He added his own five-dollar bill.

The bartender took the money and shuffled off.

"Flat?" Shafer muttered.

Wells sipped the Coke. "Completely."

"Admit it. There's pleasure in having your worst expectations confirmed. How's the Granite State?"

"Anne's pregnant."

Shafer raised his eyebrows. "You two need a television." He raised his glass. "**Salud.** I'd ask if you have any idea what you're doing but I know you don't, John. I guess you figured out where to put it, though."

"Be nice or I'll hug you again."

Suddenly the bartender muted the music, switched the television in the corner to CNN, the crawl at the bottom of the screen reading SENATOR PAUL BIRMAN, SPEAKING IN TENNESSEE . . . IN WAKE OF DALLAS ATTACKS, CALLS FOR TIGHTER RESTRICTIONS ON MUSLIM IMMIGRATION . . .

"We gotta watch this?" Shafer said.

"He spits it straight," the bartender said. "You don't like it, go on. Plenty places in this town got ESPN."

Wells had never seen Birman speak before. Now he understood why Duto was nervous. Birman was handsome, a crowd-pleaser. A populist with a preacher's drawl. Everything Duto wasn't. Anybody who could win over both the bartender at Shirley's and an arena of business owners could be president.

"Not at home," the bartender said when Birman was done. "That's right. No more nonsense."

"Watching that speech was thirsty work—" one of the guys in the booth said.

"Yeah, I got it." He brought them four fresh beers.

"Car accidents kill thirty-five thousand people a year in this country," Shafer muttered. "Alcohol a hundred thousand. This guy wants to turn our foreign policy upside down because idiots with AKs got loose at a basketball game. Sometimes the solution is worse than the problem."

"People want to be **safe**."

"Closer I get to the cliff, the more I see that's an illusion."

"Everyone dies, so why bother? That today's special, Ellis? Hope Duto's got something better."

"Guess a mosque will have to get firebombed before you hear the dog whistle. Birman's **dangerous**."

"Think he's going to introduce a war resolution like he says?"

"Yes. Might pass, too. So what's Duto want?"

Wells explained.

"Bogotá," Shafer said. "Long way from Dallas. You think it's real?"

"I can't figure why anyone down there would know anything. I think Duto's grasping at straws." As soon as he spoke, Wells knew he was right.

"What do you need from me?"

The moment Wells had dreaded. "Know an ops officer named Julie Tarnes?"

"She's all right. What about her?"

"Duto wants me to go through her from now on."

Shafer shook his head. "**Et tu, John-nus.**"

"I said only if it was okay with you."

"No you didn't. Because you knew it wouldn't be." Shafer poured himself more rotgut from a mysterious brown bottle. "How'd he sell it?"

"You can guess." Strange to think that only a couple years ago, Shafer had seemed unstoppable. But then, a couple years made a real difference at seventy.

"They're sick of us being **right**, John. Want to pretend that we didn't save their asses in Paris. They can't make me retire. Not even Duto."

"No one's making you retire, Ellis. He just wants me to use her for the operational stuff."

"You think Duto's looking out for you? Tarnes is his. This puts you under his thumb even more than you already are. You don't care if it means you get a fake passport five minutes early. Let me tell you, you get yourself stuck in a French jail, you think this woman's gonna save you?"

"I'll tell her no."

"You had your chance." Shafer slipped off his stool, strode out, leaving the door to slam.

The bartender turned at the noise, frowned at Wells. "Hey . . ."

"Don't worry. I got his tab."

"What'd you do to him, man?"

======

Wells walked up New York Avenue, a depressing slog past train yards and strip clubs. Finally, he found a Holiday Inn Express, where he spent the night staring at the ceiling. He'd committed no shortage of sins. But he'd never thought of himself as disloyal. Until now. He told himself Shafer had no cause for complaint. Wells couldn't help the fact Shafer had angered so many people at Langley. Or that Shafer was old.

But the words didn't stick.

Not how he wanted to start this mission.

Around 5 a.m. he gave up on sleeping and went down to what passed for the hotel's gym. Two rickety treadmills and a cheap weight machine. He nearly tore a cable out of its socket working his lats. Birman's speech was the lead story on every channel. **The Republican Party has a new front-runner . . . President Duto has always said he couldn't go to war against the Islamic State even if he wanted to because Congress hasn't given him the power. This resolution would change that . . . What does Birman's rise** mean for Muslims in the United States? We'll talk to two imams . . .

All this after just one attack. What about next time?

Wells arrived at Compass Coffee showered and scrubbed and wanting to be angry at Tarnes. She stood out front, a tall woman, mid-thirties, short blond hair flat against her skull, a prominent chin, the start of sun damage around her brown eyes. She wore a gray pantsuit that showed off her long legs. A striking woman. Wells imagined she'd had to deal with her share of unwanted advances in Pakistan and Iraq.

"Should we walk?" Her voice was quiet and confident. Husky. She led him east down P Street, past a giant school, uniformed kids running for the doors.

"How do you know Vinny?" Wells said.

She gave him a searching look. He wondered if she and Duto were lovers. Duto was thirty years her senior, but presidents got what they wanted. Then Wells realized they weren't. But the question had come up before, and Tarnes was tired of hearing it. All this without a word spoken.

"Every few months, a bunch of us go across the river for a chat."

"Rising stars."

"Something like that."

"I'm sure Ludlow appreciates Vinny pretending he's still DCIA." Peter Ludlow was the agency's director. He'd failed to catch a traitor who had betrayed the CIA to the Islamic State, but Duto had let him stay on. In part because the mistake belonged to Duto, too.

The traitor was gone now, his secrets buried with him. Even within the agency, only a handful of officers knew what had happened. Wells didn't know if Tarnes was among them. The agency was a gossipy place, but some stories didn't spread.

"I have no idea what the director does or does not appreciate. But last week the President brought me in again, asked me if I was ready for a special assignment." Another hard look: **Don't say it. Don't even think it.**

"Any idea why he chose you?"

"None." The denial a touch too fast. She had an idea. Wells let the hint go.

"You were in Pakistan?"

"I was."

"What was that like?"

"**You** know."

"Tell me anyway."

"I don't think I had an honest conversation in three years."

"No different than Langley, then."

She gave him a smile and then whisked it off. "I actually preferred being at the combat outposts with the operators. At least out there we knew who the enemy was."

"Maybe."

"Maybe. You really Muslim?"

"Indeed I am."

"I have a hard time seeing you in a mosque."

"Now you're just being argumentative." Wells couldn't help himself, he liked this woman. "So you're my fixer now, Julie?"

"Call me what you like."

"And still have your day job. So what happens if I need you, you're in Islamabad or whatever?"

"You're my priority, John. The President made that clear."

"Can you call him Vinny for me?"

"I cannot."

"Will you be asking me why I need what I need? Gear, cash, op support, anything else?"

"I will not. Tell me or don't, your choice."

"And if I choose to tell you and you think I'm making a mistake—"

"I will tell you so and then deliver what you've requested."

"Sounds perfect. Except for the part where you tell Vinny everything."

"You think he doesn't find out if the ask comes

from Shafer? You think all that cash and all those guns don't get logged?"

Point, Tarnes. Wells liked to pretend the agency's help came for free. It didn't.

"You do what I ask **before** you tell Vinny. You okay with that?"

"Yes."

"Don't say yes unless you're sure."

A pause. "Okay."

Wells decided to trust her. A little. "Vinny tell you anything specific about what I might need?"

She shook her head.

"Clean pistol, a clean passport, and, say, fifteen thousand dollars delivered to a hotel in Bogotá tomorrow."

"I thought you were going to ask for something complicated." She tapped his hand with two elegant fingers, her touch light enough to mean anything he wanted. "Any preference on the pistol?"

"Loaded." Wells thought of Anne, pregnant with his son. Was he flirting with this woman? He didn't want to be, but he couldn't seem to help himself.

"The best kind. You have the hotel yet?"

"I'll let you know." He stood. "Nice to meet you, Julie. Don't screw me."

She saluted. And grinned.

4

Nothing had ever come easy for Tom Miller.

His dad split the day after Miller turned five, ditched him and his mom to move to Florida. **Time to start fresh,** he said. Conveniently forgetting what he'd already spoiled. Veronica and Tom spent the next decade near poor. Like poverty was a place, a barren land easy to enter, hard to leave. They were never evicted. But sometimes they moved in a hurry. Tom never went hungry. But sometimes Veronica came home with a pizza on Tuesday, and he knew it would have to last them both until her next check on Friday.

Lucky him, she didn't eat much.

They lived in Chula Vista, Phoenix, Las Vegas. Dusty, overgrown desert cities where dreams went to wither, in apartments built to code but never better. By ten, Miller knew what they'd

look like before he saw them. Two little bedrooms, a toilet that needed careful handling, a
kitchen with a wall-mounted microwave and an
electric range.

Veronica mostly worked telemarketing. When
Miller was in ninth grade, she met a trucker named
Jared over the phone, pitching life insurance. Jared
lived in Colfax, the southeastern corner of Washington State, and to Colfax they went. It was a
town of three thousand people, better and worse
than the desert cities Miller knew. It was pretty.
Not the forests he'd expected, more open. Big rolling hills that rose to the Idaho mountains.

But it was seriously hick. The nearest city of
any size was Spokane, sixty miles north. And
Spokane hardly counted, anyway. At least in
Vegas, Miller and his mom went to the Strip once
in a while, checked out the limos and the strip-
pers handing out nudie postcards. Once, outside
Caesars, a guy in a Hawaiian shirt pushed two
tickets on Veronica—**I can't,** he said. **Long story,
my wife. Anyway, Cirque du Soleil, the Bellagio. You look like you could use it. Go.**

For an afternoon, life was magic.

Nothing like that could ever happen in Colfax. Colfax was white guys in pickup trucks.
Miller was brown. His mom was Mexican. He
had a white name from dear old Dad, the only

proof the guy had ever existed. Miller didn't make friends easily, had never bothered to try since he always figured he'd be moving again soon enough. The handful of Hispanic kids at Colfax Junior-Senior High didn't know what to do with him. The white kids ignored him.

He had acne scars and a voice so quiet the teachers asked him to speak up. He was sturdy, though, and tougher than he looked. After his first fight, the bullies left him alone. He was physically exceptional in only one way, his eyesight, 20/9, the edge of the curve. He could see the spin of a baseball as soon as it left the pitcher's hand, though he still couldn't hit it. In a luckier life, he would have been a fighter pilot.

He was an average student, lousy at math. A slow reader with his good eyes, though he loved to read, loved it all the more **because** he was slow. The Harry Potter books gave him a full year of pleasure. Senior-year English he wrote looping strange stories. After a while, he realized they weren't good, and he didn't know how to make them better. He was devastated. He'd thought about community college, trying to write. He realized he'd have a better chance at being an astronaut.

Jared had a house, the first time Miller had lived in a house. Even had a lawn. But it didn't feel like his. His mom was home all the time. She said she was tired of working. And Jared made enough money for them, anyway, so why bother? Once in a while, he'd hear them screwing and wonder how they managed. Jared was three hundred pounds of rest-stop fried chicken and waffles. He couldn't possibly be lying on top of her. Were they on all fours? **Gross.**

Jared was all right otherwise. He treated Veronica decently. But he'd made clear he wouldn't be paying for college or anything else for Miller.

Time to go.

Miller decided to enlist. He'd probably wind up in Afghanistan, the war was hotting up, but why not? He wondered if his mom would try to talk him out of signing up. She didn't. Jared was all for it, of course. Miller checked out the Marines first, but they were a little in love with themselves. **The Few. The Proud.** The whatever. Miller wasn't that proud. He went with the Army and, from the start, he liked it. He didn't mind the yelling. The sergeants seemed to care about him. Or at least about making him a better soldier. **Case you didn't notice, there's a war on, dummy!**

After Basic, Miller signed for the infantry, the real Army. He spent 2011 patrolling villages in Kandahar Province. March through October, the insurgents showed up for firefights once a week. Like they were punching a clock. Maybe they were. Two guys from the company died in IED attacks. A sniper paralyzed another. It wasn't fun, exactly, especially when the Talibs got around to mortaring their combat outpost, but it was fine. Miller's eyesight came in more than handy. On patrol, he spotted bombs and hidey-holes everyone else missed. Enemy fire didn't rattle him. If anything, he felt calmer after the shooting began. Confirmed kills were tough to come by because the Talibs pulled their corpses after skirmishes, but he wound up with two. He was pretty sure of three more, even if the Army didn't give him credit.

On base, he found the Game of Thrones series, five beautifully long novels. After a couple months reading about Sansa Stark, he made the mistake of telling a couple of the guys that he was a virgin. Women had always been a foreign country to him. The mockery that followed was good-natured but relentless. It peaked when Miller's platoon sergeant, a Kentucky fireplug with the up-country name of Willie Coole, paid a late-night visit to his hutch, leading a donkey wearing a big red ribbon.

Got her greased for you, PFC. No soldier of mine dies without getting his dick wet. 'Course, you'll have to wear this. Coole wagged a condom at Miller. **Maybe you didn't know, but Mexicans and donkeys can breed.**

He was surprised to realize that the guys liked him, and he liked them. He would realize later the tour had been the best year of his life.

When it ended, Miller's captain told him he should go to Sniper School, a five-week course at Fort Benning. Soldiers didn't have to be in the Rangers or other elite units to apply. Regular infantry needed snipers, too.

Think I can be a Ranger, Captain?

Start with Sniper School.

====

The shooting wasn't the problem. His eyesight gave him a natural advantage. But his ghillie suit never looked quite right. And though he was great at spotting enemy positions, he couldn't figure out the best spots for his own hides. **Just try to imagine what they're seeing,** his instructors said. **What you'd see if you were on the other side.** He tried. But he couldn't. He knew he was bumping up against the limits of his brain. He remembered those stories senior year, how flat they'd seemed when he reread them. He couldn't make them work, couldn't figure out how to tell the world what was in his head.

He wished he was smart enough to understand. Or dumb enough that his failure wouldn't bother him.

Still, in the real world, snipers set up inside buildings and on rooftops, where a ghillie suit didn't mean much. And no one could argue with his aim. Miller passed, barely. Three months later, he signed for Ranger training. Back to Fort Benning. He survived the preliminaries. The instructors liked him. But he couldn't lead patrols for all the money in New York. He moved his men the wrong way, called in artillery on his own positions. He was overwhelmed rather than afraid. But from the military's point of view, the reasons hardly mattered. After he flunked the second time, he thought about begging for one more shot.

But he knew he'd fail again.

He told himself he didn't care. He did. Being a Ranger would have meant really succeeding for the first time in his life. The Army respected its Rangers. Instead, Miller would be just another grunt who couldn't earn his tab.

While he was at Ranger School, the Army broke up his company. He was reassigned to the 1st Cavalry Division, at Fort Hood, Texas. He'd been there seven long months when his phone buzzed with a middle-of-the-night call. A 509 area code. Colfax.

"Mr. Miller?"

Strange to hear **Mr.** rather than **Specialist.** "Yes, sir."

"This is Deputy Drew Caprin of the Whitman County Sheriff's Department. Any chance you can come down to headquarters?"

"I'm in Texas, sir."

"In that case, I have some bad news."

Deputies had found his mother and Jared dead in their living room. Heroin. At least now Miller understood why Veronica had acted so weird the last time he'd seen her. Sleepy, mumbly, hardly interested in what he was saying.

"What about your mother's body? Should we hold it for burial?"

Miller hesitated, realized he was furious with her for leaving him this way. "Cremation's fine."

He flew to Colfax to clean out her stuff, got one surprise. Jared and Veronica hadn't married, so Miller wasn't entitled to anything of his. Veronica's life savings consisted of two thousand dollars he found stuffed in her panty drawer.

But Jared had bought a new pickup a month before the overdose. A Ram 1500 Quad Cab with all the trimmings. Fifty-five grand. Jared had borrowed against the house instead of taking out a note, so it was free and clear. And for reasons only Jared and Veronica knew, they'd titled it in her name. Jared's crummy kids moaned to high heaven when they found out, since the pickup was worth more than the house. But the sheriff left no room for argument. Her truck, so it belonged to Miller now.

On the way back to Fort Hood, he stopped in Vegas, dumped Veronica's ashes into the Bellagio fountain. Maybe the lights and the noise would give her something to do. Inside, he met a girl. Chloe, so she said. She was taller than he was. Long brown hair. Breasts too perfect to be anything but fake. Sixty seconds in, she whispered, **Six hundred for an hour, two grand for the night.** Her fingers stroked his wrist, and he wanted her as he'd never wanted anything. Even the Rangers.

In the room, she made him show her the money before she undressed. He blurted out that he was a virgin, and she laughed. **Nobody's a virgin.** Miller hadn't cried since his sixth birthday, when he'd realized his dad wouldn't be coming home to take him to McDonald's. He didn't cry now. But he wished he could. His mom hadn't been perfect, but he'd loved her. He'd trusted her. Wrong. He couldn't trust anyone. Not even a woman he'd bought and paid for.

Chloe must have seen he was telling the truth and decided to go easy on him. **Guess it's your lucky day, then, soldier. No condom. Normally, that's double.**

An inheritance well spent.

Three months later, the pickup was in storage, and Miller was back in Kandahar. The war had changed, for the worse. Fewer soldiers, more insurgents. The Talibs were bolder, the bombs bigger. And this time around, Miller's company captain was a jerk. Guy seemed to think he could win the war all by himself. **We're taking it to them**, he said. **High ops tempo. Move to contact.** So they moved to contact. Which mostly meant IEDs. They rode in mine-resistant armored protecteds, MRAPs, heavy trucks with steel plates underneath to deflect blasts. But a big enough bomb could bust all that steel.

The first hit came two months into the tour. Miller had taken off his helmet. Dumb. But the truck's air-conditioning was out, and he was sweating like a pig, and they were on a stretch of road that had been safe. He heard a whoosh as the truck, all eighteen tons, went airborne. His head slammed against the truck's steel wall. The world went dark.

When he came to, he couldn't figure out where he was. For a few seconds, he was almost giddy.

"Miller . . . Miller!" A round white face, his sergeant, though Miller couldn't remember his name—

Nausea replaced euphoria. Miller tried to vomit, came up with only a thin stream of sour drool.

The blast had blown the truck's rear axle, leaving it stuck. Miller watched as the back gate dropped and the rest of his squad piled out. He couldn't move. He felt like he was inside a video game and whoever was playing him had dropped the controller. His sergeant grabbed him, wrenched him out. The Afghan sun clawed his eyes. He hid them behind his palms and sagged until his knees touched soil.

At the outpost, the company medic prescribed rest and darkness. Three days passed before his captain came to his hutch and asked how he felt. Miller made the mistake of telling the truth. He still had some buzzing in his ears, but the dizziness was gone.

"Good. We're setting a checkpoint on the road to Helmand, and you're gonna overwatch. I've had enough of you lying in here." The captain looked like he was made of blocks, a square head on square shoulders that filled out his perfect neat uniform.

The checkpoint was set to last four days. The first three days went fine—they even caught a couple guys—but on the fourth it turned out the Talibs had been watching them, too. The IED was dug deep by the side of the road, a quarter mile before the checkpoint.

This time, Miller was wearing his helmet, but it didn't seem to matter. He fell down a hole and vanished. When he woke, his head hurt like somebody had cranked a vise around his skull. A black man in a white coat stood near the bed. "Specialist. How are you this morning?"

Miller could feel the words forming in his head before he said them. Uncanny. "Head. Hurts."

"Believe it or not, that's a good sign. Remember me?"

Miller tried to shake his head, decided he'd better not. He was sure he'd never seen this man before.

"I'm Dr. Morgan. I've treated you since you were brought in last week."

"Where I am?" The wrong way to say it, but he didn't know the right one.

"KAF." Kandahar Airfield. "Remember anything?"

The MRAP's engine rumbled in his ears. "IED."

"Good. More than yesterday. You'll start making new memories soon."

The thought didn't particularly please Miller. He looked around the clean white room. "Sir."

"Call me doc."

"Doc. When do I go back?"

"Soon as you're fit to fly." Morgan rested a hand on Miller's shoulder. "Your war's over, Specialist."

=====

Morgan was wrong. Miller's war had just begun. He spent a month at Walter Reed, where he was officially diagnosed with a moderate traumatic brain injury and post-concussive symptoms. He received a medical discharge four months later, at Fort Hood. His sensitivity to light had faded. But he still had regular headaches and anxiety attacks.

The Veterans Administration gave him a sixty percent disability rating, entitling him to a little more than a thousand dollars a month. Miller had never believed that the military would take care of him for life. Being a soldier was a job. No one had made him sign up.

Even so, the payment seemed stupidly small. Almost disrespectful. His mood swung from angry to depressed to empty. The emptiness scared him most of all. The military shrinks called it **loss of affect**. He even stopped reading. For a while, he couldn't make the words stand still. Then his brain recovered enough to put them together in sentences. But they felt as silly as a Halloween costume. Heroes and villains, swords and sorcerers, when the reality was buried bombs and ice-pick headaches. For this, the United States government saw fit to give him not even forty bucks a day.

After his discharge, he went back to Colfax. He wanted quiet and green. Between the pay he'd saved and the disability check, he figured he could rent a trailer and get by. Wasn't like he had fancy taste or a wife to worry about. He could always sell the pickup, if cash ran low. Plus the VA had a clinic in Lewiston, just over the border in Idaho. He wouldn't have to go too far for his meds. The shrinks at Fort Hood had made a point of telling him, **Stay connected to the community, isolation kills more soldiers than anything else.**

To which Miller wanted to answer, **Try IEDs.**

Mostly, the shrinks gave him meds. They'd put him on half the alphabet: Ambien, Celexa, Depakote, Imitrex, Klonopin, Paxil, Risperdal, Seroquel, trazodone, Valium, Wellbutrin. Usually, he was taking at least four at once. He didn't know if they made him better or worse. They fogged him up so much that he stopped them cold turkey. Then he couldn't sleep, and the panic attacks came back. He wound up mixing old and new prescriptions, a one-man psychotropic clinical trial.

In Colfax, Miller found himself a clean enough trailer east of town for six hundred a month. It had four acres, nestled between a hill and a stream, so he couldn't see his neighbors. He spent the rest of his monthly check on beer, pizza, and pot. Eastern Washington was home to some of the best dope in the United States and it was now legal. Not medicinal marijuana. Fully legal, thanks to the wisdom of the voters of Washington State. Anyone over twenty-one could buy weed.

Miller hadn't smoked much growing up. But he found marijuana took his headaches away better than the pills. Bad news was that it killed whatever motivation he had left. Made him a little paranoid, too. Maybe **paranoid** wasn't the right word. He found himself watching the Weather Channel for hours, hitting his bong and wondering what it would be like to **control** the weather. Then he'd start thinking he did control the weather. Because he knew exactly what the forecasters were going to say. No great secret why. They repeated themselves every hour.

Plus he put on twenty-five pounds in six months. One day, he realized his gut stuck out so far, he couldn't even see his little man. He decided to quit smoking for a while. Which wasn't easy. His headaches came back, though not as bad.

Worse, he now had to waste all those hours

some other way. Pot had helped him forget how lonely he was. He'd lost touch with everyone but Coole, his old platoon sergeant. Coole was out of the Army now, too. He'd invited Miller east a couple times, but Miller just couldn't deal with being anyone's charity case.

Lucky for him, he had the Internet, the greatest time waster and friend substitute ever invented. He joined a vets-only message board. Guys posted about how the VA was killing them all, how much civilians sucked, how they wished they could go over again and this time they wouldn't go light on the **hajjis**. In truth, the boards could be whiny. Miller said so. **I was a sniper,** he wrote. **Bet most of you never even got off KAF.**

Sniper, my ass, a guy whose handle identified him as **82vetlittlerock** wrote back. **Prove it.**

Miller posted a pic of his certification. Then, showing off, a pic of his best shooting ever, a three-round cluster, four inches at a thousand yards.

At the end, he'd figure out that's how she found him.

———

A VA therapist put him in touch with a vet who lived south of Colfax. Fred Urquhart. A few years older. He'd done his time in Baghdad instead of Kandahar. But he was infantry. He knew the drill. Once in a while, they met up at the Hyde Out Tavern to drink beer and not talk. Urquhart was as close to a friend as Miller had found since that first tour.

Six p.m., and **Thursday Night Football** was about to start. The Bengals and the Falcons. One of the benefits of living on the West Coast. Miller could watch the game and be home by ten. He was three beers in. Light beers. He'd lost fifteen pounds, but he had ten to go. Or maybe a little more.

A woman came in. Blue eyes, blond hair, tight sweater, long legs in black pants. Urquhart's head swiveled to follow her like he was a radar dish and she was a missile.

"Kidding me? Do you see that?"

Miller saw. The first, last, and only time Miller had been up close with a woman who looked like her had been that night at the Bellagio. Still the only time he'd had sex. There was a secretary at the VA in Lewiston who'd asked him to a movie. But she weighed two hundred pounds. Miller thought sometimes he'd made a mistake losing his virginity to Chloe. Tough for a regular girl to compete. Anyway, sex—the act itself—had seemed like **work** since that second

IED. Even when he was taking care of business himself, he lost the thread sometimes, couldn't focus long enough to finish.

The blonde sat down by herself two tables over. Every guy in the room looked her over like she was the daily special. Miller saw the wariness in her eyes: **Leave me alone, okay?** She looked up at the door like she was waiting for someone. Miller knew she wasn't. Up close, he saw the hints of wear and tear. A faded thumbprint bruise on her cheek. A tiny pimple from too much makeup on her chin. Suddenly he thought he could help her, if she'd let him close enough to try. He **wanted** to help her. The first time since that second bomb that he'd cared about anything.

Urquhart gave up looking after a minute. "Chicks like that, forget it," he muttered. "Waste of time."

"Yeah." But Miller already knew he wasn't leaving until she did. Even if he couldn't imagine working up the nerve to talk to her. He drank slow and careful and peeked at her while she nursed a Jack-and-Coke and a basket of fries. Then, at halftime, two guys came over to her table.

Miller knew them from high school. Their names, anyway. Don and Rob. They'd been seniors when he was a sophomore. The kinda guys who had parties Miller didn't hear about until a week later. Don's dad owned the biggest dairy in the county, if Miller remembered right. They wore purple University of Washington caps. Heresy around here, and a status symbol. Washington State was in Pullman, fifteen miles away. UW was in Seattle.

She shook her head.

"Come on, babe," Don said. "We don't bite."

"I'm waiting for somebody."

"I'm Don." Don reached for his wallet, tilted it toward the woman so she couldn't avoid noticing that it was thick with bills. "What's your name?"

"Allie."

"Tell you what, Allie. I'll buy you a drink, tell you a joke. You don't think it's funny, we go back to the bar, you can drink alone. Until your friend comes, I mean."

"All right." Her voice small. Like she didn't have the energy to argue.

"Knock, knock!"

"Who's there?"

"Dwayne."

"Dwayne who?"

"Dwayne the bathtub! I'm dw-owning!"

Rob chortled. The dutiful wingman. They pulled up chairs and spent the next two hours pushing drinks on her, patient and skillful as wolves separating a lame deer from the herd.

One shot. One won't hurt. How about Jäger? That goes down smooth—

You're from L.A.? Cool, a buddy of mine from Seattle's an actor there. He's been in commercials, wants me to move down, but I tell him this is God's country—

Yeah, I was dating someone for a while, but she just wasn't the one. I mean, she was pretty, but I didn't think she understood me. In fact, I feel more connected to you already. Believe it, 'cause it's true—

All the old, tired crap, like if Don kept shoveling, he'd build a pile high enough to jump over her walls. Allie laughed dutifully. A few times, Miller thought she was trying to catch his eye.

As the Falcons game ended, she went to the bathroom. She took mincing steps between the tables, the way Miller had in the first weeks at Walter Reed. She came back with her face still wet from the water she'd splashed on it to sober herself up.

"I gotta go."

"We'll take you."

"It's okay. Few blocks."

"No trouble, really. Wouldn't want you to get into any trouble." Don showed her his milk-white teeth.

Miller had seen enough. Why did rich people always think they could have whatever they wanted? They were going to wheedle her until she gave in or exhausted herself saying no.

Suddenly he was next to her. He hadn't moved that fast since Ranger School.

"She said **no**."

Don looked up with genuine shock. Like a beer bottle had started talking. "The fuck are you." Not a question, because Don's tone made clear he couldn't have cared less.

"You don't have to do this," she muttered.

"You want them, I'll go."

She laughed, a flash of the cool girl she'd once been. "Do I **want** them? What do you think?"

"Tell you what she doesn't want," Don said. "A little brown man with holes in his face."

Miller flashed back to Kandahar, sighting on a Talib and squeezing the trigger, the guy spinning sideways, legs splayed, gray-brown jacket flaring out as he fell.

He stepped around the table, stood over Don. Every conversation in the bar shut down at once.

Don's lips twitched in an **I can't believe this** smile. He pushed himself up. He was six inches taller than Miller, broad-shouldered, stinking of aftershave. "Three seconds, amigo, two, one—"

Don swung his meaty fist in a looping roundhouse. He was big and strong, but alcohol had dulled his reflexes. Miller remembered the sergeants at Basic: **Get in close and end it. If you're not winning, you're losing.** He ducked, shoved Don against the wall, wrapped his right hand around the bigger man's neck, squeezed the thick flesh there, feeling the Adam's apple beneath his palm.

Don grabbed for Miller's wrist, but now being smaller helped. Miller held on as Don flailed. After five long seconds, Miller twisted away, wrapped his left arm around Don's shoulders, wrenched him off the wall, stuck out a leg to trip him. Don fell on all fours, his breathing shallow and ragged. Miller needed every bit of the discipline the Army had taught not to kick him in the ribs and do real damage, the kind that would get him arrested. Urquhart shadowed Rob on the other side of the table. Miller had known Urquhart would have his back.

Don pushed himself to his feet, rubbing his throat, coughing wetly.

"Want her that bad, Romeo? Go for it. Take it from me, get her tested first."

══════

Miller had kept his trailer tidy even in the worst of his depression. Some remnant of military discipline. He was glad now. Allie slept on his couch. But just before dawn, she slipped into his bed. Still dressed. He didn't know what she wanted. And he was afraid to betray his ignorance. She smelled of sweet, cheap shampoo. He wanted to bury his face in her hair, but he couldn't move.

A little brown man with holes in his face. And he thought he deserved her?

"Tom Miller. Real name?" Her voice was low. With a hint of a European accent, though Miller couldn't be sure. Like she'd been born here but her parents somewhere else.

"Yes, ma'am."

She was silent for a minute that felt like an hour. "Thank you, Tom Miller."

"Got tired of the way they were looking at you."

She took his hand, wrapped her long fingers around his. "I'm so tired." Her breathing softened, and she was asleep. As sudden as an infant. And he slept, too.

===

When he woke, he half expected her to be gone. Maybe the truck, too. But she sat at the trailer's kitchen table, drinking apple juice. She'd taken off her sweater. Her bra wasn't fancy. It didn't need to be. She had the most beautiful breasts

Miller had ever seen. Not too-round, like Chloe's, but full and real. A faded yellow bruise stretched down her right bicep.

She'd opened the trailer's back windows. Miller heard the stream rushing, the jays outside.

"I think I'd like to stay a while."

She could have told him that she was a murderer who had just escaped from death row and he would have said yes.

———

They moved her stuff from the motel that morning. She didn't have much. A backpack and a little roller bag. She'd told him she'd gone from L.A. to Seattle and then realized Seattle was the same. Too many bars, too many nights she couldn't remember. Or wished she couldn't. She'd picked Colfax for its name; she'd lived in Denver, once upon a time, and remembered a bar she liked on Colfax Avenue there.

"Back then, I was beautiful. I thought I'd make it. There's five thousand girls in L.A. just like me."

"Shut up."

"More. So I left. Guess what? I get here and I can't even sit and watch the game without the whole thing starting again. What is it about me? I would have let them, you know. It's like—"

She went silent. He was already used to her silences. He liked them.

"Like I forgot I even had a choice."

———

He offered her his bed. She insisted on the couch. On her fifth night, she crept in with him, as she had the first morning. "You don't like me, Tom."

"Is that what you think?"

"Then why don't you try?" She leaned in, kissed him.

The thought of being with her panicked him. Like looking into the sun. "You don't have to."

She kissed him again, her tongue darting into his mouth. "Let me."

So he did. She was gentle with him. Kind, even when the first time ended almost before it started.

"I'm not much of a lover." He couldn't remember ever saying the word before.

"You'll get better."

"What about—" He had a box of condoms in his bathroom cabinet. He hadn't even thought about them. "You know." Crazy for him to be shy, considering how many guys she must have been with, but he couldn't help himself.

She touched his fingers to her bicep so he could feel the capsule inside. "Norplant."

Miller felt a tinge of disappointment that he couldn't make her pregnant. And, naïve as he was, he knew he was lost.

======

She smoked pot every afternoon. The only thing he would have changed about her. He couldn't tell her. Instead, he smoked with her. She had her own stash. When it was gone, they bought more from a head shop in Pullman. She liked the high-THC stuff, a brand called Mind Eraser. Truth in advertising. They'd light up around 2, sit on the couch, watch soap operas. Try to watch them, anyway. The afternoon would vanish. Around 5 or 6, they'd come down. She'd snuggle in his arms until he microwaved some pizza.

Until the night he felt her hot tears on his arm. Her face was pale. Despairing.

He stroked her hair. Thought of the newborn mice who lived under this trailer, tiny and mewling. He feared she'd vanish if he said the wrong words, whatever spell keeping her here would end.

"I'm dirty inside," she said.

"You're the most perfect person I've ever met."

"Do you ever think they used up all the good in you?"

Miller didn't need to ask who **they** were. "You're safe now."

"What if I'm not? What if they're watching?"

"No one's watching."

"They don't even have to. You know what I mean?"

He did. They were always watching. Waiting to see how much more they could take from him. He wondered what they'd taken from this woman.

They weren't the police. They **owned** the police.

"Maybe."

"Like wanting to punish God," she said. "No point even thinking about it."

"Forget it, then."

But she shook her head.

———

To balance the afternoon munchies, he started exercising hard in the morning, running and push-ups and sit-ups—simple stuff. He couldn't fix his skin, but he could get himself in shape. He bought her boots, and they went for easy hikes near Spokane, around the Columbia River.

He bought one of those **Be a better lover** pornos, too. One night she said, **Yes, that's it. Yes, please.** She wrapped her arms around him and moaned, and he thought, **If I die right now, it's okay. Better than okay.**

He kept waiting for her to ask for money, but she didn't. Still, he knew the bill was coming due.

Winter now. A new year. They were each other's whole world. They hardly went anywhere. He'd never seen Urquhart after that night at the Hyde Out. Allie didn't want him to tell Urquhart that she was still in Colfax. **I want to vanish for a while. Be nobody. Nowhere.** So he was nobody, too.

They were in bed. Wednesday night. One week after those terrible attacks in Dallas. She put a hand on his stomach, tracing the new muscle there.

"If I leave, Tom—"

"What?" He was out of the bed on his feet. Watching. Hyperaware.

"If I leave, I want you to know it's not you."

He wanted to tell her, **You can't, never.** But he'd imagined this conversation before, the way he'd imagined his own death. He'd promised himself he wouldn't beg. Or threaten. Wouldn't join the endless ranks of men telling her what to do.

"Baby." All he could think to say.

"What if it's not safe here either?"

"We'll find someplace."

"You don't know what I'm talking about, Tom. You think you do, but you don't. If I go—"

"Don't say that, Allie, please—"

"Promise you won't try to find me."

He lay back beside her, but he couldn't sleep.

In the morning, he went for a run. When he came back, the truck was gone. The note on the counter said he could find it on Main Street, outside the hardware store where the Greyhounds stopped.

> Remember what I said. Don't try to find me. There are things I haven't told you, things I can't tell anyone. They make me too angry. They make me dangerous.
>
> These months have been the best of my life, Tom. I can't forget you, and staying away will be the hardest thing in the world, but I want you to forget me.
>
> Always yours, always faithful,
> always love,
> Allie

He was dizzy, and the words danced the way they had when he'd tried to read after the IED.

He tore the note to pieces. He wanted to do the same to the trailer. He would never hurt her, but right then he wanted to kill her. How could she take herself from him? The cruelest of the world's tricks. He'd been furious when his mother died. Now he wanted to lie on his bed and close his eyes and will his heart to stop.

In the bathroom, he checked the little orange bottles. Fifty Klonopin. A good start. About twenty Ambien. Plus the liter of Smirnoff in the freezer. Yeah, that would do—

Then he thought of what she'd written . . . **staying away will be the hardest thing in the world . . .**

No. He wasn't taking the easy way out. The coward's way. He would wait for her. Even if he had to wait his whole life. Because she was coming back.

When she did, he would do what he needed to make sure they were together. Forever.

5

BOGOTÁ, COLOMBIA

Hurry up and wait—the motto of soldiers and spies. Wells had arrived in Bogotá four days before, checked into the Hotel de la Opera, in La Candelaria, the city's oldest quarter. For five hundred years, the neighborhood had survived earthquakes, fires, and civil wars. Seemed like a decent bet. It wasn't where Wells had told Julie Tarnes he'd be staying. He still didn't entirely trust her.

First, always, local burner phones. Wells bought two, called Enrique Martinez.

"Soon, my friend."

Wells realized what Martinez wasn't saying.

"This man, he's not even in Colombia, is he?"

Martinez's silence gave Wells his answer.

"Tell me where, I'll go to him."

"Just wait, please."

Like I have a choice.

———

The next morning, Wells called Tarnes.

"Where are you?" She sounded irritated. "Our guy tried to deliver your stuff."

"Noon today. Outside El Campín, the west side."

"El Campín?"

"El Campín." El Campín, officially known as Estadio Nemesio Camacho, was the biggest **fút-bol** stadium in Bogotá. "I'll be the gringo in the Red Sox cap."

"Sounds like you'll fit right in. Why so complicated, John?"

"Noon."

Wells arrived a half hour early. Colombians loved soccer almost as much as Brazilians, but none of the teams that shared the stadium were playing today. The plaza was nearly empty. Wells bought a red **Independiente Santa Fe** jersey and hat, walked slowly around the stadium. If he had watchers, he couldn't find them.

Fifteen minutes later, a motorcycle weaved into the plaza, pulled up beside Wells, the engine still idling. The rider wore a **Speed Racer**–style white helmet covered with stickers for bands that

Wells didn't know. He was in his late twenties, skinny, light-skinned Hispanic. An olive green backpack sat between his legs.

"Mr. Walton?" His accent was more Florida than Colombia. He handed over the pack. Wells peeked inside, found a pistol, extra magazines, a Ka-Bar knife, an auto pick, three-inch squares of duct tape with adhesive backing, and other goodies. Everything he'd asked for.

"**Gracias.** What's your name?"

"Tony."

"I may need more help, Tony."

"Long as you have more money."

Kids these days . . . "No worries."

"In that case." Tony scribbled his number and passed it to Wells.

═══

For the next three days, Wells called Martinez at noon. Each time, Martinez said only, **Nothing yet.**

Wells wanted to like Bogotá. It was bigger than he'd expected, just over eight million people, and pretty, overlooked by a green mountain ridge to the east. Though it was only a few hundred miles north of the equator, it lay almost nine thousand feet above sea level, so it was rarely too hot. It had a new airport and a bustling downtown. On Sunday mornings, the city even made some streets bicycles-only, turning them into a rolling open-air party called the Ciclovia.

But its extremes of wealth and poverty were inescapable. The rich lived in the north, in fortress houses and apartment complexes hidden behind razor wire. They shopped at heavily guarded malls that offered the usual overpriced brands and stayed out late dancing to DJs who'd flown in from Miami.

Meanwhile, the poor clumped in barrios of mud-and-brick houses in the south of the city. Ironically, the poorest barrios, like the most expensive apartments, occupied the mountainsides. But where the wealthy paid for fantastic views of Bogotá's sunsets, the poor were forced up. The hill slums lacked basic services like sewer systems. Every necessity had to be carried in. And though crime in Bogotá had fallen since the torment of Colombia's civil war, the police were still overwhelmed. They protected the rich and left the barrios to their own justice. Once or twice a week, mob vigilantes beat suspected murderers or thieves to death.

The Ciclovia was practically the only time that Bogotá's rich and poor came together.

Wells felt oddly exposed in Bogotá, too. In Muslim countries, he didn't stand out. His fluent

Arabic gave him the chance to pass as Lebanese or North African. But Arabic didn't help here. Colombia had barely ten thousand Muslims. And Wells's Spanish was limited to Taco Bell basics— **uno, dos, tres.** Wells knew that gangs watched the streets of La Candelaria. He would attract their attention soon, if he hadn't already. He would give them more trouble than they expected. But he preferred to avoid that fight.

He began to wonder if Duto had sent him to Colombia as a diversion. The idea didn't make sense. Why bother? But the conspiratorial thoughts proved his frustration with this open-ended delay. Worse, the trail to the Dallas killers was fading by the hour.

On his fifth morning, Wells realized he was done waiting.

"Enrique. Time to talk. Face-to-face. **Now.**"

A pause.

"All right. We're coming into our pied—" Wells didn't get the word at first, though Martinez's accent was perfect. "I'll send someone for you."

=====

Martinez's **pied** turned out to be a four-bedroom penthouse apartment in the mountains above Calle 140, fifteen kilometers and a million miles from La Candelaria. Even with Martinez's body-guard vouching for him, Wells had to submit to a pat-down from the building's doorman.

To Wells's surprise, Martinez opened the door himself. He was a squat man with a bullfrog's jowls and short gray hair. A general gone to fat. He grinned when he saw Wells. The woman be-side him was half his age, six inches taller, and blond. A boy of five stood behind her.

"Simon, say hello." The boy dashed off. "And this is Vanessa. **Mi amor.**"

"I'm certainly his wife," she said.

"I'm John. Didn't know I was meeting the family. Would have dressed better."

"Vanessa was Miss Colombia nine years ago," Martinez said.

"His first wife was only Miss Bogotá," she said.

"Next time, Miss Universe."

"I'll leave you men to your important busi-ness." She flashed a hundred-tooth smile to let Wells know she was in on the joke.

Martinez led Wells through the apartment and up a staircase to an enormous sunroom that seemed to have been built on the roof. For the first time, Wells grasped Bogotá's scope. The city sprawled across the plains until it disappeared into the smog at the horizon.

"First time in Bogotá?"

"Sí."

"You like it?"

Wells found his manners had vanished along with his patience. "I think it proves that if rich folks have enough barbed wire and shotguns and no conscience, they can live great even if they're surrounded by miserable poor people."

"You needed to come here to learn that?"

"I look at this, it's my nightmare for what the United States might be one day."

"I'm sorry you're frustrated. I expected him by now, too."

"Now's when you tell me his name."

"It's complicated. I've known him a long time. A socialist. At least he used to be."

Socialist. Probably Venezuelan, then. The country shared a long border with Colombia, and the left had ruled it for two decades. "And an intelligence officer?"

"Not exactly."

"I'm not playing Twenty Questions, Enrique."

"He called me the day after the attack in Dallas. Asked me if I still knew Señor Duto. I told him yes."

"How could you be sure Vinny would remember you?"

"I was first off the helicopters to rescue him."

A generation before, Colombian rebels had

kidnapped Duto and held him for months in the jungle. Duto preferred not to talk about the experience. During the presidential campaign, he'd batted down interviewers who asked. **Ancient history. You know how you get stuck in a big line at airport security? It was like that. I didn't want to be there, and I had to take off my shoes and belt, but it was fine.** The patent absurdity of the analogy left no room to follow up.

"My friend, he asks me, can **El Presidente** send someone to meet him? I said why not just arrange it himself? He said no, what he has, it's complicated. And anyway, he doesn't want to talk to anyone active in the CIA."

So the source was worried about being compromised. He feared someone at Langley, someone high enough to have access to compartmentalized information from stations all over the world. **Again?** The agency couldn't have another mole in its top ranks.

Unless it did.

"He tell you what he had?" Wells said.

"Only that it was about the attack. Something no one would expect. The details, face-to-face only."

"And here I am."

"I called him. Every day. He's not answering."

Wells waited for more, but Martinez seemed to be done.

"Come on, Enrique."

"I'll tell you one more thing. He said whoever came should be prepared to grant him U.S. citizenship."

"He thinks it's that good, he's either delusional or has the answer to Dallas. Either way, I need his name."

"He told me I wasn't to tell you under any circumstances."

"You want a finder's fee?"

"You think I need money?" Martinez appeared genuinely offended.

Wells tried to find a polite way to sweat Martinez. And failed. "You may think you're Duto's buddy, Ricky, but if you don't tell, he'll make sure you never see the United States again. Or your family. No Miami shopping trips for Vanessa. No UCLA for Simon. He doesn't forget, our President. You'll be on the naughty list forever." **And if he asks my opinion, I'll tell him I agree.**

"I'm sorry."

Wells stood—

"But. I'll give you the address of his safe house in Bogotá."

Exactly what Wells hadn't wanted. A fishing expedition. Still, the National Security Agency might have records for the address in a database. A deed, an electric bill, almost anything would do.

"Fine."

"But I warn you, it's in the slums. A neighborhood called El Amparo."

An odd location for a safe house. "Any idea why?"

"I think it was his personal place."

In other words, more of a **stash** house than a safe house. A place for Martinez's anonymous buddy to hide money or drugs or other contraband. The guy sounded less and less like an intelligence officer and more and more like a criminal.

"Fine," Wells said. "I'll leave you to your happy home."

———

Back at the hotel, Wells called Tarnes.

"I need to know if our databases have anything on the owner of an address in Colombia. Also, call data on phones down here."

"Address?"

"Number 35 Carrera 81L, El Amparo."

She read it back. "81L?"

"Yeah, it's like a substreet."

"That doesn't sound confusing at all. El Amparo?"

"A little district in southwest Bogotá." Wells had looked it up.

"And the phone numbers."

"The first is the mobile belonging to the guy I came here to meet. Enrique Martinez." Wells passed it to her. "The others, I don't have, but they belong to his wife, kids. I'm looking for an incoming call the day after the Dallas attacks followed by short outgoing calls back to the same number for the last several days."

"Would the caller also be on a Colombian phone?"

"Probably not. Guessing Venezuelan but not sure. The pattern is the most important part. Find the pattern, find the phone."

She typed for a few seconds, then: "All right. If Martinez used his own phone for the calls, I'll have an answer within the hour. Otherwise, it's trickier. We'll have to find the family's numbers first, go from there. But I'll call you tonight either way."

If Wells had asked Shafer for help, he would have waited at least a night for answers. "Thanks."

"My pleasure."

———

Wells tucked his concealed carry holster into the waistband of his jeans, broke the brim of his **Independiente Santa Fe** hat so it wouldn't look so new, pulled it down to hide his eyes. He pulled on a cheap black sweatshirt that hung low enough to keep the holster invisible. He stuffed duct tape squares and flex-cuffs and auto picker in his back pockets. He left everything else in the closet. And pulled the door shut behind him.

His adrenaline rose as he walked north, to Calle 19, the city's original commercial artery. One of the city's ubiquitous yellow cabs pulled over as soon as he raised his hand. Wells glanced inside to be certain it didn't have a security camera before slipping into the front passenger seat.

The driver was heavy, with wavy jet-black hair. He frowned at the address. "American?"

Wells didn't answer.

"You know what we **rolos** say? **No dar papaya.** Know what this means?" His English was heavily accented but understandable.

"Don't **dar** the papaya?"

"Don't walk with money in your hand. Someone buys you a drink, open the bottle yourself."

"Don't be stupid."

"**Sí.** El Amparo, it's **peligro. Muy.**" He stared at Wells. "Especially if you aren't from here." The cabbie squeezed his nostrils with thumb and forefinger, offered an exaggerated inhale. "That what you want, **cabrón**? I get it for you. No need to go there."

"No thank you." Wells sounded almost prim

to himself. He had overheard enough conversations in La Candelaria to realize that many visitors believed no trip to Colombia would be complete unless they sampled the country's most famous export.

"What then?"

"Take me or not, up to you." Wells could have found another cab, but he'd have a version of this conversation with almost any driver. He lifted his loose black sweatshirt and leaned forward in his seat far enough to expose the butt of the 9-millimeter. Without another word, the driver turned up the radio and eased into traffic.

———

El Amparo wasn't one of the mountain slums. It was west-southwest of downtown, part of a larger neighborhood called Kennedy. A million people lived there on swampy plains that had been covered with cheap apartment buildings.

El Amparo—**the shelter**—lay in Kennedy's smogged heart. It was only a few miles from La Candelaria, but Bogotá had some of the world's worst gridlock. By the time the cab pulled over, it was past 4 p.m., and the sun cast long shadows. Wells would have to move fast if he wanted to be out before dark.

The neighborhood's street grid had looked

simple enough on Google Maps. Carrera 81L was a couple blocks down from this boulevard. Wells couldn't be sure about the building numbers. But he guessed number 35 would be at least a block in.

"Fifty thousand pesos," the cabbie said. About sixteen dollars.

Wells passed him a fifty-thousand-peso note. "Will you wait for me?"

"**Una hora**, no more, another fifty thousand."

"Give me two hours, I'll pay you two hundred." Wells had no idea how long he'd need, but the extra time couldn't hurt.

"All right. But I'm not driving in. You come back to me."

"That bad?" The neighborhood looked rundown but not fierce. Across the street, a dozen kids played soccer in a trash-clogged lot alongside an appliance store.

"Bad enough."

———

The cabbie was right. The vibe changed when Wells turned left onto Carrera 81L. The street was unpaved and eroded, barely wide enough for a car. Two- and three-story brick buildings with tin slats for roofs hemmed it in. Electric wires dangled low, and the stink of urine hung in the air. Tiny glassine envelopes littered the dirt.

For a moment, Wells wondered if Martinez had lied, sent Wells here to be robbed or worse. But trouble for Wells wouldn't benefit Martinez or his family. Anyway, Wells thought he was basically honest.

Ahead, a pair of hard-faced men in their early twenties stood in the middle of the street, making sure anyone who passed knew the block was theirs. They tilted their heads as Wells stepped around them, hawks checking out a squirrel.

"Cocaine?" the man nearer Wells said. He wore a bright yellow Colombian national soccer jersey that was a size too small, the better to show his ripped torso. "Cheap, amigo."

Ignoring the guy would only make him bolder. Wells stopped, squared up, locked eyes with him, let him see the truth: **Don't mis-underestimate me, friend.**

The guy looked away first. Wells decided to push the point. He stepped close. "Thirty-five? **Treinta y cinco?**"

The guy pointed to a four-story concrete building. Then dropped his hand like he couldn't believe he'd let Wells order him around.

"Gracias, amigo."

The front door of number 35 was steel, with a

narrow, grate-screened window. It had two locks. The auto picker popped both in seconds. A few years before, the pickers had been balky and difficult. Now they were no larger than Swiss Army knives and easily opened all but the most sophisticated locks. One of Wells's favorite tricks from the Directorate of Science and Technology.

Wells peeked back as he opened the door. A third man had now joined the others at the corner. The new guy caught Wells looking and lifted his sweatshirt so Wells could see the pistol tucked into his belt.

Oh, goody. You have one, too.

═══

The first-floor hallway was bare concrete, with two doors on each side. Typical tenement layout. Televisions played in apartments, the voices low and fast. Wells jogged up the stairs.

Apartment 8 occupied the back left corner of the building. Its door wasn't flush with the hallway. As Wells approached, he saw a ribbon of light from inside. Curiouser and curiouser. Could Martinez's source be hiding here as he waited for some final piece of information to shop to the agency?

Wells put his ear to the door. He heard nothing, no voices or running water. Maybe the lights had just been left on accidentally. Wells put picker to the lock, and the bolt slid back with a thunk that echoed in the hallway. He stuffed the pick in his jeans and hustled inside.

The living room was sparely decorated, just a black futon and coffee table. A flat-screen television was bolted to the wall, and it was on, playing a muted Spanish music video. Beside it, a closed door led to what had to be the bedroom. Wells pulled his pistol, held it by his side, moved toward the door.

It opened, swung toward him—

A woman stood in the doorway, young, brown-skinned, thick-hipped, wearing only a thin white T-shirt and panties. She looked at his face as though she wasn't entirely surprised to see him. Then her eyes went to the pistol, and her mouth opened—

Wells dropped the pistol. A dangerous move, but he needed both hands to control her. As the pistol clattered down, he stepped to her, grabbed her neck with his right hand. He covered her mouth with his left, leaving her nostrils free so she could breathe. He looked around to be sure no one else was in the apartment, no one to jump him from behind or run into the living room and grab the pistol. Nope. Her T-shirt rode up, exposing her soft belly. Wells shoved her against the wall. He hated himself for the terror he'd put in her eyes. But he had to keep her quiet.

"I'm not going to hurt you."

She kicked at him, tried to scrape her nails across his face. Wells wondered if she knew any English.

He lifted his hand from her mouth, just a fraction, and her scream burst out. He covered it again.

"No peligro. Silencio. Sí?"

He looked into her eyes until she nodded.

He lifted his hand. Again she screamed.

No choice. He had to choke her unconscious. This was the risk of running missions in a country where he didn't speak the language. He had no margin for error. But he wasn't the one who would pay. He slid his hand up so that it covered her nose as well as her mouth and clamped it tight. Her lips were soft under his palm. He couldn't avoid knowing the carnality of what he was doing. She fought for air, shaking her head side to side, but she had no chance against his strength. He held her until her eyes rolled back and she went limp.

He laid her down, trying to be gentle. Then he taped her mouth shut and flex-cuffed her wrists and ankles. Gently, of course.

In the living room, he collected his pistol and

looked around. The apartment might not be an official government-owned safe house. But it had a similar feel, minimal furniture, and no personal items. The way the woman had paused when she saw him was telling, too. She hadn't seemed entirely surprised that an armed stranger had materialized inside the apartment. As though it didn't belong to her either.

The kitchen drawers held nothing but silverware, plates, and two half-empty bottles of **aguardiente**, a local liquor. No phone or electric bills, nothing with a name. Back to the bedroom. Here, Wells found a few personal items that all seemed to belong to the woman. On the bedside table, a Bible and two worn copies of **Cosmopolitan en Español.** A plastic bag of loose coca leaves. In its natural form, coca was a mild stimulant, useful for altitude sickness. Colombians chewed the leaves or brewed them for tea.

Under the bag, Wells found a Samsung phone that looked nearly new. He tried to look through it, but it was password-protected. The lock screen photo showed the woman who was on the floor. She wore a modest black bikini and a wide smile and stood on a beach. Wells didn't recognize the backdrop, but Bogotá was hundreds of miles from any ocean. This woman wasn't poor or friendless. She owned a fancy phone, had gone on vacation.

Most people in El Amparo couldn't do either. Maybe she was the daughter of Martinez's source.

The woman groaned under her duct tape, though her eyes stayed closed. Wells couldn't leave here without talking to her. Even if she didn't go to the police, he'd never see her again. He had to have a translator.

He reached for his phone.

Four rings, voice mail, a blur of Spanish. Wells tried again, and this time the phone was answered.

"Tony. It's John. From El Campín. Can you come to El Amparo?"

"El what?"

"It's in Kennedy."

"You get lost?"

"I need a translator."

A pause. Then: "Five million pesos." More than fifteen hundred dollars.

"Fine." Duto could pay him back. "How soon can you be here?"

"Give me the exact address."

Wells did.

"Forty-five minutes."

"Call me when you're downstairs." Wells would have to open the front door to let Tony inside, and he didn't want to leave this woman alone longer than a few seconds.

Wells went back to searching the apartment. By the time he was done, he was certain the woman didn't live here. Her only clothes were in a suitcase in the closet, T-shirts and jeans, nothing fancy. The suitcase also held twenty hundred-dollar bills in an envelope hidden in the lining. The money wouldn't survive a TSA-style scan but it might escape a robber's notice. If she had a wallet or passport, Wells couldn't find it.

He did find one surprise tucked behind her clothes, a two-foot-high steel safe with a dial lock the auto picker couldn't touch. The safe was too heavy for Wells to move by himself. Unless the woman knew the combination, he'd need a safe-cracker to open it.

Finally, the woman's eyes fluttered open. When she saw Wells, she twisted wildly, kicking her heels against the floor. Wells grabbed her by the ankles and lifted her upside down. The move was absurd but effective. She stopped fighting immediately.

He put her down, squatted next to her. "Silencio. Por favor."

With nothing else to do, he carried her into the living room, plopped her on the couch. **See? If I meant to hurt you, would I let you watch Spanish MTV?** They sat silently as Pitbull rapped

in Spanglish. **Dale mami, para mi taxi / I met
her in the back seat of a taxi . . .**

Finally, Wells's phone buzzed: Tony.

"I'm about to walk into 81L. Which building?"

"Block and a half down, north side. What's
the Spanish for just talk?"

"Solo habla."

Wells hung up, flipped the woman on her
stomach. He pulled back her legs, flex-cuffed her
wrists to her ankles so she couldn't kick at the
floor or try to run. He couldn't risk a neighbor
spotting her as he dragged her to the front door,
so he had to leave her in the apartment. Thus, he
had to hog-tie her. Of course.

"Solo habla. No peligro."

She muttered under the tape as he carried her
to the bedroom and set her down.

He stuck the Bible in the apartment door to
prop it open, ran to the building entrance, pulled
open the front door as Tony arrived. The last sliv-
ers of daylight were fleeing the sky. Night would
be on the slum by the time they left. The guys on
the corner were still there, too.

First things first.

6

For two days, Ellis Shafer sulked.

He and Wells had been through the wars together. Okay, Wells had been through the wars. Shafer had been through headquarters, the occasional trip to Tokyo or Paris notwithstanding. Still, he'd risked prison for Wells, saved Wells's life more than once.

How had the man paid him back? By falling for the first bauble Duto threw his way. **Julie Tarnes.** Even more than most guys, Wells was a sucker for pretty women. The normal explanations didn't hold. Wells wasn't insecure, and he was plenty handsome, one of those lucky men who'd gotten better-looking past forty. No, Shafer blamed another part of Wells's personality. Wells might not believe he could make much difference, but he couldn't stop trying. He was a romantic, though he'd never describe himself that way.

Maybe seeing himself as a knight-errant, a modern Don Quixote, was the only way Wells could survive his past. But that chivalry colored the way he reacted to women. They liked him, and he liked them. Especially the good-looking ones. Like Julie Tarnes.

Duto was nothing if not an acute observer of human nature. He'd known what he was doing when he put Wells with Tarnes. And Wells had plenty of excuses to dump Shafer. The agency **was** sick of Shafer. Shafer **was** years past mandatory retirement age. He hung on because his hunches were right more often than they should have been. But no one did him any favors. If Wells needed quick help in the field, Shafer wasn't his best bet.

But the obstacles weren't new. And they had never stopped Wells from working with Shafer before. Until now. Wells had pretended to agonize over Duto's offer. In truth, he'd dropped Shafer fast. Especially once he met Tarnes.

Worst of all, Duto knew Wells's disloyalty would eat at Shafer, and Duto was just nasty enough to get a charge from tearing up their friendship.

For forty-eight hours, Shafer stewed in silence in his office, skimming the reports coming out of

Dallas. No one asked his opinion on the investigation. He wondered if he should resign.

But on the third day, Shafer's fever broke. He woke up angry. With himself. For letting Duto manipulate him and try to push him out. For his absurd sentimentality. He wasn't quitting. Not now, not ever. Forget Julie Tarnes. And Wells, too. Time to focus on Dallas.

———

That day, the next, and the next, Shafer stayed at Langley past midnight. Fast as he read, he couldn't keep up with everything the FBI and the intelligence community produced. Forensic reports, intercepts, gossip—thousands of pages already, hundreds more every hour. Still, Shafer did his best. He focused especially on the FBI 302s, the summaries of witness interviews from the Bureau's agents.

But the more he read, the more puzzled he became.

The police had killed three jihadis inside the arena. The fourth man had driven the attackers' car. He hadn't gone inside. Video showed him reaching into the trunk when the bomb inside detonated. No one knew why. Maybe the timer had failed. Maybe he'd wanted to have the glory of causing the explosion.

The blast had obliterated his body completely, but the cameras had caught the car's license plates. It was a Hyundai registered to Ahmed Shakir, a cousin of one of the other jihadis. Shakir's face matched the video surveillance of the fourth man, and no one had seen Shakir since the attacks. Thus—as Duto had told Wells days before—the investigators assumed Shakir was the fourth attacker, most likely the leader.

The theory was plausible. But it raised even more questions, and no one had answered them.

El-Masry and the other attackers had left online traces of anti-American views. The FBI had them in what it called its T4 database, the broadest of its terror lists. The database included anyone who had ever followed a known Islamic State account on Twitter and made statements supporting terrorism. The FBI didn't have enough agents to track all sixty-two thousand people on it. The Bureau used it as an early warning system. If local police arrested someone on it for a crime, even one unrelated to terrorism, the database was supposed to alert the FBI. That way agents could ask the local cops about the arrest and interview the suspect, if they chose. But el-Masry and the others hadn't ever been arrested, so the FBI had never spoken to them.

Further, as broad as that watchlist was, Shakir

didn't appear on it. He'd been a **cleanskin**, agency jargon for an operative who'd offered no hints of his terrorist sentiments before he attacked.

To unravel the mystery, the Bureau had sent eighty of its best counterterror agents to Dallas. They'd paired with a hundred ten Dallas police detectives and officers. The group had torn apart Shakir's house and car, scoured his phone records, credit cards, bank account. The NSA had cracked his only known email account, though it hadn't officially shared that information with the FBI to preserve the Bureau's ability to make criminal cases against other conspirators, if any were found. Investigators had interviewed Shakir's neighbors and friends. His high school classmates. The mechanic who serviced his car. The pet store owner who sold him cat food.

Within hours of identifying him, they learned of his cocaine dealing. Within days, they convinced a couple of his buyers to talk. The Drug Enforcement Administration was trying to trace his upstream connections, so far without success.

Yet the investigators still had no idea who or what had driven Shakir to attack. If he had ever expressed anti-American or pro-terror views, no one had found them. Not online, and not in real life. The NSA had found no evidence that he had talked or emailed with anyone inside the Islamic State, much less been an active jihadi taking orders. He'd never tried to go to Syria or Iraq. He didn't even have a passport. Nor did he seem particularly religious. Unlike the other three attackers, he had never belonged to a mosque.

As far as the investigators could tell, Shakir had been assimilated into American society, a small-time drug dealer with a Facebook account and a cat. Until a few months before the attacks, when he cut off his friends and clients while spending more time with his cousin. That investigators found that decision suspicious. Shafer agreed. It was really the **only** suspicious move Shakir had made. But the investigators couldn't find evidence that he'd met any jihadi recruiters or made any other preparations for the attack. His electricity and credit card bills and phone records showed he still lived in his house in East Dallas. He vanished in plain sight.

Until he, his cousin, and two of their buddies went to a basketball game and killed three hundred people.

The Bureau had investigated the other attackers thoroughly, too, of course. Agents had talked to the imam and congregants at the South Dallas mosque where they prayed, as well as their families and neighbors. But they interested Shafer less. They fit a more standard jihadi profile. They'd expressed anti-American views for years. They belonged to a conservative mosque. They were poorly educated foot soldiers. Throwaways.

Shakir held the key.

Jihadis had "self-radicalized" and come out of nowhere before. But never on this scale. Further, the deadliness of the attack—and the fact the jihadis had used C-4—suggested that Shakir and the killers had received substantial training. Terrorists normally made bombs from TATP, triacetone triperoxide, an explosive any college chemistry student could make in a kitchen. But TATP's volatility made it as dangerous to bombmakers as to their targets. It had a nasty habit of blowing up on its own. C-4 was far more stable, the reason the American military used it. But buying or stealing C-4 was nearly impossible. Making it required expensive equipment.

Where exactly had Shakir gotten hundreds of pounds of it?

The FBI had concluded the four attackers had acted on the orders and with the help of an as-yet-undiscovered Islamic State cell inside the United States. Which raised the most uncomfortable question of all: **Were other attacks in the works?**

His murky status at the agency notwithstanding, Shafer had every classified clearance the government offered. Now he wanted to see Ahmed Shakir's last moments for himself. Shafer didn't even have to leave his office to watch the videos. The FBI had uploaded them to servers at its headquarters. Fiber-optic cables went to Langley, Fort Meade, the White House, and the Pentagon, a private Internet solely for classified traffic.

Of course, the Bureau wouldn't have been the Bureau if it hadn't added fifty hours of video from every conceivable angle. Quantity over quality. But Shafer eventually found what he was looking for, cuts of Shakir's Hyundai turning off the highway . . . making its way through the game-night traffic . . . Parking close to the arena . . . el-Masry and the other two jihadis getting out the car . . . Shakir following a few seconds later . . . The other three grabbing assault rifles from the trunk . . . starting to shoot, muzzle flashes clearly visible . . . moving quickly away from the car before it blew . . . A silent horror movie that turned Shafer's stomach.

Unfortunately, the video coverage wasn't great. The cameras outside the arena focused on the pedestrian plaza, not the roads. More than a dozen cameras had caught the shooters as they approached the turnstiles. But only three showed the car itself. Only one had a direct angle on Shakir as he went to the trunk. None offered a view of Shakir's hands inside the trunk. The entire sequence lasted barely forty seconds, start to finish. Still, the video mesmerized. Shakir stepped out . . . looked around . . . went to the trunk . . . reached down . . .

And the screen went white.

Shafer watched it a dozen times. And a dozen more.

With every viewing, he became more puzzled. The video was black-and-white, and the camera had been about fifty yards away, so the resolution wasn't great. Shafer couldn't make out Shakir's facial expressions clearly, much less read his lips. But he could see which direction Shakir was looking. As Shakir stepped out of the car, he didn't go directly to the trunk. In fact, he took two steps the other way. Then he stopped, looked around. Not just around. Up. Like he was looking for a plane. Or a helicopter.

Only after el-Masry yelled to Shakir did he move to the trunk. The other men quickly reached inside, pulled out the AKs. Not Shakir. He froze again. As the shooting started, he shivered. Jumped, really. The others moved and fired. Shakir stayed in place, almost crouching, looking side to side. He still seemed to be waiting for someone. After another five seconds, he tilted his head as if he'd heard something. Finally, he came out of his reverie. He turned back to the trunk and reached inside.

In their report on Shakir, the FBI's profilers had noted his odd behavior. They'd dismissed it as the last-second panic of a suicide bomber. A CIA/Mossad analysis of suicide attacks had found that one in three bombers failed to pull the trigger. Most analysts believed the percentage would have been higher if not for bomb belts that were remotely detonated and thus blew even if the attackers changed their minds. **After a brief hesitation, SHAKIR detonated the bomb,** the profilers wrote.

But when Shafer watched the video cold, pretending he didn't know Shakir was involved in the attack, reacting only to what he saw, the scene played out differently. Shakir seemed scared, yes. But he also looked surprised at least three times. First when he stepped out of the car and didn't see whatever he was expecting. Then when his cousin started to shoot. Finally, just before he reached into the trunk.

Why the surprise? He'd surely known what was about to happen.

Unless he hadn't. Unless one of the other three had tricked Shakir into driving them over. But how would they have explained the AKs or the bomb in the trunk? Or had they fooled him into loaning them the car while they loaded it up? Shafer couldn't find an answer that made sense. He knew the FBI didn't care much about Shakir's last seconds. It was focused on tracking his contacts, building cases against anyone who might have known about the attacks.

But Shafer found himself desperate to understand Shakir's psychology. Maybe he'd read too many Agatha Christie mysteries growing up. He found himself imagining Hercule Poirot, the little Belgian twirling his mustache . . . **My friends, back to the mind of the killer. For it is there we find the answer. Yes, there.**

———

Shafer returned to the interviews of Shakir's friends and family. Small-time coke dealing was lonely work. Lots of fake friends, few real ones. His parents had died years before. He didn't work in an office, so he didn't have coworkers to check up on him.

As a result, his vanishing produced little reaction. His clients found new dealers. The employees at the bars where he dealt claimed they'd hardly noticed. A waitress at a fine-sounding place called the Dirt Hole told agents she assumed Shakir had been arrested.

Of course, considering what Shakir had done, people might be playing down their relationships with him. But for the most part, they talked to the FBI willingly, and agents reported they were cooperative.

Then Shafer saw a new 302, one that had landed only a few hours before.

```
JEANELLE PITTS, date of birth
September 9, 1995, was in-
terviewed at DENNY'S, 4400
NORTH CENTRAL EXPRESSWAY,
DALLAS. After being advised
of the identity of the in-
terviewing agent and the pur-
pose of the investigation,
PITTS was asked why her name
repeatedly appeared in AHMED
SHAKIR's mobile phone records.
She stated the following:
    She dated SHAKIR between
mid-June and October of the
previous summer. The rela-
tionship was sexual but not
exclusive—
```

Oh, those relationship experts at the FBI. Shafer read on. Pitts met Shakir at a bar in June.

They had sex that night. Over the next four months, they saw each other a handful of times, always at her apartment. She believed he dated other women but had never asked him. She knew he dealt cocaine but claimed she had never used it with him or seen him use it. He had never spoken about Islam to her, never seemed in any way religious or expressed any political views at all.

Then the surprise:

```
PITTS stated that in Octo-
ber, SHAKIR told her they
would need to stop dating for
an indefinite period. SHAKIR
stated he had gotten in "law
trouble" and would need to
stop dealing drugs for a
while but that everything
would work out. SHAKIR said
she should not contact him
but that he would contact
her. When PITTS asked SHAKIR
what he meant by "law trou-
ble," he declined to answer,
and later asked her to "for-
get it."
    PITTS stated she believed
SHAKIR meant he had been ar-
```

rested when he referred to
"law trouble." She expressed
disbelief when she was informed that SHAKIR had not
been arrested in the previous five years. She said SHA-
KIR might have invented the
story as a way to break off
their relationship but that
she did not believe so. She
and SHAKIR had always agreed
either of them could end the
relationship at any time.

PITTS stated that she had
not seen SHAKIR again. She did
not know his exact address,
and, in any case, preferred
to respect his wishes—

Again Shafer had to smile. He'd hand in his resignation this afternoon if Pitts had used the phrase
respect his wishes. The rest of the interview offered nothing of note. Pitts had not seen Shakir
again. She was shocked when the police said he
had been one of the attackers. If she remembered
anything else, she would call the agents, she said.

The 302 concluded with a somewhat unusual
note. Following the interview, the agents had re-

checked arrest records in Dallas and nationally. They found no arrest reports for Shakir. The Bureau pulled Shakir's fingerprints and DNA from his home. It would have found him in the national arrest database even if he'd used an alias.

```
PITTS appeared willing to aid
the investigation; it seems
likely that SHAKIR lied to
her in order to end the rela-
tionship.
```

Another plausible theory. The FBI had interviewed more than a hundred people who knew Shakir. Pitts was the first to mention an arrest. She was surely wrong.

Unless . . .

Shafer pulled up the report from the waitress at the Dirt Hole. Lauren Hobart. She said she assumed Shakir had been arrested. The 302 report didn't indicate if the agents who interviewed her had followed up. Probably not. They knew Shakir dealt, and they knew Hobart knew. They'd figure she had mentioned an arrest as the best explanation for his disappearance. Sooner or later, drug dealers got busted and went to jail.

But what if Hobart had a specific reason to believe Shakir had been arrested? What if she'd seen something at the Dirt Hole that made her think he'd been targeted?

Shafer considered calling the agents, asking if they had pursued that thread. But they wouldn't talk to him without an okay from someone senior at FBI headquarters. Talking to Hobart and Pitts face-to-face would be faster and easier.

Unfortunately, the last Washington-to-Dallas flight of the day took off in less than ninety minutes. Between D.C. rush hour traffic and the security lines, Shafer had no chance of making it. So be it. He could fly out in the morning. Knocking on doors at midnight was a mistake, anyway. Better to wait.

He booked a flight and headed home to tell his wife, pleased with his progress. Wells wasn't the only one who could handle the field. Shafer didn't need Julie Tarnes to run interference for him either. So while Wells sunned himself in Bogotá . . .

7

Wells led Tony into the apartment, opened the door to the bedroom. The woman lay on her back, staring at the ceiling. She tried to scream as she saw them, but the tape over her mouth throttled her.

Tony turned to leave. Wells blocked him.

"We're just gonna talk."

"I'm from **Tampa**, man. I deliver bags. Don't even look inside them."

"Give me ten minutes."

Tony's eyes blinked greed. "Ten million pesos." Three thousand dollars.

"Done."

"We talk, then we go? Promise?"

"Promise." Wells maneuvered Tony into the bedroom before the younger man could change his mind. "Tell her I'm going to cut her arms and legs open." He pulled his knife. The woman squirmed wildly—

"What?"

"The hog-tie, I mean." The knife wasn't helping. Wells sheathed it. "Take as much time as you need. Tell her I'm sorry, I have to talk to her. I don't speak Spanish, I couldn't explain. I'm not going to hurt her. Swear on the Bible, if you have to. Swear on my life. My kids' lives."

Tony knelt beside her, offered a stream of Spanish.

After five minutes, he gave Wells a tentative thumbs-up. Wells cut her loose. "Tell her I'm pulling the tape. But if she screams, we'll have to do it again."

Another chat.

"I can't promise what she'll do when you take it off," Tony said.

Wells had to take the chance. This woman hated him more every second. He wasn't going to torture her, so he needed to convince her to talk before she locked him out completely.

Nobody offered advice for these moments at the Farm.

═══

Wells eased off the duct tape. She cleared her throat—

And hawked saliva at him. The gob orna-
mented his nose, warm and wet. Wells wiped it
away. Her eyes met his: **Gonna hurt me, tough
guy?**

"Had that coming."

His lack of anger seemed to calm her. She gave
Tony a long speech, the words trilling together.

"Her name is Elena. She's not happy. To say
the least."

"This her apartment?"

A short back-and-forth.

"Her boyfriend."

So Martinez's friend had moved Elena here as
he prepared to sell his secrets and start a shiny
new life in the United States.

"She's from Venezuela? Caracas?"

Elena shook her head when she heard the city's
name. "Quito."

Quito. The capital of Ecuador, which, like
Venezuela, had a hard-left government.

"The guy's from there, too? When did he move
her here?"

The back-and-forth was longer this time.

"Yes, Quito, too. Last week, he called her, told
her to come." **After Dallas.** "He'd brought her
here three times before. He's married. He liked to
take her to Bogotá when he was working."

So the apartment was more a love nest than a

conventional safe house. Now Wells understood the location. The boyfriend was spending his own money, so he'd picked somewhere cheap. And out of the way, with no doormen or guards to pry.

"This time?"

"He called her, gave her money for a ticket, told her to come and wait for him. He promised that after this, he'd bring her to the United States."

So Martinez's source expected his tip to convince the United States to accept not just him but his **mistress**? Maybe he was just nuts.

"Ask her what's in the safe in the closet."

"**La caja fuerte?**" Tony said. "**En el armario?**" She shook her head.

"She doesn't know."

"Thanks, Tony."

Tony asked something else. "Doesn't know the combination either."

"**Quién es el nombre?**" Wells said to her. "Come on, what's his name?"

"Let me handle the Spanish," Tony said. "You mangled that about four different ways."

"Tell her he's missing, I want to talk to him. He has information, and I'll pay for it." **Tell her I'll buy her a unicorn. Tell her whatever. Just get the name.**

But nothing about this day was going to be easy.

"**Chinga tu madre,**" Elena said to Wells. The words slow and clear so he'd understand.

"Not very ladylike."

"**Y tu padre.**"

"You know what that means?" Tony said.

"I know what that means."

Now she was talking again. "She says she knows men like you, men with no hearts, who enjoy being cruel, menacing the innocent with your knives—"

"I get it." Tony's translation had become a bit enthusiastic for Wells's taste.

"She says you want to cut her throat, it's fine, but she has pride and she'd die before she tells you."

Sure she would. They were in soap opera territory now. This sort of over-the-top bravado rarely survived the first cut. Lucky for Elena, Wells wouldn't be finding out. No more hurting this woman. Instead, he grabbed her smartphone from the bedside table.

"Locked, señor." Her first English word.

"She'd die, sure," Wells said to Tony. "Like all good **telenovela** heroines. But would she give up her phone? Because if she won't tell me, I'm taking it so we can break in, check the call log and the texts."

She started to squawk as Tony explained.

"I just want his name, where he lives, when he

said he was coming here," Wells said. "**Por favor.** I'm trying to help. Tell me, I'll give you a thousand dollars for your trouble, you'll never see me again."

Tony translated. As the answer came, he pulled a reporter's notepad and wrote.

"His name's Hector Frietas. F-R-I-E-T-A-S. He lives in Quito. Married, two kids. Both grown, she thinks." He handed Wells the pad. "His mobile number and address."

Wells tore the sheet, tucked it away. **Hector Frietas.** Must be the guy's real name if he was planning to take her to the United States with him.

Tony opened a browser on his phone. "Hector Frietas, Quito . . . I'm coming up with the Deputy Manager for Operations of the Banco Central del Ecuador." The bank's website revealed an unsmiling man in a gray suit. Late forties, maybe. He sat behind a desk, hands folded, like he was about to deny a loan. Elena nodded when Tony showed her the picture.

A socialist banker. Odd. "Was he connected to the security services?"

A short question that led to a long answer.

"They never talked about his job. She says he's nice, always kind to her, he loves her. He promises in the United States he'll leave his wife, they'll be together, have a family—"

"It's a wonderful life," Wells said. "Did he tell her what he knew that would get them to the United States?"

A short question, a longer answer.

"Nothing like that. He called once after she got here, the day after she came. He said he thought he would see her in three or four days. Since then, nothing. And he doesn't answer his phone."

Not what Wells wanted to hear. Still, Elena had given up the name. And Wells believed her. For the first time since he'd seen her in the apartment, the knot in his stomach unclenched. A few glasses of **aguardiente,** she'd be good as new.

"What's I'm sorry—"

"**Lo siento.**"

"**Lo siento, Elena. Muy siento.**" To Tony: "Tell her I thank her, the United States thanks her—"

"How about I tell her to stay here and keep her mouth shut until we're clear."

"Let's go with that."

Wells counted out ten hundred-dollar bills from his pocket, left them next to the phone on the nightstand. He wanted to take the phone, but he worried she might yell. Anyway, he'd promised.

"I really am sorry."

Her answer needed no translation. He saluted her as Tony turned for the door.

———

Tony was still ahead of Wells as they reached the stairs.

Below, the building's front door opened. The men from the corner walked in. The guy in the soccer shirt, the one Wells had stared down, was in front. He saw Wells, raised his pistol in a sideways gangster grip, loose and sloppy. Showing off for his buddies.

Tony stopped so quickly that Wells almost knocked him over. The guy downstairs yelled something.

"He says put our hands on our heads."

Wells stepped beside Tony. "Back up. Behind me."

Tony ignored Wells, raised his hands.

The Colombian put a foot on the bottom step, maybe twenty-five feet away. He grinned at Wells, wagged his left index finger, the sentiment universal: **Who's your daddy now?**

"Talk," Wells murmured to Tony. "Keep him busy."

"Do what they say—"

"**Sí!**" Wells yelled down the stairs. "Surrender!" He lifted his hands, slowly and showily. The

Colombian looked over his left shoulder and muttered to the men behind him. The break Wells needed. He had to act before they realized he was armed.

He dropped his right hand, reached behind his waist for the pistol, dropped the safety as he pulled it forward. He shouldered Tony left, against the wall of the building.

A half second late, the Colombian turned back. Wells squeezed the trigger, knowing he didn't have time for warnings, the first shot might be the last. The Colombian fired, too, the two shots echoing as one off the concrete walls—

A neat hole appeared low in the Colombian's yellow shirt. The pistol slipped from his hands and clattered down as he groaned. Wells fired again. This time, the round caught the guy in the forehead and tore through his skull, an inhuman sound, and he collapsed instantly—

The second Colombian stepped forward, lifted his pistol—

No morality in Wells now, no hesitation, a cat with claws outstretched. He fired again. The round tore into the guy's chest. The Colombian stumbled back, looking up with real surprise. As if he could undo what had happened by refusing to believe it. He went to his haunches, and his head drooped. Wells took aim at the third Colombian, about to pull the trigger, when the guy turned and ran.

Wells safed the 9-millimeter and shoved it into his waistband—and felt a wet spatter on his neck.

He turned—

Tony slumped against the wall, hands pressed high and prayerful to his sternum. Arterial blood dribbled through his fingers. His light brown skin was already fading, turning to papyrus, his life vanishing heartbeat by heartbeat. He was panting lightly, and his eyes were open. The fear in them told Wells that Tony had a chance if a surgeon could close whatever artery the bullet had hit.

"You'll be all right, get you to a hospital—" Wells chattering, trying to keep Tony conscious. "Walk with me and talk to me and say you'll be my friend." Wells put his arms under Tony's knees and shoulders, carried him down the stairs as fast and sloppy as an overzealous groom.

The acrid smell of gunshots lingered as Wells stepped over the dying men at the base of the stairs. He silently cursed Enrique Martinez for sending him here, for making him a killer twice more. All this for Hector Frietas's name, a name Martinez should have given him. Wells wondered if Martinez had refused simply to prove that he wasn't beholden to Wells or Duto or anyone else.

In which case, the failure belonged to Wells, too. Maybe if he'd gone at Martinez differently . . .

Wells expected to hear someone calling the police. But the building was quiet, its residents hiding in bedrooms and bathrooms, waiting for the plague to pass.

At the front door, Wells listened, heard nothing. Probably the third guy was still running.

Outside, he found Carrera 81L dark and empty. "Not far, Tony, I promise." Tony didn't answer. The blood sopping through his T-shirt.

Wells turned right, hoping the cabbie had stayed. Otherwise, he'd have to hijack a ride to the nearest hospital. Tony couldn't afford to wait for an ambulance, even if one would come here.

Back on the boulevard, life went on. Women in housekeeping uniforms hurried home with thin plastic bags of groceries. Laborers in dusty T-shirts stood at a minibus stop. Wells expected someone would offer to help. But when they looked at him, their eyes slid to the pistol in his waistband. Then they looked away. **No dar papaya.**

After a few more steps, Wells was panting, too. The Bogotá air felt insubstantial in his lungs. Not so much thin as diet. He wondered if the golden hour when surgeons could save gunshot victims was half that at this altitude, at least for people who didn't live here and hadn't adapted to the air.

A break. The cab waited. Wells grabbed the back door. Locked. The cabbie lowered the window.

"He's shot?"

No, bad sushi. Wells was ready to pull his pistol, but the lock clicked open. He had no time to be subtle as he stuffed Tony inside. The younger man moaned, and his eyes fluttered open in agony. Wells had no first-aid gear, not even gloves. He put his hands over Tony's and tried to compress the wound. If Tony had some blood-borne disease, Wells deserved to share it.

"Which hospital?" the driver said.

"Whatever's closest." Even the best surgeons couldn't save a corpse. Anyway, the local hospital probably handled plenty of gunshot cases.

"El Hospital de Kennedy, then. With the traffic, fifteen minutes."

With one hand still on Tony's chest, Wells reached for his phone, called Tarnes—

"Julie. Problem."

As if to prove the point, Wells's phone slipped from his bloody fingers. He reached for it as the cabbie swerved through traffic.

"You there?"

"The guy you sent me, he's been shot." Wells hoped Tony couldn't understand. "Going to a hospital now."

To her credit, Tarnes didn't ask the questions that were irrelevant at this moment: **What happened? Where were you? Why was he there? Who shot him?** . . . "Which hospital?"

"El Hospital de Kennedy, it's called."

"I'll call the station, we'll get someone there. You gonna stay with him?"

"Can't. There were two Kia." Wells despised himself a little for using the passive voice, made himself say what Tarnes had probably guessed already. "I killed them."

"Police? Anyone important?"

Important. Wells admired and hated her brutal honesty. "Drug dealers."

"You injured?"

Tony trembled in Wells's hands, his body shaking—

He hung up, pressed both hands on Tony's chest, his only move. The compression seemed to help. Tony stopped shaking, and his breathing stabilized.

"We're gonna get you there, buddy—"

The driver laid on his horn and accelerated into a gap in oncoming traffic, ran a light—

Under his hands, Wells felt something **tear** in Tony's chest, a blood vessel giving way, Wells could only guess at the anatomy, but the effect was immediate. Tony had been dying slowly. Now he was dying fast. His mouth opened, and he grunted, but no words came. His breath sped, and his chest trembled. His blood seeped onto Wells's hands. Not enough of it, it was getting lost inside him now.

"Nothing to be afraid of, I promise—" **Lies, lies, lies.**

Tony moaned, helpless, guttural, raised his hands, grabbed Wells's wrists—

And stilled. Wells waited, counted to ten, knowing he could have counted to infinity and changed nothing.

He pushed down Tony's eyelids, folded his arms across his broken chest. Tony from Tampa. Wells didn't even know his last name. "Pull over."

"**Muerto?**"

"**Sí.**"

The driver turned into an empty lot. Wells heard a lone siren in the distance.

"Now, señor?"

Catch the first plane home. Never come back. Tony hadn't known the risks. Wells could still hear how his voice had trembled in the apartment as he'd said, **I deliver bags.** He'd been an errand runner, hoping to parlay the work into a full-time agency job. Or not. Wells had killed him as surely as if he'd pulled the trigger—

Enough. He could mourn, beat himself up,

send Tony's parents a sympathy card. He could drown his sorrows with Duto's expensive bourbon or hug Emmie and hope he felt better. He could do anything or nothing. Later.

Now he had to move. "Take him to the hospital."

"And when the nurses want to know why I have a dead man in my back seat?"

"He got in by himself, you don't know—"

"You don't think anyone saw? This man, he's American, I see that. The police won't let this go. Even our police."

"Give me your phone number."

"Why?"

Wells had walked out of his hotel carrying five thousand dollars. After what he'd given Elena, he had four thousand. He pulled the cash from his pocket, peeled off two hundred-dollar bills with his bloodied fingers, handed the cabbie the rest. The guy held the money between his fingertips like it was tainted.

"Give me your number, keep your mouth shut, you'll get more."

The cabbie scribbled a phone number on a scrap, handed it over.

"Stick to the story, you'll be fine."

Wells pulled off his bloodied sweatshirt, turned it inside out, wrapped it around his waist so the stains would be less noticeable. The reason he wore black shirts and dark blue jeans on these missions. He took off his hat, too. He couldn't do anything about his height, but at least on first glance he wasn't exactly the man who'd been carrying a dying man on Carrera 81L.

He reached into Tony's jacket, found the ring of keys he needed. Get a man killed and steal his motorcycle. He looked once more at Tony, tried to think of a prayer in English or Arabic. Couldn't.

"Go," the cabbie said.

═══

Wells hustled back toward the building. He'd seen Tony's motorcycle outside Carrera 81L on the way to the cab, a thick, plastic-coated chain looped through its front wheel. His phone buzzed again and he grabbed it and leaned over, trying to hide his bloodied hands.

"You all right?" Tarnes.

"Fine." Wells ducked into a doorway and watched as a police car pulled up outside Carrera 81L, its wan blue lights flashing. **No dar papaya** might work in his favor now. The locals would want no part of helping the police find the man who'd killed two drug dealers. Wells would bet that Elena hadn't hung around either. "Tony's dead. The driver's taking him to the hospital, but he's dead."

"That guy was **American**, John—" She caught herself. "Want to tell me what happened?" Her voice soft, and yet heavy, as if she had only now realized the risks of involving herself with Wells.

"Not particularly." The cops were still in their sedan. Probably waiting for backup. He hoped they'd move soon. Tough for him to grab the motorcycle with them watching.

"Okay. **Later.**" She emphasized the second word, making sure Wells knew he would have to give her at least some explanation. "I'm going to tell the station not to send anyone to the hospital, then. Let the cops notify us. It'll look weird if someone just shows up there."

Wells wanted to argue. He didn't like the idea of Tony's body going unclaimed for even a few minutes. But Tarnes was right. The police would call the embassy as soon as they realized Tony was American.

"What about you?" James said.

"If I can make it to my hotel clean, I'll grab my stuff, get on the first flight out. Doesn't matter where."

"I'll find flights while you're getting back to the hotel."

"And I have a name for you to run. Hector Frietas. An Ecuadorian banker. Lives in Quito. He's the one who asked Martinez to set the meeting. No idea where he is. His girlfriend says he isn't answering his phone."

Another police car approached, sirens blaring. A crowd had begun to gather. Wells was a couple hundred meters away. Not far enough.

"I'll let you know what we get," Tarnes said.

She was his cousin in mission-at-any-cost efficiency, and, at this moment, Wells hated her nearly as much as he hated himself. "I have to go."

The second police car pulled up, and Wells knew he would have to leave the motorcycle, find another way back to the Hotel de la Opera. Wells had deliberately hailed the cab far from the hotel so the driver wouldn't know where he was staying. And the cab didn't have a camera. And the cabbie might not talk, in any case.

Still, if the police looked hard enough, they'd find him. Even a casual witness would have noticed Wells was eight inches taller than the average Colombian. And that he didn't speak Spanish. Hotels were the obvious place to start. Wells was registered at the Hotel de la Opera under a fake name, with a passport with a photo that had been altered to make him look five years older and twenty pounds heavier. But if the cops found his room before he cleared it, they'd find two passports and twenty thousand dollars in the safe, plus a backpack with a combat knife. The agency would have no chance to contain the story. Instead of a random drug killing in El Amparo, it would turn into an international mystery, with two Colombians and one American dead, another American suspected.

No, his best bet was to clean out his room and vanish.

———

Wells ditched his sweatshirt and pistol in the alley. Tarnes could always get him a new weapon, and he didn't plan on another gunfight tonight. He walked away from Carrera 81L. The sidewalk had emptied as night settled onto the streets. The bigger stores were now closed, security grates pulled over their windows. Bicycle riders had taken over the sidewalks, their red taillights flashing in the dark.

A **bike.** A bike would be faster than a cab, the quickest way to the hotel. He had the money to buy one, if his semicoherent Spanish didn't doom the deal. A man rode slowly by, but the bike looked too nice. Wells needed a junker. He kept moving. A block on, he came to a one-room bodega, still open. Its front shelves were stocked with bags of sugar, flour, cornmeal, the staples of the poor. A bike waited in front, locked to a post. It was black, with oversized bald tires and a few missing spokes.

Wells sidled inside, grabbed an oversized bottle of water, enough to wash his bloody hands. "**Cuánto cuesta?**"

The man behind the counter was small and dark and hawk-nosed. The boy beside him was half his size, with the same strong Indian features. They stared at Wells's hands. "**Dos mil,**" the man finally said.

Wells understood that, anyway. Two thousand. He dropped two coins in the man's hand. **Great. Now we're doing business.** "Ciclo." He nodded at the bike.

The man's eyes were half closed against whatever scam Wells was running. **The conquistadors have screwed us for five hundred years, nothing new here.** "Ciclo."

"**Cuánto cuesta?**"

"**No se vende.**"

Wells fished a hundred-dollar bill and all his pesos from his jeans. Much more than the bike was worth. "**Ciclo, por favor.**"

The guy looked at the bike, back at Wells, gauging risk and reward.

Finally, he nodded. He swept up the money,

handed it to the boy, pushed him toward the door at the back of the store. When the boy was gone, he reached under the counter, handed Wells a key. "Ciclo."

—————

The potholed sidewalks made pedaling flat-out impossible. Wells picked his way east, tracking his progress against the big white church at the top of Monserrate, the mountain that overlooked the city center.

At last, he reached Carrera 7, a run-down, pedestrians-only street a few blocks from the hotel. He left the bike against a wall, knowing it wouldn't be there in a few minutes, and walked to the hotel. He heard no sirens, saw no police officers, only the impossibly young-looking soldiers who guarded the Colombian Foreign Ministry, which was across the street from the hotel. They ignored him.

Hotel de la Opera was nice, four stars. Which meant it had a full-time doorman and front desk clerk. Wells wished he'd chosen somewhere less fancy. He'd washed all the blood he could off his hands and face, but he doubted he'd cleaned himself completely. He brushed past the doorman, didn't break stride.

"Señor?"

Wells kept moving, knowing the doorman knew Wells was a guest and probably wouldn't stop Wells if Wells didn't stop on his own.

"**Buenas noches,**" he said over his shoulder.

"**Buenas noches,**" the man said uncertainly, and then Wells was gone.

———

In his bathroom mirror he saw a reddish brown smudge of blood on his neck just over the collar of his shirt. He wiped away the blood as a heavy knock rattled his door.

"**Señor?**" A woman. Wells made sure the blood was gone, went to the door.

The desk clerk stood in the hall, the doorman behind her. She was round and pretty. And frowning.

"Are you all right, Mr. Walton?"

"I didn't want to say, but I was mugged." His best play.

Her mouth opened. "I'm so, so sorry—"

"It's all right."

"Would you like us to call the police?"

"No, my fault, I got lost. I was walking around, I didn't know where I was. Stupid. These two men came out, I hardly even saw them—" the words tumbling out of him as if he was reliving the incident. He stopped abruptly. **Okay, enough, don't**

gild the lily. "Listen, I think I'm done with Colombia. I'm going to check out, stay by El Dorado"—the fanciful name for Bogotá's international airport—"tonight. Can you call me a cab?"

"Of course. We can even refund the room—"

"Don't worry about it. If it's all the same to you, I'd just like to leave." The beaten American tourist, trying to keep his dignity. "Tell the cab I want to go to the airport, I'll figure it from there."

"Whatever you'd like." She murmured in Spanish to the doorman, hurried back to the elevator. The doorman didn't move. He reached out, tapped Wells's wallet in the front pocket of his jeans.

"Mugged. They don't take this?"

Wells closed the door in his face. The doorman knew, but he couldn't prove anything. At a hotel like this, he'd have to defer to the clerk, and she would be more concerned with making sure Mr. Walton didn't post a one-star review on TripAdvisor.

———

Wells walked out, his clothes loose in his luggage, his knife and cash and passports zipped into the false bottom in his backpack. He'd have to ditch the knife before the airport. An X-ray machine would pick it up immediately. But he hadn't wanted to leave it in the room.

A black radio cab waited. The doorman glowered at Wells but held the door open. Wells slipped a hundred dollars into his hand. A big tip might buy goodwill. The guy's eyes widened as he looked at the bill. "**Señor?**"

"See you soon, amigo."

=====

Halfway to El Dorado, his phone rang. "Far as I can tell, you're still clear," Tarnes said without preamble. "The cops just called the embassy, said an American had been brought to a hospital dead. Nothing more. You clear the room?"

"Yes."

"I didn't know how long it would take so I put you on two flights, eight-twenty to Quito and ten-fifteen to Lima."

It was past 7 now, so the 8:20 was a long shot, but Wells appreciated the effort.

"As for Frietas, I was surprised, but we've got a file on him. He was in the Defense Ministry until four years ago. Deputy chief of procurement when he left. He wound up at the Central Bank. It's a pretty"—she hesitated—"nonstandard résumé for a banker. But you know, Ecuador's on the dollar—"

"Meaning?"

"Meaning it doesn't have its own currency

anymore. No pesos. Or anything else. It uses the dollar."

"Ecuadorians get paid and spend in American dollars? How can that work?"

"I don't know how it works for your average Ecuadorian, John, I'm just thinking it must be easier to move money around, launder it—whatever—when everything's in dollars."

Maybe Frietas worked as a high-end bagman for Ecuador's generals and politicians. Maybe he helped the country's cartels launder money. Wells still didn't see the connection to the Dallas attack.

"But the girlfriend's right. That number she gave you for his phone, it's been off for four days. Nothing incoming or outgoing. The last time it pinged was in Quito. And before you ask, it doesn't seem like it was his main number. Not too many calls, and they're mostly with her. Nothing interesting in the others. At least not yet."

Wells waited for more, but Tarnes seemed to be finished.

"Thanks, Julie."

"John—"

He wondered if she planned to press him again about what had happened to Tony.

"Good luck."

Wells slouched in his seat as the cab fought the weeknight traffic. He had to have someone who knew Spanish. Someone he trusted. Someone who could handle a gun. Someone who would come to Quito and chase Hector Frietas on no notice. Otherwise, Wells should just go home. He couldn't stomach getting another contractor killed.

Winston Coyle.

They'd met near the end of Wells's last mission. Coyle was a Marine who, at the time, was guarding the American embassy in Paris. Wells liked to call him an embassy Marine, more concerned with keeping his shoes shined than anything else. In reality, Coyle was tough and smart and unafraid. He'd served in Helmand Province. He was watchful and quiet. And he'd grown up south of the 10 in Los Angeles and spoke fluent Spanish.

After the mission, Wells had convinced Coyle to leave the Marines and join the agency. He was in training now. But he was **game**. Wells didn't doubt he'd ditch the Farm and take the first plane down.

Coyle picked up after one ring.

"Hello?" His voice deep, sonorous.

"Winston."

A knowing chuckle. "Oh, **no**. John Wells."

8

The MGM National Harbor Resort & Casino had brought big-time gambling to the edge of Washington, not even ten miles from the White House. To match the capital's low skyline, the casino stretched wide and long, a beached cruise ship. An eight-level, five-thousand-space garage was hidden underneath, a last indignity for losing gamblers. **You've given us your money. Now find your car and get gone. Drive carefully! À bientôt!**

Anton Petrov hadn't lost. Then again, he hadn't played. He circled the garage's lowest level, looking for the black Dodge Challenger with its Tennessee plate. **There.** He found a spot two rows away, parked his gray Kia Sorento. The most forgettable of vehicles. Perfect. Petrov glanced around, found he had the garage to himself. No surprise. People didn't linger down here.

He burrowed his head into the hood of his red Nationals sweatshirt and turned for the Challenger. Like all casinos, National Harbor had surveillance cameras everywhere. Petrov preferred to keep his face in shadow. He could have been a poker pro. But he had no interest in poker. He specialized in a riskier game.

He slipped into the Challenger.

Classical music, dark and heavy with violins, rang from the speakers. Petrov didn't know the composer. The man in the driver's seat jabbed at the dashboard touch screen until the violins were a whisper.

"Adam," the man said.

Petrov had lived in the United States for thirteen years, arriving legally from Moscow for a graduate program in computer science. He dropped out after his first year. But he never went home. He now lived as Adam Petersen, a Swede with a driver's license and a half-dozen credit cards. He had a face just this side of handsome, short brown hair, a narrow nose. He'd smoothed his accent for two years before leaving Russia. He still didn't sound native, but he didn't necessarily sound Russian either. He could pass as Swedish to an American ear. Not that people here cared about his origins. In all his time in the United States, he'd been asked where he was from only once. Americans regarded the question as bad form. Of course, a real Swede would see through his cover, but he'd never met one.

He supported himself writing software. Good coders never ran short of work. He picked up most jobs through Craigslist or other websites. The people who paid him never saw him. He lived in a two-bedroom rental apartment in Clarksburg, a Maryland exurb thirty miles northwest of Washington. Far enough from the city that he didn't have to worry about bumping into professionally curious FBI agents.

He lived alone. He couldn't risk even a casual girlfriend. He relied on Tinder on those rare occasions he wanted sex with someone other than himself. When he wasn't coding or playing Xbox, he puttered with his aquarium, his only hobby. He owned a commercial-grade twelve-by-four-by-two-foot model. His favorite fish wasn't a fish at all but a black-and-white eel, a muscled, toothy creature that hid in the gray reef and ate anything foolish enough to come within striking distance.

A bare existence. But he didn't mind.

Petrov was the SVR's top undercover operative in the United States. The CIA called its undercovers **non-official**. The SVR—the **sluzhba vneshney**

razvedki, the Russian foreign intelligence service, equal to the more famous FSB on the Kremlin's org chart, though not in reality—referred to them as **illegals**. The SVR's description was closer to the truth. Most Russian and American agents worked out of embassies, with official diplomatic protection. If they were caught stealing secrets, they were given a **persona non grata** letter and sent home.

Undercovers lived as ordinary citizens, subject to the justice of the countries where they operated. Petrov had taken the act a step further. He'd hidden not just his identity but his nationality— a tricky game in a world full of databases. He couldn't have passed as American-born, so he'd taken a smaller leap. A Swedish programmer was less likely to attract the attention of the FBI or CIA than a Russian of any stripe.

Petrov had been careful at every step. Most important, he hadn't rushed. He'd taken the years he needed to **live** his new identity. The effort had paid off. In SVR jargon, he was a **200**, a foreign operative with a completely clean cover. The SVR went to great lengths to keep him sterile. Petrov ran with almost no face-to-face oversight. Emails and other coded comms were his primary connection to the service. Though a couple senior operatives in Washington knew about him, his handler was based in Spain rather than the United

States. Petrov saw her only once a year. On the rare occasions he had to pick up money or hand over packages, he used old-school dead drops.

The SVR was bureaucratic as well as paranoid. Its willingness to let Petrov operate with such independence proved his importance. The SVR had only two 200-rated operatives in the United States. It saved them for its most valuable missions.

Like running the man in the Challenger.

———

The agent's code name was Grad, the Russian word for **city**. The Russians used the simplest code names for their most important spies. Petrov hadn't recruited Grad. In fact, the man's existence had come as a shock to him. Three years before, he'd received an email from his handler telling him to book a cruise out of Miami on the Royal Caribbean **Harmony of the Seas**. He was to sit by the ship's main pool on the cruise's third afternoon. Nothing more. He wondered if he was being told to run. Maybe the CIA or FBI had discovered him. But he'd seen no unusual activity around his apartment, and the **Harmony** didn't leave port for a week.

The **Harmony** was the world's biggest cruise ship, longer than an aircraft carrier and twice as heavy. It included an ice rink and a fourteen-hundred-seat theater. And it was full for Petrov's voyage, eight thousand passengers and crew members roaming its decks. Petrov had no hope of figuring out who belonged or who didn't. He didn't try. He relaxed. After so many years undercover, Petrov understood his truest camouflage came from eliminating the gap between actor and role. He didn't play at being a vacationing programmer. He **was** a vacationing programmer.

He covered his skin in sunblock and lined up for the hundred-foot waterslide. He leafed through a boring manual on C++ coding. He drank margaritas and ate nachos. Americans weren't good for much, but they led the world in tasty ways to fatten themselves. Mostly, he sat behind his sunglasses and watched women. College girls in bikinis, moms chasing their kids, divorcées wearing oversized hats to hide their wrinkles. The college girls were out. He wasn't interested in the moms. Maybe he'd have a chance with the divorcées. But trying would be too much trouble. Both Adam and Anton were content to look.

Petrov knew he wasn't a deep thinker. Way back during SVR training, he'd seen the recruits who were. They tied themselves up over spying's moral quandaries. They didn't last. Maybe Americans could afford such nonsense. Not Russians. Russians had learned sometime between Genghis

Khan and Napoleon that survival was its own moral imperative. And Petrov didn't like the United States. It had humiliated his people after the Soviet Union collapsed. To this day, it took every opportunity to tell the world how weak and untrustworthy Russia was.

On the third afternoon, he felt himself stirring. The gap between his twin selves opened a fraction. He wondered how his masters would signal him. What they'd want. The hours passed. The humidity rose, and the sun disappeared behind a scrim of clouds. The pool emptied out. Petrov nursed his margarita, the day's third. He must have dozed because he woke to a cold shower. His controller, Julianna, dumping water on his head.

"Hey!" The shock of being woken meant that the word formed in his mind in Russian, but he pushed it out in English.

Julianna took the deck chair beside his. She had long blond hair and ropy muscled arms. Her girlfriend, Shira, stood at the other end of the pool. Shira's pregnant belly popped from her black one-piece. The SVR had correctly gauged that even if the CIA's Madrid Station realized Julianna was a Russian agent, it would pay her little attention. Langley would assume the SVR wouldn't give important jobs to a lesbian with a Jewish girlfriend.

Petrov had known Julianna eight years. He liked her, but her foolishness today nettled him. He toweled off his face. "What if I'd yelled in our old language, Julianna?"

"Swedish, you mean." She grinned. She was half drunk, he saw. Fortunately, no one was within fifteen meters.

"You're taking your cover a bit far, don't you think?"

"I think this ship is filled with people who care more about their next meal than anything else in the world. I could wear a hat that says **Russian Spy** on my head and no one would notice."

Petrov waved at Shira. "Is it yours, Julianna?"

"Is what mine?"

"The baby, of course."

"I always knew women's insides confused you."

"I don't care enough for them to confuse me. How are you these days?"

"Come to our room at nine, I'll show you. Ninety-two thirty-six, the ninth deck."

"Nine-two-three-six."

"That's right. And don't eat too much at dinner. You're getting fat, Adam."

═════

At precisely 9 p.m., he sat on the edge of Julianna's bed, reading a thin file. She sat beside him.

Shira was off doing whatever an eight-month-pregnant woman did when she wasn't allowed in her room.

"This is real?" he said when he was done.

"No, I made it up."

"Men like him, they don't betray their countries." He was whispering. He knew Julianna was right: No one on this ship was listening. No one had the faintest idea who they were or what they were doing. But given what he'd just read, he couldn't help himself.

The American had offered to betray the United States on his own, without even being recruited. The CIA called traitors like him **walk-ins**. The SVR term was **kamikazes**, because they all blew themselves up sooner or later.

Naturally, the SVR had considered the possibility that the man was a dangle, a fake mole offered by the CIA as a way to feed false information. But he was too senior to be used that way. And his first dump of information had been too valuable to be anything but real. Petrov flipped through the file again, checked the pictures. A successful, handsome man. A celebrity, of sorts. American royalty.

At a dinner at the French embassy in Washington, this man slipped a key and a piece of paper to the SVR's deputy chief of station, Dmitri Zlobin. An address and number, nothing more. The address led to a self-service storage facility in Northeast Washington. The number to a ten-by-ten locker.

Zlobin opened the locker himself. At first glance, it seemed empty. An odd prank. Then he saw the flash drive taped to the base of the back wall.

Now the American had a new name.

The drive included a two-page letter from the American with instructions on making contact and his demands for payment, as well as a brief explanation of his motives. **I know you may question my sincerity** . . . The letter and a Russian translation were included in the file Petrov held. The man wanted two hundred fifty thousand dollars a month, paid into a Panamanian bank account controlled by a Cyprus-based trust.

On the surface, the money explained Grad's betrayal. But he had millions of dollars already. As Petrov read the file, he decided the money was a smoke screen. The American's real motive was jealousy.

Petrov didn't understand jealousy. What difference did anyone else's success or failure make? But then, Petrov had realized long before that he didn't have feelings the way other people did. He wasn't exactly a psychopath. He wasn't inclined toward cruelty. But he'd suffered no remorse about shedding his identity and taking on another. He didn't miss his parents or friends or his old life. If he had to give up this new life, he wouldn't miss it either. And though he'd never killed, he was sure he could if the SVR ordered him to do so.

Julianna rested a hand on his leg. The move would have been flirty from another woman. "You don't believe?"

Petrov read the man's letter again, decided he did. Not because of what the American said. But because he had set out his motives in **bullet points**. Such inartfulness could only be real. "I do. Anyway, what I think doesn't matter. You want me to run him, I'll run him."

On that score, the orders were clear. Petrov would give up his other agents. From this point forward, Grad would be his only responsibility. Proof the SVR believed in this man.

"It's the oldest story, what he's doing," she said. "Read the Bible."

"You know what the Bible says about women like you?" He pushed her hand off his leg.

"You're a cold fish, Anton."

"Who's Anton? My name's **Adam**." Petrov was already looking forward to this job.

———

Grad's letter had set the time and place for their first meeting. Prince William Forest, a Virginia park close by the FBI training center at Quantico. Petrov disliked the location. What if an overzealous trainee went for an early morning hike? But he couldn't change it. So on a Tuesday, just after sunrise, he parked and made his way into the forest. The ground was level, and the trail easy to follow, but after a few minutes he found himself huffing. Julianna was right. Too many long nights stuffing himself with Oreos as he sat typing code on his laptop. He promised himself he would start to work out, lose his gut. **Tomorrow.**

The American was where he'd promised, the third tree marked with a yellow blaze along Quantico Creek. Petrov stopped beside him. He was trim, in his mid-fifties, salt-and-pepper hair. The photos in the file hadn't conveyed his power. Even standing still, he radiated a coiled energy.

"Do you know where I can find the green trail?" Petrov said.

The man hesitated, like he might pretend not to understand. Though he must know he had no choice.

"Down this way. I can show you."

After a few minutes, the trail opened into a small picnic area, empty now. They sat at a splintery table, staring at each other, as the jays and finches twittered around them. Petrov couldn't deny this moment thrilled him. He would have to establish control over a man who was used to giving orders rather than taking them. Build trust with a man who was betraying his country.

He started simply. "We've accepted your offer." He unfolded a paper from his pocket, slipped it across the table. An alphanumeric string, nothing else. "Your account is set, as you've asked. Five hundred thousand in it to start. Another two hundred fifty thousand on the tenth of every month. It's yours without restriction, but we recommend you tell us if you want to bring it back here. We can help." In fact, the SVR had no plans to let the American touch the money. He would trap himself if he tried. If he made a fuss, the SVR would find a way to move it for him.

"I don't."

The answer confirmed Petrov's belief that the money wasn't the real motive. "Next. As a rule, we'll contact each other electronically. Nothing fancy. Your people look hard at encrypted communications anywhere near Washington. The better the encryption, the harder they look. We'll use standard Gmail and Hotmail accounts with simple codes, keywords you won't forget. When we have information to pass, we can use short-range encrypted wireless links. Or flash drives. Simple handoffs—you leave it in a newspaper at a Starbucks, I pick it up. No cutouts."

"That seems risky. Physical handoffs."

"You know how many people have clearances at your level in Washington? Tens of thousands. Active surveillance is reserved for suspects. You're not a suspect. You're not going to be. From now on, you don't contact our people in Washington. Never. Not for any reason. I handle you. If you feel pressure, if someone's watching, something's wrong, you tell me. We'll figure out what to do. If you come across something important, time-sensitive, we have to know right now? Me again."

"Don't want to share the credit?"

"You're too valuable to be run through our usual channels."

"Is this the part where you tell me how important I am? I'm helping both our countries?"

"Would that make you happy?"

The man smiled. "What if I call, you don't answer? What if I wake up one day, see on CNN that the FBI has arrested you?"

"The FBI doesn't know I exist. They won't unless you tell them. But—" Petrov slid across another piece of paper. "Two emergency phone numbers, two email contacts." One email and one number went to Julianna in Madrid, though the American didn't need to know her name. The other two were monitored continuously in Moscow. "A simple code for emergencies. Even if I'm gone, we can have you out of the United States in four hours."

"And spend the rest of my life in Russia? I don't think so."

Petrov didn't bother to argue. If the man was confronted with what the FSB and SVR called **trudnyy put'**—**the hard way**—he might reconsider. Until then, better to steer him from such unpleasant thoughts. "Memorize this paper and destroy it."

The man stared at the paper for a minute and then pushed it back.

"You're sure you'll remember."

"It's only my life."

"Tell me, then."

The man did. Perfectly. "Now, do I have the honor of knowing your name?"

"Adam Petersen."

"You can do better than that."

Petrov slid over his Maryland driver's license.

"This is real?"

"Come to Clarksburg, you'll see where I live."

The American handed back the license. "Why show me that? No diplo protection for you, my friend. If I'm fake, you've just given yourself up."

"If you're fake, there's a hundred FBI agents watching us. And I wouldn't get back to my car anyway. Do I look like I have the skills to hide in the forest?"

The man grinned. "I thought Russians were tough."

"Besides, you're not fake."

"No I'm not. But suppose they catch me? Aren't you worried I'll give you up?"

"I trust you to protect me."

Petrov saw his words land. They both knew he was voluntarily sharing the risk the American faced. With those last two sentences, he had jump-started a relationship that normally took years to build.

"Fine. You handle me. Any other rules?"

"Don't be greedy. For information, I mean. Let it come. If we need something specific, we'll ask. But don't start poking at things that never mattered to you before."

"Adam. I didn't know you cared."

After that first meeting, Petrov and Grad developed a routine. The SVR was wise enough not to burn the American by pressing too hard. The man was in an unusual position. He wasn't a case officer, so he didn't have access to individual agents. He would have raised suspicions if he pushed for details of ongoing operations.

But he had latitude to demand after-action reports, as well as top-level analyses and the secret appendixes that detailed the raw intelligence behind them. Not just about Russia. All over the world. The topline assessments were valuable, but the appendixes were the real prize. They provided the specific intelligence sources supporting the verdicts.

Even with his security clearance, Grad had to read them in secure rooms. An agency minder checked whatever notes he'd made before he could leave. But as he'd said, Grad had an excellent memory. In his first big coup, he'd helped the FSB find spyware the NSA had planted in its computers. A few months later, he told the Kremlin that the CIA's Moscow Station was stepping up its recruitment efforts, including several specific targets.

Petrov met Grad once every three months or so. They got along. The American was brisk and businesslike. Petrov mirrored his attitude. He didn't ask for personal information or interrogate Grad about how he was feeling. Petrov felt those questions might only cause the American to reconsider his decisions. The man seemed content with the arrangement. The money piled up in his bank account month by month. He never mentioned it, and Petrov knew he hadn't tried to take any out.

Julianna hadn't told Petrov of Russia's long-term plans for the American, or even if it had any. But a few months before, she had ordered Petrov to find out what the CIA, FBI, and NSA knew about the SVR's operations in the United States. **Aside from hacking or other cybercrime, do the agencies fear that Russia is planning attacks on the United States homeland? Are the FBI or DHS tracking Russian teams on American soil? Does the CIA have a retaliatory plan if the United States finds out that Russia has attacked its citizens?**

Petrov passed along the questions. Twelve hours later, Grad signaled, the first time he had ever asked for an off-schedule meeting. They met the next day at a long-term parking lot near Dulles, a scorching summer afternoon.

"Nice car." Petrov hadn't seen the Challenger before.

"It's all right. What's this new list, Adam?"

"What they want, they want. They don't tell me why."

Grad stared at Petrov with hollow-point blue eyes. "Then put me in touch with someone who can."

"What's the problem?"

"Don't play dumb. It doesn't suit you. These questions—the only reason to ask them is if your people are planning something here."

Grad was right, of course. "Maybe."

"Not what I signed up for."

Petrov's turn to stare. Did the American really think he could pick his assignments? He belonged to the SVR now. Petrov needed to make him understand without saying so.

"You don't want to answer these, don't. I'll tell them."

"Then what?"

"Probably nothing." As vague as possible. Not even a threat.

The American nodded as if the reality of their relationship had hit him for the first time.

"We're not friends, our countries," Petrov said. "You knew this when you signed up." He leaned across the front seat, put a finger in the older man's shoulder. "It's why you came to us in the first place."

Under the hood, the big engine hummed and

ate gasoline. Through the vents, the air conditioner blasted an arctic jet stream. Global warming wasn't even a dream in this car. Petrov sat back and waited.

"Yes," the man finally said.

"So don't pretend you care now. Whatever we do, it's what you want."

Petrov knew he was taking a chance pushing the American this way. Grad was breathing hard, like he'd run one of those marathons he liked. He reached across Petrov, opened the door. "Out."

"Think carefully—"

"Out."

The hot soft pavement sucked at Petrov's sneakers as he watched the Challenger wheel away. He cursed himself for overreaching. He'd overestimated the American. The man wasn't ready to face the extent of his betrayal.

———

Driving home, Petrov realized how much trouble he might face. Grad might demand a new controller. Anger and pride might even spur him to walk, figuring the SVR had too much invested in him to burn him. In that case, Julianna and everyone else would make sure the blame stuck to Petrov. The SVR would order him back to Moscow. It might even try him for dereliction of duty.

He wondered when he would have to admit to Julianna what had happened, decided to give himself a week. He waited six miserable days before his burner phone buzzed him awake. A blocked number.

"Did you tell your bosses I told you to get lost? Bet you didn't." Pause. "It's okay. What you said, you were right. I'll get what you asked for." Then he was gone.

=====

Yet the answers that Grad eventually passed hardly seemed worth the trouble. The agencies didn't think that Russia would risk a full-scale operation in the United States, given the risk of blowback. They thought more hacking was the most likely strategy. Petrov sent along the information, waited, heard nothing more. The months ticked by, a new year began.

Then: Dallas.

Petrov hadn't known the quiet American suburbanites around him could be so furious. The morning after the attacks, he saw three white guys screaming at the Arab clerk who ran the 7-Eleven on Perry Road: **Go home, we've had enough.**

Lived in Maryland all my life, the man said.

Not anymore. One reached out and slapped him.

These Americans wanted blood.

Petrov wondered if his people had been involved with the attack. Before the Russian presidential election in 2000, bombs killed three hundred people in Moscow and other cities. The Kremlin blamed Chechen terrorists. But most observers, then and now, believed the FSB had carried out the bombings. The service wanted to make sure that its preferred candidate—who was running on a law-and-order platform—would win the election. Intelligence agencies called such operations, carried out by one country but blamed on another, **false flag** attacks. And if Russian security forces would kill **Russians** that way, they would certainly kill Americans.

But a false flag attack on United States soil risked huge blowback. The move was too risky if Russia's only goal was to rile Americans against Muslim terrorism. Anyway, the attackers in Dallas were obviously genuine jihadis. Petrov didn't see how Russia could have found them, much less given them orders.

Then he saw Senator Birman's speech in Nashville. A guess at what his masters might be planning came to him. The next morning, he found a message from Julianna ordering a meeting with Grad. With a new list of questions. Petrov nodded as he read them over. More evidence supporting his theory.

Unfortunately, Grad was on a hunting trip in Texas. They couldn't meet until the following Monday, more than a week after the attack.

———

But it had passed, and here they were, under the National Harbor Casino.

Classical music, dark and heavy with violins, rang from the speakers. Petrov didn't know the composer. The man in the driver's seat jabbed at the dashboard touch screen until the violins were a whisper.

"**Adam**," the man said . . .

"Colonel," Petrov said.

Colonel Eric Birman (Retired). Decorated veteran of the Special Forces. Chief of staff for his cousin Senator Paul Birman. American hero.

Spy for Russia.

"What couldn't wait?"

"Your cousin's speech."

Petrov handed Eric the list of questions from Julianna. Eric studied it in silence for two long minutes, handed it back. Petrov didn't need to ask if he'd memorized them.

"I'll get back to you as soon as I can."

"All right. One other question. Your cousin— is he going to run for president, do you think?" Petrov would need to handle this conversation carefully. If Eric Birman had become a spy out of jealousy over his cousin's success, hearing that the Russians were hoping to make Paul president wouldn't improve his mood.

Birman turned up the music and they sat in silence.

Finally, Petrov turned off the radio. "So, yes?"

"He'd run for emperor, if he could."

"You should have been Russian. You hate with a majesty."

"Maybe he even thinks he can win."

"Why wouldn't he?"

Birman drummed his fingers on the steering wheel.

"Imagine. A long time ago, in a galaxy far, far away—California. My cousin was sowing his oats. Fervently. He was twenty-six, twenty-seven. He got a girl pregnant. Sixteen. Henry tried to take care of it—"

"His father?"

"Yes, Adam, his dear old dad. The original Senator Birman. Uncle Henry. Sent lawyers to get her to, you know, terminate. Offered a million bucks. She had the baby. Papa don't preach. Signed a confidentiality agreement. I think we pay her five thousand a month, sixty grand a year."

"But if it's stayed secret for so long—"

"Running for your daddy's Senate seat is one

thing. Hometown boy, hometown papers. You go for the White House, reporters tear open your whole life. They'll find her."

"The confidentiality—"

"Even if she sticks to it, it doesn't cover the kid. It can't. He wasn't born when it was signed, and he couldn't sign away those rights. She wasn't supposed to tell him. But if she hasn't, she will now. Wouldn't you tell Junior that your father is gonna be president of the United States?"

"Can she prove it?"

"You mean, was there a DNA test? I don't know. But it doesn't matter. The kid looks just like him. And there may have been another girl, too. If there was, she took the money and had an abortion, which is why I can't be so sure, but Bobby—"

"Who?"

"Robert. My other cousin. Paul's brother. He hinted about it a couple times. Back in the day."

"But why would Paul run, then?"

"You don't understand how the world looks to my cousin. He'll convince himself it won't come out, that no one will believe her, that maybe the kid isn't his after all, that people will look past it. But they won't. People in this country, they'll put up with a lot from their politicians, but not this. It's not just that he knocked up a teenage girl, it's that he never took responsibility. So you can tell your bosses that if they're hoping I'm going to ride Paul to the White House, they'd better come up with a Plan B."

"I see." Petrov saw something else, something he would keep to himself. If reporters didn't find out about Birman's love child on their own, Eric would tip them. He couldn't abide the idea of his cousin becoming president.

"Good. I'm glad. My turn, Adam. The thing in Dallas, was that yours?"

"I don't know. Truly."

"I know, you're just the water boy. But you know your people. What do you think?"

"It's possible."

"Because I'll tell you, the agency, the FBI, they're freaking. They can't figure the C-4 or how Shakir got radicalized. And they think more's coming. But like I said, if the point is to get Paul elected, then you're killing people for no reason."

"I understand."

"Anything else?" Eric jabbed at the touch screen and the violins came up. "Otherwise, I have to go. Since the speech, things are crazy. He picked up two million Twitter followers in a week. Say this for my cousin: He's the man of the moment."

9

COLFAX, WASHINGTON

Three a.m., but every light in the trailer blazed. Tom Miller sat at the kitchen table, reading about Roswell. He had slept no more than three hours a night since Allie left. He was starting to wonder if he was dead already, waiting in Purgatory for Allie to resurrect him.

If she didn't . . . he would stay here until he ran out of money and the sheriff's deputies made him leave. Three, four years tops. Then he'd have nothing left of her. Not even the memories this place gave him, that first night she'd stayed over, the first time they'd made love. The way they'd walked along the railroad tracks, feeling the steel vibrate as the big trains rolled close.

On the day they kicked him out, he'd drive west until he came to the coast south of Cape Flattery, the big cliffs over the Pacific. He'd bust the Highway 101 guardrails and see if that fancy pickup could fly.

Problem solved.

Meantime, he had empty hours to fill. He smoked the pot Allie had left. He reread his Sniper School manuals. He delved into the Internet's dark corners, the ones filled with conspiracy theories about Masons and Jews. **Them.** He couldn't stop thinking about that last conversation, the night before Allie left. What she'd said. And left unsaid.

I'm dirty inside.

Like trying to punish God. No point even thinking about it.

What hurt the most, Allie hadn't trusted him to protect her. She knew he'd fought in Afghanistan. Was she afraid he didn't love her enough to do the same for her? Or that he wasn't big enough to face the truth?

He went looking for it. He learned that the Illuminati were working to establish a New World Order. That the Mafia had assassinated John F. Kennedy. That the World Health Organization had invented AIDS to destroy Africa. That President Bush had ordered the September 11 attacks, and the Mossad had carried them out.

In Miller's lucid moments, he understood that he was filling his brain with junk as a way to avoid thinking about Allie. But with every bong hit, the fantasies wormed their way deeper into him. They weren't true.

Unless they were.

He tried to call Willie Coole, his old platoon sergeant, to talk. The number was out of service. Maybe Willie had troubles of his own.

Tonight, he was reading about Roswell, UFOs. Even high, he couldn't buy the UFO stuff. A bunch of aliens were smart enough to build space-ships. Then they got lost in New Mexico and let the government lock them up. Miller knew first-hand the U.S. military could barely handle a bunch of ragheads. It wouldn't have much chance against the eight-eyed monsters of Alpha Centauri SEAL Team Infinity.

Most analysts think the aliens were moved to a secure facility at Area 51, in the Nevada desert—

One ironclad rule: The weirder the font, the weirder the conspiracy theory.

A knock on the trailer's front door jolted him from his reverie. His first stoned thought was that the aliens had come. He grabbed the 9-millimeter that he kept under the sink.

"Who's there?"

"Tom?"

———

They sat side by side on the couch, not quite touching. Like their first night. She reached for the bong, pushed it away. Miller wanted to smash it. He didn't need to be high anymore. He didn't need anything but her.

"Everything in my life that's good, I blow it up."

"There's nothing you can say to blow us up."

"Guess where I went?"

"Back to L.A.?"

"Sioux Falls. South Dakota. Ever been?"

"It's on my top ten list."

"You're funny. Twelve hundred miles. A day and a half on the bus. I got there, seven o'clock at night, I found a motel, cleaned myself up. And I did what I always do: Went to a bar—an after-work place—let guys buy me drinks." She closed her eyes. When she opened them, she was crying.

"It's okay, babe." Although the thought of her being with someone else, some insurance agent in a suit, made him want to set the world on fire.

"It's not what you think. I could only think of you. I had to leave."

Somehow, he knew the story didn't end there.

He wanted to tell her, **Whatever it is, don't say it, I don't want to know.** But he didn't.

"I went back to the room. I couldn't sleep. All night. I was waiting for a sign. Then I saw him on TV, and that afternoon I went back out. And I didn't go anywhere nice, I went to the worst place I could find and I—"

"Stop."

"Wasn't even any pleasure in it—"

"**Stop, Allie.**"

"Forgive me."

He loved her more than he ever had. Hated her, too.

"After a couple days of that, I knew I had to come back to you or die—those were my only choices—and I wasn't ready to die yet. Here I am."

"What did you mean, you saw him on TV? Who's **him**?"

She shook her head.

"I've only told this to three people ever and none of them believed me. They said I was **crazy**, Tom."

"You're not crazy."

She reached for the bong and lighter and then put them down.

"You know how I told you I grew up in San Antone, my parents got divorced when I was twelve, me and my mom went to Chicago?"

"Sure."

"It's too **bright** in here, Tom, I can't do it this way."

He turned off every light but one and came back to her.

"The truth is, when I was eleven, both my parents died. Car accident. Three of my grands were dead, the fourth had Alzheimer's. My dad didn't have family; my mom had one sister up in Illinois. Terri. She was a few years younger than my mom, maybe thirty-one, thirty-two, when my folks died. I only saw her a couple times growing up. Looking back, my mom didn't want me near her."

"But they sent you to her?"

"She was my closest relative, she put her hand up, she got me. She must have wanted the money; my dad had insurance from his job. She was divorced, no kids. She worked at a law firm, lived in an apartment on the North Side, the rich part of Chicago. But she'd always had a coke problem, and the insurance made it worse. Took her six months to burn through the money and then she started looking around for what else she could sell."

"Allie."

"Think I'm pretty now, you should have seen me then. A twelve-year-old with a twenty-year-old's body. She let me try coke. Of course I loved it. She told me we'd have fun—she'd do it, too, we'd be like sisters—the men were rich, they'd take care of us. I should have said no, Tom. I let her, I did. I wanted it—" her voice sliding now like a Ferrari on ice.

He wrapped his arms around her, and she shuddered against him. "You were **twelve**."

"Yeah, it started a week before my thirteenth birthday. I'll never forget, this apartment high up, taking off my skirt, looking out the window at Lake Michigan, and the wind was blowing, rattling the glass—"

"I'll kill her."

"You can't."

"I was a **sniper**, Allie, I'll shoot her from a half mile away and she'll be dead before she hits the ground."

"She's dead, Tom. OD'd years ago."

"I'll kill her again."

She smiled in the dark, wrinkled herself close to him.

"We got on the circuit."

"The **what**?"

"It's funny, I forget sometimes you can't read my mind. All over the Midwest and the South, guys who would pay five or ten thousand for a night with me. I never saw any money, but I heard Terri talking about it. There were politicians. And religious guys, too—"

"Religious guys?"

"I remember two different—what do they call them?—**megachurches**, and one bishop, Catholic, Terri told me to call him Bishop, said he liked it. He's actually a cardinal now. I mean, I don't want to exaggerate, it wasn't hundreds, maybe thirty guys. Forty. I stopped counting. One day, I woke up and realized it was my fifteenth birthday, and I knew I couldn't do it anymore. I would throw myself out the window or cut my wrists, whatever, but I was **done**. I told my aunt I would tell the police. She told me no one would believe me, they'd say I was troubled, a druggie looking for attention. They'd lock me up in a crazy hospital. I guess I believed her."

"It wasn't your fault, Allie."

She started to cry again. "I should have told someone, not just for me, because right now, this week, this month, there's another girl getting broken in. That's what my aunt said when we were riding the elevator up that first time: **Don't worry, they'll break you in easy.**"

Miller thought of his rifle, sighting down the scope.

"I stole a thousand dollars and two of her rings and I took a bus to L.A. Been running away from myself ever since. But, you know, wherever you go, there you are. The worst part is, I still see some of them on television sometimes. They got famous. They made me into **this** and nothing happened to **them**. They have their lives and their families, and they're probably **still** doing it."

"Who are **they**?"

"I **told** you." Her voice small and desperate.

"Names, Allie. Who's the one you saw on TV in Sioux Falls?"

She must have heard the murder in his voice. "Doesn't matter—"

He put his hands on her shoulders and squeezed. "Tell me."

"Please. **Tom**." Her voice was calm, but her eyes were wide and panicked.

"If you didn't want me to do anything, why come back? So you could live here until you freak out and take off again? I didn't know I was such a good lay."

"Please—"

"I'm on your side, Allie."

The pistol was on the table by the couch. She stood, grabbed for it, aimed it at his chest. A two-handed grip. A professional grip. One of the few mistakes she ever made, though he didn't realize at the time. He watched, not moving, as she eased off the safety.

"Do it. Doesn't scare me. You leaving again, that's what scares me."

The pistol drooped in her hands until finally she put it down and knelt on the floor in front of him. "Maybe you're not scared, but I am, Tom. I hear them laughing every day."

"Then let's make them stop."

———

At the end, he'd realize what a perfect mark he'd made, how perfectly she'd played him. **She'd even said no when he first offered to kill.** She'd led him as easily as a child.

Even at the time, though, he felt a glimmer of doubt. An interstate sex ring that played on pre-teen virgins? An evil cokehead aunt? The convenient lack of any other relatives? He could have checked her story, he knew. He could have asked for details.

But when she looked at him that night, he knew he wouldn't. **Something** terrible had happened to Allie. She'd come to him for help. Wasn't his place to question her. The others had called her crazy. Not him. He would believe her. He would protect her.

He would be her knight.

10

S hafer caught a morning Dulles-to-Dallas flight, rented a car, drove straight to the address Jeanelle Pitts had given the FBI. Just before noon, he found himself in East Dallas, an L-shaped, two-story brick apartment block called Parkside Gardens. Though Shafer saw neither park nor garden, only dumpsters at the end of a cracked parking lot.

Jeanelle lived in apartment 224, according to the FBI interview form. The top end of the L. Shafer heard a television as he approached, Judge Judy's nasal voice blaring. He jabbed the buzzer. He hadn't called Pitts in advance, hadn't wanted her to know he was coming. He wondered if he'd made a mistake. The door notched open, and a shirtless black man in his early twenties peered out, scratched his chin. "What you want?"

"Jeanelle here?"

The guy shook his head as if Shafer were speaking Hebrew.

"Jeanelle Pitts. Lives here?"

The guy reached up to close the door. Shafer stuck a toe inside.

"Don't do that."

"I have this as her address."

"Don't live here. Me and my girl do. Now, go on before I get upset." The guy opened the door enough for Shafer to see the pistol stuck in the waistband of his shorts. **Texas.**

Shafer stepped back, peered around the guy into the apartment. He glimpsed a pair of black legs stretched out of a blue dress. "Jeanelle?"

"My name Quintana," the legs said.

The man put his hand on the butt of his pistol. "Come **on.**"

"One more question, I'll stop bothering you."

"Quick. She gonna say who won."

Meaning Judge Judy, not the woman on the couch, Shafer assumed. "When did you move in?"

"Last year. All right?"

"Any idea where I can find Jeanelle? Did she leave a forwarding address?"

"She win the Powerball. Live in Preston Hollow now. Over by **Bush.**" The guy closed the door.

"I can pay!" Shafer yelled. He wished he'd made the offer sooner.

No answer. Shafer lifted a fist to knock once more, changed his mind. The property management company would surely have a forwarding address.

———

On the way to the manager's office, Shafer checked his phone, discovered Preston Hollow was the fanciest neighborhood in Dallas. Shafer would bet the farm, the house, and his rented Ford Escape that Jeanelle Pitts wasn't living there.

The office was tucked under the building's main stairway. The waiting area was hot, no air-conditioning, and empty aside from three metal chairs and a desk with a few application forms stacked in a basket. Two posters provided the only decoration. One featured an overhead shot of the building and promised PARKSIDE GARDENS: A GREAT PLACE. SECTION 8 ACCEPTED. The other announced RENT DUE 3RD OF MONTH. NO EXTRA TIME! DON'T ASK!

"Hello?"

"Hold on." A man, from the inner office, his voice strained. "Give me a few—"

The office door was closed. **William Powdy, Property Manager**, a brass nameplate proclaimed in script far too fancy for this room. Beneath it, a hand-lettered sign warned KNOCK BEFORE ENTERING! Shafer had seen enough of Parkside Gardens. He knocked and simultaneously pushed open the door. The lock held for a second, but Shafer shoved until it gave.

He found a lean white guy in a white T-shirt staring at a laptop whose screen showed three men engaging in carnal acrobatics.

Powdy's jeans were around his ankles. He was somewhat busy, too.

"Mr. Powdy, I presume," Shafer said. "Bad time?"

Powdy saw Shafer, twisted away. "Get out!"

"When you're ready." Shafer closed the door.

Two minutes later, it swung open. Powdy stepped into the doorway, pants buttoned. "You can't read, mister?" He was in his late forties, with a country face, narrow and lined and weather-beaten, the solid shoulders of a man who worked with his hands.

"Didn't realize self-love was on the job description."

"Fucking asshole."

"Ironic, considering what you were watching."

Powdy stepped into the waiting area. Now Shafer saw the rage in his dark eyes, the expandable police baton in his right hand. And the wedding ring on his left. Shafer doubted Powdy's wife knew of his fondness for gay porn. Powdy most definitely was not in on the joke. He was humiliated. And furious.

After a career of mouthing off, Shafer had made the wrong guy mad. He was in trouble, he saw.

He lifted his hands. "Sorry, buddy. My bad."

"Not your buddy. You looking for an apartment?"

"No—"

"Didn't think so. You ain't from Texas." Powdy moved toward Shafer as if being from another state was an offense punishable by death. His whole body vibrated with rage. Shafer wondered what else had gone wrong for him today. Maybe his wife had filed for divorce. Maybe a Mercedes cut off his pickup. Maybe the Mexicans at the drive-thru didn't get his order right.

Probably nothing. Shafer was enough.

Shafer took a half step toward the door, looked over his shoulder. No one could see in here. The stairs shielded the office from the parking lot outside. He wondered if he should run.

"Not another step. You lefty or righty?"

"Righty."

"Put out your left hand. Palm down."

"Please."

"Put it out or I'll shove this baton up your ass. You already admitted you weren't here on legitimate business. My door was locked. That's breaking and entering. I can shoot you, if I like."

"In the middle of the day, in an open office?" Even now, Shafer couldn't keep his mouth shut.

"You don't know much about this state, mister."

Shafer wished he could blink three times and summon Wells to take care of this closet case.

"Three . . . Two . . ." Powdy raised the baton. "One—"

Shafer turned away and broke for the door. He didn't think Powdy would hit him in public.

But Powdy moved to intercept him. Too late, Shafer realized Powdy had wanted him to try to run, an excuse to hit him in the back—

No, Officer, he broke into my office. He saw me, took off. I hardly saw him, didn't know how old he was—

He heard the baton whistling behind him—

Lightning at the back of his skull—

And nothing.

11

QUITO, ECUADOR

Wells pulled up outside the arrivals hall at Quito's international airport as a thickly muscled black man in wrap shades stepped through the sliding glass doors. He carried only a laptop case and a backpack, no bags. Packing light. Once a Marine, always a Marine.

Wells leaned over to open the passenger door. He was driving an old Toyota compact, faded green paint, no power doors, standard Ecuadorian plates. Nice and low-profile. "Winston Coyle. As I live and breathe."

"Cuánto a Quito, señor?"

"For you, my friend, on the house."

Coyle tossed his stuff in back, sat beside Wells. The sun was a few minutes from disappearing behind the vast ridge of mountains west of the airport, Mariscal Sucre International. It had opened in 2013 after one-too-many close calls at Quito's original in-town airfield.

"**Buenas tardes, Juan Wells.**"

Wells was surprised how glad he was to see Coyle. Maybe he thought of Coyle as lucky after their long-shot success in Paris. This mission needed all the help it could get. "You could pass for a native. If the natives were black and could bench four hundred pounds."

"**Solo tres ochenta. Todo el crédito a Taco Bell. Delicioso y sano!**" Coyle spoke with the exaggerated precision of a pitchman on Univision.

"Yeah, sure. But, unfortunately, Spanish is not in my skill set, so let's make America great again and go English only for now."

"**Sí, señor.**" Coyle grinned. "Time to get to business, as the white folk say."

"You know I'm white."

"I'm not sure what you are."

When they spoke two nights before, Wells had told Coyle only that he was headed to Ecuador and needed help. **You know I'm still at the Farm, right?** Coyle said. **I won't let Ms. Ratched send you to the principal's office,** Wells said. That fast, Coyle promised to be on the next plane down.

But with Coyle here, Wells found he wasn't ready to talk about Enrique Martinez and Hector Frietas just yet, explaining the mess he'd made in

Bogotá. For a few minutes, he wanted to keep the fiction that they were on a South American road trip, **Johnny and Winston's Excellent Ecuadorian Adventure.** Childish, but even Wells needed a break from the truth once in a while.

"How'd you like the Farm?"

The Farm—the agency's famed training base at Camp Peary, in southeastern Virginia—had changed in recent years to align with the agency's new focus on the War on Terror. Case officers spent less time practicing cocktail party recruitments, more on survival exercises and drone handling.

Still, the place retained its summer-camp-like quality. Recruits lived and ate together. Even those who would spend their entire lives behind desks at Langley practiced at the firing range. Like all initiations, the exercises were designed to build cohesion among diverse recruits. In less fancy terms, the agency hoped new officers would leave Camp Peary thinking that the CIA was **cool**.

Wells visited the place once a year to take questions about deep-cover work. The trips were his last formal connection with the agency. Recruits were told only he was a former field operative who had spent time in Afghanistan, a true but wildly incomplete version of his résumé.

"Farm's all right. Lots of toys. You know, you're a legend down there."

"Hope not."

"You think that aw-shucks routine works with me?"

"The fewer people who know me, the safer I am." **Anne and Emmie, too,** Wells didn't say. Foreign intelligence services like the SVR rarely targeted the families of CIA officers. No one wanted to start a cycle of retaliatory attacks. But groups like the Islamic State didn't care. With Coyle's help, Wells had narrowly thwarted a Daesh attack during his last mission. Anonymity was his best protection.

"These are our guys, John."

"And?" Wells reminding Coyle of the secret they shared: An agency mole, a senior officer, had betrayed the CIA to the Islamic State.

"Point taken. Gonna tell me why I'm here, or should I guess?"

"Let's drop your stuff at the hotel, take a walk, I'll show you what you need to see."

"Long as the room has two beds. You brought me down here hoping I'd be your rent boy, we're both gonna be sorry."

They came over a ridge, and the lights of Quito came into view. "How did you know?"

Quito was one-fifth the size of Bogotá, and five times as nice. The Ecuadorian capital occupied a narrow valley ten thousand feet above sea level. Mountains and volcanoes surrounded it on three sides. The city center dated to the Spanish Colonial era, and, unlike La Candelaria, it was largely safe, even after dark. Ecuador was poorer than Colombia, but Ecuadorian culture was much less violent than its northern neighbor's. The country's murder rate was one-fourth Colombia's.

The travel guidebooks and magazines had taken notice. Quito was a regular stop on the Lonely Planet backpacker circuit. Wells spoke quietly as they walked southwest from their hotel toward the city center. He didn't want to chance an American overhearing them, likelier here than in Bogotá. On the other hand, the tourist population meant that he and Coyle stood out less.

"Wish you'd called a week ago," Coyle said after Wells finished explaining what had happened in Bogotá. Including the death of Antonio Guerro, a/k/a Tony from Tampa. Meaning: **You screwed up, but it's done now. Just try not to get anyone else killed down here, John-O. Especially me.**

Best part of talking to a Marine who'd fought in Afghanistan was what didn't have to be said. "Me too."

"This guy Guerro, his family under control?"

"Looks that way so far."

Tarnes had ordered the chief of Bogotá Station to tell Guerro's parents he'd been in El Amparo on agency business. The CIA couldn't say anything more about what had happened because it was still investigating, and Guerro's mission was classified. Meantime, Mom and Dad would come to Langley to see a star for their son added to the CIA's Memorial Wall. Lies upon lies. And the station chief wasn't happy covering for an operation that he hadn't known about, Tarnes told Wells. But at least Guerro's parents would believe he'd died a hero.

Empty gestures seemed to be all Wells had.

=====

Wells had told Tarnes about the safe in the apartment in El Amparo, of course. Under normal circumstances, the agency would have sent in a safecracker. But a field op from Bogotá Station had checked out the building the day before and reported detectives were talking to residents. Asking the Colombian Ministry of the Interior directly about the killings would be a mistake. As a rule, the CIA didn't much care about street crime in Bogotá. Showing interest in this shooting would raise unanswerable questions.

Guerro's death was different. He was an American citizen. The Colombians would expect the United States to be interested in what had happened to him. The Bogotá cops had told their FBI liaison they believed Guerro had been alive when he got into the taxi, but the cabdriver who dropped Guerro's body at the hospital was not a suspect. They'd also said they believed the murder might be tied to the killings of two men in a slum nearby.

The cops figured if the shootings were connected, they resulted from a drug deal gone wrong. Guerro had gone to El Amparo for coke, wound up in a firefight. The fact Guerro wasn't carrying a pistol when he was delivered to the hospital didn't bother the police. They assumed he'd ditched it before he got in the cab.

The possible connection with Guerro meant that the cops were showing more interest in the El Amparo murders than they typically did in a slum shooting. Thus, the door-to-door interviews in the building. Still, Wells figured he was safe. As far as he knew, only three people had gotten a good look at him: the taxi driver, the third drug dealer, and Elena. The cabbie had kept his mouth shut so far, no doubt hoping for more money. The other two had their own reasons to keep quiet.

Even so, with the cops still investigating and residents on edge, Wells and Tarnes thought trying to crack the safe would be a mistake for now. Especially since as far as they knew Frietas hadn't been to the safe house in months. Wells and Coyle would have to look for answers in Quito first.

━━━━━

Now they crossed Avenida 12 de Octubre, a wide, traffic-choked boulevard, and walked down a hilly, tree-lined street flanked by walled homes on both sides. The sidewalks were crumbling, but the neighborhood reflected Quito's gentrification. A new apartment building rose beside a salon advertising organic facials and a vegan restaurant whose windows revealed communal tables made of driftwood.

"Quito," Coyle said.

"Yeah, who knew?"

"Frietas lives around here?"

"Next block. But he doesn't seem to be home."

Wells explained he'd arrived in Quito the afternoon before, picked up the car and a pistol from the CIA station here. He spent the morning watching the house. Frietas's wife had left around

9 a.m. But Wells saw no evidence of Frietas. The NSA said his phones were still dark.

"You have a plan to find him? Knock on his door tonight?"

"Let's wait on that. Start with the Central Bank in the morning. You call, ask for an appointment."

"Why would he see me? If he's deputy director for money laundering, or whatever?"

"Because you're a Harvard professor researching South American central banks. His name came up as a regional expert. Everyone loves Hah-**vahd**."

"You look at me, you think Harvard professor?"

"You meet him, great. If not, at least you find out if he's at the office, give us a chance to follow him home or wherever. I'm gonna watch the house again in the morning. With any luck, I'll see him. Or a chance to get inside easy. In the afternoon, we'll knock on doors, talk to the neighbors. If he's around, someone will know."

"They'll tell us because . . . ?"

"Because we're investigators from New York that a nameless U.S. company has hired to find Mr. Frietas."

Wells handed Coyle a photo identification from Kroll, a high-end private security company. It identified him as William Coil, and it came with a New York State driver's license to match. Wells had his own badge and license. All courtesy of Tarnes.

Coyle flipped the identification back and forth in his hand. "Still seems like a long shot."

"Only takes one person who feels like talking. Anyway, if we strike out on that, we'll maybe knock on his door, see if his wife feels like chatting. Somebody knows where he is. Or, at least, when he went missing."

"What's the wife's name?"

"Graciela. I got a decent look at her this morning. For a woman with a missing husband, she was awfully dry-eyed. This is her, by the way." Wells showed a photo of Graciela, a tall, hard-looking woman with a helmet of black hair and deep-set eyes.

"I'm guessing Elena didn't look like that. Maybe Graciela thinks Hector took off with her."

"Or she knows he's laundering drug money and isn't surprised he got hit. Their house is nice. Nicer than it should be. It's up here, see for yourself."

———

They turned left onto Calle José Tamayo, a quiet street that sloped southwest toward the big park that held Ecuador's national museum. Frietas's house, number 318, was a tall two-story, set back

behind an eight-foot-high brick wall topped with
steel spikes. A heavy gate protected a narrow
driveway along the edge of the property. A big
gray Mercedes sedan was visible inside. Behind
the wall, a dog barked loudly. Not the over-the-
top security Wells had seen in Bogotá, but more
than the other houses on the block.

"What's Graciela do?" Coyle said.

"Statistician in the Ministry of Public Health."

"Nobody's paying for that house on a bureau-
crat's salary. Or even two bureaucrats'."

Wells couldn't disagree. Frietas depressed him
before they'd ever met. The guy was an adulterer
and most likely a money launderer. Fine. Wells
wasn't winning any humanitarian prizes either.

What Frietas didn't seem to be was a terrorist. The NSA had found no links between
Frietas and Muslim terror groups. His bank accounts, at least the two the NSA and Treasury
had found, had about one-point-three million
dollars in them total. He was rich, but not cartel rich. He hadn't touched the money in the
last few days.

In fact, the accounts showed no unusual cash
withdrawals in the last couple years. The big ex-
penses were his mortgage, which ran six thousand
dollars a month, and two monthly automated
transfers of fifteen hundred dollars each to Au-

tolider Ecuador, which turned out to be a Mercedes dealership in northern Quito.

Frietas wasn't paying those bills on his Central Bank salary. Instead, every so often, he added forty or fifty thousand dollars to the account. The big exception came a year before when he'd added nine hundred fifty thousand dollars to one of them in one big cash deposit. That was by far the biggest deposit he'd ever made. Had he been paid for laundering? Skimmed from a cartel?

In his hours watching Frietas's house, Wells had seen no other surveillance, no black SUVs making slow loops, no drones whirring. No one cared about Hector Frietas. Aside from Frietas's boasts to Enrique Martinez and Elena, Wells had no evidence Frietas had anything to tell the CIA. Maybe Frietas had found himself in trouble and decided his best way out was to scam the United States by blowing up the importance of some tidbit he'd overheard. A dumb move, but desperate people made dumb moves. Maybe he'd thought better of the idea and taken off.

Or maybe whoever was after him had caught him and dumped him in the jungle.

Coyle seemed to read Wells's mind. "I know I'm new at this, John, but I don't see how this guy plays."

If Frietas had been from Colombia, Wells

could have asked Tarnes to have the FBI liaisons in Bogotá check with the Colombian intel agencies about him. But Ecuador's president, Rafael Correa, was an old-school leftist who couldn't stand the United States. When Fidel Castro died, Correa oversaw a memorial service with full color guard honors. Whatever they might know about Frietas, the Ecuadorian security forces wouldn't do American investigators any favors.

Wells and Coyle were stuck going door-to-door.

———

The next day was a slog. At the bank, Frietas's assistant made Coyle wait for ninety minutes, then told him that Frietas was traveling. No, she didn't know where he'd gone. Or when he'd be back. Frietas didn't answer emails. His work and phone voice mails were jammed and not taking messages. Back on José Tamayo, Wells watched as Frietas's wife emerged from the house, locked up, went to work. Coyle came back around noon, and he and Wells knocked on doors.

But the neighbors seemed unimpressed, or maybe too impressed, with the Kroll badges. The few who would talk through their gates claimed they didn't know much about the house at 318. **The dog, it barked whenever I walked by. I**

didn't slow down, a middle-aged woman five houses down said.

Did you ever see anyone visiting?

They kept to themselves.

Late afternoon, two blocks down, a shop-keeper at a narrow bodega left over from an older, poorer Quito nodded at Frietas's picture.

"You know him?" Coyle said in Spanish.

The shopkeeper was a small man who had pale brown skin, yellowed eyes, greasy black hair. He looked away, muttered at his dusty shelves.

"He says his memory is as empty as his pockets. Poet and he don't even know it." Coyle fished a five-dollar bill out of his wallet, put it on the counter.

The man looked at the bill. **"Cinco?"** he said softly. Wells laid a twenty beside it. The man tucked the money into his pocket, began what was a very involved story. Coyle listened, didn't say much. Finally, the shopkeeper petered out, and Coyle turned to Wells.

"Frietas was a drinker. Medium-heavy. Used to come in a couple times a week and buy **aguar-diente,** the local liquor, those down there—" Coyle pointed at the two-hundred-milliliter bot-tles, small enough to tuck in a coat pocket, on the bottom shelf. "The kind you buy to suck down on the walk back to your house, before your wife sees. He was usually by himself. But maybe a year ago, he came in twice with a group. Not Ecuadorian. White."

"Some Ecuadorians are pretty white."

Coyle said something. The shopkeeper interrupted, waving his hands, excited for the first time. "He knows what his people look like. These weren't from Ecuador. Anyway, they weren't speaking Spanish—"

"**Inglés.**"

The shopkeeper shook his head. "Not English."

"Could it have been Arabic?" Wells offered some Arabic to the guy, received a blank look in return. "German? **Alemán? Ich bin ein Berliner?**" The shopkeeper shook his head. "Russian? **Ya russkiy? Privyet? Spasibo?**"

This time, the shopkeeper murmured to Coyle.

"He says maybe the last one. It was a year, he can't be sure."

"These people, how many were there?"

The guy tapped his head even before Coyle translated. Wells handed him another twenty-dollar bill, and he started talking again.

"Two women, he thinks, and five or six men. They looked like us."

"Like us?"

"**Policía.**" The guy held his hands wide and apart. "**Soldados.**"

"Right. How could he be sure Frietas was with them? And did he ever ask Frietas about them?"

A short question, a very long answer, with lots of gesturing toward the store shelves.

"They came in together, they bought liquor together, **aguardiente** and vodka and wine, Frietas paid for all of it. This was over a period of at least a month, maybe two. It was a lot of money, so it stuck with him. Another time, two of them came in on a run without Frietas, and Frietas paid later. He did ask Frietas about them after, he hoped they'd come back. Frietas said they'd gone. That was all he said, and it looked like he didn't want to talk about it, so that was it."

"When was the last time he saw Frietas?"

The answer came back fast.

"Maybe two weeks ago. He seemed excited. Nothing specific, he just seemed happy."

"Thanks." Wells passed him one more twenty. "Anything else?"

"**Algo más?**" Coyle said.

"**Nada.**"

========

The sun had vanished behind the fifteen-thousand-foot volcanoes west of the city when Wells and Coyle emerged onto Calle José Tamayo.

"You got any good reasons why an Ecuadorian

banker would hang with Russian soldiers?" Coyle said.

"And maybe get paid by them, too." Wells explained the huge deposit Frietas had made the year before. "Time to ask his wife." Wells was sure now that Frietas wasn't in Quito, much less at home. Guys like him didn't just stop drinking.

They walked back to 318. The dog wasn't in the yard. A fish-eye security camera watched the front gate. Through its thick grille, Wells saw lights behind barred windows. He pushed a buzzer mounted next to the gate. Inside the house, the dog went wild with deep, throaty barks.

No answer. Wells buzzed again.

"Yes?" A woman's voice. In English. Accented but understandable. "What do you want?"

"We're investigators. Looking for your husband."

"Investigators from where?"

"New York." Wells lifted the Kroll badge to the fish-eye.

A pause.

"You come. The other one stays outside."

"Racist," Coyle muttered under his breath.

The gate's deadbolt shot back, echoing on the street.

"You heavy," Coyle said.

"You know I'm not." Wells had left his new

pistol in the room safe. "She's just nervous. Wait here." Without waiting for Coyle's answer, Wells pushed open the gate and stepped inside.

The yard was long and narrow, stretching eighty feet between the side walls, and twenty-five from the gate to the front door. Wells pushed the gate shut. As it locked behind him, flood-lights mounted on the corners of the house clicked on, revealing a landscaped garden with what looked like a koi pond on the left and small flowering trees with beautiful purple blossoms on the right.

Wells lifted his hands, walked slowly down the path to the front door. The dog yammered. If it was as mean as it sounded, Graciela wouldn't need any other weapon.

When he was ten feet away, the door swung toward him. Graciela stood just inside the door, the dog next to her, a German shepherd, ninety pounds of fur and teeth. The shepherd lunged for Wells. Graciela needed all her weight to tug it back. She said something in Spanish, and the shepherd sat. Unwillingly. Its mouth still open.

"Are you armed?"

"No."

"Sit down. Now." Precise, careful English, from years of language training. She wore a shapeless dress, and up close her face was solid, unattractive but dignified. **Look at me or don't, I don't care.**

Wells went to a knee, his hands still up.

"On your bottom. With your hands on top of your head."

A posture that would ensure Wells couldn't escape if she unleashed the dog. Nonetheless, he sat.

"You okay, John?" Coyle said from the street.

Coyle might as well have been in another galaxy, for all the good he could do. Wells ignored him. Graciela stepped out of the house. She stopped when she was five feet away, the dog a foot closer. It opened its mouth wide and ran its big pink tongue over its lips. Like an offensive tackle at an all-you-can-eat buffet.

Career stuck in a rut? Time to try something new?

"What's your name?" Wells said to the dog.

"Rosa," Graciela said.

Rosa grunted and sat. Wells, also sitting, could see unmistakable proof Rosa was male. "Doesn't that mean **pink?**"

"Yes. My husband thought it would be funny. What is it you want?"

Wells made himself ignore the shepherd. "Your husband called a mutual friend a few weeks ago. Said he had information he wanted to sell. I came down to see him, but he disappeared."

"Information for your company?"

The truth seemed like the best option. "For the U.S. government."

"You said you were a private investigator."

"In this case, I'm working for the Central Intelligence Agency."

She shook her head. "Why would I talk to you?"

The usual reasons. Money and favors. "Besides the fact that we're trying to find your husband? We can pay if you help us figure out what he wanted to tell us."

"I don't know what you mean."

Wells needed to control this conversation. He couldn't do it sitting on his butt with an attack dog making eyes at him. "I promise, I'm here to talk. Nothing else. I'm going to get up now. Don't sic the dog." Before she could argue, Wells popped to his feet, his hands still on his head.

Rosa growled, but Graciela held his leash.

"Beautiful house," Wells said. "You work for the Ministry of Health, yes? Your husband works for the Banco Central?"

Her face tightened against the implicit question: **How do you pay for it?** Wells couldn't tell yet if she wanted to protect Frietas or would turn on him.

"You said CIA business?"

"That's right. You know, Hector has a girl-friend. Her name's Elena."

Her smile didn't make her any prettier. "Hector has lots of girlfriends."

"This one, he brought her to Bogotá with him. He owns an apartment there."

"I don't believe you."

"I'm sorry, ma'am, I've seen it."

A long pause. "Do you think I stayed married to him for the money?" she finally said. "I was raised to believe that divorce is a sin. A **mortal** sin."

Even the Pope doesn't think that anymore. "Ms. Frietas. The only reason I mention Elena is that I met her last week in Bogotá." **And when I say** met, **I mean** tied up.

"Good for you."

Wells decided to press. "She said Hector had promised to take her to the United States with him."

"You're lying." But she said the words without heat, seeming to know he wasn't.

"Whatever information he had, he thought it was valuable. Enough that he could get a visa for himself. And Elena, too."

She led the shepherd inside, slammed the front door. Wells stood in the yard, replaying the conversation. It puzzled him, down to the most basic fact: **Why had she let him in?**

A minute later, the door creaked open. Wells tensed, wondering if Graciela was about to set Rosa on him. But she walked out. Alone. Wearing a jacket big enough to hide secrets. Or a pistol. "This may sound strange, but I love Hector. **Más vale estar solo que mal acompañado,** my mother said. But he made me laugh, and it's hard to make an ugly woman laugh. Are you telling me the truth? About the girl?"

Wells saw: Graciela would betray her husband if Wells stayed out of her way. "Yes."

"I don't know what he knew or where he is, that's the truth. But the last few weeks, he's been upset. Nervous. He was coming home late, asking me if anyone was watching the house."

Wells wondered why Frietas hadn't touched his bank accounts if he was in trouble. Maybe he'd made a mistake so big that a million dollars wouldn't begin to fix it. "Was anyone? Watching?"

"Once I thought I saw someone, but I wasn't sure. Then, maybe two weeks ago, his mood changed. He was happy. Wouldn't tell me why. He never told me anything about where the money came from. He said it would be safer for me, and I believed him."

Wells didn't believe her. Maybe she hadn't known all the details, but she had to have known the money wasn't clean. He didn't argue, but she seemed to see his skepticism. She pushed past him.

"Come on, let's get your friend off the street." She pulled open the gate, waved Coyle inside.

"**Gracias.**"

"Stick to English," she said to Coyle. "So, no, he didn't tell me anything. But he was in a better mood, I could tell. Then he disappeared. This was eight days ago. He told me he was going to Bogotá."

Another reason she'd believed Wells about Elena. "You weren't surprised when he didn't call?"

"Not at first."

Wells thought now that Frietas's disappearance was unrelated to whatever he'd been trying to sell to the United States. Or related only because it made him take a chance that had gotten him in trouble. Like someone had spotted his name on an airline manifest.

"You have any idea where he might be?"

She shook her head.

"Was anyone helping him launder money? Inside the government, maybe?"

"If there was, I don't know who. Truly, he kept it away from me."

And you never asked. But the question of what Graciela had known was a distraction from the real issue: **What had Frietas wanted to tell them?** "Last year, did he bring any Russians over?"

"No."

"Excuse me, ma'am," Coyle said, grabbing her attention, "but did your husband have a safe house here?"

"A what?"

"I mean, is it possible he owned another house in Quito? Or rented one? The reason I ask is that we've been told he spent time with Russians about a year ago. Maybe they weren't staying in a hotel."

Wells didn't like the interruption, but Coyle was right. If the Russians had been in town for as long as the shopkeeper remembered, they would have been conspicuous in a hotel. Wells doubted they'd stayed at the Russian embassy either. The apartment in Bogotá proved Frietas liked his own properties. Why wouldn't he have had one in Quito, too?

"Another house?" Graciela weighed the idea. "I don't know. I don't think so."

Wells thought she was protesting too much. From the way Coyle looked at Wells, he thought so, too.

Maybe they'd touched a nerve, or maybe Graciela was tired of talking. She nudged Wells toward the gate. "Now, please. You need to leave."

"Just a few more questions. Your husband was no fool. He thought his information would be worth millions of dollars and a U.S. passport. Help us, they're yours."

"Fine. Two minutes."

"Just to be clear, when did you last see Hector?"

"The morning he said he was going to Bogotá. Eight days ago. Normally, he would go for three or four days."

"Did he give you any reason to think this trip would be different?"

"No. But then he didn't call. Three days ago, I started to worry. I called his secretary, friends at the bank. No one's heard anything."

"He drove himself to the airport?"

"Yes. He has a Mercedes like mine."

In the U.S. and Europe, luxury cars often came with automatic emergency roadside assistance programs that used the car's own cellular link to broadcast their location in case of an accident. The link could also be used to find the cars if they were stolen. But Wells didn't know if Mercedes offered the program in Ecuador or if it would work if the car had been turned off since the previous week. He'd ask Tarnes to find out.

"Can you give us the plate number?"

"I'm sorry, I don't know. Now, listen, you really must leave." She shook her head. "Whatever's happened to Hector, I don't want to talk about this anymore."

She shoved them toward the gate. Wells didn't want to upset her, not with the shepherd inside and neighbors all around, though she didn't seem upset. He couldn't read her at all.

═══════

The gate slammed. Wells and Coyle looked at each other.

"Weird," Coyle said.

"For lack of a better word. Let's walk and talk."

They worked their way down José Tamayo while Wells filled Coyle in on the first part of the conversation.

"Why let us in at all?" Coyle said when he finished. "She doesn't know us, her husband's missing, she knows he's into something. We're obviously not local. The sun's down. Why?"

The same question that stumped Wells.

"And, okay, she has the dog, but then she puts him away and lets me in, too. Two of us."

"By then, she figured we weren't a threat."

"How, exactly, did she figure that?"

Wells stopped mid-stride.

He had all the pieces of the puzzle, he'd just needed Coyle to shake them loose. Why Frietas had insisted on having the meeting outside normal agency channels. Why he and Graciela openly lived so richly. Why he hadn't touched his money.

"Statistician, my ass," Coyle said, beating Wells to it.

Graciela was an Ecuadorian intelligence officer. One senior enough to have a cover identity. She had let her husband make the dirty money, keep it in his name, pay for the house and the cars. He took all the risk. Maybe she'd grown tired of his affairs. Or lost her temper when she learned he was running off with his mistress. He'd wanted to keep the meeting secret because he was afraid she'd find out. But she had anyway. Or maybe he'd blurted out the truth the morning he was headed for Bogotá. Either way—

She'd played Wells and Coyle decently, though she'd professed her complete ignorance too many times. Even the most naïve wife had some idea how her husband was making money. She'd agreed to talk because she would want to know why a pair of Americans were looking for him.

Wells wondered if Graciela would set the security forces on them now that she knew what they wanted. He didn't think so. She wouldn't want too many questions about what had happened to dear old Hector.

"You think she killed him?" Coyle said. "Father of her children?"

"Possible." More than possible.

"What did she do with the body?"

"Stuffed it in the Mercedes, went for a drive. Parked it in that flophouse of his. Notice how fast she sent us packing after you brought that up?"

The theory made sense to Wells. If she'd killed him in the heat of the moment, she wouldn't have an alibi or a plan to dispose of the corpse. She was a strong woman, and Frietas a small man. She was big enough and tough enough to have stowed his body in the trunk while she figured out her next move. Maybe she had already driven into the Ecuadorian jungle, set the Mercedes on fire, left her husband's corpse as a feast for the jaguars and the wild pigs. But she couldn't have taken the Mercedes very far off road. Someone would have spotted it already. Which meant the car and Frietas's body were probably still close by.

"Here's the thing. I don't care if she killed him. I only care if she can help us."

"Meaning?"

"Meaning, if we find the body, or figure out where it is, we make a deal with her."

"No justice for Hector?"

"Hector should have kept it in his pants. Next question. How do we find him?" Wells explained his idea about the Mercedes. "It's a long shot, but it's probably the best place to start."

"Can we try the guy at the bodega first?"

"How so?"

"It slipped past me at the time, but remember what he said about how they came in without Frietas and he paid later? Let's say they bought a couple weeks' worth of booze. Let's say the house isn't close. Maybe it's way up one of these hills. They walk down. Are they going to want to drag a bunch of bottles all the way back up themselves? No, they're going to have our friend bring it for them."

"Maybe they took a taxi."

"Maybe. Never hurts to ask, though."

———

Back at the bodega, the shopkeeper was closing. He didn't look thrilled to see them, but he nodded them inside. Wells handed him another twenty, and Coyle started asking questions. Even before the shopkeeper finished his answer, Coyle's smile told Wells they were onto something.

"He says they told him to deliver it on his motorbike that time. They gave him the address—"

"Coyle. I'm starting to like you."

"Hold on. He can't remember where exactly, but it was on this side of the valley, high up, where the streets end."

"We need an address, not a sonnet."

"He thinks he can find it if we take him around. He wants two hundred dollars."

"**Dos cien,**" the guy said, flashing his yellow teeth at Wells. "**Dos cien dólares.**"

"We can manage that," Wells said. "Let's go. **Vamonos.**"

"**Mañana.**" The guy shook his head and spoke to Coyle.

"He says he has twin girls, they turn ten tonight, he won't miss it, doesn't care how much we pay him—"

"Fine." They would lose a night to the daughters of an Ecuadorian bodega owner. Wells could live with the delay, considering how much progress they'd just made.

Long as the guy didn't change his mind overnight.

12

Wings. Beer. Sports.

The televisions in the Buffalo Wild Wings were tuned to English Premier League soccer this afternoon, thin gruel for sports addicts. The night's first pro basketball and hockey games were still hours off. Eric Birman was happy to see the place was mostly empty. Eric didn't like meeting the man he knew as Adam Petersen so soon after their last encounter in the casino garage, but at least he didn't have to worry about running into a congressional staffer having a drink after work.

Adam sat alone in a corner booth, a computer programming manual on the table. Beside it was an oversized menu, open to pictures of entrées. As if B-Dubs didn't trust its customers to know what wings looked like. This place catered to the idiots who enthusiastically supported his cousin.

It wasn't until Eric left the Army that he realized what an elitist he'd become. Why not? He and his men spent years apart from their families. They risked torture and death to protect the sheep at home. They couldn't tell anyone, not even their wives, what they'd done.

In truth, most civilians knew nothing about military service and cared even less. The okay ones thanked him, bought him a beer, left him in peace. The armchair warriors were the ones he couldn't stand. The ones who wanted to hear about Black Hawk rides in the Empty Quarter, pretend they were soldiers, too.

His cousin had that streak. Paul liked to hunt. Once a year, he made Eric go with him. As if killing animals made him Eric's blood brother. **They can't shoot back, idiot.**

A decade ago, on one of those hunts, Paul had told Eric that he'd decided to run for the Senate. Take his dad's seat. At the time, Eric was still in the Army. He hadn't known what to say. He had always thought **he** would be the next Senator Birman. Henry was smart, but neither of his sons had inherited his brains. Paul barely scraped through the University of Tennessee, and spent twenty-five years cashing checks from the Birman family malls.

He called himself a real estate developer. Like he'd ever developed anything other than tendinitis from playing too much tennis. His younger brother, Bobby, made him look good. Bobby spent most of his time dodging statutory rape charges.

Naturally, Paul was Henry's favorite. Paul was living proof that it was better to be lucky than good. And of course he had grown bored with the mall business at exactly the right time.

"What do you think, cousin?"

That you're the most fortunate sumbitch who ever walked the earth. That I'd like to have an accident with this Mossberg 500. Though even the dumbest sheriff's deputy in McNairy County might wonder how a decorated Joint Special Operations Command officer had so much trouble with a shotgun.

"Sure people aren't tired of having a senator named Birman?"

"You're kidding me, right? They gonna love me even more than Henry."

Paul was right. His aw-shucks conservatism played perfectly. Despite his wealth, he connected to average voters. **I'm just like you, my fellow Tennesseans, only richer. Way richer.** He rooted for the Volunteers, had a pretty wife, nice kids. He didn't use big words or talk down. He listened to both kinds of music—country **and** western.

Ultimately, folks liked him. The unteachable gift.

===

Eric should never have gone to work for Paul. His fatal mistake. After Eric left the service, he figured he'd hang out for a while. Then hook up with a defense contractor or maybe go into politics. But he found spending time with his family next to impossible. He no longer understood his wife or kids. If he ever had. Their back talk made him grind his teeth. He was used to giving orders, not negotiating with a seventeen-year-old about her curfew while his wife yapped he was being too strict.

The contractors were the next disappointment. He met with executives at Boeing, Northrop, Lockheed, all the biggies. The guys who'd served were okay. Most hadn't, though. They spent their lunches bragging about their golf handicaps, the money they made playing the stock market. When Eric talked about problems with weapons and systems, they steered him away. **The engineers can handle the details,** they said. **From you, we're looking for the bigger picture. The right people to talk to down in Tampa**—at MacDill Air Force Base, where Central Command was headquartered. In other words, they wanted him for his connections, nothing else. He walked out of their fancy clubs feeling like a high-class whore. He didn't return their follow-up calls.

That left politics. But Tennessee's governor was popular. Eric had no shot to unseat him. And the thought of shaking hands for years to worm his way into Congress made his stomach ache. Even if he won, he'd be one of four hundred thirty-five representatives competing for attention. Decades from having any real power. He couldn't wait decades.

The Senate. That's where he belonged. Senators had national platforms. Senators became presidents.

But Paul was in his way. Lucky Cousin Paul. Tennessee was happy to have one Senator Birman. Not two.

Eric figured the only saving grace was that Paul would tire of the Senate after a few years. Paul liked hanging out at home. Home. A nice way to describe a twenty-acre estate with a garage full of hundred-thousand-dollar cars. So when Paul asked Eric to be his chief of staff, Eric agreed. In a term, two at most, Paul would quit. Meantime, Eric would make the important decisions.

But Paul had a nasty habit of making up his

own mind. Eric would never forget the day he'd told Paul the United States didn't need new visa rules because of the Ebola epidemic.

"We shouldn't stop aid workers from going. It'll be counterproductive." They were in Paul's palatial office in the Dirksen Senate Office Building in Washington.

"Counterproductive." Paul made the word sound like a curse. "Folks back home don't want Africans bleeding Ebola all over them. That simple."

"The public health—"

"Public health where? The Congo?"

"The Congo is two thousand miles from West Africa." As soon as he spoke, Eric knew he'd made a mistake.

"I don't need **geography** from you, cousin. Let me explain exactly what's going to happen with this stupid Ebola. It's about as big a public health emergency as hemorrhoids. Something for CNN to talk about while they're waiting for something else to talk about. In a few weeks, we'll forget all about it. Until then, the people who voted for me don't want any brown people getting them sick with the E-bola or the AIDS or anything else. Understand?"

"Yes."

"Now out. And the next time you have some-

thing you think I need to know, a teachable moment, you don't call me **Paul**. You call me **Senator**.
Better yet, keep your mouth shut." He was shout-
ing. Eric knew the staffers in the big office outside could hear.

Worst of all, Paul was right. A few weeks later,
everyone **had** forgotten Ebola.

━━━━━

Eric could have quit, of course. Maybe he should
have. But now that he was a few years out of the
Army, his connection with Paul was his best selling point. He needed Paul more than ever.

He couldn't stand needing Paul.

He started to think about the Russians. They'd
approached him after he retired from the Army,
of course. They approached every important officer. Their pitch was public and relatively subtle.
A St. Petersburg–based think tank called the Federation for Defense Cooperation offered him two
hundred thousand dollars to speak at a conference. The group's president, Gennady Petyaev,
was a retired general smooth as a talk show host.
Eric merely had to give a forty-five-minute speech
about the way the United States military viewed
the world, Petyaev said. And answer questions afterward.

"What questions?"

"Nothing surprising." Then Petyaev mentioned that his group could pay far more if Eric attended other conferences. "These would be smaller events, and more tactical issues would be discussed."

"Sounds like you'd want me to disclose classified information."

"No, Colonel. Never. Only what you're comfortable with."

Even then, before his hatred of Lucky Cousin Paul became overwhelming, the offer had a surprising pull. As a soldier, Eric admired the Russians for their uncompromising approach. When they decided to fight, they **fought**. They didn't worry about civilian casualties or whiny journalists. They understood that too-strict rules of engagement could prolong wars and, ultimately, cost soldiers their lives. They'd lost twenty million of their own people in World War II, after all. And beaten the Nazis.

In Syria, Russian fighter jets had done what the United States couldn't: Stop the Islamic State from toppling the Assad regime. Bashar Assad was a butcher, Russian bombing had killed thousands of civilians. But did anyone doubt that letting Daesh take Damascus would have been far worse?

The money was appealing, too. Eric's branch

of the Birmans had missed out on the mall fortune, thanks to his idiot granddad Philip, who refused to invest with the rest of the family. But Eric ultimately decided that taking money from Petyaev's group would make defense contractors wary of him, an option that still seemed viable at the time.

Now that he worked for his cousin, he couldn't possibly take Russian money openly. Anyway, he'd decided that he was past the winking corruption of a think tank. Like the Russians themselves, he had no interest in half measures. Fortunately, Lucky Cousin Paul's seat on the Intelligence Committee gave Eric nearly complete access to CIA and NSA secrets.

He memorized the details of a program he knew the Russians would like, rented a storage room in Northeast D.C., and waited for the moment when he could meet a Russian intelligence officer without being obvious. It came at a dinner to celebrate the French president's visit to Washington. The food was always excellent at the French embassy, and its dinners were always crowded. During cocktail hour, Eric spotted Dmitri Zlobin, the SVR's deputy chief of station, in a line for the bathroom.

The rest was history.

The Russians had run him cautiously. Still, he knew the risks. Almost every agent was discovered sooner or later. Despite what he'd told Adam, Eric had decided that if he was found out, he would flee to Moscow. The Kremlin would take care of him. Russia treated its spies well. And his wife and kids would hardly notice he was gone.

Plus, if he was discovered, Paul's political career would end. How could Senator Birman survive the revelation that his cousin, a man he'd appointed as chief of staff, had betrayed the United States? So if it all went wrong, Eric would wind up alone in an apartment in Moscow. But Lucky Cousin Paul would be disgraced, too.

Eric figured he could live with that trade-off.

Now Eric sat in the Buffalo Wild Wings across from Adam.

"I hope you like wings. I ordered two platters. Barbecue and Hot Sauce."

Eric glanced over his shoulder. No one was in earshot. "Maybe you've acclimated a little too well."

"Don't pretend you don't enjoy the crunch of a frozen chicken wing fried in oil."

Eric tapped his wrist: **Let's get to it.** "First. The FBI is still stuck on Dallas."

"Are you sure they're telling you everything?"

"They've briefed us twice this week, and they seem edgy. Without coming out and saying so, they're hinting they've asked the NSA and CIA for help, which is dangerous, because it could mess up any court cases. They'd only do that if they were desperate."

"They haven't mentioned my friends?"

"Not once. And that's the kind of tidbit they would give us. **See how hard we're pushing, we're even looking at—**"

Adam looked over Eric's shoulder, a warning. "Hey there, bud—"

"Straight from the fryer," the waiter said. "Give 'em a second to cool." He put down two plates of wings and nodded at Eric. "Get you a drink?"

Eric shook his head, just a fraction.

"We have an afternoon special—"

"I said **no.**"

Something in Eric's eyes must have scared the waiter. The guy backed away. Civilians.

Adam grabbed a wing. "You were saying."

"I have to watch you eat?"

"I came here to eat. And study novel concepts in advanced C++ programming. You should eat, too."

The last sentence was half suggestion, half order: **You'll draw attention to yourself if you don't.** Eric didn't like grease. At JSOC, he'd prided himself on being able to outrun soldiers half his age. He forced a stingingly hot barbecue wing into his mouth.

"Good, right?"

No. Eric finished three wings, anyway. **Satisfied with my cover, fatso?** "Second, if your friends are hoping they can stampede Duto into an alliance, they're wrong."

For years, the Kremlin had proposed the United States work with it in Syria. After Dallas, it was making the case increasingly loudly. The Russian foreign minister had spent the last ten days in the United States, appearing on every media outlet that would have him. **Whatever our differences, our countries have this terrible enemy in common,** he said. The argument conveniently ignored that the United States was already fighting Daesh.

"Duto won't be president forever."

Words that made Eric sit up. The Russians couldn't possibly be thinking about trying to kill the President. "Tell me **that's** not on the agenda. You'd start World War Three. Anyway, this isn't some dissident in Moscow. You can't get to him."

"I'm just stating a fact," Adam said primly. "Look at the polls." Duto's approval rating had fallen almost fifteen percentage points post-Dallas. "He got elected to keep the country safe. Look what happened."

Almost but not quite admitting that the Russians were behind the attack.

"What about your cousin?" Adam said. "Does he understand the benefits of an alliance?"

"Doubt he's considered it either way. He thinks one sentence at a time."

"Could you convince him?"

The wings had left Eric's mouth coated with a sugary aftertaste. No wonder these places sold beer by the gallon. "What does it matter? I told you last time, he can't win."

"He can put pressure on Duto. People listen to him."

Don't I know it. Eric was almost sure Adam had just given him the real reason for this meeting. He didn't love the idea of pitching his cousin to make a pro-Russian speech. Pushing too hard on Paul could be dangerous. Still, Paul liked strong men, and the Russian president was nothing if not strong. **Look how they handled their own Muslim problem. They don't screw around.**

"It would be good to do this as soon as possible," Adam said.

"What's the rush?"

Adam shrugged.

"Fine. I'll try."

"I'm sure you'll succeed. He trusts you, yes?"

"Why wouldn't he? We're blood."

13

DALLAS

A few hours before, Shafer had opened his eyes and found himself on a pure white cloud. He wanted to believe he was in Heaven, but considering his feelings about God, or the lack thereof, a hospital seemed more likely. Second by second, the world pulled him in, the beeping of a heart monitor, the burn of a needle in his elbow, the controlled chaos of an emergency department outside his door.

He tried to sit up, wished he hadn't. The motion set his head on fire. He lay back, closed his eyes. When he opened them again, he found himself looking at a uniformed Dallas police officer.

"Mr. Shafer. I'm Officer Thome."

"Where?" The word stuck in his mouth.

"Presbyterian Hospital." Thome pointed at

the floor as if he worried Shafer might question existence itself. "In Dallas. We brought you in about an hour ago. Do you know why you're here?"

Because I had the misfortune to stumble on a good ol' boy pleasuring himself to man-on-man-on-man action. Despite the pain, Shafer's memory was surprisingly clear. He realized his left wrist was cuffed to the metal rail of his hospital bed. So he was under arrest.

He decided to keep his version of events to himself for now. "Not sure."

"An apartment building manager caught you trying to burglarize his office. He struck you with a baton. The doctors say you have a hairline skull fracture."

"Hurts."

"I'll bet. I'm not a doctor, obviously, but my understanding is you should make a full recovery. What worries us is, a few minutes before, you'd harassed the residents of an apartment in the complex. You insisted someone else lived there. A woman named Jeanelle. Do you know that name?"

"Not sure."

"You have the right to remain silent, sir. But given that your driver's license identifies you as a Virginia resident, and we haven't found any relatives anywhere in Texas, I need to ask if you have any history of Alzheimer's disease and if we should notify your relatives."

Of course they wanted to pin Alzheimer's on him. Like he was ninety-five. Shafer stifled a curse as Thome knelt beside the bed.

"Sir? I know this is complicated. I'm hoping to keep you out of the system if that's possible. Are you following me?"

Yeah, I'm following you. I'm a CIA officer with a direct line to the President. I came to Dallas because I have a lead on the bombings that the FBI's too stupid to see. Even with the CIA identification in his wallet, Shafer had a feeling that answer wouldn't convince Officer Friendly here. Plus he hadn't told anyone at Langley about this trip.

"No Alzheimer's."

"Is Jeanelle someone important in your life?"

"Call my wife." Shafer didn't like asking the police to involve Rachel in this mess, especially since the version of events they gave her would freak her out. But he had to make the charges go away immediately so he didn't have to worry the cops would drag him to jail. He could use a lawyer, but having Rachel here would speed the process. And he wasn't sure the hospital would let him drive after he was discharged.

"Jeanelle is your wife? Why did you think she was in Dallas?"

Oh, come on. Shafer tried to shake his head, an even bigger mistake than trying to sit up.

"Were you trying to find her, Mr. Shafer? Did you travel with her to Dallas when you were younger?"

Shafer had never met a cop so nice. Or so clueless. "Wife . . . Rachel," he said through gritted teeth. "In Virginia. Call her."

"Your wife is named Rachel. And you want us to contact her."

"Yes." An overwhelming tiredness took Shafer. Too much thinking too soon. He sank back in the bed, closed his eyes.

———

Rachel arrived that evening, fear cutting lines in her round, pretty face. Shafer was at once glad and sorry to see her.

He was no longer cuffed to the bed, and Officer Thome was long gone. The Dallas police had decided that he wasn't a flight risk. After an afternoon of rest and morphine, he felt better. Slightly.

"Ellis." Rachel came to the bed, hugged him awkwardly, touched her lips to his. Then stood above him, tears flowing. "What **happened** to you? The police—"

"Are idiots."

Ten minutes later, she was still crying. But

laughing, too. "All those years being a jerk caught up to you."

"I'm not a jerk."

"You are **such** a jerk. You should have knocked, Ellis."

A trim redheaded woman in a white coat walked in before he could answer. "I'm Dr. Tyler." She extended a hand, and Shafer managed to lift his own. "How are you feeling tonight, Mr. Shafer?"

"Been better."

She leaned over, shined a penlight in his eyes. "Do you know where you are?"

"Dallas. Presbyterian Hospital."

"Can you count back from one hundred by sevens for me?"

"One hundred . . . ninety-three . . . eighty-six . . . seventy-nine . . ."

"Good. You seem to be recovering nicely. As I'm sure Dr. Hansbro told you, your CT showed no signs of internal bleeding, and your pupil response and your vitals are normal. Must have a hard head."

"The hardest," Rachel said.

Tyler looked at her. "You're his wife?"

"Yes. Rachel."

"In all seriousness, the blow caught him on the thickest part of the skull, which was a lucky break. We're going to keep him overnight, but assuming that he's fine in the morning, we'll discharge him then. The bigger question is why he wound up in that office at all. Has he recently displayed any other memory lapses or odd behavior, Mrs. Shafer?"

I'm right here, Doctor. You can ask me. Being ignored by your own physician, reason one million twelve that getting old was no fun.

"No more than normal."

Tyler didn't smile. She must be used to spouses protecting each other from these questions.

"Do you know why he came to Dallas?"

"He's always been interested in the Kennedy assassination."

Rachel delivered the line deadpan, forcing Shafer to bite his lip to stifle a laugh. **Nicely done, Rach.**

Tyler looked to Shafer. "How about you, Mr. Shafer? Do you know why you came here?"

"No idea." True enough. At least in retrospect.

"That concerns me. I can't speak to the legal issues, but considering what I was told about the case, if anything, you strike me as the victim. But you must promise to see a neurologist after you get home."

"Of course."

"Mrs. Shafer, make sure he doesn't forget."

Tyler reached over, squeezed Shafer's hand. "I'll check in on you again in the morning. Assuming everything's fine, we'll arrange your discharge. We will let the police know in case they want to—you know . . ."

"Book me?"

She nodded. "I'm sure they won't . . . Feel better, Mr. Shafer."

"I already do."

———

"She's nice," Rachel said after Tyler left.

"The Kennedy assassination."

"Thought you'd like that."

"Can I have your phone? I need to call Duto."

She laid a hand on his chest. Soft and full over his bones. He'd been used to the warmth of her palm for two-thirds of his life. "Ellis, when they discharge you, we're going home. You understand that, right?"

He stared at her, letting her know that he understood nothing of the sort.

"You have a **fractured skull**, Ellis. Let someone else talk to these women. The FBI."

What had he expected her to say? But he knew the Feds would immediately bury his theory. No conspiracy necessary. It would fall victim to not-invented-here syndrome.

"You don't want to help me, I'll get a lawyer." He wanted to say more, but ten words at a time seemed to be all he could manage.

"You are too old for this, Ellis. Running around pretending you're a field officer." She leaned over, lowered her voice. "This theory of yours doesn't make sense, anyway. The cops arrested a cocaine dealer, told him if he blew himself up, they wouldn't charge him? And he went for it? Why? And why would they do it?"

"You're right. It doesn't make sense to me either. That's why I don't like it."

"Because if you in your genius can't figure it out, it must be wrong."

"Make you a deal. We find Pitts and the waitress. If we don't get anywhere with them, that's it. I'll even go to a neurologist back home."

"You just want me here because you're going to have a bandage on your head and you're worried no one will talk to you."

"Chauffeur."

"Of course, right. You can't drive with a fractured skull."

=====

She stepped away from the bed, sat in the corner of the room, and looked at him with an expression he'd known for forty years. Her head tilted, a smile creeping across her lips, vanishing, creeping back. A smile that said **I don't know why I find you charming, Ellis Shafer. I don't know why I love you, but I do.**

"I'm only doing this because I'm worried that if I don't let you, you'll make my life so miserable I'll end up strangling you." She handed him her phone, kissed his forehead once more.

"You're the best, Rach."

"And you're the worst. The **worst.**"

14

QUITO

In the morning, the shopkeeper waited in front of his store, wearing a clean button-down shirt for his big adventure. Wells handed him a hundred-dollar bill, and he practically hopped into the back seat of the Toyota, chattering to Coyle.

"Tell him he gets the other hundred when we find the place."

"He says he told his daughters they can have new sneakers with the money we gave him—"

"Heartwarming. Does he happen to know where he's taking us?"

Coyle sat beside the guy, showed him a map of Quito. Wells watched in the rearview mirror as the man's finger darted at random across the map's right half.

"He says he's sure it was somewhere between Parque Itchimbía, that's a few hundred meters south, and Bellavista, that's a rich neighborhood maybe four klicks northeast."

Wells couldn't tell if the guy was being difficult or was simply confused. "That's a congressional district, not a neighborhood."

More talk. "It was near the top of the city. Like a castle."

"Meaning a moat and a drawbridge?"

"On one of the higher streets, the edge of the grid, where the city runs into the hills." Coyle led the guy out of the car, pointed up, east. The guy nodded.

"We go up there, he thinks he can figure it out."

"If he's so confused, how'd he find it in the first place? How can he have no idea of the route he took?"

"He doesn't go up there much. He used a map on his phone. Even with that, it took him a while—"

Life in the age of GPS. "Where's the phone?"

"I was about to tell you he doesn't have it anymore. He lost it."

"**Lo siento**," the guy said.

"Makes two of us." Wells turned on the Toyota.

———

Trying to take a systematic route along the edge of the Quito street grid proved more difficult than Wells hoped. The eastern ridgeline wasn't a solid mass like the flank of Volcán Pichincha on the other side of the valley. It was made up of small hills broken by gullies and streams. Walled houses and mid-rise apartment buildings dominated the lower sections. The upper hillsides included an odd array of mansions, cinder-block shacks, monasteries, and parks. Wells even saw signs for a zoo, although it seemed to be gone. Streets changed names and directions as they followed the topography of the hills. A few roads extended over the hills before dropping into the valley to the east.

Wells drove slowly, making sure he didn't miss any turnoffs. He tried to stay patient. If the guy felt pressured, he might pick a house at random. Still, Wells didn't understand how anyone could be so geographically challenged. His sense of direction had saved his life more than once.

After a half hour, he pulled over beside a one-pump gas station at the city limits. "Any ideas?"

"Nothing in this section. Maybe farther north."

Wells wondered if the guy might be lying, taking them on an expensive sightseeing ride. But he surely wanted the extra hundred dollars. After another twenty minutes, they'd almost reached the north end of the neighborhood. Wells made a right, up a steep pitch—

The guy squawked at Coyle.

"This seems familiar."

Wells reached a T junction with high-walled houses on both sides.

"Izquierda." The guy pointed left, the first time he'd given Wells any directions. A hand-lettered sign dangling from a wall proclaimed the street Calle Ignacio. The hillside here was steep, and the houses hemmed in on small plots. A few hundred yards north, the street abruptly ended at another T junction.

Beyond the junction, the hillside dropped away into a deep gorge. The slope wasn't quite a cliff, but it was too steep for trees to take root, only brush. On the opposite side of the gorge, Bellavista, the next district north, occupied a hill of its own. An arched bridge to the northwest spanned the ravine and connected the two neighborhoods, but it couldn't be reached from here without doubling back.

"Derecho." The shopkeeper jabbed a finger right.

"Right," Coyle said.

"Thank you, Sergeant."

Wells turned right, along a road that had been carved into the hill. This area had clearly been developed as an enclave for the rich. The road was paved. A billboard offered a rendering of an idealized neighborhood filled with expensive SUVs. Just as clearly, the rich had stayed away. The billboard was peeling. The street had only a handful of houses scattered among empty plots of land.

The road dead-ended at an ungainly two-story concrete house. A wall topped with concertina wire surrounded the place. Though it seemed to be located on the edge of the wilderness, it was, in reality, no more than three miles from the bodega. Even with the winding roads, they could be back in ten minutes.

Wells knew he should be pleased they'd found it, but he was annoyed the guy had wasted their morning. "This didn't stick? It's literally the last house in the neighborhood."

"He did mention his sense of direction," Coyle said.

"Glad we're not lost in the jungle with him."

"Aquí," the guy said.

Wells pulled up. A rusted chain and combination lock held the front gate tight. A neon yellow poster warned PELIGRO! NO ENTRAR. Behind the gate, the house appeared unlit, its windows barred.

"If I were hiding a bunch of Russians, this wouldn't be the worst place," Coyle said.

"Or a body. We'll take our friend back, figure out a way inside."

"Cien dólares."

"Yeah, yeah."

======

Wells and Coyle spent the afternoon shopping for supplies and checking out Google overheads of the house and the land around it. The aerials confirmed what Wells already knew after seeing the place firsthand. The house was in a bad spot for a break-in. He and Coyle would be conspicuous coming down the dead-end road.

Worse, they had no good exit routes once they reached the house. The ravine was a trap. Even if they reached the bottom without falling and breaking bones, they'd have a tough climb out. Their best bet for escape would be the other way, up the hill south of the house. Once they topped out, they could track southwest, toward the city. But they would have to traverse several private properties to get back to the grid. Wells suspected that Ecuadorian landowners would shoot first and ask questions later.

"We'll go at dusk," Wells said. "Dark is too obvious. Peek inside and get gone."

"**Pistolas** tonight?"

Wells nodded. This trip might turn messy, no point in pretending otherwise.

———

With the sun vanishing, Wells piloted the Toyota along Calle Ignacio. Two cars had trailed his Toyota, but they'd turned off. Coincidence, most likely. Now his rearview mirror was empty. He turned right at the T junction, parked in front of the house. No reason to be subtle. The lights of Bellavista sparkled to the north. To the west, the sun disappeared behind the Volcán Pichincha, and all of Quito slipped into shadow at once.

"Prettier than Helmand," Coyle said.

"Anyplace is prettier than Helmand."

They didn't have any fancy gear for this mission, no night vision goggles or concussion grenades. They had picked up a sledgehammer, pliers, gloves, and masks from a construction supply store. At a shop that catered to Western hikers, they'd bought powerful LED headlamps that strapped to their foreheads, leaving their hands free. Wells had his auto pick. They had their pistols in inside-waistband holsters.

Wells took one more look down the empty road. "Ready?"

"That a rhetorical question?"

"Big word, for a Marine."

Coyle offered Wells a two-fingered salute.

They could have climbed the wall and cut the razor wire. But Wells wanted the gate open in case they needed to make a quick exit. He grabbed the sledgehammer from the trunk, took a three-quarters swing that clanged off the gate rather than the lock. His second try rattled the lock, didn't break it. Wells knew if he didn't bust it with the third swing, Coyle would ask for a chance.

No way.

Wells lifted the hammer over his head, ignoring the twinge in his shoulder. He lined up the swing, brought the hammer down. The lock split with a metal ping that echoed down the empty street.

"Impressive, sir."

Wells didn't need to ask if Coyle was being sarcastic.

The yard had no koi ponds or fancy trees, just bare dirt and bits of broken bottles. The house loomed over it, with an American-style attached two-car garage. Wells wondered if the Mercedes was hidden there. But the garage door was solid, no way to see inside.

Through the narrow window beside the front

door, Wells spotted an alarm panel. It was dark. He suspected it wasn't connected. He put the auto pick to the door. The bolts swung back quickly. When Wells opened the door, the panel stayed dark, and no alarm sounded. Wells switched on his headlamp, pulled on latex gloves, stepped inside, with Coyle a step behind.

The house had a mansion-style floor plan, with a big foyer and a wide central staircase. But it was unfinished, the floor bare concrete. A faintly unpleasant smell seeped through the air, seeming to come from the garage.

"Just a clogged toilet, right?" Coyle said.

"No doubt." Wells wanted to check the rest of the house first. If the smell was a body, once they unearthed it the stench would be unbearable.

Wells picked his way up the stairs. The stink wasn't as bad up here, and the house was more finished. The second floor had a master bedroom suite left of the stairs, two smaller bedrooms in the middle, a den on the right.

Someone had been looking after the house. Glue-style mousetraps dotted the corners. The rooms were furnished with cheap but functional couches and beds. Someone had lived here, too. At least for a while. Wells found a box of condoms in one bathroom, a couple pill bottles without labels in another. But nothing of value. No leftover laptops or flash drives.

The third bedroom had a twin mattress on the floor. Wells nudged it aside—and found a paper-back book, its cover embossed with a pair of crossed AK-47s, its title in Cyrillic.

He showed it to Coyle, then stuffed it in his in his pocket. Maybe the agency could trace it. Maybe its owner had even written his name or left notes inside. Unlikely, but possible. They'd check later.

Unlike the other closets, the one in the third bedroom was closed. Coyle pulled it open—

Clothes. Mostly men's. Jackets, pants, shoes. Coyle poked through labels. "Cyrillic. Figure they left the stuff because they were going some-where they didn't want people to know they were Russian?"

Wells nodded. Only one place made sense, the good ol' United States of America. "Take two minutes, see if you find anything besides lint in the pockets. I'll look downstairs."

———

Downstairs. The sour smell strengthened as Wells walked into the kitchen. He looked through the refrigerator and freezer, found only a single, half-full bottle of vodka. He heard pattering behind him, spun, pulled his pistol—

Realized the house did have at least one other occupant, a rat in the walls. He holstered his pistol as the animal scuttled off.

Coyle came down the stairs. "Rat?"

"Call it a big mouse. Might account for the smell, if they're dead in the walls."

"Might." Coyle handed Wells a phone, an old flip. "Found it in a jacket. Battery's dead."

"Nice." Wells stuffed it next to the book. The phone might be a shell, its SIM card gone and memory erased. It might be incredibly valuable. They wouldn't know until someone at Langley broke it open. "One dead phone, one paperback book."

"Speaking of dead, how about the garage?"

"Don't sound so excited." Wells had a jar of Vicks VapoRub in his pocket. He dipped a finger into the waxy jelly, lathered it under his nose, a soldier's trick to cover terrible smells. He put a dust mask over his mouth and handed the jar to Coyle.

A door off the kitchen led to the garage. Wells opened it, stepped down—

And stumbled on a tire iron that someone had left by the stairs. He cursed as he went sprawling.

As he pushed himself up, the light of his head-

lamp clanked off the long metal jelly bean of a
Mercedes sedan. The stink of decay was stronger
here. Still, the acrid scent wasn't as strong as Wells
would have expected, not if Hector Frietas was in
the trunk of the Mercedes. Death was never subtle, certainly not after a week. He would have expected to hear flies buzzing, too.

The sedan's doors were locked. Wells grabbed
the tire iron, smashed the driver's window. He
pulled open the door, popped the trunk.

―――――

The stink was harsh, but the trunk was empty.

Almost.

Wells swung his headlamp side to side, captured smears of gray and a chunk of bone in the
back corner of the trunk. The bone was the size
of a silver dollar and still had bits of scalp attached. Plus four sad strands of hair that gleamed
black under the lamp's stark white glow.

Wells had seen plenty of death. Still, the skull
fragment tightened his stomach. Graciela had
killed her husband, made his body vanish, pretended to care when Wells asked about him. The
father of her children. The impersonal violence
of war seemed almost honest compared to the intimacy of this evil.

Wells pushed aside the thought he was making excuses for his own killing, drawing a line that made no difference to the corpses left behind. He picked up the bone. "Pretty sure this is what's left of Hector Frietas."

"Guess we won't be asking him what he wanted to tell us."

"Not without a medium."

Wells plucked a single greasy hair from the skull fragment on the unlikely chance that they would need Frietas's DNA. He dropped the bone back inside the trunk, ran a hand across the coarse black fibers of the Mercedes's trunk mat. They were stiff with dried blood. As he touched them, the stink worsened. Not just blood. Something sharp, too. Gasoline or lighter fluid. Wells's hand stirred a cloud of flies. Coyle coughed under his mask.

"She shot him, put him in the trunk. Dumped his body in the jungle, most likely. Based on the lighter fluid, maybe barbecued him, too. Then stashed the Mercedes here while she decides what to do next."

"Remind me not to make her mad."

Wells slammed down the trunk lid. "Wonder if she left anything in the car."

The front seats were empty. The glove compartment held nothing but an insurance card. But a black nylon gym bag was tucked on the floor behind the back seat. Coyle pulled it out. Underneath the bag, a single folded piece of paper. Wells opened it, found a single name. **Anatoly Vanin.**

"John." Coyle held open the unzipped bag. Inside, two thick stacks of hundred-dollar bills. Maybe a hundred thousand dollars, if the stacks were hundreds all the way through. And something else: a gold flash of metal. Wells reached for it.

A badge. FEDERAL BUREAU OF INVESTIGATION / U / S / DEPARTMENT OF JUSTICE in embossed letters, surrounding a stylized eagle with outstretched wings. If it wasn't real, it was a very good fake. Wells showed it to Coyle.

"That real?"

"Let's hope not." Wells dropped it back in the gym bag.

"Leave the bag?"

Wells shook his head. They would need the bag to confront Graciela. And real or fake, the badge might be evidence.

Wells squatted down, reached under the seats for a passport, a driver's license, or some other goody. He came out empty. "One more look, then let's get gone. Figure out the next move back at the hotel."

They checked the corners of the garage, under

the Mercedes, didn't find anything. They'd been in the house fifteen minutes, ten too long.

They hurried through the kitchen, out the front door and into the yard—

And heard an SUV speeding toward them, its engine rumbling in the quiet Quito evening, lights glaring through the filigree in the gate. By the time they reached the gate, the vehicle was barely a hundred yards away, a Ford Excursion flaring its brights. Blue security lights flashed in its grille. Coyle opened the gate. Wells pulled him back. They were too late. And the Toyota couldn't outrun the Excursion, anyway.

Wells put himself against the wall, reached for his phone, texted Tarnes their GPS coordinates. Nothing more. If something went wrong, Tarnes would understand.

Wells wondered how Graciela had known they were here. Maybe the alarm had been silent and connected to the house back on Calle José Tamayo. Maybe she'd installed a pinhole camera that he and Coyle hadn't noticed. But what was her plan? She wasn't looking to arrest them. She couldn't risk drawing attention to the Mercedes. Did she think she could make them vanish, too? Wells wanted to believe that the fact she had brought only one vehicle meant that she wanted to talk instead of shoot.

But maybe she'd decided that killing suited her.

The Ford stopped with its snout pointed at the Toyota. Graciela was in the driver's seat, a man beside her. He opened his door and stepped out. He was brown-skinned, small, barely out of his teens. He wore a black uniform, and slung an AK. Not a real soldier. A paramilitary, an order taker. His uniform top had the hidden bulk of a bullet-resistant vest. The vest worried Wells as much as the AK. It would stop a subsonic round, which meant that the pistols Wells and Coyle carried were about as useful as the fake FBI badge they'd found.

"Go back to the house," Wells said. "Get a firing position. You hear me whistle, start shooting."

Coyle ran back to the front door. No questions. Good man.

As Coyle disappeared, Graciela stepped out of the Ford. She wore a thin police-style, bullet-resistant vest over a black T-shirt. Wells wondered how he'd ever mistaken her for a statistician. **Confirmation bias,** the social scientists said. A fancy name for seeing what you wanted to see instead of what was in front of you.

The soldier knelt behind the hood of the Toyota, covering the gate with his AK. Graciela stood beside him. "You're trespassing!" she yelled. "Come outside!"

Guess again. Wells took three sideways steps away from the gate, pulled his pistol, crouched low against the wall. He hoped the concrete was thick enough to protect him from an AK barrage. Two pistols against an AK wasn't exactly a fair fight. But Wells and Coyle had the advantage of cover. Wells figured they could hold Graciela off until the real police showed up. If they did.

"You're under arrest. Do you understand?"

Wells understood she didn't want a firefight either. He relaxed. Slightly. He didn't answer, and after a few seconds, she continued in her oddly formal English.

"I will count to ten, then we come in—"

"And when the cops find the Mercedes?"

"The Mercedes you and your friend set on fire? After robbing this house?"

Wells supposed she could sell that story. Especially if she was really a senior intelligence officer. But she'd spend the rest of her life waiting for the CIA to come after her. "Your friend out there speak English?"

A pause. Then: "No."

"Walk to the gate, I'll meet you, let's parley." She didn't answer, and he realized the word had confused her. "**Talk.** Face-to-face."

He heard her whisper in Spanish, and the man beside her say, "**Sí. Sí.**" Then her footsteps, crunching on the road. The city's noises rose from the valley, cars rumbling over the bridge to Bellavista, a violin playing sweetly in the distance. Wells stepped to the gate, peeked around the edge. She stood a few steps away.

If she ducked aside, he'd be meat for the guy with the AK.

"Closer," Wells said. She took two steps closer, still out of reach. He holstered his weapon.

"Where's your friend?"

"In the house. Watching us."

"How did you find this place?"

"Luck."

"**Bad** luck."

"I meant what I said last night. You killed him, I don't care. I have to know what he had for us."

She shook her head.

"The truth is the easiest way to get rid of me."

"If I knew, I'd tell you."

Wells stared at her in the darkness, and she met his eyes without blinking. Her eyes were deep and black and pitiless. Wells believed her.

"What about the Russians?"

"They came last year, stayed here, left. They needed money moved to the United States. A lot. Too much to do quickly, even for Hector."

"How much?"

"Almost twenty million dollars. They were going to go through Venezuela, but then they decided they couldn't trust anyone in Caracas, which was smart of them. If they put the money into a Venezuelan bank, they'd never have gotten it out. So they came here."

"Your husband laundered money for the cartels."

She nodded: **Of course.**

"So why was this more complicated?"

"That money, it runs around South America and Mexico. The narcos, the smart ones, they know they have to wait at least twenty years before they can buy apartments in Miami, anything in your perfect country. Their money just needs to be clean enough that our banks, or the Brazilians—whoever—can handle it. For a BMW in Cartagena, a house in Rio, things like that."

"Can't be cash in suitcases."

"That's right. We call it **electricidad**. Meaning it can **run through the wires**. But this money, it was going **into** the United States. So it has to be much cleaner. **Blanco—**"

"White."

"What a scholar you are. Yes, white enough to pass the Treasury Department. White enough to spend in the United States without anyone blinking. To do that, even for ten or twenty thousand dollars, is complicated. To do it for twenty million is impossible, at least from Ecuador. Hector needed help from someone in Mexico."

"A banker."

"Yes. But before you ask, I don't know his name. Hector called him Z."

"Like Mr. Z? Or like Z was a code name?"

"Just Z."

"Which bank?"

"Maybe Banamex. He'd used them before."

Graciela sounded like she'd been deeply involved in Hector's money laundering. Wells resisted the temptation to push on the subject. Only the Russians mattered.

"So I'm clear, he told you explicitly that the Russians were headed to the United States?"

"No, but nothing else made sense."

"Did you help them get fresh identities, anything like that?"

"No. I asked Hector if they needed Ecuadorian passports, and he said no, European."

Another clue that the Russians were headed for the United States. Travelers from most European countries did not need American visas, a courtesy that the European Union and United States offered each other.

"Did you ever meet them?"

She shook her head. "Hector kept them here. But I heard him on the phone with them."

"Did you know if they were FSB?"

"I never asked."

"Okay, they came, they stayed here a couple months, and then?"

"One day, they left. I don't know where they went, but I think Mexico."

"They flew?" The NSA could probably find the flight manifests and the immigration records.

"Not from Quito, I don't think. I think they took a bus to Colombia, then maybe flew to Havana and on to Mexico City. But it could have been the other way, down to Guayaquil and then by ship to Lima and then Acapulco."

"Seems like a lot of trouble if they were already getting fresh passports in Mexico."

"Maybe they worried about someone like you coming to look for them. Anyway, Hector told me at the time that they paid three hundred thousand dollars. I found out later he was lying. They gave him almost two million."

That why you killed him? She was staring at Wells as if she was expecting him to ask.

"And after they left?"

"He didn't mention them again. Until the end. He told me the Russians had given him a gift. That he was going to be free from me." She tilted her head down. Wells couldn't tell if the memory weighed on her or if she was acting. He wondered if she'd really loved Frietas or if she'd killed him out of wounded pride.

"He say where he was going?"

"Only that he was leaving me."

"Did he say anything at all about Dallas?"

"No. But it was only a day or two after the attack."

"So Hector said he was leaving. And you shot him."

Her head snapped up. He waited for her to jump out of the way, tell the guard behind the Toyota to open up with the AK. But, ultimately, she only patted Wells on the cheek.

"You found the bag in the car, with the badge?"

"Yes. What about his laptop?"

"I left it with him in the jungle."

"So it's burned." Wells couldn't afford to assume and be wrong.

She nodded.

"Too bad."

"I know. Now you, your friend—you take what you found and drive away. I watch you go. You never come back. Around midnight, there are flights to the Estados Unidos."

Wells suspected she planned to torch the Mercedes. And the whole house, too. No matter. The

Quito cops would have to handle justice for Hector Frietas.

"Fine. But before we come out, you drive back down the road."

"You think I want to shoot you? Why would I have told you all this?"

"So I'd trust you."

She smiled, said something in rapid-fire Spanish to the guy with the AK. He argued for a moment and then ran back to the Excursion. "All right?"

"One condition. One murder's enough. You leave his girlfriend alone."

"And how would you know?"

"Try me."

She turned, walked to the Excursion, slowly, not bothering to look back.

Wells yelled to the second floor. "Coyle! Let's go!"

———

On the way to the airport, Wells recounted the conversation.

"She killed him," Coyle said. "Nice lady. We gonna do anything about it?"

"Not a chance."

Coyle looked at Wells, at the road, back at Wells. His big shoulders sagged a little under his sweatshirt. Wells understood. The game could be rough.

"These Russians come to Quito, Frietas moves money for them. They go. A year later, the attack happens in Dallas. Somehow, he connects them to it. I missing anything, John?"

"Maybe Frietas lied to her, and it wasn't the Russians, he stumbled onto something else. But I doubt it. And there's no evidence that he was moving money for the Islamic State, anything like that. Plus he couldn't have sold that to us, he'd be implicated, too. And he was sure he had something, so sure he told Graciela he was getting out."

"ISIS hates the Russians," Coyle said. "Can't see them doing business."

"Maybe they made a deal. Enemy of my enemy." But Wells couldn't see it either.

"So what's next?"

"Soon as we land in Houston, back to Mexico City." Wells would call Tarnes, ask her to run the name on the piece of paper, Anatoly Vanin. But Wells wasn't expecting much. They had to figure out how to check the phone Coyle had found, too, either themselves or by sending it to Langley for the techs to examine. Above all, they had to find Z, the banker who had helped Frietas.

"One thing we do know," Coyle said. "These

comrades, they went to **mucho** trouble so they and the money would be clean when they got to the United States."

Coyle was right, Wells saw. The care the FSB had taken was the best piece of evidence yet that it was behind the Dallas attack. Russia knew the United States would retaliate if it found out.

Coyle seemed to be thinking along the same lines, because after a minute he said, "John. Suppose it was the FSB. What then?"

Wells had no answer. He wished he could call Shafer. Maybe he should. Shafer loved this sort of puzzle. But Shafer was a proud old man. No doubt he was at home, licking his wounds, stewing over Wells.

15

DALLAS

In the end, walking in on Powdy cost Shafer almost two days. The cops weren't the problem. Barely an hour after Shafer called Duto, a Dallas police officer showed up in Shafer's room.

"No charges. Sorry for the misunderstanding." Given the speed with which the officer had shown, and his obvious nervousness, Shafer suspected Duto might have called the police chief himself. Duto liked making those calls.

But, the next morning, the skull fracture was the gift that kept on giving. Shafer woke with a nasty headache. Dr. Tyler insisted he have another CT scan before he could go. Waiting for the scan cost four hours, waiting for a radiologist to read it three hours more. By then, Shafer's headache had faded, with the help of two Vicodin, but so had the day. It was 6 p.m. when he

signed the discharge forms and walked out with
Rachel.

He'd called Jeanelle Pitts three times already,
left three messages. He was wondering if he'd
have to ask the FBI to find her real address when
his phone buzzed with a blocked number.

"Who's this? Calling me **all day**." She had a
syrupy Dallas accent—half Southern, half Texan.

"Ms. Pitts? My name's Ellis Shafer." Shafer
wished he could ease into this conversation, but
Pitts was already irritated. "I wanted to ask you
about your FBI interview."

"You work for the FBI?"

"CIA."

"Stop it now."

"Truth, it's easier to explain face-to-face."

A pause. "You know where I did the interview?
I'll be there tomorrow morning at nine." She
hung up.

Shafer hated to admit it, but he didn't mind
having one more night to rest.

———

He arrived at the Denny's a half hour early, ordered a Grand Slam. Normally, he liked Denny's
bacon, tiny crispy pieces that seemed almost syn-
thetic. But his appetite was still on the fritz this
morning. **A bad Jew are you,** the Yoda voice in

his head told him. He'd wanted two Vicodin when he woke up, forced himself to take only one. Better to be in pain and sharp. Not for the first time, he wondered how Wells endured the punishment he took. But even past forty, Wells trained as though his life depended on his strength and agility. Because it did.

Shafer sat alone in the booth, Rachel directly behind him. Shafer had decided not to try to explain her presence.

Pitts showed a few minutes late. She was in her late twenties, black, pretty, tending toward heavy, wearing the chunky jewelry that bigger women seemed to favor. Shafer intercepted her as she waited to be seated. "Ms. Pitts?"

"**You?** This a joke?"

"No joke, ma'am. I'll show you."

At the booth, Shafer handed over his identification and a copy of her Form 302 that he'd printed.

"You really CIA?"

"We can call them, if you like."

"What happened to your head?"

"I went to Parkside Gardens, looking for you. The manager didn't like me much." Shafer was taking a chance, but he couldn't imagine that this woman would be a fan of William Powdy.

"Powdy? Keeps the place clean, but he is one nasty mother."

"I walked in on him watching gay porn and he popped me."

"Hold on. You said **gay** porn?"

"Extremely."

She grinned. She had a cute chipped front tooth. "Heard him once saying he wasn't gonna have no **sodomites** in his apartments."

"Those are always the ones."

"You know it. So, Mr. CIA . . ."

Shafer would have to send Powdy a thank-you note. He had given Shafer an instant bond with Pitts.

"I wanted to ask you about what Ahmed said about being arrested."

"FBI told me he wasn't. Told me he just got tired of me. Got religion. Got crabs. Who knows."

"You didn't think so."

"He wanted to bounce, he didn't need no story. He knew that."

More or less what she'd told the FBI.

"He ever talk about Islam? Ever see him praying?"

She laughed, a sweet, low tinkle that cut through the workday restaurant noise and lightened the place for a moment. "Shake didn't care about none of that."

"Maybe he hid it from you."

"I remember once we were at my place watching TV, Creflo came on. Creflo Dollar. You know who that is?"

"Preacher, right?"

"Yeah, from Georgia. Says how believing in God will make you rich. Shake—"

"You called him Shake?" The nickname hardly made Shakir sound like a hard-core terrorist.

"Shake and Bake. Shake saw him, said how does anybody believe any of this stuff? He wasn't talking about Christianity. He meant all of it. He slung coke all night and slept all day, Mr. Shafer. Had no time for **Allah**."

Two sentences that summed up everything Shafer had read about Ahmed Shakir. The waitress came over, and Pitts ordered coffee. "Watching my weight."

"You look fine to me." He heard Rachel cough behind him. "So what happened? How'd Ahmed wind up at that basketball game?"

"No idea. And I've thought about it plenty. Maybe his cousin tricked him somehow. Just drive us downtown tonight, help me out."

"That wouldn't explain how they got the bomb in his car."

"No it would not. It wasn't much of a car, that Hyundai, but he liked it. Took care of it."

The coffee arrived, and she poured in a half cup of cream. She caught him looking. "Said I was **watching** my weight. Watching it go up."

"One thing age teaches you, you get old either way, might as well enjoy yourself."

She smiled: **I accept your apology.** "Anyway, Shake told me he got arrested."

"He said so explicitly? That wasn't in here—" Shafer tapped the 302.

"The real reason those FBI wanted to talk to me, they was wondering if I knew what Ahmed was gonna do 'fore he did. **Accessory.** They asked me I ever texted him? I said sure. They asked could they see? Didn't have nothing to hide, so I showed them. They took a look. After that, they didn't care much 'bout what I had to say."

"It's standard procedure to look at anyone who was in contact with Ahmed."

"Okay, sure, I wasn't mad. I tried to help even after that. But they didn't pay no attention. And the thing was, Shake said it wasn't the local cops who got him."

"The DEA?"

"He didn't say flat out. But I felt weird that these two didn't know about it already. I hinted around about it, and they shot me down. You see?"

"Yeah." What Shafer saw was that the agents

had blown the interview. They'd made her feel like a suspect and then ignored the information she tried to provide. Agents faced overwhelming pressure on an investigation like this. Once they'd cleared her, they would have wanted to move on as fast as possible. An understandable mistake, but in this case a big one.

"Tell me exactly what Ahmed said. About the arrest." He still couldn't bring himself to call the guy Shake.

"Last time we got together, he came over, we didn't fool around. He said he couldn't stay, he just wanted to tell me he couldn't see me for a while. I asked him why, he said he made a mistake. Got greedy. I asked him when, he said two nights before. I asked him how he got out so quick, he said he couldn't talk about it. He said he'd be back in a few months."

She smiled.

"What?"

"You really want to know?"

Shafer nodded.

"He said, **Keep it sweet for me. 'Cause I'm gonna miss it.** That sound like a guy who was about to blow himself up? I said be careful and he told me not to worry, he could handle it. Made me promise not to call him. Then he took off."

"And you never saw him again."

"Not once. After a couple months, I kinda forgot him, to be honest. You know, dating somebody else, all that. Then one night—"

She shivered. No need to explain.

"What did you think he meant when he told you it would be okay?"

"What do **you** think I thought? Thought he was dropping."

"Dropping a dime? Becoming an informant?"

She rolled her eyes: **Do we need to talk like white people?** "How else he get out in two nights. Wasn't like he had a million bucks lying around for bail."

Her logic made sense to Shafer. But if the Drug Enforcement Administration had arrested Shakir and released him as an informant, the DEA agents would have kept a **closer** eye on him, at least for a while. He would have had to have paperwork, too, a cooperation agreement and a lawyer to represent him. **Miami Vice** notwithstanding, these deals weren't done on a nod-and-handshake basis.

Could the DEA have tried to make the agreement disappear once it realized its informant had carried out the most serious attack since September 11? Possibly. But a cover-up would be insane. Months had passed. The case would have moved ahead since the arrest. There would be court filings. Sealed, but not under the DEA's control, and impossible to erase. Anyway, Shakir's lawyer would have come forward, to the FBI, or the media, or both.

"You think he got angry at the way the DEA was treating him?" Shafer said.

"And did **that**?" She shook her head.

The other possibility, that someone had targeted Shakir in a **fake** sting, seemed even more unlikely. "I don't get it." Shafer's head was starting to hurt again, as if thinking too hard had damaged the fracture.

"I'm telling the truth." The real reason she'd agreed to meet with him. She couldn't figure out what had happened to Shakir either, and the mystery was eating at her.

"I believe you." He did, too. Mainly because Jeanelle Pitts had no reason to make up this story.

"Listen, I have to go." Seller's remorse, now that she'd told him.

"If I have questions—"

"Call me." She stood, chugged off.

———

When the door had closed behind Jeanelle, Rachel came around, sat beside him.

"**You look fine to me**," she said, mocking him lightly. "Didn't know that was your thing."

"Variety is the spice of life." In fact, Shafer had slept with only one other woman in his life, his junior-year college girlfriend. Almost five decades now he'd stayed true to Rachel. He'd never felt he was missing out.

"Like you'd know." She squeezed his hand. "Now what?"

"Now we're staying in Dallas."

"That story she told didn't make any sense, Ellis."

"Exactly. Why it matters." He turned to look at her, and a white flash of pure uncut **pain** exploded in the back of his head. The brain might not have nerves, but the skull sure did. Shafer reached for his own coffee cup, held it tightly in both hands, hoping Rachel wouldn't notice it shaking.

"Ellis." She gently took the cup from his hands, put it on the table.

"Vicodin." The bottle was in her purse.

She tapped out a pill, then one more. He choked them down with a slurp of coffee. She looked at him with the cool anger of a parent at a misbehaving child.

"Is this worth dying for, Ellis?"

The wrong question. "Why don't you ask those folks at the game?"

16

ST. PETERS, MISSOURI

Finding the right hide had always been Tom Miller's biggest weakness as a sniper.

No more.

The bed on the Ram 1500 extended almost six and a half feet behind the cab. Miller was five foot seven in sneakers. Plenty of room for him back there, even with his Remington beside him.

At an AutoZone off I-90 in Spokane, he bought a tonneau, a fancy name for a pickup-bed cover. He chose one made of thick but breathable black mesh. It unspooled in seconds from a rod attached behind the cab. Extended, it hid the Ram's bed and everything in it. Three hundred sixty-five dollars plus tax. Miller paid cash. Already covering his tracks.

Back home, Miller drilled a quarter-sized hole through the truck's tailgate, left of the centerline, four inches above the bed. Then another hole above the first, this one the size of a half-dollar. The bottom hole for the muzzle of his rifle. The top for the scope.

Covering the holes proved trickier. Miller tried plastic first. He cut a tarp in strips, four inches long, two inches wide, and taped on the strips. But even from twenty feet away, they looked obvious and weird.

"Bumper stickers," Allie said. "Two, one on top of the other. I peel them off when you're back there and ready to shoot. Put them back on when you're done."

At the Walmart in Pullman, Miller bought a dozen bumper stickers: American flags, DON'T TREAD ON ME, LIVE FREE OR DIE, THE CLOSER YOU GET . . . THE SLOWER I DRIVE!

He slapped a HORN BROKE: WATCH FOR FINGER tag on the Ram's bumper and a couple UNITED STATES OF AWESOME tags above them. "Going full redneck."

"Full what?"

"Redneck." He was surprised to see she still looked puzzled. "You know, a country boy. What's thirty feet long and has sixty teeth? A bus full of rednecks."

"Hah. Redneck." She rolled the word around her mouth. "I didn't hear." She leaned over, put her lips to his before he could say anything. Her kiss was sweet and light. He stopped wondering why a woman who'd grown up in Texas didn't know what a redneck was.

━━━

Miller spent the afternoon in the hills east of his trailer, making sure he had the rifle zeroed. His first two shots barely grazed the tree where he'd tacked the targets. He feared his concussions might have ruined his shooting. He forced himself to breathe deep, relax.

As the sun moved behind him, his training from Fort Benning came back. Adjusting his head to keep his cheek flush with the rifle, making sure his view through the scope aligned with the muzzle. **You don't have to know how to spell** parallax **long as you know how to make sure it doesn't happen to you,** one of his instructors liked to say.

Pulling the bolt back smoothly, popping it home firmly but not too fast. **Haste makes an empty chamber.** Squeezing the trigger on the pause between breaths. The sudden crack as the pin struck home. The gun kicking into his shoulder, the scope staying perfectly on target even with the recoil.

He remembered now. Sniping was beautiful.

He'd been good at it, too. Lousy at finding cover, but not many guys could outshoot him. After four hours of fine-tuning, he put three straight shots within one inch at a hundred yards. He was ready.

But as he packed up the Remington, the world spun. He closed his eyes, sagged against a tree. He'd pushed himself too hard. The concussions had made him more fragile than he'd realized. His earplugs didn't fully protect him from the thunderclaps that came with each shot. The pain was centered behind his eyes. He focused on the pine bark scratching his back. Anything to remind him that he existed as more than this agony.

After a while, the vise opened, and he stumbled home.

———

He found Allie vacuuming the trailer, a rumble that did his headache no favors.

"You look sick, Tom." She brought him to their bed, pulled the curtains, turned out the lights. He must have slept, because when he opened his eyes he was alone.

"Allie?" He felt better, though still tired.

She came in, sat beside him. "Maybe you shouldn't do this."

He forced himself up. No way would he let

her think he couldn't protect her. "I shot great. Just wore myself out at the end."

She nodded. He couldn't help feeling that he'd passed.

"Good. Because I know where to start."

She tilted her phone to him. Miller found himself looking at the web page for the Abundant Life megachurch, an evangelical congregation in St. Peters, Missouri, thirty miles west of downtown St. Louis. **Join our twelve thousand members in joyful prayer this Sunday!**

"Twelve thousand?" Miller said.

Allie scrolled through the website: pages titled **Tales of Redemption, Sermons & Song, Abundant Life for Children**, and **Your Abundant Life!** Video, too. A thirty-person choir belted out **So much to thank Him for** . . . as colored floodlights swung overhead. The place looked nice enough. Mostly white folk, but black and brown, too. Miller had never been the churchy type. The website made him wish he were.

Allie opened another screen, pointed at a handsome fiftyish white man, salt-and-pepper hair, striking blue eyes. **Our Pastor: Luke Hurley.** "His hair was black when I knew him. Otherwise, he hasn't changed much. The Fountain of Youth, sex with thirteen-year-olds."

Hurley looked nice enough, too. "You're sure?"

"That smile, it's a **lie**. He told me the pain would **help** me, Jesus suffered, and I needed to suffer, too." Her voice rose. For the first time since she'd come back, she was losing control. "Want to hear what he did? Would that turn you on? It turned him on. He'd tell me what he was about to do—"

"Allie." He put a hand on her back. She laughed, half hysterical.

"Even then I knew that's not how the Bible worked."

She found another photo of Hurley, standing at a table with a group of teenage girls, finger raised as he made a point. **Pastor Luke drops by the Girls-Only Bible Study Class to talk about what we can learn from Mary Magdalene!**

Allie magnified the photo. "Look at him."

Miller picked up a gleam in the minister's eyes, a curl to his lips that could have been a smirk.

Maybe.

===

Miller wouldn't be the first sniper to use a vehicle as a rolling nest. In 2002, a two-man team had terrorized Washington for a month from a sedan with a hole drilled into its trunk. Lee Boyd Malvo and John Allen Muhammad—together known as the Beltway Sniper since authorities didn't know at the time that two people were involved—gunned down ten men and women before police caught them. They had killed seven other people in other shootings earlier in the year, though those were only connected after their arrests in the Beltway case. Their run was especially noteworthy because they used an old Chevrolet Caprice with heavily tinted windows and New Jersey plates. It should have attracted attention. At one point, a police officer even stopped it near a shooting. But he let it go without a search.

Miller figured he and Allie had edges over Malvo and Muhammad. The Ram, clean and new, should draw less attention than the Caprice. And Malvo and Muhammad weren't trained as snipers. They had used a Bushmaster, a civilian version of the Army's M16 assault rifle, instead of a more accurate single-shot, bolt-action rifle like Miller's Remington. As a result, they had needed to shoot from close range, less than a hundred yards. The fact that no one had noticed them at that short distance testified to the panic that sniper attacks produced.

Miller planned to shoot from a quarter mile away or more. Even trained soldiers couldn't spot a sniper from that distance, not without binoculars or specialized radar to track shots. By the time anyone figured out what had happened, the Ram would be gone.

But Miller and Allie would be up against one big hurdle the Beltway snipers hadn't faced. Since 2002, cameras had become ubiquitous in public spaces. Smartphones had video and zoom lenses. Big intersections had cameras to catch drivers who ran red lights. Bridges and tunnels used automated toll collection systems that tracked license plates. License plate readers were standard equipment on police vehicles, too. Simple ballistics would tell the police where Miller had been when he'd fired. They would start there and work outward, combing all the surveillance footage they could find.

A pickup truck with out-of-state plates and a covered cargo bed would stand out in the footage. Its mere presence wouldn't be proof. Or even enough evidence for a bulletin. Not by itself. But when the cops ran the plates and found out the truck was registered to a former Army sniper, they'd want to talk to Miller. If the truck popped near a second shooting, they'd want to do more than talk.

Of course, Miller and Allie could always lift the plates from a Ram 1500 in Missouri. But that move came with its own risks. They had to assume the police response would increase as the shootings continued. Eventually, the cops might start locking down whole neighborhoods, running random roadblocks on highways. Stolen plates would grab their attention faster than anything else.

So Miller and Allie would have to try to avoid cameras, especially on the local roads close to the church. The good news was, they could get to an arterial highway quickly after shooting Hurley. Not just any arterial either, but Interstate 70, a crucial east–west highway. In the St. Louis area, I-70 carried thousands of cars and trucks every hour. Washington State plates wouldn't stand out on it.

The other bit of good news was, they didn't have to rush. They would have time to scout the best path once they reached St. Louis.

———

Allie wanted to leave the next morning. Miller told her he needed a dry run, taking shots from inside the cargo bed. He lay in the pickup bed as she pulled the tonneau over his head. She piloted the Ram to a railroad crossing a couple miles northeast. The nearest houses were nearly a mile away and hidden behind low hills.

When the Ram stopped, Miller flipped on a

battery-operated lantern and pulled out the rifle and scope. He heard the driver's door open. Allie pulled off the bumper stickers, allowing daylight into the covered bed, as Miller finished mounting the scope. He slid the muzzle of the Remington through the smaller hole until the rim of the scope was flush with the hole above. With the holes blocked again, Miller dimmed the lantern so it wouldn't distract him.

He peered through the eyepiece of the scope. He had a clear view through it, plenty of light for targeting. But he couldn't swing the rifle more than a couple degrees left or right. He would need to widen the muzzle hole to give himself more flexibility. No matter. The bumper sticker would still easily cover it.

For now, though, he focused on a red-and-yellow railroad sign mounted on a steel post a quarter mile down the tracks. He realized another problem he hadn't anticipated. Being inside the bed made adjusting for the wind more difficult. In the Army, he worked with a spotter who carried an automated wind gauge and could give him the correct scope adjustments. Miller could have bought a gauge for Allie. But using it would distract her before the shot. He wanted her to focus on the area around the truck, make sure no one was watching them.

Even without the gauge, good snipers learned to read the wind, the biggest variable on longer shots. How did it **feel**? Was it gusty, swirling, broken by trees along the path the shot would take? Unfortunately, the walls of the truck bed insulated Miller from the touch of the wind. Instead, he had to depend on the scope, another trick he'd learned at Fort Benning. Anything but the lightest breeze would visibly move leaves and grasses. Today, they were rustling slowly but steadily, the wind coming from the west, left to right, through his scope. Miller put the breeze at five miles an hour, enough to push the shot seven or eight inches to the right at this distance. He didn't bother to dial in an adjustment but instead simply ticked the muzzle left as far as it would go. He would settle for hitting the sign at all on this first shot.

They'd bought short-range children's walkie-talkies at Walmart. Miller hit the push-to-talk button on his.

"Clear?"

"Clear."

Miller clapped in his earplugs, chambered a round, counted to five, watched to see if the wind would pick up. It didn't. He took a breath, exhaled slowly. And squeezed the trigger.

The explosion echoed off the metal walls of

the truck bed. As if by magic, the sign quivered, and a hole appeared, an inch low, maybe five inches right of center. Not perfect, but most likely a kill shot against a live target. And once Miller opened the muzzle hole, he'd have more flexibility.

It **worked**. He could shoot from inside here. He felt weirdly proud of himself. One added bonus: If he needed to take a second shot, he wouldn't need to worry about finding the spent shell. It would be stuck in here.

He heard Allie, faintly, through the walkie-talkie. He ignored her. She had no way of seeing the hole in the sign. He pulled back the Remington's muzzle, telling her they were done. After a moment, the holes darkened as she reapplied the bumper stickers. Fifteen seconds later, the truck started up.

Back at the trailer, she unrolled the tonneau, and he slipped out and hugged her.

"You hit it, Tom?"

He nodded.

"It was loud."

"Can't help that." The .308 rounds produced more than 160 decibels at the muzzle. Suppressors, also known as silencers, were a pleasant fantasy. Buying one took months and attracted the close attention of the Feds.

"It works," she said.

"It works."

———

At dawn the next morning, they packed up. Allie made peanut-butter-and-jelly sandwiches and filled a thermos with coffee. The day was unseasonably warm, birds twittering, the sun glowing over the hills to the east. Miller felt almost festive. His headache was gone. His uncertainty, too. If Allie said Hurley had hurt her, he'd hurt her.

"I'll miss it here," Allie said.

"For real?" Miller had never thought of her as sentimental.

"It's where we met."

Miller locked up the trailer, vaulted over the tailgate into the Ram's bed. Allie unrolled the tonneau, blotting out the sky. He wanted to get used to being in back for long stretches, just in case.

The truck bounced over the dirt roads for a while, stopped, turned left on 195, accelerated. Now the ride was smoother but colder. No surprise. This bed was unheated, meant for cargo, not people. Miller crossed his hands over his chest and let himself shiver. If the Army taught anything, it was how to handle casual discomfort.

A sliver of light leaked through the bumper stickers. Otherwise, the space was coffin-black. He wondered what would happen **next**. Maybe they'd wind up someplace like Nicaragua and live on the cheap. Hang out, teach English. For once, being brown would help him.

But probably not. Probably the police and FBI would catch them sooner or later. Yet as Miller lay in the dark, the pavement rushing by underneath him, he found the idea of being captured didn't bother him. Not that he'd let the cops take him alive. No, he'd save them the trouble of a verdict, pronounce his own guilt with a single round.

Even if an eternity in Hell awaited him, he didn't care. Not as long as he could be with her now.

———

He opened his eyes to find the tonneau rolling back. She'd pulled off the road at the Lewiston Hill Overlook, where the Bitterroots opened into the plains of western Idaho. The colors below were muted, a winding gray river cutting through brown-and-green hills. The sky was pure and blue, endless and ruthless.

"You're shivering, Tom. I thought you would tell me when you wanted out."

"Who said I wanted out?"

===

They stopped for the night in Wyoming. The motel was called the Hilltop. Miller didn't see any hills, but he was too tired to argue. He lay on the bed, staring at the ceiling, as Allie washed up. She closed the bathroom door. He thought he heard her phone buzz, the back-and-forth of texts. But the faucet was running and he couldn't be sure.

"Can I borrow the truck?" she said when she emerged.

He tossed her the keys. "You okay?"

"Woman trouble. I need a drugstore."

He didn't believe her. But before he could say anything, she was gone.

After an hour, he started to worry. She didn't trust him to do what she needed. She'd left for good—

The door swung open.

"Sorry, babe. Got lost."

Whatever power he thought he had over her was an illusion. He might be the soldier, but without her, he was nothing at all.

He was afraid to ask where she'd really been.

===

In the rickety neighborhoods north of downtown St. Louis, they found a no-name motel that took a five-hundred-dollar deposit instead of a credit card. Allie rented a Chevy Lumina, and they drove around St. Peters, tracing routes around the church. **Terrain mapping,** Miller's captains in Afghanistan would have said. Unfortunately, the terrain wasn't ideal.

The Abundant Life campus included the church and four smaller buildings at the intersection of Eagle Rock Avenue and Oakhurst Drive. Eagle Rock was a six-lane boulevard that ran directly north to I-70. Along the way, it passed an intersection with red-light cameras, as well as two gas stations with surveillance cams.

Oakhurst was a curving two-lane road that ran east–west through subdivisions. Worse yet, the entire area consisted of low rolling hills, not the pancake-flat prairie Miller had imagined. And the church was set behind a huge parking lot. On a busy Sunday, the lot's cars might block his field of fire. Miller worried, too, that they had no obvious place to park the Ram while they waited. The Beltway snipers had operated with one huge advantage. They had picked victims at random. They hadn't needed to wait more than a few minutes.

"Maybe we do it at his house?" Hurley and his family lived a mile from the church.

"No. Here. On Sunday. After the eleven a.m. service, the big one."

She was insistent. Almost pouting. "We can't know he'll come out through the main doors."

"He will."

"I thought you hadn't seen him in all these years—"

"I **know** him. He'll shake hands and listen to these people telling him how wonderful he is while he thinks about what he wants to do to their daughters. If this is too hard for you, let's go back to Colfax." She left the rest of the sentence unsaid: . . . **until I take off again.**

"We'll figure it out, Allie."

She put her arms around him and wrapped him up. That fast, she was his again. For now.

Finding the right hide came first. On the west side of Eagle Rock, three hundred yards north of the Abundant Life campus, was a more modest church, brick with a white cross in front. Past the church, a service road led off the avenue to an electrical substation that serviced the subdivisions to the west. The substation was a fenced, cleared area fifty feet in diameter, screened with trees so that the neighbors wouldn't notice it. A razor wire fence protected the transformers inside. It had cameras, but they were focused only on the electrical equipment.

Allie parked the Lumina in the brick church's lot while Miller walked to the substation and scanned through the trees with binoculars. Behind him, electricity hummed through the transformers, the sound strangely alive. The spot wasn't ideal. Miller would be forced to angle his shot through the big trees. The stoplights on Eagle Rock produced predictable traffic patterns, but Miller still had to worry a car would cross his field of fire as he pulled the trigger. And if utility workers showed up while Allie was parked, she'd have no good excuse for her presence. At least the service road was paved rather than dirt, presumably so that utility vehicles didn't get bogged down when they came in. Paved meant no tire tracks, no treads for the police to chase down.

Miller thought the spot was viable. Barely. It did have one big advantage. It wasn't visible from Abundant Life. No one would immediately connect it with the shot.

He walked Allie over, showed her where to park. She brought the Lumina around, and Miller lay on the roof, which was roughly as high as the Ram bed would be, and made sure the angle was right. Start to finish, he was at the substation for forty minutes, longer than he would have liked. He waited for a nosy cop to come by, ask what they were doing. No one did.

Next step, finding a clean way out. By the end of the afternoon, they had one. Left—north—on Eagle Rock, left again on Hillside Drive. Four other roads followed, all with equally bland names. Finally, they reached Bryan Road, a big north–south boulevard about two miles west.

The route was tricky, but it reduced their risk of passing a police cruiser responding to the shooting. The cops would stick to the avenues, where they could speed. And Bryan Road was far enough from the church that the cops probably wouldn't check its cameras, busy enough that the Ram shouldn't stand out if they did. They'd head south on Bryan to Missouri 364, a state highway that merged quickly into I-64. Two miles westbound on I-64 and they'd hit I-70 at Wentzville.

By then, the cops would need more than camera readers to find them. They would need a psychic.

———

Friday. Miller and Allie had two days to fill. Miller couldn't even give himself another round of target practice. He had to assume that after the shooting, the cops and FBI would check every range within a hundred miles.

Allie was even more impatient. At lunch, she pushed for them to go to Abundant Life and meet Hurley.

"I want to see him, see if he remembers me."

"No."

"Because you're afraid."

"Because the police will know this isn't random. The first question they'll ask: Did anyone new want to meet Pastor Hurley recently? We just spent a whole day trying to beat surveillance. Now you want to show up and wave."

"Fine, we'll go to the service Saturday night. We'll blend in."

As if beautiful twenty-something women filled the Abundant Life congregation. "Forget it."

"If you won't do it, then go home."

"This guy's only the first on your list. You want to get to the others or not?"

She registered his seriousness. She pouted for an hour, but this time he knew he had her. Again, he would only see what she'd done later. How she'd made him own the killing.

———

On Saturday an ugly midwestern wind kicked up, twenty miles an hour, gusts to forty. Wind this strong deflected shots by feet, not inches. If it didn't drop overnight, they'd have to wait a week. The Weather Channel and the local forecasters said this front would pass sometime Sunday, but no one knew exactly when.

He didn't say anything to Allie. He wasn't sure her nerves could take another week of waiting. They stayed inside for most of Saturday, eating cheap pizza and clawing at each other. Until now, their sex had been respectful, even loving. Now Miller saw another side of her. She demanded he slap her, put his hands around her throat.

Miller stopped moving. "No way, Allie."

"Sissy."

"I can't hurt you. I **love** you." The first time he'd ever spoken those words. The worst possible time.

She pushed him off her as if he'd been hurting her against her will, the very opposite of the truth. She sobbed—big, silent heaves. Miller listened to the wind howl against the door and prayed to himself that Sunday would dawn sunny and windless.

====

It did. The front passed sooner than the forecasters had predicted. In the motel parking lot, Miller felt only a hint of a breeze. They ate breakfast and checked out. At 11:30 a.m., Allie parked behind a dumpster in a deserted downtown alley. Miller kissed her cheek, slid into the bed of the Ram. She pulled the tonneau down. If the mission went as planned, he wouldn't see her again until Luke Hurley was dead. His headache was returning. With the pain came the sense that he was about to do something wrong. Something unforgivable. What did he know about Luke Hurley? Nothing. He hadn't even googled the guy.

Miller dry-swallowed a half-dozen Advil and Tylenol. If he could beat his headache, maybe his doomed feeling would disappear, too.

The pickup stuttered through downtown, accelerated up a ramp. Half an hour passed before finally it slowed. It stopped for a light, and Miller knew they were on Eagle Rock. Very soon, Allie would turn onto the service road. They'd aimed to be in position about twenty past noon. Miller's watch said they were going to be right on schedule.

His heart raced. He'd never felt this way, not even on the mid-summer patrols that he and everyone else knew were headed for Taliban ambushes. Not even when he woke up in those clean white sheets at Kandahar Airfield and couldn't remember his own name. He was about to kill a man because he couldn't say no to his girlfriend.

You are whipped, he heard Willie Coole, his old platoon sergeant, say. **Whipped as whipped can be.** Out loud. So real that Miller looked around, wondering if Coole had somehow snuck into the pickup with him.

I'm protecting her.

How can you protect her when you don't know nothing about her, Miller? Call me a hick if you like, but I know when a man's thinking with his—

The pickup swung right, rumbled over the pebbled asphalt of the service road. Angled back and forth and stopped. The engine cut. The driver's door swung open. Miller flicked on the lantern, pulled out the Remington and the scope, just as he had in Colfax. Moving automatically now. Focus on the details. Let the mission take care of itself.

Too late to change his mind, anyway.

Outside, Allie peeled off the bumper stickers. Sunday light flooded inside. Miller slid the muzzle through, until the scope was flush with the higher hole. Everything happening with the fluid logic of a dream. Seeing a dragon through the scope wouldn't have surprised him.

But instead: trees, parking lot, road. The Abundant Church lot and the white façade of the central church building. It looked more like an arena than a traditional church. Allie had parked a couple degrees off-line, but Miller wriggled the muzzle of the rifle, focused the scope on a pair of smoked-glass doors, tall white crosses painted on them. The main entrance. He had a clear field of fire.

He scanned the lot, looking for security guards or cops. He saw one police cruiser parked at the south end of the lot, but it was empty. Maybe the officer was inside. A bald, beefy man in a white dress shirt and jeans stood at the front door. Miller guessed he was an off-duty cop who watched the parking lot during services.

The doors swung open. A trickle of people emerged, then more and more. The service must just have ended. Husbands and wives walked hand in hand. A white teenager pushed an old black woman in a wheelchair. A handsome young Hispanic man whose legs stopped mid-thigh swung himself ahead on crutches. Miller would have bet his life the guy was a vet. The folks walking out seemed happy. Could they all be so wrong?

Then Miller remembered all those Catholic priests who'd raped little boys. You couldn't trust anyone. Just because Hurley had followers didn't mean anything. Miller trusted Allie or he didn't. That simple.

Don't have to do this, Specialist. Coole again. **Willie—**

It's Platoon Sergeant Coole to you. And you know somewhere in that shook-up head of yours that this whole thing is FUBAR. This girl is trouble with a capital T and that rhymes with P and that stands for—

Miller's head was hurting, he'd been looking through the scope too long. He closed his eyes, tried to think.

Abort the mission, Specialist. Turn around, go home.

Coole couldn't know, but he'd made exactly the wrong play. Home was nowhere. Colfax was an empty trailer. Allie's scent on every sheet.

Miller came back to the scope. The talk with Coole had taken only a few seconds in his head, but minutes seemed to have passed. The flood of parishioners had thinned. Miller wondered if he'd missed Hurley already.

The doors opened, and the minister stepped out. Tall and handsome, blue suit, white shirt, red tie. A blonde in a modest flowered dress walked beside him. Two kids followed. Hurley stopped outside the doors, as Allie had promised he would, and chatted with a knot of men and women. His arm rested on his wife's shoulder.

Miller tapped his walkie-talkie. "Clear?"

He didn't know what he was hoping to hear, but after a few seconds, his receiver squawked. "Clear."

The rules of engagement haven't been met, the risk of civilian casualties is too high—

Miller pushed in his earplugs, but Coole kept talking. Miller didn't know if he could do this with Coole yapping at him. He watched through the scope as Hurley's wife raised her hands in a **Can you believe this guy?** gesture. She stepped close to him and kissed his cheek.

Miller cursed softly, waited. Hurley's wife reached into her purse and came up with what looked like car keys. She held them over her head, jingled them. Hurley laughed again. Then their son grabbed them and tossed them to his sister. Hurley raised a hand, and father and son high-fived. Somehow, Miller had stumbled into an episode of **America's Happiest Family.** Seeing them like this infuriated him. He couldn't blame Allie—he **hated** them. No one got to be this happy.

Who did this kid think he was to have a **father—**

Miller's pulse pounded in his throat. He made himself breathe deep. **The shot comes if you're ready,** the instructors at Fort Benning liked to say. **If you're in place, zeroed, your breathing is right. It** always **comes. Patience, grasshopper.**

Hurley's wife kissed him once more, stepped away. The kids followed. Hurley turned to the parishioners. He was in three-quarter profile to Miller, not perfect, but at this range, on a windless day, Miller knew he could land the round. Anyway, he was sure Hurley was going to turn, sure as he'd ever been of anything.

Don't, I'm ordering you, Specialist—

A last yelp from Coole. Miller ignored him. Hurley turned to his right, offering his chest to Miller, a perfect target—

17

MEXICO CITY

For generations, Mexico City had been called the DF, short for Distrito Federal. Now, to establish its independence from Mexico's corrupt central government, it was busily rebranding itself as CDMX. The boldface initials popped up on billboards, buses, park benches. But by any name, the city was tough. Exciting and vibrant, sure, but traffic-choked, crime-riddled, earthquake-prone, and, as an added bonus, running out of water.

Then there was Polanco.

The neighborhood lay just north of Chapultepec Park, a seventeen-hundred-acre park that offered an oasis of green in the center of the twenty-million-person metropolis. Mexico City had hundreds of thousands of residents who were rich by any standard. Many of the wealthiest lived in Polanco, whose central boulevard, Avenida Presidente Masaryk, could have passed with a squint for Rodeo Drive. Chanel? Check. Louis Vuitton? Check and double-check. Porsche? **Vroom!**

Wells and Coyle walked down Masaryk now, 1 p.m. on Sunday, skies blue and sun warm. Pale-skinned women in two-hundred-dollar sneakers jogged past.

"Don't look like the Mexicans I know," Coyle said. "These people are **white**."

"The Mexicans you know snuck over the border to get away from these people."

"Mowing lawns in the land of the free."

Wells's phone buzzed before he could answer. He tipped the screen to Coyle.

"Tarnes?"

"The one and only."

═════

Wells had called her thirty-six hours before from the airport in Quito while Coyle stood at the United counter booking them on a flight to Houston. Though it was almost midnight on a Friday, Tarnes answered within two rings, ready to work. No need to explain she was in a bar or to ask someone in the background to turn off the television. In her ability to focus, she reminded Wells of Exley. But where the job had nearly overwhelmed Exley, Tarnes seemed more careerist. Wells sensed she would have worked just as hard at a law firm or a software company.

Wells told Tarnes what Graciela Frietas had said about her husband's money laundering and the mysterious banker named Z. Plus the mobile phone, the list of names, the FBI badge, and the paperback he and Coyle had found.

"FBI badge?"

"We think it's fake."

"You **hope** it's fake. What about Frietas?"

"Gone. Permanently."

She didn't ask. "And the wife's given us what we're going to get?"

"Correct."

"So the Russians are running an op with the Islamic State."

Wells wondered if he heard sarcasm in her voice, decided he didn't. Shafer had always been preoccupied with motive. And Shafer would push back hard if he thought Wells was following the wrong trail. Not Tarnes. At least not yet. Wells realized he wouldn't have minded more resistance. A little more.

"Whoever was in that house was Russian, and Hector Frietas definitely thought they were connected to Dallas."

"I'll run the names, see if we or NSA have anything on a banker code-named Z in Mexico."

"He might be at Banamex. The banker."

"Right. What else?"

"We're going through Houston on our way to Mexico City. Can we hand the phone to someone there, give the basement a chance at it?" The hackers at the Directorate of Science and Technology worked out of the basement of the Original Headquarters Building.

"Done. The badge and paperback, too."

"You want our flight number?"

"Guessing there's only one flight from Quito to Houston at midnight. What else?" For the first time, she sounded ready to be rid of him and back to whatever she did on Friday night. Wells thought about asking her to arrange pistols for them in Mexico, but if he couldn't figure out a way to talk to a banker without being strapped, he ought to go home.

"Anything new from Dallas?"

"Not much. Your buddy Ellis is out of the hospital, and the cops wiped the arrest, but you already knew that."

"Arrest?"

"You didn't know?"

"Haven't talked to him since I came down

here." Wells didn't mention that Tarnes was the reason.

"He went down there, looking for something, I don't know what, but he got hurt, and the police picked him up. I only heard about it because he asked Duto for help."

"Hurt how?"

"Someone banged him up. He was out of commission a couple days."

"You know what he was looking for?"

"Not a clue. I think he's still down there, though." Tarnes didn't say anything else, but Wells heard the questions, anyway: **How come this is news? Aren't you two pals?** "I'll let you know if I hear anything about the banker. Fly safe. By the way, we finally got someone to break open that safe. Empty."

Wells had figured as much. Then she was gone. Wells was glad Coyle was still at the counter buying the tickets. He felt like Shafer had betrayed him, though the reverse was more accurate. He called Shafer, got voice mail. He didn't leave a message.

———

The Quito–Houston flight landed at 5:50 a.m. It was not even 7 a.m. Saturday morning when they cleared immigration. Still, Wells was not surprised to see a beefy guy in jeans nodding at him as he walked into the arrivals hall.

"Mr. Wells. Ms. Tarnes sent me."

Wells handed over the phone, badge, and book. The guy slipped everything into a black bag and walked off without a word.

"Tarnes," Coyle said.

"Yeah, she doesn't play."

Wells called Shafer again, got voice mail again. They were booked on a 9 a.m. to Mexico City, but as Wells looked for the departure gate, he realized United had canceled the flight. The next flight wasn't until noon. An annoyance, though they wouldn't have much to do in Mexico until they had found Z's real name. Wells almost wanted to go north, to New Hampshire. But he didn't know how long Tarnes might need, and going home for a few hours would only upset Emmie.

He called instead.

"John." Anne's voice was dry. Scratchy. "Still in Quito?"

"Houston. Everything okay? You sound sick."

"I just puked breakfast over the Maine line."

"Babe. Emmie sick, too?"

"I doubt it. Unless she's also pregnant. In which case, we have bigger problems."

Wells told himself he hadn't forgotten Anne

was pregnant. Not really. He'd just set the fact aside.

"Hold on a sec—" The unmistakable sound of retching. "Lucky me. I'm down to spit. You know what they say: **If men had to have babies, the whole human race would end.**"

"I'm sorry."

"Blame your son. The only things he seems to like are bananas. And vanilla ice cream." Anne half laughed. "I just need him to get interested in chocolate sauce. I got a prescription for Zofran this morning. I'll live. The big question. How is it possible I've gained ten pounds if I can't keep anything down? The other big question: So you're done in Quito? Making progress?"

"Maybe. We have to go to Mexico City. Talk to a member of the global banking conspiracy." Hoping to make her smile.

"You say so." She sounded more exhausted than annoyed. Like she lacked the energy to care. Not that Wells could blame her. "Emmie's right here—" Her way of hanging up on him without having to hang up.

"Hi, Dada! **Hihihi**—" No adult could ever be excited like a three-year-old. "Where are you, Daddy?"

"Houston—"

"I go to Houston all the time! With my sixty-five sisters!" Emmie insisted now that she had sixty-five sisters. Or sometimes eighty-five. **Kayla, Kaylee, Kaydee, et al. . . .** "I fly there!"

"Yeah, it's a long drive. You like Houston?"

"It's called **Boos**ton, actually. Not **Hous**ton."

"Booston."

"Yes, Booston. It's okay. But **boring**. Okay, I have to go, Dada. My sixty-five sisters! Love you. Bye!" She hung up before Wells could ask her to give the phone back to Anne. He found himself grinning, his usual response to these chats.

"She sounds sweet," Coyle said.

"The best. One day, Duto's going to call. I'm going to look at her—"

"And answer."

"Maybe. You'll see when you have kids, Coyle."

"No kids for me."

"Because of your brother?" Coyle's younger brother, Lincoln, had died years before, hit by a car as he bicycled through Inglewood to watch Coyle play baseball. Not coincidentally, Coyle joined the Marines shortly afterward. "He wouldn't want you to give up your chance for a family."

"How do you know what he'd want, John? You never met him. And guess what? You never will." Coyle shook his head. **This portion of our conversation is over.** "Now what? Team-building exercises while we wait for the flight?"

"Go ahead. I'm taking a nap."

"Oldster."

"I think of myself as seasoned."

———

In Mexico City, they booked themselves into the NH, a shiny business-class hotel in the Zona Rosa. The area was a once-swanky but now slightly run-down neighborhood not far from Polanco.

A Google search revealed that Banamex, the second-largest bank in Mexico, was owned by Citigroup and had recently changed its official name to Citibanamex to emphasize the relationship. Everyone still seemed to call it Banamex, though. In 2015, Citi had paid a one-hundred-forty-million-dollar fine for money laundering at the company's American subsidiary and shut it down as part of the settlement.

But the search for Z proved fruitless. The Internet revealed nothing about a banker named or nicknamed Z at Banamex or any other Mexican bank.

"So much for the easy out," Coyle said. "How else do we find this guy?"

After years watching Shafer work, Wells had some ideas. **WWSD: What would Shafer do?** "Here's one idea. I'll bet these places have live phone operators in their high-net-worth divisions because rich people like to feel special, and touch-tone keypads don't make anyone feel special."

"So we just start cold-calling these banks on Monday, ask for Z, see if anyone connects us?"

"Not we, amigo. You're the one who speaks Spanish."

"Lucky me."

"If it comes to that. Let's get some sleep, see if Tarnes has something in the morning."

"I may go out. If that's cool with you."

Wells wanted to ask where. But Coyle was a grown-up, and they weren't in the Marines. What the man did with his nights was his own business. "Have fun."

"Oh, I will."

===

Whatever Coyle got up to, he was showered and shaved and knocking on Wells's door at 7 a.m. while Wells was still doing his morning push-ups. Youth. Coyle didn't say where he'd been. Wells didn't ask.

===

Now they were in Polanco, Tarnes calling. "Sorry it took so long."

"Thirty-six hours. You're losing it."

She didn't laugh. "We didn't have anything, NSA didn't either. This morning, I tried DEA. Lots of Mexican cartel guys with names or nicknames that start with Z. Zorro, Zapata, of course the Zetas. No bankers. But three years ago, part of a big money laundering investigation, they opened a file on a banker named Alina Mendoz."

"A woman."

"Last I checked, women could launder money, too. She's in what Banamex calls its mid-high-net-worth division. Three to thirty million."

"Alina Mendoz. That's it? Her last name ends with z?"

"That's not it. She was on the accounts for three suspected traffickers. Guess what? Two were Ecuadorian."

"What'd she say to the DEA?"

"Nobody ever talked to her. The cross-border stuff made it messy, and they had a hundred bigger fish."

"No direct evidence, then."

"Didn't realize you needed me to find the diary entry that says **I laundered Russian money today.** I'll email you her file. It's not much. And I'll text you her address. And I'll keep looking, Your Highness."

She was gone. Wells wondered if she was annoyed, decided it didn't matter. One thing he already knew about Tarnes, she would do her job either way.

Mendoz's address hit his phone. No surprise, it was in Polanco, a few blocks northeast. Calle Hegel. Many streets in the neighborhood were named after philosophers and scientists.

The phone buzzed again, a CNN alert:

Missouri megachurch pastor killed in sniper attack outside church.

Police say "expert sniper" carried out attack, warn area churchgoers to be wary.

Wells showed Coyle the screen.

"Doesn't have to be terrorism. Maybe the guy was having a two-person Bible study group with somebody's wife."

"Maybe."

———

Five minutes later, they stood outside Mendoz's property. The security here was as tight as in Bogotá. Behind narrow sidewalks, both sides of Calle Hegel were lined with ten-foot walls topped with barbed wire. Every house had security cameras. The big ones had their own guardhouses.

Wells peeked through Mendoz's steel gate at the 7 Series BMW in the driveway. The sedan rode low on its frame. A Rottweiler roamed the yard. It came to the gate, growled at Wells, a rumble more menacing than any bark.

"Car looks armored," Wells said. "Dog might be, too."

"Maybe we should just ring the bell."

Wells considered. **Me and my buddy are thinking about buying in the nabe.** But bankers for drug traffickers didn't open their doors to men they didn't know. Not if they wanted long healthy lives. And trying would cost Wells and Coyle any chance of surprise. Even standing here for more than a minute or two might hurt their chances.

As if to prove the point, a police cruiser stopped beside them. The passenger window dropped, and the officer in the passenger seat waved Coyle over. Wells couldn't understand the conversation that followed, but Coyle stayed cool. Finally, the cruiser pulled away.

"We good?"

"Long as we're gone when they come back."

Wells mulled their options as they walked back to Avenida Masaryk. The house was out. The idea of trying to snatch Mendoz on the way to work was equally far-fetched. She'd have a driver. Probably a bodyguard, too. Rich Mexicans built their lives around the constant threat of kidnapping.

"It's going to have to be her office," Wells said. Not ideal. They'd have a hard time making a threat stick. Mendoz would know she could get rid of them simply by yelling **Call Security!** to her secretary. Anyway, why meet them at all? Wells assumed most of her clients came through word of mouth.

"I don't see Banamex just letting us in. Unless you have five million bucks lying around to impress her."

Wells realized that Coyle had the answer. "My man. You think you're joking, but you're not."

———

Back at the NH, they watched CNN for news of the Missouri shooting:

Preacher Luke Hurley shot to death in front of congregants . . . Worshippers describe terrifying scene, as preacher collapsed without warning . . . Governor Roy Steiner says police believe sniper shot from "hundreds of yards with pinpoint accuracy" . . . FBI, police to hold press conference at four p.m. . . .

Then:

No claim of responsibility as yet, but Muslim groups sharply criticized Hurley last year after he said the United States had "a duty to protect Christians from Muslim barbarians . . . Any

Muslim who disagrees isn't a real American and doesn't belong here. As a pastor, I have a duty to stand up for Christian values."

"Still think it's not terrorism?" Wells clicked open the dossier Tarnes had sent on Mendoz.

As Tarnes had warned, it was thin, a basic biography, with a single passport photo. Mendoz was forty-eight, had two teenage kids. She'd married in her late twenties to a plastic surgeon, divorced him a decade later. The pic revealed a dark-haired woman, thin-lipped, self-possessed. Property records showed Mendoz had moved into the house in Polanco about seven years ago, long after the divorce, implying that she paid for it herself.

All in all, Wells didn't think Mendoz would be in a hurry to give them the truth. He called Tarnes, who picked up on the first ring. As usual. Wells wondered if the phone was plugged into her brain.

"We need a Colombian passport for Coyle and five million dollars. Tomorrow, if possible."

Silence from Tarnes. Wells was happy to have stumped her, if only for a minute.

"May I ask why?"

"We think the only way to get to Mendoz is officially through Banamex. There's plenty of black Colombians, and Coyle's Spanish should get us in the door."

"What about you?"

"I'll be his American lawyer. But we're pretty sure she'll want to see cash before she says yes."

"Can't you just tell her you're selling Girl Scout cookies?"

"You can't do it, let me know."

"Didn't say that."

Her voice slightly acid, letting Wells know she didn't like being told what she couldn't do. As he'd hoped.

He heard her typing. "Lucky you. There's a one a.m. nonstop from Dulles to Mexico City. We'll put the passport together tonight and courier it to you. It may not be live, but it'll look real enough to convince the bank. The money—I don't know. I assume this is a bank account, right? Not straight cash. Not even sure how you'd carry that much money around."

"Yes. But not a U.S. bank. The Caymans, someplace shady but not completely dark. Somewhere they know they can deal with. Shouldn't be in whatever name you give Coyle either. Make it a trust. Nobody with five million dollars to hide has a personal account."

"I get it. I know someone at Treasury who can help, make it look right."

"I'm sure you do," Wells said.

"Is that a question?"

"This is. You hear anything about Missouri?"

"They found what they think is the hide. Five hundred yards away. Single shot, center chest. Hurley was dead before he hit the ground. Plus whoever did it made sure there were no cameras anywhere."

Details that added up to a pro job, a police- or military-trained sniper. You couldn't learn to shoot that way from YouTube, no matter how many videos you watched.

"How'd the shooter get away?"

"Good question. Whoever did it was local or had a car. They're pulling video. But the betting is the guy scouted his exit route in advance. Lot of local roads with no cameras. Before you ask, no chatter. Now the idiots are tweeting about how it was Allah's will. But nothing from the official Islamic State accounts."

Yet the fact Tarnes knew so many details proved terrorism was on the table. Fifty people were murdered in the United States every day. Nobody called the CIA.

"You hear anything big—"

"I'll let you know. I'll start on the bank account right away. I may need you to sign something saying you're not going to touch the money."

"There goes my retirement."

Tarnes didn't laugh. "I'll call you tomorrow, John."

"Julie? Thanks."

Wells called Shafer again. Still nothing.

"Ellis. It's Sunday afternoon. I heard you ran into trouble in Dallas. Call me, let me know you're okay."

Six hours later. "Ellis. I know you're old and mad—and nobody does mad like you—but this isn't about you. I'm in Mexico City with Coyle. Remember Coyle? Marine? Good with a shotgun? We may have something."

As they went to bed, Shafer still hadn't called. By now, Wells figured Shafer didn't have anything real. Nothing he'd locked down, anyway. If he did, he would have called. If only to gloat.

Wells found out he was wrong the next morning as his phone buzzed him out of a confused dream about a minor-league baseball team. Related to Coyle, he assumed. The bedside clock said 5:48 a.m.

"Hello, sunshine. I wake you? I'm calling to tell you I've decided to forgive you for your many sins."

The monotone grumble of a late-night radio host at the end of his shift. The words not so much layered with irony as built from them. **Shafer**. "Too bad you aren't God."

"Can you really be sure?"

Wells flipped on the lights. This call was turning into a little too much Shafer a little too soon.

"Ask me why I'm up so early, John."

"Why are you up so early?"

"A very bad man broke my head. It wouldn't even make your top twenty, but I'm not sleeping much. So I heard your pathetic messages and decided I'd say hello."

"I can't imagine why anyone would ever want to hit you."

A choked snort. "Don't make me laugh, John. It **hurts**." Shafer briefly fell silent. "Ask me what I was doing in Dallas."

"We have to do it this way?"

No answer.

"What were you doing in Dallas?"

"Following a hunch about something weird the feebs turned up but couldn't put together. I was right."

"Of course you were."

"Ahmed Shakir's girlfriend said he was arrested a few months before he went **Boom!** FBI checked the arrest records, didn't find anything. They decided she was wrong. But I interviewed her, and I'm telling you someone arrested him. And there's a waitress at one of the bars where Shakir dealt coke who thought he got caught in some kinda sting, too. He went out one night, didn't come back, she never saw him again. Her exact words to me were: **Everybody gets tagged sooner or later.**"

———

Wells could almost feel the FBI badge in his hand. He and Coyle had solved half the puzzle. Shafer had given them the rest. **The Russians hadn't been working with the Islamic State. They'd figured out how to make their own terrorist attacks.**

Wells shivered like an arctic wind had snuck south and infiltrated his hotel room. At their best, if **best** was the word, the Russians played the intel game with an exquisite and precise cruelty, inducing paranoia in the innocent and guilty alike.

The Kremlin liked poison as a murder weapon for just this reason. Opponents had a tough time staying focused when they had to worry that any meal might kill them. Exploiting weakness was another Kremlin specialty, and the FSB agents had found the perfect victim in Ahmed Shakir.

They'd arrested him, then given him a fake route to freedom.

Shafer mistook Wells's silence for disbelief. "Trust me, John. Somebody has a file on this guy, we just need to shake it out. They pushed him too hard, he went nuts. Now they're trying to hide it."

"No. They weren't real cops, Ellis."

"This guy had been dealing a while, no way someone could have faked him."

"What if it was a team? With twenty million dollars?"

"Explain, please."

"Let me call you from a sat phone." Wells didn't trust unencrypted lines for this call.

For once, Shafer didn't argue.

"I feel like I got hit in the head again," Shafer said when Wells was finished. "But it fits. They, quote, **arrest**, unquote, Shakir, tell him to lure his cousins into an attack . . ."

"Yeah."

"We tell no one, John. When we're ready, we stovepipe it straight to Duto."

Wells understood. What they'd found was worse than a Kremlin–Islamic State conspiracy. The Russians were killing Americans. They'd put

Duto in a terrible place. If Duto openly accused them, the public would want war. But if he kept the truth secret, the Russians might think they'd won.

Then Shafer sighed. "We're missing something. We're already helping them in Syria. Maybe not as much as they want, but the risk on this is off the charts. There's another endgame here, even if we can't see it."

Shafer, always thinking ahead. He was right. The Russians wouldn't risk war just for Assad.

"You think this thing in Missouri is part of it?" Wells said.

"If it is, it's got to be a different con. The key with Shakir was that they blew him up before he could tell anyone what was really happening. They didn't do that with the sniper. He's still out there. Which means they think they can control him for as long as they need him."

More logic Wells couldn't fight. "Reassuring."

"So when do you meet the banker?"

"Still working on it."

"Hope it's before next Sunday."

18

MOSCOW

Moscow lay five thousand miles away and eight time zones ahead of Missouri. The difference meant the reports of Luke Hurley's shooting reached the Kremlin just after 9 p.m. local time, snow falling on the famous onion domes, the air a balmy four degrees below zero. By midnight, terrorism had taken center stage as a possible motive. Sergei Fedin, the president of the Russian Federation, called the White House.

The President is in emergency meetings, the chief Oval Office scheduler told his Kremlin counterpart. **He'll try to call before he goes to bed. Midnight here, seven a.m. tomorrow in Moscow. Best he can do.**

Fedin wished he could call Duto's mobile directly. But he didn't have the number. The President had never given it to the Russians, presumably to avoid the risk of being hacked. Fedin wondered if Duto was sending him a similar message even before they spoke. **I don't trust you, even if all you're doing is offering condolences.**

The Russian president wasn't sure he wanted to talk to Duto so late in Duto's night. The American had a temper. Then again, exhaustion might loosen his tongue. The Kremlin had heard rumors of Duto's drinking, though no one had any real evidence other than the bourbon Duto famously offered visitors to the Oval Office. At public events, he was always composed, his suits pressed, ties perfectly knotted. If nothing else, the man could hold his booze, a trait that Fedin respected as much as the next Russian.

The fact that Duto had spent so many years working for the CIA, the main enemy, didn't bother Fedin either. At least Duto was no soft-headed liberal. After his experience as the station chief in Colombia during the depths of the drug wars, Duto surely knew different countries needed different systems. The so-called **virtues of democracy** made for chaos in a place like Russia. Outside Moscow and St. Petersburg, the Russians were still serfs in their dark, drunken hearts. They needed strong and capable men—and only men—to protect and lead them. So Fedin didn't overreact to the squawking of Pussy Riot and

Garry Kasparov and the rest, whether they were in Moscow or exile, whether they called themselves journalists or human rights activists.

Just as long as they didn't go after the money Fedin and his men had made. Millions, yes. Even billions. So? The average Ivan **wanted** his leaders to be rich. He gloried in their hundred-meter yachts and London mansions. Even if he never saw them, even if he was never allowed anywhere near them, even if he would have his face smashed in if he looked too long at them, their mere existence gladdened him.

But the reporters and the other troublemakers didn't understand. They bleated about **theft** and **corruption**. When they sniffed too closely after the money, they had to be put in their place. A year or two in jail wouldn't do for those. Ten years. Or a beating, the kind that put the recipient in a coma. If those warnings didn't do the trick, a few grams of lead, strategically inserted into the cerebellum.

As far as Fedin could tell, Duto understood. He wasn't afraid to live well, and he accepted the Kremlin could and would rule Russia however it liked.

———

So in the months after Duto's election, Fedin told the others at the Kremlin he hoped he and the

American could build a respectful relationship.
Even a **beneficial** relationship. Russia had plenty
of men who would invest in Duto's post-
presidential ventures. Or simply pay him millions of dollars to speak at their corporate retreats.

But Duto disappointed Fedin. Duto insisted
on limiting Russia's influence to its own borders—
its ugly, shrunken, post-1991 borders. Like the
other CIA men who'd come of age at the end of
the Cold War, Duto mistakenly believed the West
had won forever, that Russia would permanently
be a third-class nation.

Russia. The world's largest country, even after
territorial losses nearly as big as the United States
and China combined. For a thousand years, Russia had saved Europe from the hordes of Asia.
And in the twentieth century, Russia saved Europe from **itself**. More Russians died fighting
the Germans for Stalingrad than Britain and
the United States combined lost in all of World
War II. The British forgot because they never remembered anything that didn't benefit them.
The Americans forgot because they never remembered anything, period.

Thus, Duto refused to see the obvious truth.
Russia's decline in the 1980s had been temporary,
the result of low oil prices and a broken political
system. No, Russia would never match China or

the United States economically. But it had vast natural resources. It had highly trained scientists. It had the world's largest nuclear arsenal. And a resurgent army. It could hold its own. And it would. It would protect its citizens in Ukraine, no matter what threats NATO made. It would make sure that the bureaucrats in Brussels stopped worrying about expanding the European Union. It would dominate Central Asia.

But Duto refused to accept the appropriate Russian sphere of influence. He armed the Ukrainian government. He supported the rebels fighting Syria, Russia's steadiest ally in the Middle East. He tried to destabilize Iran. He set his CIA and NSA dogs on the Kremlin, distracting Fedin's security forces from their work against the Moscow troublemakers.

Worst of all, he showed no inclination to remove the sanctions and travel restrictions that the United States had imposed on Russia. Even during the Cold War, when the United States and the Soviet Union threatened to destroy each other, they'd respected each other's leaders. Fedin and the men around him—and their wives and mistresses, too—were tired of having to beg for visas to visit Paris or St. Barts, much less buy houses in London or Los Angeles. They were tired of sneaking around like they were criminals instead of the richest men in the world. They were tired of worrying that the American Treasury Department might try to seize their money, or the Justice Department might seize **them**.

The risk was real, as the men of the Fédération Internationale de Football Association had learned in 2015. Americans had quickly forgotten the FIFA arrests. Not Fedin. The prosecution was infuriating. The supposed corruption involved FIFA, a **Swiss** federation managing its own World Cup tournament. How exactly did the way the Uruguayan Football Association voted in a FIFA election fall under American law? No one in the United States even cared about **fútbol**. They called it **soccer**.

The world's policeman.

The phrase sickened Fedin. Whatever his supposed CIA sophistication, Duto had shown himself as dim as his predecessors. No American politician had the courage to tell his people, **Russia is our equal. Our partner. These crazy jihadis, they're the real threat.**

Fedin and the men around him feared they would never find an American leader to make that case.

Then Eric Birman appeared.

Fedin heard about Eric's approach to the SVR deputy chief in Washington a day after it happened. Of course, the Russians had other agents in the American government. But from the first, the Kremlin realized Eric was in a different class. The SVR had targeted him when he left the Joint Special Operations Command and been surprised he did not immediately dismiss the idea of speaking in Russia. But, ultimately, he turned down the offer, and the SVR decided not to touch him for a couple years. Give him time to simmer, grow tired of civilian life.

Instead, out of nowhere, he touched them.

The Kremlin quickly dismissed the possibility the CIA was offering Eric as a dangle. From the first, his intelligence was gold. The fact that his cousin Paul was a senator only added to his importance, especially after Paul became an early favorite to challenge Duto. Paul's rise surprised Moscow. The Tennessee senator seemed absurd, a so-called **man of the people** who'd spent his life cashing checks.

In Russia, Paul's career would have been controlled. The Kremlin stage-managed elections now as thoroughly as it had in the Soviet era. No one wanted a repeat of the 1996 election when a Communist had almost beaten Yeltsin. But the United States wasn't Russia. Somehow, Paul Birman had broken out. Russians might want to fear their leaders, but Americans seemed to want to **like** theirs. And Eric was Paul's closest advisor. For the first time in its history, Russia might have an agent at the very center of American power.

Still, Fedin knew Paul was a long shot to win the White House. The election was years away. Politicians came and went in the United States. Paul would have to survive a brutal primary and then beat Duto. The threat of terrorism played well with Paul's base, but most Americans were more concerned with health care and the economy.

—————

Then the Kremlin's top spy, Oleg Nemtsov, came to Fedin. Nemtsov headed the FSB, the internal Russian secret service. The SVR—the external Russian spy agency—was the equivalent of the CIA. The FSB was the Russian equivalent of the FBI. Theoretically, the FSB and SVR were equal partners, both descended from the KGB.

In reality, the FSB was senior. The reason was simple. The men inside the Kremlin feared internal threats even more than they feared the United

States. The FSB guaranteed Fedin could sleep without worrying that he'd wake with a pistol pressed to his neck. Further, Fedin and his top advisors all had come out of the FSB. The agency's importance to the Russian government couldn't be exaggerated. In many ways, it **was** the Russian government.

Thus, the FSB did what it liked, including operating on what should have been the SVR's turf outside of Russia. The FSB let the SVR handle the grind of conventional espionage and focused instead on what it called **leverage campaigns**. If Fedin decided to kill a mouthy dissident in London, or ruin an unfriendly French diplomat in Brussels, or give the Russian rebels in Ukraine a hundred surface-to-air missiles and the training to use them, the FSB did the job. Usually, the campaigns were meant to be deniable, sometimes completely secret.

The plan Nemtsov proposed to Fedin fell in the latter category. If anyone else had suggested it, Fedin would have laughed him out of the room. Then arrested him.

But Nemtsov wasn't anyone else, and Fedin knew better than to laugh. They'd worked together for thirty years, starting in the KGB's station in Prague in the 1980s. They'd watched Czechs fill Prague's streets to protest their Communist rulers and the Russian overlords behind them. As the protests grew bolder, Fedin and Nemtsov waited for Mikhail Gorbachev to order the Red Army to break the demonstrations, as it had done in 1968. But Gorbachev knuckled under instead of killing a few protestors and restoring order. The Poles, the East Germans—they understood the lesson. All those Soviet tanks and soldiers didn't mean anything because the men who commanded them wouldn't use them.

Within a few months, Russia lost Eastern Europe.

That experience, and the miserable decade that followed, taught Fedin and Nemtsov the value of order. Order was the foundation of society, more important than freedom, even more important than law. When people couldn't leave their homes for fear of being attacked, when businesses couldn't open their doors for fear of being robbed, a society was hardly a society at all. **Political** order was just as important. Better to have one strong leader, even a cruel one, than gangs fighting for power in the streets.

Fedin and Nemtsov hung tight, stayed out of politics, built a core group of a hundred or so officers inside the FSB. Good men. Rough and fearless. Russian patriots, not seduced by the West's supposed superiority. They bided their time as the chaos spiraled and vodka destroyed

Boris Yeltsin. Finally, at the end of the nineties, with Moscow near anarchy and the economy collapsing, the rich men came to them and begged for help, begged for the FSB to do what only it could do.

Fedin was happy enough to oblige, on one condition. **Make me president.** An audacious demand, but the oligarchs didn't have much choice. Anyway, Fedin knew they saw him as a figurehead, no different than Yeltsin. **We have the money, the companies, the media, our own bodyguards and banks, let him pretend to rule.**

But Fedin knew they were wrong. He and Nemtsov had an iron alliance. Once Fedin led the FSB inside the Kremlin, it would never leave.

He took over in 2000. Within two years, he'd consolidated control of the government, putting his own men in the judiciary, the Interior Ministry, the army. He broke the gangs and the terrorists, quelled the violence in the streets. For a while, he left the oligarchs alone. As long as they were making money, they wouldn't notice what was happening inside the Kremlin.

Meanwhile, he made sure the voters knew he was more than the heir to Yeltsin and Yeltsin's weakness. He went on raids with Special Forces units to kick down the doors of Chechen gangs. He rode horses on the steppe and fly-fished in the Urals, every catch he made televised. He greeted the cosmonauts when they returned from the International Space Station. He stood in front of a mock-up of a new aircraft carrier and promised it would join the Russian navy while he was president. The Moscow wags joked that he would need to be a hundred before Russia had the money. But then, the Moscow wags laughed at everything he did. They thought he was a cartoon. **Super Sergei**, they called him, in English. Fedin didn't care. The people, **his** people, lapped up his every move. In the next election, in 2004, he won by a landslide, seventy percent of the vote. No need for vote fraud.

Finally, the billionaires realized what had happened. But, by then, they were too late. Fedin no longer needed them. He went after them one by one. Breaking them was easier than he expected. Every one of them was a thief. Without exception. Russia had no clean fortunes, no great inventors creating world-changing businesses. The first generation of oligarchs had simply scooped up state-owned companies during the years when the state barely existed. Ever since, their companies had disrespected the Kremlin, failing to pay even a kopek in taxes.

Fedin gave them a choice. Become partners with the state, with **his** state. Pay their share.

And, more important, give him and his men a piece of their enterprises. Or lose everything. The oligarchs scoffed. They thought they were above the law. Yet they thought the law would protect them, that their Moscow attorneys would bury the courts in paper. They thought Fedin wouldn't want to scare away Western investors by coming after them too hard. They were wrong in every way. Fedin used the judges they no longer owned to take their networks and banks and oilfields. If they argued too much, he sent them to prison or forced them into exile.

Soon enough, the fight was over. He made deals with the smart ones and broke the rest. Russia was his.

His and Nemtsov's.

Fedin feared no man. So he told himself. But he wasn't sure Nemtsov was a man. The FSB director had a welterweight's body and a full head of wavy gray hair that he wore swept back, his only affectation. He wasn't married. When he'd been younger, there had been rumors he was gay. Those rumors had vanished. Russians spoke about Nemtsov as little as possible. They weren't true, in any case. Not exactly. Nemtsov was neither gay nor straight. He played no favorites. Mainly, he liked to make his bedmates scream. And not with pleasure.

Fedin learned of Nemtsov's tastes not long after they met. The KGB residents in Prague sometimes drove their Ladas across Hungary to northern Romania, a stretch of Europe so backward it wasn't Europe at all. Forget dollars. The East German mark passed for hard currency in those hinterlands. The officers called the excursions **hunting trips**. The local women would do anything for eighty marks. The gypsies made the local women look like virgins. Nemtsov invited Fedin on a trip four months after Fedin arrived in Prague. He had a fiancée in Russia, but of course he agreed.

The station's operations chief, a drunk named Gennady who died of exposure in St. Petersburg two months after the Soviet Union dissolved—a lot of that went around in the winter of '92—pulled Fedin aside the day before he left.

"The hotel's going to be empty. Whatever you do, don't stay next to that psycho Nemtsov."

"Why?"

Gennady lifted his index finger, let it drop. "What you hear will put you off your feed."

═══

Ceaușescu's Romania wasn't high on tourist must-see lists. Arad, a city of a hundred fifty thousand, had a single two-story hotel, the President. Fedin and Nemtsov were the only guests. The clerk gave them rooms 209 and 210, across the hall from each other. Fedin thought about asking for a different room, but he couldn't say anything without being obvious.

An hour after they arrived, Nemtsov knocked on Fedin's door.

"The women are here."

"What women?"

They went down to the lobby, where twenty women waited, in all shapes and sizes. The game almost disappointed Fedin. It wasn't even hunting, more like plucking birds from a cage. The two Fedin picked said they were nineteen, and maybe they were. They were beautiful, as long as he didn't look too hard. He'd brought a pack of condoms, Ritexes from West Germany. He wasn't taking chances with local rubbers.

Nemtsov stood at the other end of the lobby, talking to a chubby woman with a boil on her nose. Not Fedin's type, but maybe Nemtsov liked witches. Fedin wandered over, tapped Nemtsov's shoulder.

"See you in the morning, then—"

Nemtsov turned. For a blink, Fedin saw something darker than murder in his eyes, something that stripped Fedin's very humanity. **Like a man looking at a bug he's about to**

stomp. Then the look was gone, replaced by a plastic smile.

"Have fun, Sergei."

The hotel's walls were a single three-centimeter layer of plaster. They might as well have been cotton. Fedin and his girls were in the middle of playing when a moan from across the hall tore through their room. They looked at one another: **Did you hear that?** Then another moan. Louder, and definitely not pleasure.

"**Spasibo, spasibo . . .**"

Fedin had brought a Walkman with him. Gennady had told him, **Bring a Walkie and you can screw the whole family and the dog, too. You don't even have to give it to them, just let them listen.** He reached for it now, but the begging stopped as abruptly as it had started. **Different strokes for different folks.** He went back to playing.

A minute later: the unmistakable screech of a cracked whip. Followed by the slap of leather cutting flesh. Followed by a muffled sob. Nemtsov must have gagged her; otherwise, she'd be screaming her lungs out. The girls grabbed their clothes and ran. Fedin didn't try to stop them.

For the next two hours, he sat on his bed and listened to Hell's soundtrack. Whimpers, muffled moans, begging. Slaps, punches, kicks, and the occasional low grunt of satisfaction. The whip cracked three more times. Why only three? Nemtsov must save it for special occasions. Fedin wondered if Nemtsov planned to kill her, but in that case why choose a hotel? The desk clerk stayed on duty all night, and their arrivals had been logged. Going across the hall and knocking on Nemtsov's door didn't even occur to Fedin. He'd have sooner booked a one-way ticket to Chernobyl.

Finally, the door across the hall opened, and someone stepped out. The woman, probably, because the tread was slow and unsteady. Fedin closed his eyes, tried to sleep.

———

The President offered a so-called full breakfast: chunks of soft gray flesh that it called sausage, brownish yellow powdered eggs, a fluorescent orange drink that was supposed to be juice. Even by Eastern European standards, the stuff was inedible. Fedin pushed it around his plate with all the enthusiasm of a line worker at Heroes of the Revolution Tractor Factory No. 6. Across the table, Nemtsov was fresh as the winter's first snow.

"Did you enjoy yourself last night, Comrade Fedin?"

"I did, Comrade Nemtsov. And you?"

"Such a **treat**."

Like they were talking about a trip to the Bolshoi. Fedin wondered if he could find an excuse to go home early.

"Not much to do in Arad," Nemtsov said, seeming to read his mind. "Perhaps we should drive back to Prague."

Fedin nearly said yes, then stopped. Nemtsov knew what he'd heard. This was a test. Fedin wasn't sure why he cared. Nemtsov might speak perfect German and French and have a degree in physics from Moscow State University, but he was a psychopath. Maybe that was **why** Fedin knew he couldn't give in. "I like it here."

"I knew I could count on you." Nemtsov pulled a plastic bag from his pocket, slid it across the table.

Inside, three pairs of earplugs. **Now we're both in on the joke.** Nemtsov grinned at Fedin. He seemed to have too many teeth. If a shark could smile.

=====

Over the years, Fedin had learned more about Nemtsov's tastes. He engaged in these sessions every few months. And he paid for them, though not always well. The FSB director had a cheap streak that his hidden billions couldn't cure. Or maybe he just wanted his victims to know how little he valued them.

He had never killed any of his conquests, as far as Fedin knew—**knew** being the operative word. Fedin had heard rumors of pretty Chechen fighters of both sexes captured in off-the-books FSB operations and never seen again after Nemtsov took custody of them. But no one had ever confirmed those stories. The few journalists who tried had an uncommonly high mortality rate.

One fact Fedin did know: Nemtsov had put in a special interrogation room at the FSB's Lubyanka headquarters with a concrete floor and a drain in its center. Agency officers called the room **Nemtsov's Stable**, a name the FSB director seemed to like. Fedin had watched interrogations there and realized that the most terrifying aspect of Nemtsov's personality was that he remained absolutely calm no matter what he was doing. He eliminated his humanity and thus did the same to his subjects. How could any human beat the Devil?

Yet after all their years working together, Fedin trusted Nemtsov. Best to think of him as a guard dog with a nasty streak. A Doberman. Keep him fed and quartered, give him plenty of rabbits to chase down, and he wouldn't turn on his master. He might not even realize he **had** a master. Plus

Fedin was sure Nemtsov knew he couldn't do Fedin's job. He couldn't hide who he was. Even the dim sunlight of Russian politics would destroy him. The Ivans had a taste for cruelty in their leaders, but they would recoil from Nemtsov. His darkness, his **otherness**.

Nemtsov's absolute amorality came in handy in another way, too. He would never protest that Fedin was going too far. For those questions, Fedin had other advisors. And despite his cruelty, Nemtsov was fair. He allowed everyone at the FSB one mistake, as long as it wasn't kept from him. He had a commitment to the truth, at least internally. Fedin understood. He lied shamelessly in public, but he demanded honesty from his advisors. In a democracy, a politician who didn't know where he stood might lose an election. In Russia, he'd lose everything.

As long as Fedin had Nemtsov, he had the FSB. For the simplest and most primal reason. The men inside Lubyanka saw Nemtsov up close. They feared him more than anyone else, and they respected Fedin because he **didn't** fear Nemtsov.

===

All this in Fedin's mind when Nemtsov called him, asked to meet. A secret tunnel ran from Lubyanka to the Kremlin, along the way passing close to the tourists who lined up to visit Lenin's tomb. The tunnel was lit, heated, and wide enough to accommodate two cars. During the Soviet era, the KGB joked it was really only one-way. KGB officials could use it as they pleased, but any Kremlin official sent to Lubyanka would not be coming back.

"I have something for you, **Sudar.**" The word was the original Russian form of **czar.** Fedin never knew if Nemtsov was using it sarcastically. A question best left unasked.

"Of course, Oleg."

"Four p.m.?"

"Perfect."

Nemtsov was famous for his punctuality. He arrived at Fedin's office precisely at 4. Fedin hugged him, kissed his cheeks, closed the heavy wooden double doors behind them.

"The usual?" Fedin poured two generous shots of pepper-flavored vodka.

"L'chaim," Nemtsov said, their usual toast, its origins lost to history. Neither man was Jewish.

"L'chaim." They clinked and drank and sat on Fedin's new couch. It was black, with subtle silver striping, made by a French company that special-ized in one-of-a-kind furniture. It had cost two hundred thousand euros. It felt the same against Fedin's rear end as every other couch.

Nemtsov wasn't much for small talk. The year before, Fedin had asked after Nemtsov's mother, Martina. Nemtsov had tartly said, **Yes, she has cancer, of the ovaries. They found it two months ago. She's at the hospital in Petersburg, she'll die in a few weeks**, with all the emotion of a man talking about his dinner plans.

"The American spy," he said now.

"The colonel, yes." At this point, Eric Birman had been working for them for more than a year.

"If his cousin Paul is president, he'll be at the center of it."

"And if a horse could hire a tractor to plow, it would."

"The cousin can win."

Knowledge of democratic politics wasn't Nemtsov's strong suit. "The only way he gets elected is if the jihadis blow up New York, Oleg." To Fedin's enormous surprise, Nemtsov smiled. "Don't tell me you know there's an attack coming."

"Better, Sergei."

For the next half hour, Nemtsov outlined his plan. Put an FSB team of illegals into the United States with plenty of clean money. Ideally, the team would find Muslims and other Americans who could be fooled into carrying out attacks. If not, they would go ahead themselves, although in that case the attacks, obviously, wouldn't be suicide.

"The risks, impossible."

"Not if we bring the money and the team in cleanly. The Americans will be happy to blame jihadis."

"You think this alone will be enough to elect Birman?"

"You're the expert on politics. But it surely won't help Mr. CIA."

That much was true. Duto's great claim to power was the way he'd kept the United States safe from terrorism, first as the CIA director, now as president. At the least, a new wave of attacks would make him respond against Muslim terrorists. And Russia would offer to help.

For a price, of course.

If Duto wouldn't cooperate? Nemtsov was right. A big attack couldn't help but boost Birman. Terrorism was all he talked about, terrorism and Mexico. Too bad the FSB couldn't come up with **Mexican** terrorists . . .

"You're sure they can't trace the money?"

"We both know there are ways to make money untraceable, Sergei."

True. "This team, they can pass for American? Even if they're arrested?"

Fedin saw he'd asked the right question. Nemtsov poured them both another shot of vodka, smaller ones. He raised his glass. Fedin didn't.

"In daily life, yes. Not if they're arrested," Nemtsov finally said. "But they won't be. They're too good. They find the right **polezniye duraki**, wind them up." The term literally meant **useful idiots**. During the Cold War, the KGB had used it to refer to Communists in the West who parroted Soviet positions. "Then they disappear."

"Killing American civilians." Fedin didn't particularly care about a few hundred dead, even a few thousand. But if they were caught . . . what would the Americans do?

"They won't be caught, Sergei." After so many years, Nemtsov could read Fedin's mind. "But if they are . . . they were a rogue unit, they vanished, we don't know who they were working for. Like the plane." Nemtsov meant MH17, the Malaysia Airlines 777 that a pro-Russian Ukrainian militia had shot down in 2014. Two hundred ninety-eight passengers and crew had died. But no one had gone to war over MH17. No one had even stopped doing business with Russia over it.

The Americans wouldn't go to war either. Not without ironclad evidence. They'd be furious, yes. But these unconventional operations denied the enemy a clean answer. They provoked inquests and reports and fact-finding commissions. Not war.

"It'll be a treat, Sergei."

A treat. A strange phrase for this operation. Fedin couldn't remember when Nemtsov had said it before. Then he could. In Romania.

Another thought, unexpected, snuck into his mind. If everything went wrong . . . maybe the failure would give him the chance to rid himself of Nemtsov. Replace him with an FSB director who would be loyal not by choice but from necessity. Necessity was better.

Fedin tried to banish the idea. He didn't even like having it with Nemtsov just a couple meters away. As if the man could read his very thoughts. But there it was.

Fedin sat back against his ridiculous couch. Raised his glass. "Don't get caught, Oleg."

———

Nemtsov had told Fedin little about the FSB's progress since that conversation. Fedin preferred not to know. Ignorance made his conversations with Duto easier. Besides, Nemtsov would come to Fedin only if he had a problem.

So the attack in Dallas surprised Fedin as much as anyone. Naturally, he called Duto to offer his condolences. Duto accepted them tersely. Fedin didn't say anything about remaking Russia's relationship with the United States. He'd have more chances later.

Fedin expected Paul Birman's popularity would rise. Even so, the strength of Birman's surge surprised him. Suddenly the Tennessee senator was the Republican front-runner. His warnings of terrorism were now prophetic, not fearmongering.

═══

The bigger surprise came a few days later, at what Fedin expected would be a routine meeting with Nemtsov.

"There's a problem with Grad." Eric Birman. "His attitude toward what's happening with his cousin is not what we expected."

"Meaning?"

"He doesn't want Paul to be president. In fact, his controller suspects he would sabotage Paul himself."

Fedin didn't bother to ask how Eric would stop his cousin. Something sexual, no doubt. Men like Paul Birman always had histories. The more they said they loved their wives, the more sure Fedin was. Fedin wondered about killing Eric, but then they'd simply lose their source. "Can we pressure him?"

"Controller says no. Family, you know." Nemtsov's tone was dull. Humans. So emotional. So difficult. "There is another way."

Suddenly Fedin wanted a drink. He knew before Nemtsov spoke that whatever Nemtsov was about to propose would be dangerous.

"A surgery." The FSB euphemism for **assassination.**

"Of Eric? But he's our source."

"Not Eric. **Paul.**"

"Paul—"

"Imagine it. This man, cut down by a sniper's bullet as he speaks about Islamic terror. His cousin beside him, trying to save him, covered in his blood. The cousin already a soldier, a hero of the War on Terror. Now he runs for president to carry on his family's legacy."

"He understands this possibility?" Meaning: **Is Eric Birman all right with our killing his cousin?**

"His controller thinks so. We'll check."

"Madness."

"Eric Birman, President of the United States. **Our agent.** Even if he doesn't touch any of their policies, he'll give us every secret."

"And if we're caught—"

"If we were going to be caught, we would have been already, with the bomb. This is simple. This sniper we've found, he's an ugly man. We're giving him the sweetest honey of his life. He'll do whatever we ask. He **wants** to. He's in love."

"Enough to shoot a senator?"

"Happily. His first target's a priest." Nemtsov smirked. "Tell you what. After he does that one, you call Duto. If he gives you what you want, forget it."

"I need to think about this, Oleg. Remember, we've already won. The Americans are furious at the Muslims. Better one step too few than one too many."

"As you wish, **Sudar**."

Fedin sat alone. He'd been worse than foolish to think that he could control this operation. His old friend had boxed him in like a rat. If he backed off, Nemtsov would make sure the top of the Kremlin and FSB knew, **Fedin lost his nerve, missed a once-in-a-hundred-years chance.** If he fired Nemtsov, he'd provoke open war inside the FSB. Fedin might win, since Nemtsov had no base outside the agency. More likely, some new shark would take advantage of the power struggle to ruin them both.

Still. A United States senator. The head of the Senate Intelligence Committee. A presidential candidate.

Why was Nemtsov forcing this choice on him? Fedin feared the most banal of reasons. Nemtsov was **bored**. The Kremlin wasn't open to him. He had long since accumulated all the power he could have inside FSB. He had no wife, no children or grandchildren, nothing to soothe his slow descent into his sixties, the sun far from set but its downward arc unmistakable. Despite his billions of dollars, Nemtsov took no pleasure in yachts or cars or art. His only hobbies were chess and making whores bleed. A false flag operation to put a Russian agent in the White House: Here was a project worthy of his talents.

Fedin wondered if he should call Nemtsov back to his office, if their alliance could survive an honest conversation about motives and power. **In the end, I have the country and the army, Oleg. Even if you keep the FSB, the best you can do is destroy us both.** But Nemtsov would only insist that Fedin was wrong: **You can trust me, Comrade Sergei, now and forever.** He'd walk back to Lubyanka—underground, where he belonged, where he was comfortable. Fedin would spend the rest of his life waiting for his counterattack.

Maybe Nemtsov was right. The bombing had been the more complex mission, more chances for mistakes. Fedin had seen the FSB's honeypot operatives. If one of them had her hooks in this poor sap of a sniper . . .

As a rule, Fedin was willing to take chances. Even when missions went wrong, like when those idiot Ukrainians shot down MH17 and **bragged about it**, he didn't second-guess. But the stakes were so high this time.

Maybe Duto would save him from having to make it.

Now the sniper had done his work in Missouri. **A perfect shot**, the reporters said. Fedin slept restlessly, dreamed he was watching television, Nemtsov whipping a woman until her skin was a carpet of blood. Fedin tried to change the channel, but he couldn't find the remote.

At 6 a.m., he gave up on sleep, showered, shaved, felt better immediately. Outside, the day was black and cold, but Fedin didn't mind. A Russian winter morning. Five hundred such mornings had done in the Germans. Fedin headed to his windowless private office to drink coffee and wait for Duto's call.

It came just at 7. Both sides had translators available, but usually the two men spoke in English. Fedin's was more than passable. "Mr. President."

"Mr. President." Duto's voice was low and gravelly, as if he were too tired even to hide his exhaustion. "You called to tell me how sorry you are."

"I called to tell you that we need to make this stop. In your country and mine."

"How do you propose we do that? Since we aren't even sure yet who did this."

"Russia is your ally."

Fedin could hear Duto's breathing. A wounded bear.

"In return?"

"This isn't the moment for that."

"Let me guess, Sergei. Cooperation on Ukraine. Cooperation on Syria. Maybe let you buy our best software so you can design that fifth-generation fighter you've been promising for twenty years."

"To be treated with respect, yes."

"And dropping the sanctions. How could I forget?" Duto made a noise that was half growl and half groan. The sound of a man who'd put enough liquor in himself to say what he thought. "Thanks, but we'll find whoever's doing this all by ourselves. I would hate to think Russia was using dead Americans for its own benefit."

"We only want to help—"

"Then let me sleep, Sergei. While you and

Oleg Nemtsov do what it is you do all day. Bite the heads off chickens or whatever. That way, I can pretend this conversation was a bad dream."

You'll regret this, Fedin almost said. **To speak to the president of the Russian Federation this way.**

"As you like. Good night."

Duto hung up without another word.

<hr />

Fedin laid down the phone. How could he ever have imagined Duto would listen to reason? The Americans and their arrogance.

He'd made a mistake. He needed to correct it.

He punched in a number.

Nemtsov picked up after two rings. "Comrade Fedin?"

Fedin didn't answer right away. They were both silent. Nemtsov's home had no background noise. No surprise, it never did. Fedin sometimes imagined he lived inside a vault. It was possible. Even Fedin had never seen the inside of Nemtsov's home.

"To what do I owe this honor?" Nemtsov finally said.

"I should never have doubted you, Oleg."

19

Even the makeup artists in the television green rooms treated Paul Birman differently these days. They took their time, used the hundred-dollar foundation, the stuff that smoothed his pores without giving him a clownish glow-in-the-dark tint. They no longer chatted while they worked either. Like he was too important for them to bother him with their petty thoughts.

Paul talked to them instead. **At** them. They nodded their heads at his brilliance like he was Moses bringing down the Commandments. Paul liked having his ass kissed as much the next rich guy turned senator. But he already saw how this much flattery could be confusing. When he reached the White House, the bubble would be even worse.

If. Not when. He hadn't won anything yet.

Though he knew he would.

He was making the rounds of the morning shows to start the week. The calls to his press secretary had begun not even twenty minutes after the Associated Press flashed a bulletin about Luke Hurley's death. Fox and CNN and MSNBC wanted to interview him on Sunday afternoon while the body was still warm. Paul talked it over with Eric. They both agreed the answer should be no. Not just because the timing was vaguely ghoulish. Before Paul shed tears for Hurley as a modern-day Christian martyr, they should be sure the guy hadn't been screwing choirboys. Anyway, if the sniper really had shot Hurley for his religion, the story would only get bigger.

So it did. By late afternoon, the bookers were practically begging. Normally, the shows wanted exclusivity—or at least semi-exclusivity, meaning no more than one appearance on a competing network. Not this time. Paul hadn't had this many pretty women on their backs for him since he left Los Angeles thirty years ago, a time in his life he tried his best to forget, though he couldn't pretend he hadn't enjoyed himself back then.

Then the Intelligence Committee staff told Eric that the FBI agents combing through Hurley's past had found no skeletons in their first pass. The guy paid his bills, loved his family, drove a minivan, mowed the lawn at his church-owned house. He even ministered once a week at a homeless shelter in St. Louis. Of course, the investigation might find something in a week or two, but real trouble usually popped up almost immediately.

Paul and Eric decided he would start with Fox, his base, then hit the rest in order of audience size.

———

He woke up with the sentences he was going to speak already chiseled in his head. His first hit was at 7:30 a.m. Eastern. He arrived early, had the makeup room at 400 North Capitol to himself. Eric was outside, doing his chief of staff thing, talking or texting or both at once. Paul's driver and bodyguard waited unobtrusively in the corner as the makeup woman, a chubby fifty-something—Samantha, Sabrina, he'd been here enough times, he should remember—gave him one last touch with her brush.

"You're good."

"Am I?"

"Senator, I wouldn't lie to you."

"Thanks to you, Selena." **Selena. For the win. And, yes!**

She gave him a sheepish smile—**You remem-**

bered!—as the Fox producer stepped into the room. "Three minutes." Lesser guests endured what the bookers called pre-interviews, discussions of their expertise, what they planned to say. The elite showed up, had their faces painted, and walked on.

"Thanks." Paul said **Thanks** more than ever. His good Tennessee manners at work. The word the magic carpet on which he floated through his day. He stood, smoothed his suit, craned his head so a tech could attach a tiny microphone to his suit. The new mics were so reliable that the producers could dispense with the **Can you count to ten for me?** routine that had been a staple for decades.

"You'll have two segments, but if you want to go longer, that's fine."

"Thanks."

═══════

They put him in the chair as the show went to commercial. **Fox & Friends** was filmed in New York. Under normal circumstances, not being on set with the anchors could be dangerous. It gave the hosts the power to dictate interviews. They could make guests look deer-in-the-headlights helpless, staring at the wrong camera, trying to answer one question as the next rolled in.

But Paul knew they were on his side today, and he planned to use his isolation, the chance to speak unimpeded, to his advantage.

"Back in five . . . four . . . three . . ."

The screen to Paul's right filled with the face of Steve Doocy, the show's senior host, grave and serious. Paul stared straight at the camera.

"We're here with Senator Paul Birman of Tennessee, chairman of the Intelligence Committee. To talk about the tragic shooting in Missouri yesterday, the killing of Pastor Luke Hurley as his family watched. Senator, we know the FBI is considering terrorism as a motive in this case. What can you tell us?"

Showtime.

"Steve, thank you for having me on. First of all, let me say my thoughts and prayers are with Pastor Hurley's wife and children and his parishioners. By all accounts, he was an exemplary man, a true Christian leading a Christian life." Always work **thoughts and prayers** in first. Besides, this time Paul might even be telling the truth.

"Of course, Senator. We're already hearing about his good works. And then, yesterday, to be cut down **outside his own church—**" A perfect lead-in. Paul didn't have to watch the monitor to know Doocy was slowly shaking his head.

"Yes, Steve. We can't be sure yet, but the early

indications are that Luke Hurley was killed for his religion. We need to let the authorities investigate. But here's what we know already. Terrorism is a cancer spreading across the United States. President Duto's inability to face this threat head-on gives these killers aid and comfort. Nearly a month has passed, and we have no evidence as to who ordered the attack in Dallas. No plan to bring the perpetrators to justice. I don't want to think that in a month I'm going to be back here talking about how Luke Hurley's shooter is still on the loose, still terrorizing Christians all over this country. Yet I fear that's exactly what will happen. President Duto needs to step up or get out of the way."

"Are you saying the President should resign?"

"I don't want him to resign. I want him to **act**. And, by the way, if he's so confident that we have the terrorist threat contained, it would be nice to see him join us commoners outside the White House security bubble."

The interview went on another few minutes, but Paul already knew he'd won. Fox would run **President Duto needs to step up or get out of the way** fifty times today. He was happy with his dodge of the resignation question, too. Saying Duto should resign would have sounded ridiculous. Presidents didn't resign. But flat out saying

no would have disappointed his hard-core supporters. He'd found the perfect middle ground.

———

He came out of the studio to find Eric, arms
folded, frowning. "Everything okay? I thought I
killed it."

"Someone called in bomb threats to your offices in Tennessee this morning. And this morning Gloria and your housekeeper both heard two
shots outside the mansion. There's no sign anything hit the house, but Gloria wants you to call
right away. She's really upset."

Paul was more angry than frightened. How
dare they come after his family? Yet he felt something else, too, an emotion he needed a moment
to recognize. **Pride.**

Even the bad guys knew who he was.

"I've already called Sean Flynn," Eric said.
"We'll see him at noon."

"Who?"

"Chief of the Capitol Police. In my opinion,
you're reaching a presidential-level profile, and
they should give you full-time protection the way
they do for the leaders." The Secret Service protected the president, but Congress had its own
dedicated security force, the Capitol Police. The
police guarded the Capitol complex and provided

security details to the House and Senate majority and minority leaders. Other lawmakers didn't receive full-time protection even after the shooting of Gabrielle Giffords and Steve Scalise.

"I trust Jimmy." Jimmy Sanders, his bodyguard.

"I do, too, but he's only one guy. Let's see what Flynn says."

"Thanks, Eric."

"You're the franchise."

═══

The Capitol Police were headquartered in a handsome six-story building on D Street, near Union Station. Like the rest of the Washington security complex, the force had grown vastly since September 11. In the nineties, even the majority leaders hadn't had guards, only drivers. Now the force had more than two thousand officers, including bomb squads, undercover agents, and a chemical and biological response team. It regularly locked down the streets near the Capitol in response to threats.

Flynn's office was on the top floor, with a view southwest over the Capitol dome. The man himself was in his late forties, hearty, with muscled arms that suggested he rarely missed a day at the gym.

"Senator Birman. Saw you on Fox this morning. A pleasure to meet you in person." He gave Paul a big smile, the kind that spelled bad news. Paul decided to let his cousin handle the conversation. He nodded at Eric.

"Chief Flynn—" Eric said.

"Call me Sean, Colonel. Can I get either of you coffee?"

"I trust you've seen the reports from this morning."

"I have. The threat cycle is picking up. Fifteen members received calls to their offices today."

"How many of those had shots fired at their homes? Or were on six different networks this morning?"

Flynn raised his oven-mitt hands. "I get it, I promise. If the Senator receives a specific threat to a specific appearance, we will be there ourselves, we'll liaise with the local police, the FBI. But barring that, we have five hundred thirty-five members to protect, and you guys and gals are way more active than the President. To your credit. But it makes you tough to watch, you understand. To have even one officer watching each of you full-time, I'd need a force at least three times this size. No joke."

"We're not asking you to protect five hundred thirty-five members. We're asking for one."

"Can't play favorites. Not that your colleagues

would let me. I can just imagine what Chuck Schumer would say—hypothetically speaking, of course—" Flynn shook his head. "Good news is, I know Jimmy Sanders. He's very capable. And if you want recommendations for more body-guards, I can help."

"You think I should pay for my own protec-tion?" Paul said.

"I really am sorry, Senator."

———

"At least he was honest," Paul said in the elevator down.

"We'll hire some folks. May take a couple weeks, I want to get the right people, but we'll find them."

"My number one priority is keeping Gloria safe. And the kids. Forget me."

"Understood."

———

Eric Birman looked into his cousin's eyes, saw Paul was telling the truth. Or believed he was, anyway. Maybe for the first time in his life, Eric found himself proud of Lucky Cousin Paul.

Ironic.

Not worried? You should be, he wanted to tell his cousin. **Scared to death.**

20

Monday morning, a courier showed up at Wells's hotel room with a Colombian passport for Coyle in the name of Raul Moreno and an American one for Wells in the name of James Walsh. Plus a garment bag that held shiny silvery shirts and black jeans for Coyle, a lightweight suit for Wells. **Look the part,** the note inside said.

"I'd ask how she knows our sizes, but of course she knows our sizes," Coyle said. "She's a genie. With no wish limit."

"Don't get used to it. When this is done and they send you to Nicaragua and the station's air-conditioning kicks out twice a month and you have a broken chair and a view of a blast wall and your chief tells you to chase a lead in the Ministry of Transport and, by the way, don't lose any more receipts, this will seem like a pleasant dream."

"I'm going to enjoy it, then."

"Speaking of, let's go to the Four Seasons. I want you calling Banamex from a landline that suits Raul Moreno's tastes."

═══════

Wells spent the morning coaching Coyle on what to say. And how to say it:

Don't be too polite, you're rich, you give orders. As far as you're concerned, these bankers are a bunch of trained seals. You want Mendoz only, no one else. They're not going to like that, but stick to it. You want to buy a place in Miami, you heard she could help. They ask you why her, someone you know recommended her. No details. You and your American lawyer—no, advisor, lawyer is checkable and advisor **isn't—will tell her what she needs to know face-to-face. Nothing about where the money comes from. Make sure they know you're busy, you want this as soon as possible, but no deadline, that gives them a chance to say no.**

Coyle called, had a conversation shorter than Wells would have liked, clicked off.

"They'll call back. They asked me how I liked the Four Seasons. They obviously knew the number. Got weird when I asked for Mendoz, said she didn't meet new clients without a reference. I said her or no one. They asked me if I had proof of the money. I told them, Of course."

"Sounds good. Now we wait. For them and Tarnes."

Around 3 p.m., Wells's phone buzzed. Tarnes.

"A gentleman from the Royal Cayman Bank is going to call in the next ten minutes. He has some know-your-customer questions."

"Meaning?"

"Meaning under the new anti-laundering rules, banks can't just open accounts for anyone who walks in. The more money you want to deposit, the more questions they're supposed to ask. An American bank, an account of this size, they'd want specifics about how you make your money. What business you're in. Maybe even a tax return. If the Cayman bankers want access to the global money transfer system, they have to follow the same rules. In theory. In reality, the way it goes is, they ask. But if you won't tell them, you say you don't want to talk about your business, hint maybe you're trying to move assets in front of a divorce, they'll just go to the default question: Is the money from an illegal source? And you say?"

"No."

"Very good. No. Pure as the driven snow. You're offended they've even raised the issue. They ask a few more times. And that's it. By close of business today, Raul Moreno will be the beneficiary of an account at Royal Cayman Bank held by the Leverdeep Trust Company of Bridgetown, Barbados. The wire will hit overnight. A balance of five million six hundred eighty thousand two hundred five dollars."

Wells wondered why she hadn't gone with an even five million, realized she was right. A round number would look odd.

"That's good enough for Banamex? They know they can take it and move it to the U.S.?"

"My understanding is, the money will still be too hot to cross the border without raising flags. Maybe Banamex routes it through another bank. Chops it into a bunch of smaller accounts, trades Mexican stocks with it. Pork bellies. Piñata imports. My guy didn't really explain, since it doesn't matter, the money's just an excuse to get you in, right? If you must know, ask Mendoz when you talk to her. The paperwork will hit during the day tomorrow, but if all you need is an account number for a screen grab, you'll have that by the morning."

"I need to sign anything promising I'll give it back?"

"The big boss laughed when I asked. So I guess not."

The room phone rang. Wells hung up as Coyle answered.

Royal Cayman Bank, Wells wrote. **$5.7 million. Trust in Barbados. Account details in morning.** Coyle would have to handle the rest. Coyle's end of the conversation seemed to consist mostly of **Sí** and **No**. Then, "Frietas. Hector Frietas. **Sí, Quito.**" He listened for a while. "**Sí, sí . . . Mañana.**"

He hung up. "They'll call us in the morning to set a time."

"Why'd you mention Frietas?"

"They weren't going to bite. Said they had to have a name. I figured, he's dead, his phone's in the jungle somewhere, not like he can tell them anything. If we're wrong, Mendoz doesn't know him, we find out now. If we're right, she's his contact, his name should get us in. Sure enough, I said it, you heard. A minute later, she told me to come in tomorrow with a statement and we'd talk."

Wells realized Coyle was right. "Nice play."

"This job's not bad."

Wells flashed to Bogotá, Tony bleeding to death in the back of the cab. **Until it bites you,** he almost said. But Coyle would learn soon enough, if he hadn't already.

Tuesday morning, 6:30 a.m. Wells was stepping out of the shower when the room door rattled. He opened up, found Coyle.

"You ever sleep?"

"Turn on the TV."

CNN again, an overhead shot, SWAT trucks clustered around a stately house. Then at ground level, an epilepsy-inducing number of red-and-blue lights flashing, white sedans with CHICAGO POLICE painted in red. Behind them, a black wrought-iron fence and snow-dusted lawn.

The crawl told the story:

CARDINAL OF CHICAGO KILLED IN PREDAWN SNIPER ATTACK . . . JAMES MCDONNELL, 59, FOUND DEAD IN HIS HOME ON CITY'S NORTH SIDE . . . SHOOTING OCCURRED AROUND 5 A.M., POLICE SAY . . .

MCDONNELL HEADED CHICAGO ARCHDIO-CESE, SERVING 2.5 MILLION CATHOLICS . . . IN STATEMENT, POPE "DEPLORES" VIOLENCE, CALLS FOR CALM . . . POLICE AND FBI SAY SHOOTING "BEARS RESEMBLANCE" TO SUNDAY KILLING OF MEGACHURCH PREACHER LUKE HURLEY IN ST. PETERS, MISSOURI . . .

"Guess you were right about Missouri." Coyle hesitated. "You think this connects to Dallas somehow? The Russians killing clergy now? Stirring us up even more?"

Wells watched the CNN crawl: MCDONNELL KNOWN FOR HARD-LINE STANCE ON INTERFAITH RELATIONS: "HARD TO FIND COMMON GROUND WITH PEOPLE WHO WANT TO BLOW THEMSELVES UP," HE SAID AFTER DALLAS ATTACK . . .

"Assuming it's not a copycat. I guess so. The timing is so close." And these killings felt professional to Wells the same way the Dallas attack had. Not that his old friends couldn't do damage, but they left loose ends. They were rarely so slick.

"Shouldn't the Russians be putting out some fake claim of responsibility, then? Leaving a Quran at the hide?"

"They've got time, if that's the game. Plus, if we're right about Dallas, Shakir didn't know how they were using him. This guy, if it's the same, they want to keep it that way."

"So this sniper, he doesn't see any **religious** connection to what he's doing, killing priests?"

The theory sounded ridiculous when Coyle phrased it that way. "I don't know. Maybe they've twisted him up somehow. Shafer said last night we're not seeing some big part of this, and he's right."

"What if they're working up to their real target? Like the Pope."

"Not bad. He coming to the United States anytime soon?"

Coyle pulled his phone, tapped away. "Three months, he'll be in California and Texas."

But that theory didn't work either. The sniper or whoever was using him had to know he'd just dramatically increased the odds he'd be caught. A second shooting in less than forty-eight hours would inevitably leave clues. And the killing of a cardinal was deeply provocative, to say the least. The FBI would make this case equal to the Dallas investigation as a priority.

Under those circumstances, three months on the run was an eternity. Besides, if the sniper's ultimate target was the Pope, he was making his job harder by killing high-profile religious leaders. Even under normal circumstances, only the President had more protection than the Pope. If the shooter was still on the loose when the Pope was set to arrive, the security would be off the charts. The Vatican's own security team might even try to postpone the trip.

"I think it's something closer to home," Wells said.

"The President?"

"Nah, he's practically untouchable even when he travels. And they'll find excuses to lock him down until they get a handle on this."

Wells's phone buzzed. He knew without looking: Tarnes.

"Anything from Mendoz?" Her voice tense.

"Meeting her today. Good morning, sunshine."

"You think this is funny, John?"

"Hilarious."

"A hundred ten threats to mosques already this morning. Only a matter of time before some idiot firebombs one."

Or worse. "Have they confirmed the shootings are related?"

"Ballistics will come back in a couple hours, but the betting is yes. FBI puts the shot at seven hundred yards. And he was gone fast. They think he's got a rolling nest like the Beltway guys. You think this is related to Dallas, John?"

Wells wasn't ready yet to tell Tarnes what he and Shafer had figured out. Not until after he talked to Mendoz. "I have to guess, I'd say probably."

"That case you sure you don't want to go at Mendoz officially? Bring in the FBI? Might be faster—"

"Faster? Say the FBI jumps on this today. Which they won't be happy about, they hate this kind of lead out of left field, but Duto can make them. First, she isn't American, they don't even have jurisdiction, they have to ask the Mexican government to interview her. The Bureau is the Bureau. It wants to be sure it can make cases. Rules are rules, even when people are getting shot. Fine, the Mexicans aren't happy, they say yes, but it takes two days. Second, we ask Mendoz to talk. She says, What for? We tell her. If she has any sense, she tells us to get lost."

"But the bank can make her. Or just open the records itself."

"Sure, but they'll need a warrant, or whatever the equivalent is down here, I'm no expert. But even with a friendly judge, I'm not sure we can get a warrant in Mexico based on hearsay from the wife of a dead man in Ecuador. Not to mention that Graciela didn't even know Mendoz's name. That's another couple days gone, into next week. Then we go up the chain, tell Citi it's in trouble. Someone in New York realizes the stakes, flies here, makes Banamex lift its skirts, warrant or not. But that's, what, next Wednesday, Thursday? A week, for sure."

"In other words, you're in control, and you like it that way."

"Let's see what Mendoz says today. If Coyle and I can't get to her, we'll do it your way."

Tarnes hung up.

"You done flirting so we can get to the Four Seasons?" Coyle said.

═══

Mendoz called at 10:30. Coyle was smiling when he hung up. "Meeting's at three."

═══

The high-net-worth offices were in an oversized town house in the southern part of Polanco, near Chapultepec Park. Wells and Coyle passed through a metal detector into a waiting room, with lesser Impressionists on its pastel walls, hidden speakers playing string music. The style suggested Banamex's clients were of a certain age. Wells and Coyle were the only people waiting. Wells realized they weren't really inside the bank. Two armed guards watched the steel door between the lobby and the rest of the building. Wells suspected there was a separate entrance, maybe through the garage, for known clients.

He wondered if the security was for show. This bank probably handled very little cash. But the tension on the faces of the guards suggested otherwise. The clients themselves were the targets. A forty-something woman wearing a diamond that should have been measured in ounces rather than carats emerged from the inner sanctum. Her bodyguards gave Coyle hard looks as they passed. Maybe Tarnes had done too good a job dressing him like a narco.

Ten minutes later, the door opened again to reveal a man in a gray suit. He could have been running for Congress. He gave Wells and Coyle the pained smile of a man who'd walked into a meeting an hour late, extended a hand to Wells. "Buenas tardes. Yo soy Manuel Lagares—"

"Buenas tardes, but I think my client is the one you want."

Lagares had a conversation in Spanish with Coyle that ended with Coyle handing over their passports and a statement from Royal Cayman Bank they'd printed at the Four Seasons. Lagares looked over the numbers like they were written in crayon. He'd be in for a surprise when he called the bank.

Ten minutes after that, Lagares reappeared. This time, his smile looked at least half real. Royal Cayman had done its part. Wells and Coyle would meet Mendoz with her guard down. Downish, anyway.

Lagares led them through the security door, up a single flight of stairs. The floors were wood, and none of the doors were marked. The classical music continued. Banamex seemed to intend the offices to have the feel of an exclusive club. Wells hoped the atmosphere would work to their advantage, lulling Mendoz a little.

Lagares led them to a conference room that overlooked the town house's garden, lush and wide and deep. Three jacaranda trees stood at the back, their flowers almost hiding the barbed wire atop the back wall. Wells and Coyle turned down Lagares's offer of a drink. He walked out and Mendoz entered.

In person, she had the smooth, shiny glow that came from expensive chemical peels and a little too much Botox. She wore a dark blue suit and skirt with subtle pink piping. She looked the part, a stylish middle-aged woman whom clients could trust. Charming, not glib. Rich, not too rich. She held brochures in one hand, what looked like a contract in the other. No passports. Wells suspected their disappearance wasn't an accident and would be mentioned if they misbehaved.

"Mr. Moreno. Mr. Walsh. I apologize in advance, my English is not perfect." In fact, it was smooth, lightly accented. As well groomed as everything else about her. Her brown eyes shifted between them, a frank effort to understand who they were, why they'd come here. "Mr. Frietas sent you."

Wells had planned to approach her cautiously, see what she might give up about how she and

Frietas had operated. But now that they were here, waiting felt wrong. Although she'd agreed to meet, she was suspicious. Better to hit her hard and fast, try to shake her. Anyway, they needed records from her, not a primer on Banamex's skills at moving money.

"Is this room wired, Ms. Mendoz?"

"Wired?"

"You know what I mean."

"That's not how we treat our clients."

"We're not clients yet." Wells leaned over the table. "I'm asking for your protection. Not mine."

"I don't understand, Mr. Walsh."

"I'd like us to be friends. That'll be easier if we can talk honestly."

If Mendoz could have knitted her brow through the Botox, she would have. She looked at the door as if she was considering calling for help. Then she seemed to decide she'd better hear what Wells had to say.

"It's a fine day. May I show you our back garden?"

Up close, the garden was slightly tatty, a space meant to be seen through windows rather than in person. An apartment building loomed over it from the north, ruining its privacy. Broken paving stones were tucked in a corner where they couldn't be seen from the house.

Mendoz arranged three chairs in a triangle close to the jacaranda trees by the back wall.

"Beautiful," Coyle said. "I didn't realize the jacaranda bloomed so early."

Wells read Mendoz's mind: **Enough small talk. This isn't going to be fun, let's get to it.**

"I don't know what Hector told you," she said.

"Hector didn't tell us anything, Alina. He's dead. His wife killed him and dumped him in the jungle."

"You're lying."

"Guess again. I saw a piece of his skull."

"I remind you I have your passports—"

"Keep 'em. We'll get more."

She stood. "You need to leave."

"Sit **down**."

She didn't sit, but she didn't walk away.

"We're not looking for you to clean money. And we're not looking to arrest you. We're not DEA. We came here to talk to you face-to-face."

Now she sat.

"Before she killed him, Hector told his wife he sent some Russians to you. This was about a year ago. They needed clean accounts that they could use inside the United States. You set those up."

She smiled. Wells could read her mind. **That all you got?** "I don't know any Russians."

"They came in with twenty million dollars. Say, eighteen, if they paid Hector two. What's your cut? Ten percent? Fifteen? Three million dollars. Not bad for a few hours' work, printing out contracts. You could even use the fancy paper, the heavy stock."

"Do you have the names of these people? Their passport numbers? Anything at all?"

"Hector knew one of them as Anatoly Vanin."

"I've never heard that name."

"They were behind the attack in Dallas."

A glimmer of surprise flitted across her smooth face, a breeze ruffling a sun-dappled lake. "That was crazy Arabs. The usual."

"Those Russians tricked them into carrying out the attack."

"You have proof?"

"Yes, but I can't show you."

She hesitated, and Wells thought he caught a flash of uncertainty in her eyes.

"Do you think we showed up here to ruin your day because we care about narcos buying apartments in L.A.?"

"Mr. Walsh, Mr. Romero—whatever your names are—I can't help you. Even if I wanted to."

"Because you have to protect your customers'

privacy?" Coyle said. "We'll come back. And when we do, we'll have warrants. And this will be ten times worse."

"When that happens—if that happens—fine."

"Why not now?" Wells said.

"You want to know? Really?"

"Sí."

"Suppose I am what you say. And I help you. If my clients ever find out what I've done . . ." She trailed off.

"But they must know that you're a bank, sometimes the authorities have questions—"

"If it comes through the courts, officially, fine, I can't stop it. They may not like it, but they won't blame me. But if I personally do this, it's different."

"We understand," Coyle said. "It's okay."

Coyle was trying to do the right thing. Unfortunately, at this moment, they needed the wrong thing.

"Sergeant, give us a moment."

The anger in Coyle's eyes suggested he might argue. Then his Marine chain-of-command training kicked in, and he walked away.

Wells leaned toward Mendoz. "No one will ever know that you talked."

"You can't guarantee that."

"We're not going to tell. You sure aren't. Hector's dead. The Russians will have other problems when we find them. They've got nothing to do with narcos, anyway. And guess what? Next week, the week after, we'll come back with warrants and lock this all down."

"Then why do you need me?"

"Next week, too long. The shooting this morning in Chicago, it might be connected, too."

She shook her head.

"**Listen.** Give us what we need, I'll give you a pass for Dallas. I believe you didn't know what they had planned."

"Big promise from a man who won't even tell me his real name."

"But if you don't agree, forget whatever the lawyers tell you about how Mexico won't extradite for financial crimes. Just hope the Russians don't kill anyone else."

Wells waited, and finally she cracked.

"Why?" A frightened edge in her voice.

Wells leaned in close enough to smell her lilac scent. He had to make her fear him more than she feared the traffickers, his only chance. He stroked the back of her right hand with his left middle finger. Crude and unwanted intimacy.

She didn't flinch, but a tendon in her neck quivered.

"If they do, I'll kill you myself. I'll blow that

armored BMW of yours. Shoot you while you're at a spa with your girlfriends."

"You can't." Her voice trembled.

"You think I'm American government. You think I have rules." Wells shook his head.

"The narcos—"

"They don't care about you. They're too busy with each other. They scare you, leave the country, go to Madrid, they'll never think about you again. Not me. Four hundred people died in Dallas. I won't forget."

Wells looked Mendoz over. She'd held up, considering, but her breathing came fast. Another line crossed. He had never gone after a civilian this way. But Alina Mendoz wasn't exactly a civilian. Maybe.

======

"Wait here." She walked off, short steps on stiff legs. She left the garden, slammed the door, threw the bolt shut.

Coyle came over. Wells expected he'd protest. He didn't. "Let her off the hook too easy, didn't I?"

"She's probably coming back with the cops."

"What'd you say?"

Wells shook his head: **You don't want to know.**

He wondered if Mendoz believed his threat. He wondered if he believed it himself.

He and Coyle sat silently as a helicopter circled overhead. Jacaranda petals fluttered down, providing a counterpoint to the sirens ringing in the distance. After a while, they died out. But the quiet didn't mean a team of masked Mexican **federales** wasn't on the way over, running lights only.

Fifteen minutes later, the lock snapped back. Mendoz stepped out. She stared with frank hate across the garden at Wells, and he knew he'd won. If **winning** was the word. She'd marked him as the killer he was. She'd seen enough rough men come through this supposedly gentle place to know he was one.

She came to them. Coyle stood. "Stay," Wells said. "You get to hear, too."

"You don't care about how we do what we do," Mendoz said.

"Correct. Only where the money went. If it went to an American bank, we can find it, chase it down. How you got it clean, that's your business."

"It's within the law, I promise you. What we do is legal. Complicated but legal."

"Of course."

The hate in her eyes flared anew. "Hypothetically speaking, these accounts—"

"Accounts?"

"Yes, two. One much larger than the other. One in a man's name, the other in a woman's."

"How much money?"

She looked at them. "Here's what I can do. The stuff on the front end, you don't care about that, then we forget about it. In return, I'll let you see how they spent it. Then you never come back."

I get a lot of that, Wells didn't say.

———

She left. Another twenty minutes passed before the garden door swung open again. Lagares waved them inside.

Wells half expected they'd be jumped as they walked through the door. Instead, Lagares led them back to the conference room that overlooked the garden. Mendoz waited, carrying a leather folio.

"I'm glad we could have an honest discussion about your needs," Mendoz said. "I've brought information about account products you might like. Some of it's—" She hesitated. "I'm not sure of the word in English—**clasificados**, business secrets— so it can't leave this room. But look them over, take

notes, if you like. Take a few minutes to read. Fifteen minutes, say." She handed him the folio, pulled
her iPhone, set the timer for fifteen minutes.

Wells flipped the folder open. Found two
blank pieces of paper and a pair of gold pens. A
glossy brochure. A twenty-five-page contract in
English and Spanish. And, underneath, twenty
double-spaced pages of bank statements.

They were **close** now. Not that these pages
would necessarily enable them to stop the Russians. Or even find them. But at least Tony from
Tampa hadn't died for nothing.

The statements revealed two accounts, one in
the name of Alan Vartan, the second Annalise Fabian. Good generic European names. They could
have been French, Spanish, even German in a
pinch. Wells figured the fact Alan Vartan's initials
matched Anatoly Vanin's was no coincidence.
They both had addresses in Acapulco, and emails,
but no phone numbers.

The Vartan account was far larger. It had held
more than fourteen million dollars. A lot of that
money had been spent in big chunks fairly early
on. Millions to real estate brokers and title companies, lawyers, auto dealerships.

Nearly all of it had been spent in Texas, mostly
in and around Dallas. Wells couldn't pretend to
be an expert, but the records seemed to show the

account had been used to buy one or possibly two properties. Shafer and the FBI should be able to chase down exactly where.

The big purchases slowed down three months after the account opened, still several months before the Dallas attacks. Cash withdrawals, usually in the range of one to five thousand dollars, replaced them. Two days before the attack, the account had seen one last big withdrawal, ninety-five thousand dollars in cash. Since then, it hadn't been touched. It still held more than a million dollars.

The Fabian account was much smaller. It had been set up with two hundred thirty thousand dollars. The money had come out in ATM withdrawals, dribs and drabs, all over the West Coast, Los Angeles, San Francisco, Seattle, back to Los Angeles, Seattle again. Then eastern Washington, Spokane, several in a town called Pullman, which Wells recalled was in the southeast corner of the state. Then the account went quiet for months, until one final withdrawal in Fargo, North Dakota, a couple weeks before.

The Russians had come to Mexico City with eighteen million, left with a little more than fourteen. Wells had guessed low on Banamex's cut. It was twenty percent. Wells wondered how much Mendoz had personally made, didn't ask.

"These addresses?"

"I wouldn't count on them."

"Is it standard to open an account of this size without a phone number attached?"

"On an account like this, nothing is standard. A case-by-case basis."

"Right. We need these pages."

"These belong to the bank."

She was serious, Wells saw. She'd let them have the information but not the records themselves. Wells began scribbling names and numbers for the recipients of the Vartan account. He slipped the Fabian account statements to Coyle, and Coyle followed his lead. Mendoz poured herself a glass of water, didn't drink it. She stood against the wall, watched the iPhone clock count down. They wouldn't have time to copy everything, but Wells decided not to push for extra minutes. The timer and keeping control of the pages played the same role for Mendoz. They let her think she hadn't given in entirely. If Wells and Coyle stuck to their side of the bargain, she would stick to hers, let them walk out.

The phone's alarm beeped.

"Gentlemen," Mendoz said.

Wells swept the papers back into the folio, slid it across the table. "We're definitely interested in Banamex."

"I can't wait to hear from you." She reached into her suit and slid their passports back to them. And Wells realized what was missing from what she'd shown them.

"Our friends, what about their passports?"

"Yes?"

"You needed identification from them. Making a copy of the picture page is standard procedure, right?"

"I'm not sure how much those would help you."

Meaning the passports for Vartan and Fabian were as fake as the ones for Walsh and Montero.

"I'd like to see them, anyway."

She walked out, came back a minute later holding two creased pieces of paper, each a copy of an identification page from a French passport. Wells reached for them, but she shook her head. "Look, don't touch."

"Just the pictures, make us a copy."

She shook her head.

"What if we take a picture of the page, then?"

Another shake.

So Wells looked. Trying to sear the faces into his memory, steal the souls of the man and woman before him. Vanin, a/k/a Vartan: short hair, slightly pocked skin, narrow eyes. He wasn't smiling, but if he did, Wells guessed his teeth wouldn't be great.

A killer or a cop. He looked European to Wells rather than a native-born American. But if he spoke good English, he could probably have fooled Ahmed Shakir, who wasn't native-born either.

Fabian: Even the unnatural flatness of a passport pic couldn't hide her beauty. Blond hair, pert nose, the edges of a smile. Only her eyes didn't fit. Wide and blue, yes, but with an uncanny emptiness. They could have been holes in the page.

Wells wanted to snatch the pictures, but all the Botox in the world couldn't keep Mendoz's face steady any longer. If they pushed her further, she'd crack open. "Thanks for your help."

"My pleasure."

═══

Outside, it was almost 5 p.m. Polanco was taking on its after-work vibe, pretty young things stepping out of Ubers.

"Whatever you told her, she went for it," Coyle said.

"I'm a real people person."

"Wish she'd let us have those pictures, though."

Wells understood the implicit criticism. "She was about to start screaming."

"You think she's going to call the Russians, warn them?"

"I think she's going to hope we never come back."

Wells and Coyle weaved through the crowded sidewalks until they found a taxi on Avenida Masaryk.

"Annalise Fabian would fit in fine here." Coyle paused. "Think she could get a sniper to target priests?"

"I think she could do whatever she wanted."

The afternoon traffic was terrible, and the cab hardly moved. Wells handed the driver a fifty-dollar bill. "Come on." Now that they had a target, Wells felt faintly paranoid. What if Coyle was right and Mendoz made the worst decision of her life and panicked and called Vanin?

He emailed Tarnes to ask her to set a meeting with Duto as soon as possible.

8 a.m. tomorrow too soon? She wrote back.

Perfect.

━━━━━

Twenty minutes later, they stepped into the NH's lobby.

"Grab your stuff, Coyle. No more **noches** in CDMX."

"We going to Dallas?"

"Washington."

THREE

21

slamist terror is the darkest threat of our time. The world's nations have a moral duty to work together against it. Yet we ignore one country's contributions. Russia has fought these killers for twenty years, in Chechnya, Syria, even on its own soil. Next to the United States, no non-Muslim country has suffered more civilian casualties. And Russia has the military tools to provide real aid in this war. Its army and air force have already proven themselves in the fight against the Islamic State. President Duto must put outdated Cold War notions aside and build an alliance with Moscow for the twenty-first century—

The door to Eric Birman's office swung open. Eric knew without looking up from his screen that he'd see Paul. No one else would barge in that way. Without knocking. Like he owned the place. But then he did, didn't he? Like everyone else here, Eric served at Paul's pleasure.

"Colonel."

Eric never knew if Paul meant the title as compliment or insult. "Senator."

"Working hard?"

"On your speech."

Paul came around his desk, peered at the screen. Eric heard him murmuring under his breath, the sure sign of a weak reader. "**One country's con-trib-utions** . . . Pretty pro-Russia, isn't it?"

"I have to give you credit, Paul. You've done a great job talking about the jihadis. Duto's on his heels." **Thanks to my friends.**

"Thirty-eight percent approval this morning. Not that I noticed."

"But he's not dumb. He'll come back, say we're running drones all over the world, moved soldiers into Iraq and Syria. We've killed tons of these guys since I took office. Senator Birman talks a good game, but what will he **do** that we're not doing already? What do you say then?"

"We fight harder. Take no prisoners—"

"Empty rhetoric. He'll tear it up. A new alliance with Russia, that would be a real change. Best part is, you'd use his strength against him.

Everyone knows he ran the CIA, it gives him credibility. Here you say he's stuck in the past. Thinking like some Cold War dinosaur who always makes the Russians out to be the enemy."

"But they are the enemy. I mean, they're pretty nasty, aren't they?"

Lucky Cousin Paul showing his geopolitical understanding.

"They're tough. But they're not stupid. Why do you think the Cold War never got hot? I mean, chess is the national game over there."

"Always thought chess was for losers."

Of course you did. "When I was at Special Operations Command, we talked to the Spetsnaz, the Russian Special Forces, every so often. Traded tips on these guys. We had to be careful how much we gave up, of course, but kidnapping situations, fighting in mosques, we both had the same problems. Fedin came to the meetings once or twice. You'd like him. He looks you in the eye, man-to-man, says what he thinks. You can do business with him. The Russians, they just want to have their own sphere of influence. Honestly, who cares about Kazakhstan, whatever-stan, long as they aren't sending suicide bombers our way? Even Ukraine. In my opinion, the Russians have the right to keep an eye on it."

"How so?"

"Far as they're concerned, it's a buffer between them and Europe. They've never forgotten all those panzer divisions rolling east—"

"Fine. Sounds good. Keep writing."

Eric wasn't surprised Paul had agreed so quickly. The worst part of talking to him was also the best part. He had the attention span of a gnat. Tell him a story that sounded halfway reasonable, facts he couldn't be bothered to check, he would agree simply so he didn't have to listen anymore. That way he could return to thinking about his favorite subject. Himself.

"Will do," Eric said. "I think you should give it soon, ride this wave."

"Maybe ask Sam"—Samantha Raynor, the head of Paul's in-state office in Nashville—"to set something up this weekend."

Now that Paul had agreed, Eric wondered if he ought to talk to his controller before setting a date. The Russians might have plans of their own. "Logistics could be tricky."

"You're the one who said **soon**." Paul grinned. He loved turning the tables as much as any five-year-old. He perched himself on the edge of Eric's desk. Another move Eric hated. "Anyway, the real reason I came in: Gloria is freaking out. She said something about selling the house. Which I told her is never going to happen, that was Daddy's house and it's staying in the Birman family as long as there is a Birman family."

"Sorry, Paul."

"I want ex-Deltas for her. That'll impress her."

"Deltas run a thousand a day per guy, three guys for continuous coverage."

Paul shrugged. **Three thousand dollars a day, a million a year, who cares?** "We can look into getting full-time guys on staff in a few days, something cheaper, but right now I need her calm. She wants them for me, too."

"I'll start looking for folks this afternoon. For her first, right?"

Paul squeezed Eric's shoulder. "Colonel. I know I give you a hard time once in a while, but I couldn't do this without you. Behind every good man there's a good chief of staff."

Eric managed to wait until Paul had left the room before he cursed.

====

He had just turned back to the speech when his mobile buzzed. A blocked number.

"Captain Farragut?"

Eric knew the voice immediately. Adam Petersen. His SVR controller. **Captain Farragut** was code for a same-day meeting. "Excuse me? This is Eric Birman."

"Sorry. I'm calling for Captain Farragut. Tommy Farragut. Third Battalion, Fourth Infantry Regiment."

Eric was glad he'd memorized the codes. **Third Battalion** meant Petersen wanted the meeting in three hours. **Fourth Infantry Regiment** was a preplanned location, a Target parking lot in the Columbia Heights neighborhood, two miles north of the White House. Not perfect. Eric preferred to meet outside the Beltway. Still, the store was far enough from downtown and Georgetown that it should be safe. And **Tommy** . . . Eric was pretty sure Tommy meant Petersen would be waiting in a Toyota.

"Tommy Farrugut, you say?"

"That's right."

"Yes. I mean, no, you have the wrong number. I don't know who that is." The first word was the only one that mattered, signifying Eric's agreement. Any other answer would have meant no.

"You're sure?"

"Yes, positive. Not from the Fourth ID or anywhere else." Confirming the location.

"Sorry about that." Petersen clicked off.

"No problem," Eric said to the empty line.

———

Eric left the office two hours later, made sure he'd have time for countersurveillance. The Blue Line to Metro Center, the Red to Gallery Place, the Yellow past Columbia Heights to the Georgia Avenue exit. Twenty years ago, this part of Washington had been close to a no-go zone for the district's white residents. Now it was bustling, lined with new apartment buildings.

Eric walked north, away from Columbia Heights. He felt vaguely conspicuous in his suit and tie. But Washington had tens of thousands of lawyers and lobbyists who were paid to dress like grown-ups. No one glanced twice at him. When he was sure he was clean, he hailed a cab south to the Target, which looked like every other Target. The Toyota Camry in the middle of the parking lot looked like every other Toyota.

He knocked on the driver's window. "Do you know if there's a Sam's Club around here?" The question itself merely offered Petersen one last chance to abort. If he answered no, Eric would walk on.

"Get in."

They drove northwest for a few minutes, until Eric broke the silence.

"You worried about surveillance?"

"Not really. Though with drones, who knows anymore? Anything new from the FBI?"

"They've promised a briefing next Monday. I think they're scrambling. This is now three investigations in three states, and they don't have a lot of leads." Eric looked at Petersen. "That can't be why you pulled me out of the office."

"Have you spoken to your cousin about the speech?"

"I was writing it when you called. **Russia is greatest country in history of world, anyone who thinks different is Nazi or terrorist or terrorist Nazi.** It's easier for him to give it than talk to me about it, so that's what he'll do."

"Hah." Petersen slapped the steering wheel. He turned into a 7-Eleven parking lot, stilled the engine. "Will you be there when he gives it?"

Eric felt a prickling in his chest he recognized from Afghanistan. The adrenaline of incoming fire. The battle joined. "Wasn't planning to. Not like he needs me in the audience. Why?"

"When will he give it?"

"As early as this weekend, if we can set it up. By the way, he's going to hire extra guards soon."

"Sooner is better, then. Even better if he gives it somewhere outside Tennessee, a venue he isn't so familiar with."

"You have anywhere specific in mind, Adam?"

"What about Dallas, outside the American Airlines Center itself? Where the bomb blew up."

"Of course. So important symbolically—"

"When he gives this speech, you should be close by."

"How close?"

"As close as you can be."

They sat, side by side, with their hands in their laps. Almost too calm. Birman wondered if he was dreaming the conversation. He turned on the radio just to hear it. It was tuned to WAMU, the local NPR station. Of course. So refined, these Russian spies. When they weren't blowing up bombs.

"You want to kill me, too, then."

The words spoken now, the threat real.

"No."

"So not a bomb." Eric had wondered if the sniper belonged to the Russians. Now he knew. **Bet when I get back to the office, I find at least one hotel with rooms overlooking the arena.**

"Do you see what happens next, Colonel?"

"**Da.**"

They were quiet, listening to a calm NPR voice recounting the day's events: **The FBI is appealing for information—**

Petersen turned off the radio. "Tell me."

"You want me to **say** it." Eric imagined counterespionage agents swarming the car. But they were far, far past a sting. "Senator Paul Birman.

Chairman of the Intelligence Committee. Just as he calls for Russia and the United States to band together against jihad, he's gunned down. Killed from afar. Guessing the sniper has jihadi credentials. No idea how you've managed that, but you're clever souls. I grab Paul, pull him to cover. My cousin. His blood is all over me. All of a sudden, I'm Bobby Kennedy. Maybe I'm the wrong Birman, but I have the great advantage of being **alive**. I'm a hero, too. Everyone else ran. Not me. I went to him with that sniper still loose. So brave."

"Of course you're brave. You are a soldier."

The .30 caliber round tearing through the thin bullet-resistant vest Paul would wear for the speech. Paul crumpling, slipping sideways, as Eric cradled his shoulders, shielded him, held his head close—**Okay, cousin. Stay with me. Eyes open. Don't give up**—empty promises to a dying man . . .

Eric wasn't imagining it, he was **seeing** it, the future as it happened, the screaming, the panicked stampede of the audience, the cops finally reacting, running for Paul: **Go! Go! Go!**—

He even felt a glint of sadness for his cousin, cut down at the peak of his popularity. But Paul would be as lucky in death as he had been in life. No mortal fear for him, the cord cut in one swift stroke. No way for him to know that the White House could never be his. He would have a clean exit, join his beloved Daddy in Heaven's garage, where all the cars were classic.

"Colonel?" Petersen's voice brought Eric back to the parking lot. Could they be planning this **here**? With Big Gulps on sale for ninety-nine cents ten feet away? "You don't mind this? This man is your blood."

Petersen had mistaken his reverie for second thoughts. "If you thought I'd mind, you wouldn't be asking me."

"We don't have to, your cousin can stay in the Senate, you'll have all the information we need."

Eric's vision strayed south. Past the White House to the Lincoln Memorial. The great man, sitting, hands on knees, trying to save the Union. A century and a half later, his every word still remembered. To be president was to be a god, of sorts. And to have a god's afterlife. Do you want to be president? Do you want to be **Zeus**?

"Do I even have to answer?"

"You still have to win. You said yourself the reporters look at everything. Could anything disqualify you? Please, take a minute, think—"

Funny, now that they'd reached this moment, Petersen was almost discouraging him. Eric didn't need a minute to think. He'd always lived honorably. Told the truth even when it didn't benefit him. Led his soldiers from the front. One of his first real memories, five years old, he'd taken an extra Tootsie Roll from a drugstore. Accidentally. When he found it, he insisted to his mom that they needed to go back, pay the nickel.

"Nothing."

He'd always been a good man. **Until now.** Not so good now, was he? He was pretty sure that Honest Abe Lincoln had never plotted to kill his cousin so he could be president.

But maybe that perfect history was why he'd fallen so far so fast. Not fallen but jumped. Let gravity have its way. He liked to blame Paul. Maybe he'd looked around and realized nobody cared about his code. He was just another washed-up retired colonel, stuck working for his cousin.

He'd solved that problem, anyway. He wasn't just another anything anymore.

"Scout's honor, nothing to hide. Just make sure of one thing, Adam."

"Yes."

"Make sure this sniper of yours doesn't miss. He misses, or, even worse, he hits Paul and doesn't take him out and that SOB makes some miraculous recovery, I swear before God and Stalin I will choke him out myself on live television. And call a press conference and confess it all."

Petersen patted Eric's arm. "Let me know when you have the details of the speech. Give us an hour or two before you make the public announcement, if you can. And make it Sunday at the latest. Friday or Saturday, even better. The longer it goes, the harder it is for our man to hide."

"As you wish."

"Relax, Colonel. When all of this is over, you'll have what you want."

"And only the Kremlin to thank."

It was past 9 by the time Eric knocked on the heavy oak door to Paul's Capitol Hill town house. Some senators lived in shared houses in Washington, but not those who had nine-figure fortunes. For a while, when he came over, Eric expected to catch a mistress coming or going. He never had. Tonight, Jimmy Sanders pulled open the door.

"In the study."

The room Paul called a study was devoid of books and had been given over to a thirty-foot model train track, complete with mountains, stations, and a miniature version of Nashville. A professional model train engineer had built it. Such people really did exist, so that rich people didn't have to bother putting their own sets together. Paul watched happily as an eight-car train chugged around the track.

"Cousin, you get Gloria her Deltas?"

As if the world's most highly trained soldiers were take-out fried chicken. **Gimme two Sergeants and a Captain, extra-crispy.** "Coming up from North Carolina tomorrow. I want to talk to them myself before I send them to her."

"Cool."

"I finished your speech." Eric pulled a folder from his briefcase. Seven pages inside. "I think you ought to give it by Saturday. And not in Tennessee."

"Don't we want to be sure we have a good crowd?"

"You'll have a good crowd wherever you do it. We'll call it a major foreign policy address, a re-thinking of America's place in the world. The networks will show. Might even cover it live. Guess where I'm thinking?"

Paul's eyes crinkled in annoyance. **Employees don't make bosses guess.** "Been a long day, Eric—"

Yeah, I see you've been busy playing with trains. "Dallas. The American Airlines Center. I checked, the Mavs and Stars are out of town Friday, the weather's gonna be good—"

"Would they let me? The Mavs, I mean."

"How can they stop you? The leading voice on terrorism wants to speak at the site of a major attack. If they say no, they'll look awful."

Paul shut off the train. Eric could almost see him thinking.

"Cousin, don't mean to sound like a wimp, but you sure it's safe? With this sniper out there?"

"You'll have the Dallas police, your own security. A vest. Plus, if you haven't noticed, the guy's after priests. Unless you announce you're joining the ministry, you should be fine." Eric snapped his fingers like Paul had suddenly given him an idea, although he'd planned this line all along. "In fact, we can play up the risk, make Duto look even worse. Tell reporters you're **not afraid** to go to the site of the attack, that's the language we'll use, and Duto's in his bubble."

Paul flipped the train back on, and Eric knew he'd won.

"Cousin, I like the way you think." He smiled as the train began to chug. "Dallas, here we come."

22

Wells and Coyle caught the Aeroméxico evening flight, landed at Dulles two hours late, 2 a.m. Wednesday morning. Five and a half hours later, bleary-eyed but shaved and scrubbed, they offered their IDs and walked into the White House.

Shafer and Tarnes waited at the inner security checkpoint. A Secret Service agent promised someone would fetch them all. Shafer wore a three-inch-square gauze patch on his nearly bald head. His blue dress shirt was a size too large. But he seemed steady on his feet. A relief for Wells.

"Ellis."

Shafer ignored Wells. "Looking good, Sergeant."

"Nice to see you, sir."

"Never call me **sir**. You know, Coyle, I feel like you need an announcer every time you walk in a room. Maybe some chalk to throw."

"I believe you just compared me to LeBron James."

"Mike Trout."

"Game I play with white folk of a certain age. I call it racist or old?"

"I love all you people." Shafer winked.

"It's just the closed-head injury talking," Wells said.

"You think he bothers me?" Coyle said.

"We friends again?" Wells said to Shafer. Shafer reached his fingers under his chin, wagged them at Wells—the old Bronx curse. Wells grabbed Shafer's skinny bicep and reeled him in. "Hug it out."

Shafer puckered up, kissed Wells on the chin, his lips dry and scratchy, his breath musty.

"Ever heard of ChapStick?"

"I don't blame you for dumping me." Shafer nodded at Tarnes. "She's way better-looking."

Tarnes merely shook her head. "Children. We need to prep for this? It being the President and all." She was the only one dressed properly for the meeting, in a slim gray suit that pulled off the neat trick of being both conservative and flat-

tering. Wells wished he hadn't noticed how flat-
tering. Five hundred miles north, Anne was still
throwing up like a broken cuckoo clock.

"He might be the President to you, but to us
he's just Vinny, prick in chief," Shafer said, as
Duto's chief admin stepped into the room. Wells
refused to let himself remember the guy's name.
He was as glib, and gelled, as any Hollywood
agent.

"I'll pretend I didn't hear that." The admin
turned them away from the Oval Office corridor
and led them instead to the staircase that accessed
the Situation Room.

"No big O?" Shafer said.

"He wants to be able to videoconference Langley and the FBI just in case."

Wells suspected Duto just preferred the Sit
Room. It was a windowless, self-important conference space with lots of gadgetry. It felt more
like the agency than anywhere else in the White
House.

They arrived to find Duto at the wooden conference table that dominated the room. **The New
York Times** lay in front of him, a front-page
headline screaming SNIPER KILLS CARDINAL OF
CHICAGO IN PREDAWN ATTACK. The shooting
had happened barely twenty-four hours before,
though it seemed far longer.

"Showing your age," Shafer said. "Who reads off-line?"

"Goody, gang's all here," Duto said. Wells had told Duto only that he had urgent information. "Whatever this is, I know it's going to suck, so keep the wit to yourself until you've told me." He nodded at his admin. "Go on. Leave us."

The atmosphere changed, stilled, when the admin closed the door. The Sit Room's air was cool and odorless because it was so thoroughly filtered to remove potential toxins. The atmospheric equivalent of bottled water. The wood paneling hid concrete walls thick enough to survive a direct hit from a five-ton bomb. If the White House was a castle, this room and the offices around it were the keep. If it fell, the only refuge would be the tunnels underground. Descending into those would be a sure sign the Apocalypse was nigh.

"Begin," Duto said.

Wells had the fullest picture of what they'd found. Still, Shafer did most of the talking. Wells thought Coyle seemed intimidated. He retreated to the far end of the conference table and kept his head down, taking notes on a legal pad.

When Shafer was done, Duto looked at Coyle. "Sergeant? Anything to add?"

"No, sir."

"Sure?"

Coyle seemed to recognize that he'd better have at least one idea for his commander in chief. "I think the sooner we hit Banamex, the better, Mr. President. They may have records even Mendoz doesn't know about. Banks like paper—I know, from the time they tried to foreclose on my aunt and uncle. And, obviously, this kind of account is different, but banks are banks, sir."

"Noted. Julie?"

Wells hardly recognized this version of Duto. **Stop acting so presidential, Vinny. Watching you solicit staff opinions makes my teeth hurt.**

"Why open two accounts in Mexico? Seems overly complicated."

"Two accounts, two plots, right? Or do you think the Russians aren't running the sniper?"

"They must be. But the Russians could have started with one Banamex account and shifted the money to an American bank later." Tarnes hesitated. "What I'm saying is, they wanted to split the two plots as far up the chain as possible. They wanted the sniper to run whether or not Dallas worked. Which says to me they wanted him to be able to go on for a while."

"And?"

"So why have the sniper kill two guys in forty-eight hours? Something changed, they want to move fast. Like they have some specific target they didn't have before. The obvious choice—" She broke off.

Wells understood why she didn't want to say more. Telling the President he might be the target of a Russian assassination plot was no fun.

"I get it, Julie. Here's a fun fact nobody but the SecDef knows, as of now. I talked to Fedin after Hurley got shot. He told me how much he wanted to **help. By the way, can ve have Ukraine as vedding present, ve really like Ukraine.** I told him to get bent. I figured he was just taking advantage of the situation. Didn't realize he was making his own luck."

"Maybe he didn't like getting blown off," Shafer said. "Now he wants you gone, figures the Vice President would be more his speed."

"Has he ever talked to the guy?" Duto snorted. "But, yeah, maybe. If they thought they had a real shot and could get away clean. But they can't. Not unless this sniper is Chris Kyle resurrected. Not even then. The Secret Service is a pain, and they love them some hookers, but they're good at snipers. Fedin has to know that. And he has to know that shooting me would be World War Three."

"Unless he doesn't," Wells said.

"Can't believe I'm going to say this, but I preferred the Cold War," Duto said. "Everybody knew the rules. Three dates before you screwed, no matter how bad you wanted it. These days, it's like, **Do I swipe left or right? Do we have dinner or just go back to his place? Is he going to expect oral, too, 'cause I've got a sore throat, I'm not in the mood—**"

Duto stopped abruptly.

"What I hear, anyway. Kids these days."

"**Oral**—would that be regional hostilities?" Shafer said.

"Let's call it **limited nuclear war**. Right down their throats."

"Great metaphor there, Vinny. Screams dignity of the office."

Coyle caught Wells's eye: **This really happening? Am I hearing this?** Wells nodded: **Welcome to the show, son. Hope you can hit the curve.**

"Now that we've learned much too much about your dating habits," Shafer said, "now what?"

=====

Above Duto, the digital clocks counted seconds—Washington, London, Paris, Moscow, Jerusalem, Delhi, Beijing—not coincidentally, the capitals of seven of the world's nine nuclear-armed nations. Only a matter of time before Pyongyang showed up, too. Wells knew Duto would go from emergency meeting to emergency meeting in the next days. The SecDef would helicopter over from the Pentagon. The DCIA from Langley. The Vice President and the National Security Advisor would arrive, too, to discuss "appropriate responses" and "contingencies" and "levers of escalation."

But they'd be talking around the most important questions, the ones Duto alone could answer. **Those bastards killed four hundred Americans, same as if they'd pulled the triggers themselves. Only we caught them. That an act of war? If it is, do we start down a road that ends with the world on fire? And if not, if we're not going to call them on it, what then?**

"Anyone in the Kremlin we trust?" Tarnes said. Wells was glad to see her ask, put herself back in the game.

"No one who matters," Duto said. "But it's worth asking State if they're in touch with anyone even halfway honest. Meanwhile, beyond the bank records . . . What do we have?"

"Not much," Shafer said. "We don't know where they stayed in Texas or if they're still there. Don't know what names they used. And no, we don't know if they have more attacks planned."

"If you had to bet?"

"Put a gun to my head—"

"If only."

"I'd say no. Easier to hide one person than a team, and they have to know they pushed their luck, no matter how well they planned it. I mean, what if Shakir had just flipped them off? Gone to the Dallas cops? No, I think they're gone. Left the country weeks ago. I think it's only the sniper now."

Duto went quiet.

"But you're guessing," he finally said. "You haven't run the Banamex names through our databases. No NSA contact tracing on emails or phones. No driver's licenses or speeding tickets or court records."

"That would have meant calling the FBI and the agency officially, and we thought we'd better wait until we talked to you—"

"Because, this way, I get to decide all by myself whether to start World War Three," Duto said. "And because you hope I'll let you two run around on your own." Duto pointed at Coyle. "Sergeant, you been infected with the hero virus yet? The **I'll do it myself except when I need help and then it better come this very second** virus?"

"I know you're stressed, but take it out on us," Wells said, "not him."

Duto focused on Wells. "If he's gonna be

around a while, he should know I'm only the third-biggest ego in this room."

"Maybe you forgot, but you begged John to help, Vinny," Shafer said. "May as well know something else, Sergeant, long as we're talking 'round the campfire. El Jefe likes us because he doesn't have to sign anything when we're involved. He never buys when he can rent. We are **disposable**. You, too."

Wells flashed to Bogotá, Tony bleeding out. The cemeteries were filled with forgotten spies.

"Shouldn't you be in Florida waiting to stroke out, Ellis?" Duto said.

"Better question: If the Russians aren't after you, then **who** do they want? And, even more important, why? What could be worth this risk?"

Silence again. Wells knew Duto put up with Shafer's sharp tongue for these moments when he scissored to the heart of an issue.

"There some dissident here who's been a real problem for them?" Tarnes said.

"A hedge fund manager," Shafer said. "A couple reporters. Nothing they can't handle, nothing that needs this kind of operation."

"Agreed," Duto said.

"Plus, remember, they're trying to make this

look Muslim," Shafer said. "When we do catch the sniper, bet they've salted his house with **I love Muhammad** graffiti."

Duto drummed his fingers on the conference table. "Too many questions. And an active shooter. I know you like to play by yourselves, but not this time. I'll tell the FBI I have a private foreign intel source who says these two accounts might be connected to Dallas. They can start chasing all the stuff that you copied yesterday while Justice finds a way to get a real warrant. You can go back to Dallas, if you want. I'll tell them to let you work with them—"

"Work with them? I found this."

"Did we not just discuss your ego and the size thereof, Ellis? Plus, if you're right, the Dallas stuff is archaeology now. They're using the little account for the sniper. And that wasn't Dallas, it was mostly the West Coast, Washington State, right?"

Washington State. Wells imagined FBI agents descending on the southeastern Washington hills in their black Tahoes, rattling trailer doors with hard knocks. "Wait."

"Not you, too," Duto said.

"Let the FBI chase the big account. The real estate deals, cars they bought, money they moved. Let them see if they can figure out how these guys made the approach to Shakir. Prep a criminal case, if you decide to bring it."

"No way we're going to handle this in open court, John—"

"Up to you. All I care about, the little account. Let me and Coyle go after it."

"How? From what you said, there's withdrawals all over the country—"

"I'm not interested in **all over the country**. Just one place: southeastern Washington, Pullman."

"Why there? Nothing there worth hitting. Not even an Army base."

"Exactly."

"So?"

But Shafer nodded. "John thinks that's where they found their sniper."

"Why else go there? It's not on the way to anywhere. Not even a good place to hide—too small—and Coyle and I saw a picture of the woman who opened that account and, let me tell you, they'd notice her there. She wanted to blend, she'd be better off in a place like L.A. So she went there for a reason. And what other reason is there?" Wells didn't know if he'd convinced Duto, but he'd convinced himself.

"Say you're right . . . Even more reason to get the FBI in," Duto said.

"Up there, a lot of folks will slam their doors when they see that badge. Especially pissed-off veterans. Especially if the Feds tell them, **We're looking for snipers who've gone missing, that's all we can tell you. And, no, we don't have a name, we're depending on you for that.**"

"And they'll tell you?"

"That's my country, Vinny. Even now."

"I thought Afghanistan was your country." Duto gave Wells a sour-milk grimace.

"He's right, Vinny—" Shafer said.

"Shut up, Ellis." Real venom in Duto's voice. To Wells: "End of the week. After that, it won't matter, because Justice will get to Banamex. And when they do, the FBI will connect the two accounts."

"Sure."

"I'm only doing this because you deserve the chance to close this out." Duto smirked, not even trying to hide his real reason: that he wanted maximum flexibility.

Wells stood, offered Duto the crispest of salutes. "Won't let you down, Cap'n." **Up yours.**

"Rangers lead the way." **Right back atcha.**

———

They left the building through the northeast exit and were suddenly back in the real world, surrounded by tourists and school groups. The White House security perimeter had been extended. Again. Seemed to Wells that it was always being extended. No one was allowed to walk on Pennsylvania Avenue in front of the White House anymore. Secret Service agents, wearing black Kevlar and toting assault rifles, herded the kids back to Lafayette Square. As if they were protecting a dictator's mansion and not what Wells had always been told was the "people's house."

Tarnes was already looking at flights to Spokane. Shafer was muttering. Coyle hadn't said a word since Duto's speech to him.

Tarnes held up her phone. "Southwest, BWI, at ten-thirty a.m. Change in Denver, Spokane at two forty-five."

"We can get up there in time?" Baltimore–Washington International was at least an hour from downtown D.C., worse in the morning traffic.

"If you leave right now. While you're in the air, I'll talk to the Pentagon and VA, get the names and addresses of veterans in southeastern Washington who had sniper training. Duto may have to sign some kind of national security waiver, but I'll try to have a list to you by the time you land in Spokane."

"Don't forget Idaho and Oregon. Everyone within a hundred miles of Pullman." Wells turned to Coyle. "Coyle, you coming?"

Coyle nodded.

"Good. I guess you got the hero virus, too."

=====

Coyle was quiet until they were outside the Beltway.

"Didn't expect that. The way you talk to him. And he talks to you. The President."

"We've known him a long time."

"You trust him?"

Wells grunted.

Coyle stared at Wells. "That's a no. You don't trust him why do you work for him?"

Wells had a hundred answers to that question. And none. **Because, in the end, he usually does the right thing. And by** usually, **I mean** sometimes. **And by** right, **I mean** expedient. **Because we might have stopped a war three years ago even if he helped only because he saw a path to the White House. Because he's the president. Because I don't know what I'd do if I didn't do this.**

"Come on, Coyle," he finally said. "I need to tell an infantryman the answer to that?"

They didn't speak the rest of the way to BWI.

23

NASHVILLE

Another afternoon shading into another night in another no-name motel on the pay-day-loan side of town. They'd been in this room barely a day, on the road not even a week. Tom Miller was exhausted in mind and body and, worst of all, soul. He wanted to go **home**.

If he could decide where home might be.

Room 214 was peeling green paint and cigarette burns on the bedside table and a toilet with twin brown rings, the universe's ugliest asteroid belts. Next door, a hooker urged her clients with an endless rotation of **Do me. Harder, baby. So good.** Every so often, she threw in an **Oh, yes. God, yes** for variety. Pretty much the second the men walked out, the hooker turned on her television. She watched the Food Network. And only the Food Network. Maybe all that acting made her hungry. Maybe she'd worked at a restaurant in her previous life.

Miller had watched a lot of television himself since Sunday. CNN and Fox, mostly. They were both big on computer-generated re-creations and retired cops talking about sniper nests. Miller didn't mind those parts. But he hated hearing everyone talking about what good guys Luke Hurley and Cardinal James McDonnell had been. On CNN, the word **senseless** kept coming up. Fox focused on Islam. **They keep saying Islam is a religion of peace. This look like peace to you?**

Miller didn't know what anything looked like anymore. He hadn't minded shooting the Talibs in Kandahar. Those men were soldiers, too. Armed and dangerous. He'd slept fine after those kills.

But taking out Hurley, and especially McDonnell, had cut in a way he hadn't expected. On Tuesday night, he lay on the bedcovers, staring at the ceiling. Whatever they might have done, whoever they might be, those two dudes were **helpless** when he'd come for them. They'd had no chance at all.

Wednesday morning, he left Allie in the motel, found himself a copy-and-print store that had an Internet-connected computer. He looked for any hints Hurley and McDonnell were involved in a sex ring. Not just the regular news outlets but conspiracy sites and message boards, too.

Nothing. Anywhere. On Reddit, the posters mostly thought jihadis had killed the men. **These dudes want a religious war, I say we give it to them!** The ones who didn't said the Christian right was running a false flag operation to make Muslims look bad. **Don't fall for it.** Not one person even raised the idea that they were being targeted because they were part of a pedophile gang.

Funny part was, he and Allie were good at shooting people. McDonnell had gone even more smoothly than Hurley. The Chicago streets had been dark and empty when Miller lined up the shot. Allie had the Ram fifty miles away by the time the cops showed up. Now the FBI was basically admitting it had no good leads. Nothing about a pickup truck, nothing about a female driver or a two-person team. **This could be a long hunt, and we are hoping for the public's help,** the Chicago chief of police had said on Tuesday night. Maybe they were lying, playing down what they knew, but Miller didn't think so. Given the panic the second shooting had caused, if the cops had information, they would have shown more confidence.

Allie was standing on the motel balcony when he drove back. She waved when she saw him, almost ran down the steps. Normally, watching her move was enough to excite him. Not today.

"You okay, babe?"

"Fine." He knew what she'd say. **Of course you didn't find it anywhere. Do you think they told people they tricked out thirteen-year-old girls? Come on, Tom.** The answer made sense, too.

Then why did he have such a hard time believing it?

Being in Nashville meant he was barely four hours from his old sergeant if he was still at his old address. But if he went to Coole now, told the truth, what would Coole say? He would tell Miller to turn himself in: **You got to do what's right, Tommy. You know that.** Coole might even call the cops himself. What then? No mercy. Not that Miller deserved any. He'd shot two men in cold blood. Because some woman he didn't know had told him a story.

For the first time since he'd met Allie, he just wanted to get stoned. So stoned he couldn't move. So stoned he couldn't think.

═══════

He watched television instead. After a while, CNN made his eyes ache, and he switched to the Food Network. Why not? If it was good enough for the whore next door, it was good enough for him. The stuff looked tasty, too.

Around 1 p.m., Allie went out. He didn't ask where she was going. She was gone most of the afternoon. When she came back, he barely looked up. She lay beside him on the bed, slid a long leg over his, buried her face in his neck. She even ran a lazy hand down his chest, those fingers that had given him so much pleasure. He didn't stir.

She sat up, poked at him. A finger on his carotid.

"Tom. Look at me. **Please.**"

He turned off the television now, stayed on his back. She looked down at him with those cool-blue eyes.

"I wouldn't want to be with you if this was easy for you. You're a soldier, not a killer."

"I don't know **what** I am."

"You're purifying me. Can't you see?" She stretched her hand around his neck. Like she could draw out his life with her fingertips. He wished she could. Giving himself to her that way would hurt less than what he'd done. And then they'd be together forever, him inside her.

He closed his eyes.

"I'm too weak to do it myself, Tom."

"Maybe we should stop."

"Soon."

He'd known she was working up to asking him again.

"Not a minister this time."

"Who?"

"Paul Birman. The senator."

Miller opened his eyes, looked up at her. The pieces fit. Allie had wanted to come to Nashville, after all. And Birman had been on CNN talking about Luke Hurley like he'd known Hurley. Worst part, she was right. Birman would be easier. He was too smooth. Like everything had come easy his whole life. Miller's teeth gritted every time he saw the guy on television.

Still. Another man down.

Miller didn't ask what Birman had done to her. He didn't want to hear. Didn't want to have to wonder if she was telling the truth.

"Please, baby."

Oh, hell. What difference did another one make, anyway?

"He must have a ton of security here." His way of saying yes.

"Tom." She kissed him, chastely, her hand still close on his neck. Her way of saying she understood that he'd agreed. He felt his desire flickering once again, lightning in the distance. "Not here. He's giving a speech in Dallas Friday. At the basketball arena. Where the bombing was."

"The American Airlines Center." CNN had mentioned the speech.

She nodded.

"He'll have security there, too." Now that he'd agreed, he felt the weight off him. He was already thinking tactically, solving the problem of shooting Paul Birman. Solving the problem of Paul Birman's life. The guilt would come back later, but Miller didn't care. Not if he didn't have to think about it now.

"I googled it, and there's a hotel that looks over the arena. Just south of it. I'll show you."

Of course she'd already looked.

"We'll go down tonight. Have tomorrow to scout. Friday, too, if we need."

"Still be tricky."

"I know you can do it, Tom. You're an amazing shot. And then Mexico. The border's six hours from Dallas. No one will pay any attention to us. It'll just be **us**. You and me. "

"You promise?"

"I love you, Tom."

A few days before, he would have given anything at all to hear her say those words. Even now, they carried a power that he couldn't fight.

She kissed him, not chastely this time but openmouthed, exploring him with her tongue. And he couldn't help himself, the lightning wasn't in the distance anymore. He wanted her as badly as ever. She broke off the kiss, sat up, straddled his chest. She reached down. And when she touched him, the shock ran through him—

This is wrong, what you're doing. She's playing **you, and you're letting her. It's** wrong, Tom—

"No, stop—" But he wasn't talking to her. He was talking to himself. He didn't want to hear anything else in his head, he just wanted to feel her. And if he had to shoot Paul Birman to do it—

She smiled at him. She seemed to know what he meant, because she didn't stop. She didn't even slow down.

24

When Wells and Coyle landed in Spokane Wednesday afternoon, Wells checked his phone for the list of soldiers and veterans who'd received sniper training. Didn't find it. He called Tarnes.

"Julie, oh, Julie—"

All he needed to say. "I hear you. Even with the White House making calls, it took me all day to convince the records people to do it without a warrant."

Amazing but true, even the President didn't truly command the federal government. He could steer it. But federal workers were effectively impossible to fire. On a day-to-day basis, they followed their own rules. "They're running the names now?"

"You're funny. If there's a more bureaucratic

bureaucracy than the National Personnel Records Center, I haven't seen it. They punch out at exactly three forty-five p.m. Central Time, rain, snow, or sniper attack. Ironically enough, they're in St. Louis. Good news is, they show up bright and early, seven-thirty a.m. sharp. It won't take them long to run it tomorrow morning. With the time difference, you should have it when you get up. But don't expect any specifics about their service. That was the compromise. Names, ages, rank upon leaving the military, and addresses."

Another disappointment. Any soldier who had received a disability rating for post-traumatic stress disorder or head trauma would have jumped to the top of the list. Instead, Wells and Coyle would be working blind.

"Anything from Dallas?"

"Not yet, as far as I know. But they're on it. And say what you like about the FBI, they do work late. They plan to start knocking on doors tonight. 'Course, our friends are probably long gone—"

"But maybe someone will remember them." Having the passport pictures from Banamex would have helped. Maybe Wells should have insisted on taking them, as Coyle had wanted. Too late now.

"Shafer's getting down there tomorrow morning, so you can ask him."

"If he doesn't get his head beaten in again."

"Banamex side will take longer. I know this'll come as a shock, but the Mexican government isn't doing the United States any favors these days. By the way, we checked immigration records for the Banamex names—"

"Annalise Fabian and Alan Vartan?"

"Yes. Guess what? No entries in the last two years."

Not a surprise. Easier to create fake passports and driver's licenses than clean bank accounts, so the Russians would have done everything possible to keep their aliases out of United States government databases. They might even have hired a coyote to sneak them over the border.

"Appreciate the update."

"Any more delays, I'll call you." Tarnes hung up.

Of course, even having the names would hardly guarantee success. Veterans didn't always tell the VA when they moved. On an even more basic level, Wells couldn't be sure the woman who called herself Annalise Fabian had come here to find a sniper. But he and Coyle had to start somewhere.

They rented a Ford Explorer, drove south on the two-lane state highway that paralleled the Idaho border. Past the Spokane suburbs, the country opened up, pastures bordered with wooden fences, cows and horses lazily wandering. Coyle drove slumped in his seat, staring at the world from behind big mirrored sunglasses, clocking a steady 80 with one hand loose on the wheel. Reminding Wells how young he really was.

"Where'd you grow up again, John?"

"Hamilton, Montana. Just on the other side of Idaho. Beautiful country."

"Looks just like this, right?"

"And Malibu looks just like Long Beach."

Coyle gave a soft **Pffft!** of dismissal. "Don't know anything about that. Only black people allowed in Malibu are Will Smith's family. Maybe Kobe."

"Should have learned to surf."

Another **Pffft!** "Know the joke they like up there? How do you stop a black man from drowning?"

"Tell me the punch line doesn't involve chitlins."

Coyle turned to stare at Wells through his sunglasses, didn't lay off the gas. The Explorer drifted. "Went there, did you?"

"You started it. Eyes on the road, Sergeant."

Coyle straightened out the Explorer but didn't stop looking at Wells. "You want to know?"

"If you insist."

"How do you stop a black man from drowning? Take your foot off his head, you racist."

Wells had no choice but to laugh. "I'm racist?"

"Whole world is racist. White and black. Black people just know it better than you." Coyle pulled off his sunglasses. "You like growing up in all this nothing, John?"

"I did. The sun would go down, and it would be **dark** in the mountains. When I was little, my dad would take me for hikes. He was a doctor—a surgeon—and he always said the mountains were the best cure after a tough operation. No lights, no fire, no tents. Not in the summer, anyway. We'd bring bedrolls and blankets, lie on our backs, looking at the stars, listening to the critters. Sound carries a long way in those canyons; we heard the wolves, the foxes, the owls—all the predators. Hawks and eagles get the credit, but owls are vicious. You're a squirrel and you hear that **Hoo-hoo! Hoo-hoo!** time to jump. After I was about twelve or so, he let me go on my own—"

"Twelve?"

"I knew every stream and ridge to the Idaho

border. He figured I could handle myself. Sometimes I had a rifle, but, even without, I never
minded, I never was scared."

Coyle kept driving.

"Think I'd be lonely," he finally said. "Anyway,
there's nowhere to hide up there—"

"People have been hiding in those mountains
a long time."

"You can hide yourself, sure, but I mean your
secrets. The way you take a drink before work.
Or even something simple: You're a Marine who
likes **jazz**. Those little towns, everyone knows everyone's business. In a city, you can disappear."

"Never thought of it that way." Wells remembered how Coyle had vanished into the Mexico
City night. "You like jazz, Coyle? **Shoo-bee-doo-
bop**—"

"Maybe I do and maybe I don't. Not your
business. What would they have said in Hamilton if you'd come back and told them you were
Muslim, John?"

Interesting question. The answer wasn't as obvious as Coyle thought. Frontier tradition said a
man's home was his castle. Long as he didn't
bother anyone, he could do what he pleased. But
Coyle was right, small towns tended to be heavy
on gossip. Hamilton was no exception. Wells remembered his mother complaining about one

neighbor who always seemed to go to the grocery store at the same time as she did and spent an inordinate amount of time checking out what she bought.

Wells was still mulling his answer as they reached Colfax. Pullman, another twenty miles down, was much bigger, but Colfax was the county seat. "Let's see if the sheriff will talk to us."

———

The Whitman County Sheriff's Office was a gray concrete block conveniently next door to the county courthouse. The building looked to Wells like a place where justice would be dispatched fairly, if brusquely. A sign beside the front door warned FIREARMS BANNED AND WILL BE CONFISCATED. Underneath, a smaller sign, handwritten, added: **We Mean It—Don't Tempt Us!**

Wells and Coyle found themselves in a five-foot-square lobby, adorned only with an American flag and a framed photo of Sheriff Clay Darby. In the pic, Darby wore a dark gray uniform, a light gray tie, and a toothy smile. He looked friendly yet protective, a human Labrador retriever. Judging by a picture was a mistake, but Wells liked him.

A steel door with a magnetic lock offered the only entrance to the offices, though a thick Plexiglas window permitted a view of a single empty desk. Wells pushed the buzzer next to the window. After a minute, a deputy appeared behind it. Late fifties, with a brushy white mustache and a belly that pushed his gun belt.

"We'd like to speak to Sheriff Darby."

"Any reason you can name?" The deputy's gruff high-country accent took Wells back to his youth.

"Looking for someone."

"You bounty hunters?"

"Not exactly."

The deputy grunted, waited for more. "Names?" he finally said.

"John. And Winston."

"ID?"

Wells and Coyle slipped their driver's licenses through the slot beneath the window.

"You have warrants outstanding, now would be a good time to leave."

Wells noted the deputy had waited until he had their licenses before offering the advice. "We look like the warrants-outstanding type?"

"Lil' bit." The deputy scooped up the licenses, disappeared.

"Last time I showed up at a police station unannounced, the man put me in jail," Coyle muttered.

"That was France. Anyway, you got to hang with me. So it wasn't all bad."

"Says you."

A few minutes later, the maglock door swung open.

"Any firearms?" the deputy said.

"We saw the sign."

"That's a no?"

"That's a no."

"Come on, then."

═══

Darby's office was as bare and practical as the rest of headquarters, two laptops on his desk, a bookshelf sagging with books on criminology and crime scene investigation. The room carried the faint smell of late nights, sneaked cigarettes, and not enough deputies for all the work. Darby was a few years older than he'd been when the picture in the lobby was taken. More gray in his hair. Still looked like a good guy to Wells. "Sit, please."

They sat. The deputy stood behind them, reasonable under the circumstances. I trust you. Sort of.

"Gentlemen, Deputy Walsh tells me you're looking for someone."

Being straightforward would be their best bet, Wells saw. "Sheriff, this is gonna sound strange, but I promise we'll give you a way to confirm it. We're CIA, and we have reason to believe that the Chicago sniper is from this area. Maybe closer to Spokane, maybe over the border in Idaho or Oregon, but Whitman County is the center of where we're looking."

"**Reason to believe**—you two psychic, then?"

"Foreign source."

"How come the FBI isn't here?"

"We developed the information. Plus the source isn't the kind the FBI likes. If we can't find the guy in about three days, you'll see them, but I thought we might have a better chance coming in quiet. I grew up in Montana. FBI's been known to get people's backs up."

"Whereas everyone **loves** the CIA." Darby shook his head. "Have to be honest, gents. Even if you are who you say, I'm not buying it. I can watch CNN same as you, and everybody says it's terrorism. We're short on Muslims here. Especially outside Pullman."

Wells hesitated only a moment. "There's about five people in the United States who know this. But we don't think he's Muslim. We think someone recruited him."

"For money?"

"Not necessarily. We think it was a woman. Blond, late twenties, pretty. She showed up in

Pullman a couple months back. She may have called herself Annalise. Our working theory: Maybe she met the shooter online. He had anti-government or anti-religious leanings, and she fostered them."

"Seems like a lot of trouble to avoid the obvious explanation, that the guy is some jihadi nut."

"We have more, but I can't tell you what."

Darby reached into his desk for a Nicorette pack, popped out a piece. "Used to smoke Camels. Lot cooler than these. Then one day I woke up, and I was thirty-six and couldn't run a mile."

"Ever try vaping?" Coyle said.

Darby tucked the gum in his mouth. "What is it you want from me and my deputies? Pullman has its own PD, by the way. Wazzu, too. If this guy's on campus—"

"I don't think he goes to Washington State," Wells said. "Or lives in town. Guy like this doesn't want the neighbors too close. But sooner or later he announces himself. Swings at the mailman. Smacks his girlfriend and winds up in here for a domestic. Or just writes the local paper to complain about the United Nations. You know those guys. Especially the ones who like their guns."

"Or maybe he lives in the hills, like you said, doesn't bother anyone. And I've never heard of him."

"Sure. But we'd appreciate any names that fit the profile."

"What then? You knock on their doors, offer a hit on your vape, ask if they shot anyone lately?"

"Start by seeing who's home. The second shooting was yesterday morning in Chicago—that's two thousand miles. If our guy does live here, I doubt he's back yet. Anyway, two kills so quick, I think he has more on his plate. He's not coming home until he's done."

"Lot of guesses. Maybe somebody's away driving a rig. Or working a double shift."

"True enough, but we can talk to the neighbors. We should have a list of local veterans with sniper training by tomorrow morning. If we can cross-check it against the names you give us, we might get somewhere. Look, maybe we're wrong. But I promise if we can't find this guy, the FBI will come knocking and make a lot more noise than we do."

"You have a card?"

Wells scribbled down his and Coyle's information.

"And that confirmation. Not that I don't trust you."

Wells added Julie Tarnes's number and cia.gov and ucia.gov email accounts. "Call her anytime, day or night, she'll call you back on the Langley trunk line. Even better, just email her. Can't fake those addresses."

"I'll call you after I've talked to her. Maybe put in a call to the Pullman cops, too. A couple potential names come to mind, but honestly no one who fits the profile a hundred percent."

Tomorrow seemed to be the best they could do. Wells stood. "Thanks, Sheriff."

———

They went to a Staples in Moscow, Idaho, for a couple items Wells thought they might need, then found a hotel in Pullman. Wells wondered if he should go to the local cops, decided he was unlikely to build a better rapport with them than he already had with Darby. He'd let Darby handle them. The VA office, thirty miles south in Lewiston, was closed for the night. And when he checked online, Wells didn't see any veterans' meetings scheduled. There was one group the next night in Lewiston, another specifically for veterans with post-traumatic stress disorder in Pullman.

"That's it for tonight?" Coyle said. "Seems like we should be doing something."

"We are. We're getting a decent night's sleep and waiting for Tarnes to send those names. See you in the morning, Sergeant."

Sure enough, the list from Tarnes arrived at 7:30 a.m. the next morning. It included fifty-five names within a hundred miles of Pullman, more than half clustered to the north, in and around Spokane. As Tarnes had warned, the list included only the barest facts—name, age, rank at discharge, and address. Seven veterans lived in Pullman or Moscow, eleven more within a fifty-mile radius, scattered at random in every direction.

Given the distances and the rural roads, Wells thought they would be lucky to clear those first eighteen names before nightfall. He wanted to be back in time to meet with the Lewiston support group, which began at 7:30 p.m. Those conversations might be tricky, too. He printed out the names and maps of all eighteen addresses.

"Ready, Sergeant?"

"No, let's keep waiting."

"Bet the sergeants loved you at Camp Lejeune." Wells's phone buzzed. A 509 area code. Local. "Sheriff."

"I have three names you should know. Unfortunately, they're all over the place. The first guy lives in Hay, the western edge of the county. Not really a town at all, it has a zip code and a cemetery. Anyway, his name's Harlan Gould. He's got six kids, and a wife who keeps calling nine-one-one to say he's hitting her, and changing her mind by the time we get there. I don't think he's ex-military, but he has an arsenal. Even a light machine gun that he says doesn't work. My guys treat him carefully, and I suggest you do the same. Your buddy, even more so. Guys like Harlan often have strange notions about black people."

"Understood."

"Second guy, he's up near a place called La-mont. Name's Kenneth Brane. He lives on a farm his parents owned. I mention him because they died a few years back in a fire I'd call suspicious. We brought in the State Patrol, but they couldn't prove anything. I'll tell you a secret. Strangle your kin while they're sleeping and burn their house—unless you're dumb enough to leave out a gas can, you'll probably walk. Fires happen. He's a little bit older, ex-military. Might even have been a Ranger. We haven't heard from him in a while, but I assume he's still there."

Wells looked down the list Tarnes had sent, didn't see Brane's name. But if he'd been a Ranger, he could probably shoot even without sniper training.

"Got it."

"The third one lives east of Colfax, town called Palouse, he's Nez Perce. Palouse has a thousand people. So compared to the other two, he's a city boy. He applied to become a deputy maybe three years back. He'd won a shooting contest. It was on his application. Underlined about four times. We had to reject him because he had two psychiatric hospitalizations he hadn't disclosed. He kept emailing, asking us to reconsider. His name, believe it or not, is Milo Nighthorse."

"No wonder he's pissed. Were the emails angry?"

"More childish, I'd say. Emotionally immature. I mean, I actually drove to Palouse to see him. Not because I was worried he might do something, but because he sounded so lost. He wasn't home, I left a card with his mom. He never called. That was the end of it. Probably a long shot, but I figured you'd want to know."

"We do. Thanks, Sheriff."

"I'll text you the addresses. Remember what I said about Harlan."

Wells hung up. "The Staples stuff is going to come in handy," he said to Coyle. "Darby may have broken this open for us."

"I'll believe it when I see it."

"I'm gonna make you write him a thank-you note."

Wells decided to start with Harlan Gould. Guys like him were best approached in the morning, before the day's frustrations and the drink mounted. The drive to Hay took more than an hour, plenty of time for Wells to fill in Coyle on the three possibilities.

"Who do you think?" Coyle said.

"I guess Milo." But as Darby had warned the day before, none of the three were perfect matches. Wells didn't see how Annalise could have connected with Gould or Brane. Nighthorse might be too crazy. The Russians would want to know they could control their shooter.

The hills around Hay were crimped tight, eroded by nameless creeks that ran into the Snake River a few miles south. The maps showed that Gould's house lay at the end of an unnamed private drive. Coyle drove by it twice before Wells spotted it, an overgrown single-lane rut. The Explorer thumped as Coyle swung the steering wheel side to side to avoid the worst potholes.

PRIVATE / DO NOT ENTER, a faded, hand-painted sign warned fifty yards on.

They came around a curve to see a ramshackle white farmhouse atop a low hill. Gray-white smoke rose from a stovepipe that leaned off the right side of the house. Rusted farm equipment shared space with the front half of a white Ford Bronco and an old Mazda that looked like the only operable vehicle in the bunch.

"Washington Chainsaw Massacre," Coyle said. "Remember, the black guy always gets it first."

"You would say that."

A heavy steel chain blocked the road. UNLESS YOU ARE AN INVITED GUEST STOP, DISMOUNT AND WAIT, another hand-painted sign announced.

"**Dismount**," Coyle said. "Somebody's **fancy**. What do you think?"

"We do what we're told."

"Awful exposed." Still, Coyle stopped a few feet shy of the chain.

"Then let's be nice. Take off your sunglasses and put on your name tag."

The name tags were simple laminated white pieces of paper in generic blue holders. Coyle's read WINSTON and Wells's JOHN, cleverly enough. Wells had made them at the Staples in Moscow. He'd also bought notebooks, clipboards, and Bic pens. At a nearby Walgreens, he'd added a pair of black-framed clear-lens eyeglasses that would have been hip in Brooklyn but were just dorky here. Wells wanted to appear as unthreatening as possible, and these name tags screamed **unthreatening**.

Now he and Coyle snapped on their badges and stepped out. An easterly wind turned the air brisk and sent clouds chasing one another across the blue sky.

"We look like Jehovah's Witnesses," Coyle said.

"Exactly. Keep an eye on the upstairs windows."

"You think I need you to tell me that?"

But no one took aim from the second floor. Instead, a man stepped out of the house, shambled toward them, a rifle slung over his back and a pistol strapped to his waist. He was short and squat, with a notable limp and a perfectly round head. Kids in T-shirts and jeans followed him out. **Stay back, inside!** he yelled without looking back. They ignored him. The oldest waved and then dropped his hand quickly as if he'd made a mistake. The two littlest both raised finger pistols, aiming at Coyle.

"Hospitality runs in the family," Wells said.

"No way this guy was in Chicago two days ago."

"Agreed, but let's make sure."

Wells gave a friendly wave as the man approached, received a single shake of the head in return.

"Private property."

"Mr. Gould? I'm sorry to bother you, sir. We're conducting a road-use survey for the Department of Transportation."

"You work for the **state**?"

Uh-oh. Wells hadn't figured Gould's dislike of the government would run to the DOT. Who hated roads? Coyle bailed him out.

"Private contractors, sir. 'Fact, we don't get a dime if we can't get our surveys filled."

Gould's eyes snapped to Coyle. "Piecework. Your kind is used to that."

Coyle nodded: **Good one, you got me.**

"Hate to have to tell you this, but looks like you ain't getting paid. I got no cotton to pick neither."

A real charmer. "We know your time is valuable," Wells said. "We're authorized to offer a twenty-dollar payment for answering our questions. Five minutes, at most."

Gould smirked. "You two couldn't look more like cops if you tried. Don't know what you really want, but for a hundred bucks I'll answer your questions. About roads, that is."

"Twenty is our standard payment."

"**Fifty.** You drove all the way out here. Shame to see you go home empty-handed."

"Fine, fifty."

"Hand it over, then."

Wells gave him the bills. "About how many miles do you drive each week?"

Gould rubbed a hand through his thick blond

hair. The rest of his body was as ruined as the cars in his front yard, but his hair was magnificent.

"Three hundred miles, I'd say. You know, it's fifty just to Pullman. Used to do more, but gas ain't cheap."

300, Wells wrote on his clipboard. "And what is the primary purpose of those trips?"

"Shopping, most like."

"When was the last time you drove your vehicle?"

Gould looked back at the front yard as if the Mazda itself could tell him. "Musta been Sunday."

———

"Wasn't him," Coyle said, as the Explorer bumped back down the road.

"No. Nice line about getting paid only if we got answers. He liked that. Put him in charge."

"Bet one of his kids kills him one day."

"Only one? Brane's up next. In Lamont." Wells checked his phone. "Figure an hour and a half."

"Think he's gonna be strapped when he sees us, too?"

But Brane had no warning signs on his property. His house was new, presumably a replacement for the one that had burned. An American flag flapped high on a pole in the front yard. A woman answered Wells's knock. Heavyset, white, early fifties. In the background, a television played.

"Can I help you?"

"We're looking for Kenneth Brane." Wells was already sure Brane wasn't their shooter.

"He's out back working. I can get him if you like."

"Actually, ma'am, maybe you can answer our questions. We work for Nielsen—the TV folks—and we're doing a survey of television use in Washington State. We'd like to ask what shows you and your husband have watched over the last week. We don't need an exact list, just whatever you remember."

"We can offer twenty dollars for your time," Coyle said.

"He's not my husband, but sure. I'm Mary, by the way."

———

"Wasn't him," Coyle said ten minutes later, back in the Explorer. "Maybe he killed his parents, but it wasn't him."

"Agreed." Mary had reeled off an impressive list of shows. Even with a teleporter, Brane wouldn't have had time to kill anyone in St. Louis or Chicago.

"Two down, one to go. How far's Palouse?"

"Hour-plus." Wells checked his phone. It was already almost 11. "Let's get a snack on the way."

The snack turned out to be PowerBars and Gatorade from a gas station. The radio was mostly static, and since Coyle hadn't splurged for the satellite, they rolled along in silence.

"Land growing on you?" Wells said.

"Not really."

"I know, not enough jazz joints. You a Chet Baker guy, Coyle, or more modern? **Bip-bap-a-bam-boom!**"

"Your dad was a doctor, how'd you turn out to be such a hick?"

=====

The center of Palouse looked like a movie-set western town, brightly colored three-story buildings on a main street wide enough for angle parking. An old-timey advertisement for the local paper was painted in black-and-white on a brick building. Away from downtown, the city was less quaint but pleasant enough, homes clustered close on neatly kept lawns.

Milo Nighthorse lived on the north edge of town, a poorer neighborhood, in a long, low house, cinder blocks propping its steps. A red flag with a gold-black-and-white icon at its center hung above the front door. A Nez Perce emblem, Wells figured.

Coyle eased the Explorer behind a rusty Toyota pickup. "What's the play? Herbalife distributors? **Lose weight now, ask me how!**"

"Military recruiters. He wanted to be a cop? Rangers are even better."

"Marines, you mean."

"I mean Rangers."

"You do know even a below-average Marine could kick a Ranger's ass."

"Save it for your **Semper fi** buddies." Wells grinned and stepped out. For the first time in years, he felt like he had a partner in the field.

The front door opened even before they reached it. A fiftyish woman stepped out. She had square features and light brown skin. She looked at Wells as if she knew he brought bad tidings. "He okay?"

"Ma'am—"

"Just tell me he's okay." Up close, she smelled of skunk weed and bad luck.

"Can we come inside?"

══════

The pot stench in the living room was overwhelming. Wells wondered how long they could stay before they wound up with a contact high.

"You're Milo's mom?"

"Karen, yes. And you're State Patrol?"

"No, ma'am." Best to play this conversation as straight as possible. Karen would be too focused on her own problems to challenge them. "We're with the federal government. We're worried your son might be in trouble."

"Is this about the bear? Because that was tribal land, a tribal matter—" She paced around a card table that was home to a two-foot-tall glass bong. She might have smoked all morning, but the pot wasn't calming her.

"Ma'am, help us here."

The steel in Wells's voice had the effect he hoped. She stopped moving, focused on him.

"When did you last see Milo, Ms. Nighthorse?"

"**Taylor**, not Nighthorse . . . A week ago Monday. He said he'd be back soon. I told him don't go, but he said he had something important to do, something that couldn't wait."

"You were worried because of his prior hospitalizations."

She didn't ask how they knew. "When he takes his medicine, he's fine. But soon as he stops—"

Wells didn't point out that living in a house where marijuana was one of the major food groups probably didn't help Milo stay on his meds. "He's schizophrenic?"

"No, bipolar. He's a beautiful boy, I promise."

"Ms. Taylor," Coyle said. "Did Milo have a girlfriend?"

"No, not really. Girls liked him—" She hustled out, returned with a picture of a handsome twenty-something man with deep black eyes, standing atop the Space Needle in Seattle. "See?"

"Can we hold on to that?"

She handed the photo over.

"Do you know, was he dating anyone?" Wells said.

"He kept that stuff to himself."

"Mothers know. Maybe a blond woman, late twenties?"

She shook her head. "I don't think so. But, really, he never brought girls here. He was embarrassed he still lived at home, he thought it was lame."

"But he was trying to get a job. He applied to the sheriff?"

"And the State Patrol, a bunch of places. They all turned him down because of the hospital stuff. It wasn't fair. His dad died when he was young. I always told him, try something else, a mechanic maybe. He was good with his hands. But he liked the idea of being police."

"A good shooter, the sheriff told us."

She nodded. "He won a contest in Spokane a while back."

"He had his own rifle?" Coyle said.

"Of course."

"Did he take it when he left last week?"

Milo Nighthorse's mother opened her mouth but made no sound.

———

With its MMA posters taped to the wall and comic books scattered across the floor, Milo's bedroom looked like it belonged to a teenager, not a twenty-seven-year-old who aspired to become an officer of the law. Taylor opened his closet door and pushed aside Milo's flannel shirts. "Kept it in a case back here."

The case was gone.

"Do you know what kind of rifle it was, ma'am?" Coyle asked.

"Not sure the model, but the caliber was thirty-oh-eight."

Wells caught Coyle's eye. The sniper was using a .308 rifle. "Did he store ammunition anywhere else in the house?" They might be able to match the ammunition to the rounds the police had recovered.

She shook her head.

"Anything else missing, ma'am?"

She pulled out a metal box latched with a combination lock. "Milo doesn't know I know the numbers." She spun it open. Empty. "He kept his money in here. Maybe a thousand dollars, fifteen hundred. And his stuff."

"Pot?" Coyle said.

"Maybe a little—" She sniffled.

"Crank?"

"He said it helped him when he got down." She flipped the lid shut, kicked the box back into the closet as if she blamed it for Milo's troubles. "He's okay, right?"

"We just need to find him," Wells said.

———

"I'm not sure it was him," Coyle said, as they drove back to Colfax.

"Maybe not, but we'd best find out." Milo didn't have a credit card or a bank account. **Didn't trust banks,** his mother had said. He didn't have his own computer either. So the FBI couldn't track him that way. But she'd given them the details of his car—a burnt-orange 2004 Chevy Cavalier with Washington State tags and racing stripes—and his email account and phone.

She'd called every few hours, but the phone had gone straight to voice mail for almost a week, she said. He hadn't responded to texts or emails either. Still, between the phone and the license plate, the FBI had a good chance of finding Milo if he was still alive. It could rerun the footage it had collected near the shootings, looking for the Cavalier. Health privacy laws would protect Milo's identity if he'd been hospitalized. But if police officers had forcibly brought him to a hospital, even if he hadn't been arrested, his name ought to show up in an incident report database. Many of those databases, especially in big cities, were now indexed and available to the FBI in real time.

The NSA could dive even deeper into his phone and email accounts, as long as Duto would sign a finding, the written authorization needed to spy without a warrant on an American citizen. The plain fact was, ordinary Americans had almost no chance of avoiding law enforcement once it mobilized against them, unless they were willing to live on the streets or had the survival skills to stay alive in open wilderness.

Wells called Tarnes, explained what they'd found, and what they hadn't. Before they left, they'd asked Karen if Milo ever seemed angry with preachers or ministers. She insisted he had not, that he'd never cared much about religion. She said he wasn't violent even when he was manic. And she told them again he hadn't mentioned any new women. They asked if Milo's friends might have an idea what had happened to him. She gave them four names but told them that she'd already spoken to all four. They'd denied knowing anything. **And they wouldn't lie to me. They know if Milo takes off, it's trouble.**

"What about the seeding?" Tarnes said.

"Seeding?" Wells flashed to the NCAA men's basketball tournament: **A sixteen has never beaten a one . . .**

"What we talked about with Duto. If the Russians want to blame this on Islamic terrorists, they need to make it look like the shooter was a secret convert. Or at least had sympathies."

Tarnes was right. "We didn't see anything like that. No Quran, no ISIS flag. On the other hand, his mom lives there full-time, so it might be tough. They could put stuff in his car or load up his email account."

"So this mainly comes down to timing."

"Which is striking: He takes off six days before the first shooting."

"Let's make a deal. I'll ask Duto to sign the finding if you'll keep looking."

The first time she'd given him anything close to an order. Wells found himself slightly annoyed. "Sure."

"Don't like a woman with a mind of her own, John?"

"Let me know when you hear." He hung up.

"What now?" Coyle said. "Talk to the sheriff again?"

"My impression this morning, he told me what he knew about Milo. Let's call the friends first, see if anyone wants to talk in person. If not, let's put him aside, get to the list. FBI will find him soon enough, if he's alive."

———

By nightfall, they had made modest progress. Milo's friends insisted they had no idea where he'd gone. **He was nuts,** one said. **Good dude, but nuts. You heard about the bear?** Meanwhile, they'd visited nine of the names on Tarnes's list. Six had been home on Sunday. The other three didn't answer their doors. Of those, two had dogs, a fact that strongly suggested that they were simply at work.

The third, a guy near Colfax named Tom Miller, was more interesting. Mail was piled in his box, and the blinds to the windows on his trailer were drawn tight. Unfortunately, Miller's nearest neighbors weren't home either, so Wells and Coyle couldn't ask anyone about him. Wells figured he was worthy of another look in the morning, maybe a conversation with Sheriff Darby.

"Veterans' groups next," Coyle said, as they pulled back into the hotel in Pullman. "Never been to Idaho."

"Idaho is to Montana as San Diego is to L.A."

"Now I can't wait."

Wells's phone buzzed. Tarnes.

"I think we found Milo Nighthorse."

Her tone was so calm that Wells knew right away Milo wasn't the shooter.

"FBI traced his phone to Los Angeles last Saturday. The final signal before it went down. They asked the LAPD and the Los Angeles County Sheriff's Department to recheck incident reports for anyone by the name of Milo Nighthorse in the previous ten days. Or any non-black twenty- or thirty-something men who gave false or no names after being arrested. Turns out, LAPD picked up a guy downtown for vagrancy and public intoxication last Sunday. He wasn't carrying identification or a phone. Empty pockets. He gave his name as Emperor Jesus Young Joseph."

"Couldn't work in Muhammad?"

"Young Joseph was a Nez Perce chief from the eighteen hundreds. The guy's prints aren't in the system, so they've been holding him while they figure out who he is and what to do with him. He's reported as likely Native American, late twenties, five feet ten inches tall. They sent his booking photo, and I'm pretty sure it's the same guy as the pic you sent, though he's definitely the worse for wear. I'll forward it to you."

"Thanks, Julie. Quick work."

"Thank the Feds."

Wells passed the news to Coyle. By the time he was done, the booking photo had hit his phone. Tarnes was right. Milo Nighthorse was going by Emperor Jesus Young Joseph these days.

"Another one bites the dust," Coyle said.

"Least we have good news for his mother." Not the worst news, anyway.

―――――

The support group in Lewiston began an hour before the one in Pullman, so they went to Lewiston first. Wells might not have dared to make the approach if he and Coyle hadn't been veterans themselves. As it was, he didn't want to participate under false pretenses. He planned to ask if he could talk to the group for a minute before things started.

The Lewiston meeting took place at a storefront church a few blocks from the Clearwater River. A half-dozen middle-aged men and one woman stood around a table stacked with bottles of store-brand juice and a percolator that had been brewing coffee since Vietnam. None of them had the guarded eyes of soldiers who'd served in the infantry.

"New blood," a tall white guy said. "Nice to meet you. I'm Clyde."

"John. And this is Winston. We are veterans, but we came for a specific reason."

"What's that?"

"We're investigating a woman who might have run a scam on soldiers in the area." True enough, as far as it went. "We think she was targeting infantry. Specifically, snipers."

Clyde shook his head. "We're Guard and Air Force, mostly. I'm the only one who was Regular Army, but I was a mechanic. I mean, to be honest, we mainly get together to drink bad coffee."

"I saw there was a group up in Pullman—"

"Yeah, those guys are younger. More of a PTSD-type situation." Clyde almost but not quite saying: **To those guys, we're practically civvies, so we have our own little meeting here.**

"Thanks. We'll try there."

"Hold on," the woman said. She was forty or so, with the squint and lines that came from long days in the high-country sun. "This woman, what was her name?"

"She may have gone by Annalise. She was in her twenties, blond, pretty—"

"Three, four months ago, I was at the clinic, and I got to talking to this vet named Fred, who lives up by Pullman. He told me how he was out with a buddy, they almost got into a fight over some woman. I can't remember her name, but it started with an **A**. Blond, real pretty. His friend fell hard for her, he said. **Love at first sight. Like something from a cheesy movie.**"

"This guy Fred mention the friend's name?"

She shook her head. "I'm sure he was in the service, too, though. Just from the way Fred told the story. But that was it. I never saw the guy again—Fred, I mean. Don't even know his last name."

"What's your name, ma'am?"

"Kimberly." She scribbled down her contact information. "If you have any questions, call me." She winked at Coyle. "And you . . . You call if you have questions or not."

———

The sniper list didn't have anyone named Fred. But someone at the Pullman meeting would have to know him. If not, worst case: Tarnes could ask the military records office in the morning.

"Progress, as promised."

Coyle grunted noncommittally.

"We confirmed she was here—"

"We confirmed somebody got into a bar fight over a blonde. Maybe."

"You were right about Nighthorse, but you're wrong about this."

The second meeting was at a volunteer firehouse south of Pullman. The place had four bays and a big meeting room, where ten guys stood around sipping coffee. About half had serious ink on their arms or necks, and they all had hooded, downcast eyes. The real deal.

They, too, stirred as Coyle and Wells walked in, but the vibe was warier than in Lewiston, not exactly unwelcoming, but questioning: **Sure you're in the right place?** Wells wondered if he should mention Annalise first. But he sensed he'd only have one chance. Finding Fred was the priority.

"This the veterans' meeting?"

A tall guy turned to them, giving Wells a glimpse of the burn that scarred his right cheek. "You served?"

"We did. I was a Ranger a while back, and Coyle here just got out of the Marines. But we're really just looking for one guy in particular. Named Fred."

"We heard two guys have been knocking on doors today. That you?"

Wells nodded.

"And you work for?"

"We'd rather not say and we have good reason, I promise. You can call Sheriff Darby in Colfax, if you don't trust us."

"You're cops, then?"

"We're not, I swear, and Fred isn't in trouble. Just hoping he can help us."

The tall guy shook his head. Now Wells could see the scar tissue extended down his neck, under his shirt. "You two should go. Whatever this is, it's got nothing to do with us—"

A fireplug of a guy stepped up. "I'm Fred." To the tall guy: "It's all right, Lyndon. I'll talk to 'em outside. You hear me whistle, you come running and jump 'em." He smiled so Wells would know he was joking, though he wasn't.

Lyndon grunted: **Hoo-ah.**

———

They stood in the dark in the fire station's parking lot.

"I'm John, and this is Winston."

"Fred Urquhart." Urquhart was a little man with oversized features: a big beak nose and a chin that belonged on a lineman. He sized them up with a mix of confidence and deference, the confidence of a man who had traded fire with the enemy, the deference of a grunt who was used to taking orders he didn't necessarily like. "What brings you to beautiful Pullman?"

"This is gonna sound strange, but we're looking for a guy with sniper training—"

"Can't help you there—"

"Who met a woman a few months back."

The look on Urquhart's face said **Should have let you finish. Even bosses get it right once in a while.**

"This woman, she was blond? Great body?"

"I've only seen her face, but she was pretty, sure," Wells said. "Maybe she called herself Annalise—"

Urquhart shot a stream of curses. "Not to us. To us, she was Allie. I knew she was trouble. That whole night, the whole thing, it didn't make **sense**—" He caught himself, sputtered out.

Wells let him tell the story his own way, knowing they'd have the name soon enough.

"I'm sorry. I was at the Hyde Out—that's in Colfax—back in the fall. This woman came in. These two guys were trying to pick her up, pretty hard, and Tom stood up for her—"

"Tom?"

"Tom Miller."

Wells looked at Coyle: **Believe me now?** "He lives a little north of Colfax? Trailer?"

"Yeah, that's him. To be honest, I never actually saw his place. Some woman from the VA hooked us up—we're both on partial—she thought we'd get along, and we did. But wasn't like we were **tight** tight, we'd only known each other a few months."

"What happened that night?"

"This chick, Allie, comes in. She was more than pretty. I mean, it looked like she'd been rode hard and put away wet, but, even so, she'd stop traffic. She was alone, and these two jerks start on her. They won't let go. You know, officer types. Finally, Tom decides he's going to do something about it. And Tom's little, but he's tough, so **that** fight doesn't last long, and it ends with both those dudes walking away with their rich little tails between their rich little legs. A couple minutes later, I left, too. Tom and the girl were looking at each other like Adam and Eve, and I swear that's the last I saw of him."

Urquhart poured out the story like he'd been mulling over that night for months. Wells believed every word.

"Why didn't it make sense? He stood up for her, she fell for him. Old story."

"Yeah, and I know you're thinking I'm just mad I didn't get to her first. But I'm telling you, it was weird. First off, those guys were a-holes.

But it wasn't like this chick was **wasted**, she could have walked out. It felt to me kinda like she was **waiting** for us to poke our noses in, which at the time I figured, you know, pretty girls, some of 'em like to start stuff. Get guys fighting. Second, even beaten-down, this girl was something. Clean her up and she was a **nine**. And Tom, I liked him. I don't want to sound like a REMF here, but—" He broke off.

"Not a good-looking guy?"

Urquhart grunted like even admitting the fact hurt. "Tom was a five. On a good day. The normal move for that chick would have been to say, **Thanks. And, by the way, the door's over there, don't let it hit your ass on the way out.** But she looked at him like he'd just invented fire or something."

"So you left?"

"Yeah, I left. I figured sooner or later he'd call me and tell me how he bought her a few drinks, and she went **Poof!** Or maybe he did get lucky and had the best night of his life. But he didn't. After a week or so, I called him a few times. He never called back." Urquhart shook his head. "And I dropped it, I admit. I stopped calling. I was a little pissed. And now I'm **ashamed** of myself, 'cause that is not how infantry does infantry.

And you two look like the real deal to me. And I don't think you came all the way to nowhere to track me down, however you tracked me down, to tell me he just won the 4-H prize for best pig. And Tom: He wasn't the type to brag, but we talked a little bit about 'Stan. He'd taken down a bunch of **hajjis**. I doubt he'd have trouble playing Shoot the Cardinal at seven hundred yards."

The fact that Urquhart had guessed so quickly why they were interested in Miller was yet another sign he was their man. "Did he ever mention any anti-religious leanings to you?"

"Nah, he was a nice guy. But he was **alone** up here. No family. His dad left when he was little, and his mom died a couple years back. I mean, I was like his closest friend. And he'd had a couple nasty concussions. If this chick twisted him up—"

"Understood. You have his number or email?"

"Just his number." Urquhart gave it to them. "Want me to go up to his place with you?"

"No, we don't think he's there. And we need to talk to the sheriff, anyway. Obviously, keep this to yourself."

Urquhart nodded. "Go easy on him, if you can."

"If we can."

Back in the Explorer, Wells called Darby.

"Sheriff, name Tom Miller ring a bell? Veteran, lives in Colfax?"

"Believe it or not, yes. His mom and stepdad died a couple years back. Overdose. There was a fight over who was in line for their pickup truck—it was brand-new—and we had to get involved. Title was in her name, so Miller got it."

"How did he strike you?"

"Decent. You wouldn't know it by his name, he's Hispanic. I had the feeling he had a rough go in the service, but he never complained about it or played that card. He was happy to get the truck, though. Why?"

"He's on our sniper list, and an Army buddy of his says he got into a fight over a pretty blonde at a bar in Colfax a few months back. And he's not home, and it looks like he hasn't been for a while."

"Still seems thin."

"His buddy thought he was the guy."

A pause. Then: "I'll meet you at his trailer."

"You don't have to do that, Sheriff."

"Don't go in without me."

Darby's Explorer waited a half mile down from the trailer, running lights only. Wells stepped out to talk to him. The night was quiet, only the faint rumble of traffic on 195 breaking the silence. The sheriff sat alone in his truck, a wad of Nicorette in his mouth.

"Once I saw you weren't there already, I pulled back. Didn't want to freak him out if he is in there. Though, I agree, it doesn't look like anyone's home."

"We'll follow you."

Darby's truck rolled slowly off. Coyle followed. He hadn't said much since Urquhart.

"All right, Sergeant?"

"Hoping it's not him."

Wells understood. But hope meant nothing now.

They followed Darby down the short private road that led to the trailer. A stream cut through there, feeding a stand of trees that screened Miller's property from the main road. Wells heard it burbling in the dark. Soon enough, they reached the clearing in front of the trailer. The blinds were as tightly shut as they'd been earlier, although in the darkness Wells glimpsed the faint glow of lights inside. But they could have been on timers. The building was clean and well maintained, no rust on its metal siding. Yet its vacancy was unmistakable. It looked as cold as an empty safe.

Wells and Coyle grabbed the pistols under their seats and joined Darby in the clearing.

"Tom!" Darby yelled to the trailer. "It's the sheriff. Remember me?"

They waited. Nothing.

"You home? Tom, if you're in there, I'm gonna turn on the light. Don't shoot us!" Darby flipped on the spotlight attached to the Explorer's light bar, bathing the trailer in white. Still no movement.

"When did it last snow, Sheriff?" Wells said. A thin rime covered the clearing. Animal tracks were visible, but nothing resembling shoe- or bootprints.

"A couple inches Tuesday night. Safe to say, nobody's been here since then."

"We need to go in."

"No warrant?"

"Welfare check. His buddy hasn't seen him, nobody's picking up the mail, the truck's gone. Maybe somebody shot him, stole it."

"Maybe."

"I'm gonna take a look around back."

Wells walked slowly around the trailer, his feet crunching through the stale snow. He hoped to find something that might force the sheriff's hand, but the snow was unbroken back here, too. The blind in the middle rear window was up a couple inches.

"Fine," Darby shouted from the front. "You win. Welfare check."

Wells heard Darby and Coyle walking to the front door. "Hold tight. There's a blind up—"

Wells edged to the window, glimpsed a couch, a coffee table—

"Tom!" Darby yelled. "Just want to make sure you're okay—"

Wells looked to the front door. Fishing line had been strung horizontally from the door-knob—

Too late, Wells understood the trap. They'd been so busy catching Miller and the Russians, they hadn't seen the Russians catching them, too—

"SHERIFF—"

Wells watched helplessly as the door swung out, opening up, the line pulled taut. He could just see Darby's gray shirt—

No—

The thunderclap of a shotgun tore the night into a thousand pieces.

Darby crumpled backward and vanished.

Wells ran for the front. In the distance, he heard an owl hooting for prey.

Darby lay flat on his back in the snow. Wells didn't have to touch him to know he was dead. He hadn't been wearing a vest, not that it would have mattered. The 12-gauge shot had carved him open. He wasn't even twitching.

Coyle had been hit, too, high on the right side of his chest. He was on his knees, his hands pressed against the wound, wordlessly watching his own life stain the snow. He must have been a step down from Darby. The sheriff's body had saved him, at least temporarily, but he was in bad shape.

Wells slid his arms under Coyle's shoulders, pulled him up. The sudden movement seemed to wake Coyle. He gave a single groan, low and agonized. "Sheriff."

"We have to go."

Wells tried to turn Coyle, walk him toward the Explorer, but Coyle had nothing in his legs and sagged into the snow. Wells slung an arm under Coyle's knees and picked him up, no easy feat: The Marine was short but **dense.** Wells hauled Coyle to the Explorer as Coyle's blood painted him. He pulled open the door, shoved Coyle in. Coyle slumped against the window, glassy-eyed. Wells remembered how Tony from

Tampa had bled out in fifteen minutes, no golden hour for him. He wondered how long the hospital in Colfax would need to bring in a surgeon. It was 9:15 now. Would they even have anyone on call or would they just put him in an ambulance and send him to Pullman? The hospital there had to be bigger, better equipped. Wells would need an extra fifteen minutes to reach it, but he could call them, tell them to be ready.

He snapped on Coyle's seat belt and bumped down the dirt driveway and left onto the one-lane road that led to 195. "Sherf . . ." Coyle mumbled.

"We'll come back—"

"Sherf . . ."

"Shh. Save your energy."

Wells turned the heat on high, grabbed his phone, found the emergency room number for the Pullman hospital.

"Pullman Regional ED."

"I'm bringing in a patient with a shotgun wound to the upper body. He's conscious but in shock—"

"Sir. Slow down—"

"I'm in Colfax now—" Wells swung south onto 195, and gunned the Explorer's engine. He wished he'd taken the sheriff's truck. He could have run with the emergency lights. Too late now, he'd just have to hope he didn't come across a cop on the way south. "I'll be there in fifteen. Please, have a surgeon ready, or my friend's gonna bleed out."

"What happened, sir? Is there an active shooter?"

"No. I'll explain when I get there."

Wells hung up, slowed slightly as he passed downtown Colfax, seeing the Hyde Out Tavern on his right. He hadn't noticed it before. Funny. Hilarious. At the south end of town, the road forked, and Wells swung left and put Colfax in his rearview mirror. He wished he'd never have to see it again, though he knew he'd be back to check out the trailer. He gunned the Ford's engine until it roared. The tach needle touched the red line, and the speedometer hit triple digits. The truck shook on its frame, and Wells laid off. An accident would kill Coyle for sure.

Coyle was muttering, one word: . . . ink . . . ink . . .

Wells didn't understand. Then he did.

Not ink. Not link either.

Linc . . . Linc . . .

Lincoln, Coyle's dead younger brother. Wells grabbed Coyle's left hand with his right, squeezed it as hard as he could, dug his fingers into Coyle's palm.

"You don't get to see him yet, Sergeant. You stay with me."

Despite the overheated air pouring from the vents, Wells found himself shivering, remembering a song he hadn't thought of in a while: **This train . . . / Carries saints and sinners / This train . . . / Carries losers and winners . . .**

"Land of Hope and Dreams," it was called. Springsteen.

If Coyle died, Wells would have to quit. The truth.

Emergency lights ahead, pulsing their red-and-blue SOS into the night. Northbound. Probably one of the neighbors had called in the shotgun. Maybe one had even found Darby's body already. Wells slowed to seventy-five until the cruiser passed, then jammed down the pedal.

He called Tarnes, wishing he had done so before they went to Miller's house. Past midnight in Washington, but he knew she'd answer. She did, the second ring. "John."

"We found him. His name's Tom Miller, he's on the list."

"How do you know?"

"We know. But it's a mess here, and you need to get in front of it now—like, right now. The local sheriff is dead and Coyle's wounded, I'm taking him to the hospital."

"What happened—"

The door opening, the fishing line tightening—

"Trap in Miller's trailer, shotgun." **Why didn't we see it? Why didn't I see it?** But Wells knew. And he hated the reason. Being in the field alone was exhausting, and he made plenty of mistakes. But he never let down his guard. Tonight, he and Coyle had relaxed. Not just because they'd handled all the other meetings that day easily, even Harlan Gould. Not even because they felt they could depend on each other. Because they **liked** working together. For a minute, they'd forgotten the stakes of the game. A minute was all the other side needed. **No time-outs, no takebacks.**

Beside him, Coyle coughed, low, throaty grunts, like he had blood in his throat. Pullman was only a couple miles off.

"You there, John?"

"Just get the FBI on this guy Miller. He had a pickup and it's gone. I don't know the make or the model, but I'll bet that's their hide."

"Tom Miller?"

"Yeah, and get ready to airlift Coyle to the closest hospital with a trauma center. And pick up when the cops call you about me, I need to get back to that trailer tonight."

Wells hung up, wrapped an arm around Coyle's

shoulders, pulled him away from the window. Coyle groaned. Good. He could still feel pain. "You can't die on me, Marine—"

Coyle coughed. He was trying to talk again. **Fine . . . fine . . .** No. **Find.**

"That's right, Sergeant. I'm going to find this motherfucker." The word burned Wells's mouth like bleach. "And you're going to be there when I do."

25

Wells came back to Miller's trailer just past midnight Friday morning. Its false wooded serenity was gone. It was a crime scene now, the property of the State of Washington, to be prodded until it gave up its secrets. All its lights were on, but it looked emptier than ever.

Paramedics and sheriff's deputies had moved Darby's corpse to the morgue at Pullman Regional, leaving only a patch of bloody and trampled snow where he'd lain. In their place, two state troopers sat in a Yukon next to Darby's Explorer. The troopers told Wells they'd peeked inside the trailer to make sure there were no other bodies. They were waiting for daylight and a forensics team for a full search. Wells understood the caution, but he couldn't wait. He doubted the Russians had left more traps. They would want investigators to be able to search the trailer and find the clues they'd left.

At least Wells would be able to work in secret. The initial service calls had gone out over police radio, but no cub reporter with a notepad and an iPhone set to record was going to show up. Wells figured Seattle, two hundred seventy miles west, was the closest city where reporters were on duty all night. And no one except the cops and Darby's family knew he had died. The FBI had asked the Sheriff's Office and Washington State Patrol to sit on the shooting until morning. The deputies had told Darby's wife but asked her to stay quiet, too. The announcement they planned for the morning would say only that Darby had died overnight and that they were investigating.

Leaving out the details would buy them extra time, though by early afternoon the state papers and Associated Press would insist on knowing more. Once the word **ambush** appeared, the story would become national news. But those hours would give Wells and the FBI a chance to find Tom Miller and the woman who called herself Allie.

═══════

The details had been worked out while Wells was locked in an office at Pullman Regional. The local cops had waited for him at the emergency room entrance. No surprise, after his call. They frisked and cuffed him while the hospital techs moved Coyle to a gurney and sped him away. An officer half Wells's age asked him if he'd shot Coyle, or anyone else, then frog-marched him to an office and shackled him to a desk.

Wells stared at the ceiling as he tried to unpack what had happened. On some subconscious level, he must have recognized the trap. Otherwise, why had he circled the trailer instead of going to the door? But he hadn't taken the time to understand what his intuition was telling him.

He closed his eyes as the Muslim prayer for the sick came to him: **As'alu Allah al'azim rabbil 'arshil azim an yashifika—I ask Allah, the Mighty, the Lord of the Mighty Throne, to cure you.** Coyle would laugh at the blessing, Wells knew. Coyle couldn't stand religion. Since his brother died, he was as sure an atheist as the late, great Christopher Hitchens. Wells repeated the prayer, anyway. Arabic was better than English for these desperate pleas, faster, more guttural and primal. It dug deeper into the muck where the truth lay buried—

A long night ahead, and Wells was already exhausted, the adrenaline from the ambush gone.

He put his head on the table, floated through the walls into the operating room with Coyle. His dad, Herbert, was the surgeon, which made perfect sense. Herbert reached into Coyle's chest with neon green tweezers, and a buzzer on Coyle's nose went off. **Thought you said he was the best,** Coyle said. **Just like you.**

Before Wells could answer, the operating room door swung open. Sheriff Darby rode a BMX bicycle through. He pulled a wheelie and gave Wells a thumbs-up. **Trusting a boy from Montana,** he said. **Lookit me now.**

Lookit? Coyle said. **Did he say** lookit? **Am I already in Hell?**

You don't believe in Hell, Wells said.

Got to be better than nothing.

Come on, Dad, get to work.

What's the rush, John? We've got forever and a day, forever and a day—

Herbert began to sing, a low baritone rumble, then reached down to pull Coyle off the table, swing him around the room, a Fred-and-Ginger routine—

Better than jazz, Marine, I tell you—

The office door mercifully swung open, pulling Wells awake. He wiped sleep from his mouth as the cop walked in. The wall clock said an hour had passed, but the nap had played the neat trick of making Wells even more tired. He'd been so sure Coyle was dead. A bad sign.

The cop unlocked his cuffs. "Supposed to take you wherever you want." He sounded neither annoyed nor impressed with the fact that he'd been told to chauffeur a man who'd been a murder suspect an hour before. He was young enough not to question his orders. Wells wasn't sure he himself had ever been that young.

"I've got my own car. Anyplace around here still selling coffee at this hour?"

"Jack in the Box up 27."

"Thanks."

___

On his way out, Wells asked the nurses if anyone had news on Coyle. "Gonna be a while," the head nurse said. "But he's lucky Dr. Kenley was on call tonight. She's amazing."

Wells wanted to stay until the surgery was done, but the trailer awaited. He scribbled his number. "When she comes out, will you ask her to call me? Any hour, doesn't matter."

The nurse took the number but shook her head. "She probably won't. HIPAA."

___

The Ford stank of blood. Red smears covered its passenger-side window. Wells wondered how many units Coyle had lost. He knew he should call Coyle's parents, but he couldn't bring himself to wake them, especially when he didn't know whether Coyle would survive the night.

Instead, he called Tarnes, who filled him in on what had happened while he was locked up. She'd reached the duty officers at FBI headquarters, who'd passed a message to the Seattle agent in charge, who had leaned on the Washington State Patrol. The Feds would have their own agents at the trailer by morning. Meanwhile, the troopers guarding the trailer were expecting Wells and would let him pass.

"Thanks, Julie."

"Any word on Winston?"

Strange to hear Coyle's first name. Wells usually called him Coyle or Sergeant. "Still in surgery."

"You call his people?"

The question jabbed Wells. "Not yet. I wanted to know where he stands."

"I can do it. You have enough to worry about."

Wells almost said yes. But he was Coyle's senior officer. The job was his. "Get some sleep, Julie. I'll call them."

"Let me know if you find anything. And John . . . ?"

His name hung heavy. "What's that?"

"Not everything's your fault."

Then she was gone.

He badly wanted to call Anne. But waking a pregnant woman at 4 a.m. to make her carry his sins seemed cheap. Instead, Wells swung into Jack in the Box and ordered a combination meal, cheeseburger and large fries. Eating emotionally in his old age, soothing his soul with salt and fat. Then two more combos, though those weren't for him. No quicker way to a cop's heart.

———

Sure enough, the troopers watching the trailer perked up at the burgers.

"Twelve-gauge," the one in the passenger seat said. "Rigged to angle down the stairs. Nasty. You'll see."

"Find anything else?"

"Not much. It's empty, for sure. The door to the bedroom's open, so we looked, but we didn't check any closets. Basically, sniffed the place for bodies."

In other words, the troopers hadn't gone out of their way to find more traps. "Understood."

The trooper handed Wells latex gloves and booties. "Just don't mess it up for tomorrow, the techs are gonna shake it out."

At the door, Wells pulled on the protective gear, stepped inside. The trap that had killed Darby waited. **Nasty** was right. The shotgun had been hidden in a closet in a wall left of the front door. The killer had nailed a two-by-six to the closet floor, duct-taped a metal C-clamp to the wood, tightened the clamp around the barrel of a shotgun. The fishing line ran from the doorknob, through a pulley screwed into the back of the closet, to the trigger.

Civilians called these setups **booby traps**. Police called them **spring guns**. By any name, they were simple and deadly. This one had been positioned high and angled down, to take out not just the person who opened the door but anyone behind him. And the person who set it had left the door unlocked to make entering easy.

Seeing it set Wells's blood on fire. He knew the killer hadn't meant to target Coyle or Darby. But the randomness only made him angrier. He wondered if Miller had set the trap. Probably the Russians. They could have come to the trailer anytime after Miller and Allie left and before the snow on Tuesday night. Miller had probably given Allie the key months before. If not, she could have stolen and copied it. The police might never find the answer. The filament, C-clamp, and wood were all available at any Home Depot.

The shotgun was a Remington, a popular brand, untraceable if it had been bought used for cash at a gun show or garage sale.

Wells forced himself to leave the closet behind, turn to the rest of the trailer. The living room was spare and clean, guides to local hiking trails stacked on the coffee table, weights in the corner alongside a sit-up mat. The furniture was carefully set at right angles. Miller hadn't lost his military habits. He'd cleaned before he left, too. The toilet was spotless. The glasses and coffee cups were washed. The refrigerator was empty, aside from a jug of water, a loaf of white bread, and a package of string cheese.

Wells found no trace of Allie, no women's clothes or cosmetics or personal items. A box of condoms was tucked in the bathroom cabinet, but it was unopened. Wells suspected that if the FBI matched the serial number, the Bureau would find it predated Allie's arrival. No surprise. She wouldn't have wanted to leave any evidence of her existence.

The gun safe in the bedroom was locked tight. Wells left it. If the Russians had set a second trap anywhere, the safe would be the place. Besides, he already knew Miller had taken his rifle.

The more Wells looked, the more strongly he felt that Miller had intended to leave not just this place but his life behind when he walked out. In a kitchen drawer he found Miller's most important documents neatly stacked: discharge papers; medical records, showing the extent of his injuries in Kandahar; the title and registration to his pickup, which turned out to be a black Dodge Ram; the Veterans Administration letter explaining he'd been given a sixty percent disability rating. A dozen photographs from Afghanistan lay at the bottom. Mostly standard stuff for an infantryman, pics of Miller and his fellow soldiers at the base and on patrol. One showed Miller grinning as he sat astride a donkey that had a big red ribbon stuck to its side. A sergeant stood beside the donkey, angling a bottle of Jim Beam as if he planned to pour a shot in the animal's mouth. As Urquhart had told Wells and Coyle, Miller wasn't very good-looking: short, with pitted skin and a strange slope to his forehead. He looked happy enough in the picture, though.

At the back of the drawer, Wells found the red ribbon from the picture. Miller could have had other copies of the photos, maybe even his medical records. He didn't have another ribbon. He'd cared enough about it to bring it home from Kandahar. He hadn't forgotten it here. He'd left it.

Wells took it, left everything else for the cops.

The Russians had seeded the place relatively subtly. Wells found no ISIS flags or Qurans left open to verses that called for death to the unbelievers. But the top drawer of Miller's bedside table held a dozen pamphlets about Islam, the basic brochures that mosques and Islamic community centers left on their front tables for curious American visitors. **What does Islam say about terrorism? Who was the Prophet Muhammad? What do Muslims believe about Christians and Jews? Ramadan: The Month of Fasting . . .** The pamphlets were creased, paragraphs circled and underlined. Wells took them. Islam had enough problems in the United States without the Kremlin helping.

The second drawer contained two photographs. They both showed the bloodied corpse of an Afghan child lying on a muddy village path, his neck torn apart by a high-caliber round. The photos were taken from different angles, both close up. Wells suspected that even a forensic expert would have no way to determine where or when they had been taken, much less who had taken them. They didn't have any indication of when they'd been printed on the back.

Wells wondered if Miller had really taken the pictures, if they'd really depicted an incident from his tour. If not, the Russians were taking a chance by leaving them. On the other hand, would the FBI want to ask the soldiers who'd served with Miller about them? And if his buddies denied that they depicted a real incident, would investigators believe them? Plenty of kids had died during the war, usually by accident, occasionally in atrocities that received little attention in the United States but lots in Afghanistan.

The Russians were offering a story the investigators would understand: an angry veteran, getting by on disability, lonely, Hispanic in a rural and overwhelmingly white community, racked with guilt over a child's death. He'd grown interested in Islam, self-radicalized, decided to put his skills as a sniper to use. **I've met the enemy and he is us.** As an explanation for terrorism, the narrative was a little paint-by-numbers, but it would stick. Best of all, from the Russian point of view, it didn't require Twitter rants from Miller, or even letters or a diary. The photos and records spoke for themselves.

Of course, none of this evidence explained how the woman who called herself Allie had actually convinced Miller to shoot a pastor and a cardinal. Wells couldn't imagine her playing a true believer, considering she'd picked Miller up in a bar. He supposed only Miller and Allie knew the answer. He took one of the photos, left the second. He suspected having the picture might come in handy if and when he confronted Miller.

In the bottom drawer, more articles, these about the futility of the Afghan war, the problems at Walter Reed. Followed by stories about Luke Hurley, Cardinal McDonnell, and—

Paul Birman. Senator from Tennessee. Chairman of the Select Committee on Intelligence. Presumptive presidential candidate. And the leading voice for more American invasions of Islamic countries. Birman had been in the news plenty since the Hurley shooting. In fact—

He was giving a speech. Friday afternoon. Today. In Dallas. At the site of last month's attack.

A perfect target. Birman would have security, but it wouldn't be overwhelming. Considering the attention he was receiving, he was a target nearly as important as Duto, with a fraction of Duto's protection. The FBI and police were focused on the threat to religious leaders. Killing him in Dallas would resonate, and not just because of the bombing. The American Airlines Center was not even a mile from Dealey Plaza. And sooner would be better than later, as far as the Russians were concerned. With the manhunt for Miller intensifying, they would want to use him as soon as possible. Three shootings in a week would also force Duto to respond.

———

Wells grabbed the articles about Birman, left everything else, slid the drawer shut. Looked around once more, silently wondering if the Russians might have offered Birman's name as a fake to send investigators the wrong way. But no. The other two targets had already been shot. And the Russians wouldn't have expected anyone to find the trailer so soon. It was supposed to be discovered only after Allie tossed Miller to the sharks. Everything in it was meant to confirm Miller's guilt.

Presumably, after Miller was done today the Russians would kill him in what looked like a suicide. Maybe a bombing, his truck loaded with ammonium nitrate and fuel oil. He was on the chopping block. Allie couldn't afford to have him talking.

Wells pulled up Kayak, checked Seattle-to-Dallas nonstops. Lucky him, the route was popular. There was a 6:05 a.m. American nonstop that landed at DFW at noon local time. It was only 12:45 a.m. now. He should be able to make the flight. If not, Alaska had one an hour later.

He jogged back to the Explorer. He wasn't tired anymore. He wanted morning.

———

He called Shafer at 4:30 a.m., still twenty minutes east of Seattle, no hint of dawn, just him and the big rigs racing through the dark on I-90.

"You're up early."

"Didn't sleep." Wells explained his night. As he walked Shafer through the trap at the trailer, he realized the surgeon hadn't called him yet. Maybe she was still operating. Maybe HIPAA had stopped her. Maybe she'd finished and gone straight to sleep. Or maybe—

No. He wouldn't let himself even think the word.

"John?"

"Sorry. Good news is, I'm pretty sure I know the next target. Paul Birman. I went back to the trailer, found articles about him right next to Luke Hurley and James McDonnell."

"Birman's speaking here today—"

"I know. I'm flying down at six. Get to DFW at noon."

"You told Tarnes?"

"Not yet. Not until I get down there."

Meaning: **We don't tell anyone. We find him ourselves.**

"FBI's gonna figure it as soon as they search the trailer, anyway."

"No they're not." The reason that Wells had taken the pages about Birman from the drawer.

"John—" Shafer stopped himself. "What if your plane's late? What if we can't find him?"

"There's gonna be a hotel that has rooms with a view of the speech, and Miller and his little friend are gonna be there."

"Unless they're not. Unless there are five hotels like that. Unless he sticks with the rolling hide. You're gambling with Birman's life."

"We have time, Ellis. We can tell the Feds if we don't find him ourselves. Plus, if we tell Birman to cancel the speech, he will."

"Unless he thinks we're trying to make him look bad because we work for Duto, and he won't back down."

"We'll find him."

"Hong Kong all over again. You're making it personal."

Wells looked at Coyle's blood on the passenger window. **Of course I'm making it personal.** "I need a pistol, too." He couldn't bring the one he had with him through airport screening, and he had no time to check a bag.

"Of course you do. What do you even think you're going to do with this guy, John? Tell him how your buddy got shot, and he kneels at your feet, asks forgiveness?"

"We know more about this than anyone. Way more than the FBI. I just want to hear for myself how the Russians played him. While he's fresh."

Shafer was silent for long enough that Wells wondered if the call had dropped.

"Come on, Ellis."

"What's the car he's using?"

And Wells knew he'd won. "A black Dodge Ram four-door pickup. Three years old. Washington tags."

"All right. While you're in the air, I'll see what I can find. But if we don't have him at three, you're calling Tarnes, and I'm telling the FBI. **Three.** You hear me? Not three-thirty, not four. That's close enough."

A deadline that would give Wells less than three hours on the ground in Dallas. He wanted to argue, but Shafer was right. "When did you turn into such a goody-goody, Ellis?"

26

DALLAS

The Dallas/Fort Worth metroplex included five million residents sprawled across three thousand square miles. But the real money lay in a snug triangle in the center of Dallas, bounded by Love Field—the area's original airport—to the west, downtown's office towers to the south, and the mansions of University Park and Preston Hollow to the north.

The famous hotel now called the Rosewood Mansion on Turtle Creek sat near the heart of the triangle. Naturally, Paul Birman was staying there the night before his speech. Naturally, he'd put himself in the Presidential Suite. For a mere three thousand dollars a night, the suite offered gold taps in the bathroom and a terrace the size of a house. Eric knew Lucky Cousin Paul believed he deserved no less.

Eric was stuck three floors down with the commoners. He watched CNN on mute as he took one final pass at Paul's speech. He wished he could leave everything after page 5 blank, but even Paul might wonder why. He closed his laptop, climbed into bed. For a while, he stared at the ceiling, excited as a kid waiting for Santa. **'Twas the night before Christmas, when all thro' the house / Not a creature was stirring, not even a sniper.**

By tomorrow night, he would be the Birman everyone knew.

Yet his decades as a soldier had taught him that rest was too precious to squander, especially with action ahead. He was not surprised when he faded into unconsciousness.

His alarm snapped him awake at 6 a.m. He ran for an hour on a treadmill downstairs, came back to his room for a shower and coffee. He was finishing his second cup when the room phone trilled.

"Eric? I need you up here. Now."

=====

Eric walked into the Presidential Suite to find a hotel housekeeper ironing a handmade English suit. Paul's professed love of buying American didn't extend to his clothes.

"In here." In the bedroom, Paul was knotting a tie—muted red, of course.

"**Morning News** and local TV are setting up downstairs," Eric said. Paul had interviews scheduled to promote his speech.

"FBI director just called. He wanted me to hear it from him. They have a break on the sniper."

Eric's first thought: The fact that Paul had personally received a call showed how important he was becoming. The head of the FBI didn't waste his time giving updates to average senators.

His second thought was less polite, half-formed curses melting into a scream: **Nonooonooooo . . .**

"He say what they have?" Eric kept his voice steady.

"Just for you, okay?"

Eric looked at him: **I'm your cousin, of course you can trust me.**

"They know who it is. He wouldn't tell me how, but they're sure. They've put him in Chicago the day of the shooting. An American citizen. He wouldn't say if he was Muslim."

But Eric's friends must have put together a backstory for him, whoever he was. "They going public?"

"Not yet. They think they have enough to find him quietly in the next forty-eight hours. Maybe sooner. I don't know what, exactly. He wouldn't say, and I didn't push. But they don't want to spook him, they're worried he might start shooting randomly or blow himself up if he knows they're close. They're going to brief the committee tonight. I think I should be there."

Eric's pulse thumped in his throat. The Russians wouldn't have another chance after today. When the FBI realized that Paul had been the third target, he wouldn't need to hire Deltas, he'd have presidential-level protection. "The speech—"

"Duto will crush me if I'm not at the briefing. **Senator Birman can't even be bothered to meet the FBI director—**"

Eric saw the answer, the **only** answer. If he could sell it. "You can still give the speech. We'll move it up—say, two p.m. Takes twenty minutes, a half hour. We go straight to Love, you're back in D.C. by five-thirty, on the Hill at six at the latest."

"No one will pay attention to what I say—"

"Give it **before** they catch the guy, you have today's news cycle at least. Maybe longer. There's no guarantee they're going to find him as fast as they think. Plus I'll rework the speech to hint what might be coming, so you stay in front even if they do: **I know the FBI and CIA are doing everything possible to protect us. The problem is, the direction they're receiving from the White House—**"

"Can we even change the time this late?"

"Of course. We only skedded it this week. Look, you took the trouble to fly down here."

Eric saw the last sentence had scored. Like most lazy people, Paul hated to waste the minimal work he did put in. "All right, if you can change it and make sure we can still get an audience—"

"No worries, just tell all those local interviews you'll be speaking at two. They love you here, Paul. Nineteen hundred people already signed up on the web to say they're coming. Say you had to change it because you have a big national security briefing back in D.C. tonight, that'll get people interested."

"Think CNN and Fox will still cover it?"

"I'll start making calls right now." **Though I'll keep the first one to myself.**

===

Back in his room, Eric pulled his emergency phone, punched in Adam Petersen's number. He hesitated before connecting the call. He'd never used this phone before now. Petersen had told him the number on the other end was clean, too. But then the Russians hadn't expected the FBI to find their sniper so fast, had they? If the Feds discovered Petersen somehow, the NSA would trace this call to Dallas, and Eric would be toast.

But Eric had no choice. He had to talk to Petersen. He made the call.

Petersen didn't answer. **No.** Not the time for the Russians to fumble their emergency procedures.

Eric waited three minutes, redialed. Two rings . . . three . . . four . . . **Come on—**

"Hello."

They had confirmation codes. Eric didn't feel like using them. Petersen knew who he was. "The man doing your work today, he's sick. Very sick."

"Where do you hear this? As far as I know, he's healthy—"

For the first time, Eric heard the hint of an accent in Petersen's voice. Stress.

"I'm sure. These doctors are good. I want to reschedule his appointment. Two p.m."

A pause. "Two, yes, that will work. I'll make sure he knows. And you, are you still all right?"

"I'm feeling fine. For now."

"If that changes and you need emergency treatment—"

"I'll let you know." So the Kremlin would stick to its promise to bring him to Russia, if he asked.

"Good, then." And Petersen was gone.

Two p.m. Six hours. Eric pulled open his curtains and stared into the morning sun until his eyes burned. Either way, he wouldn't have long to wait.

Wells touched down at DFW at noon. Fourteen voice mails and twenty-three texts awaited him. Ten from Tarnes. The first couple were chipper enough. The FBI had found footage of Miller's pickup in Chicago on the morning of the Cardinal's shooting. Confirmation, not that Wells needed any.

Two calls later, she had news about Coyle. Good news.

The operation had lasted seven hours and cost Coyle the middle lobe of his right lung. But he was alive. The surgeon had inserted a tube into his chest to relieve the pressure and put him on a ventilator to help him breathe. He was in critical but stable condition. For now, he would stay at Pullman Regional. The doctors in both Pullman and Seattle believed the risks of transporting him outweighed the extra care a bigger hospital could offer. **I'll call his parents to update them,** she said, **'case you don't get this for a while.** Wells tried to ignore the implicit rebuke. He had called Coyle's family twice just before takeoff. But they hadn't answered, and he hadn't wanted to leave a message.

As the hours passed, Tarnes's messages grew more urgent. **FBI's been in the trailer all morning. They're sure Miller's their man. I know you** were there last night, John, I know you saw what they saw. The troopers said you left in a hurry. Don't play with me. You found something, and you're not in a sharing mood. Don't make me tell them to put out an APB for you, too.

Then a message from Shafer. **Google says your flight is on time. Hope it stays that way, sahib. I have something, but we're cutting it close. While you were flapping your wings over Idaho, Birman moved up the speech. Two p.m. He's saying the FBI wants him back in D.C. tonight. I'm guessing they want to brief the Intelligence Committee on the sniper. Oh, the irony.** Shafer was excited, the words coming even faster than usual. He'd found Miller. Or thought he had.

Finally, Duto. **You're being a very bad boy, John, not answering Julie. No idea what you're playing at, but whatever it is, it stops now. Pissing me off. And if something happens that you could have stopped, I will make you pay. You hear me?** The clipped fury of a man who wasn't used to being ignored.

Wells wondered if FBI agents might be waiting for him at the gate with a material witness warrant. He'd booked the flight under his own name, and the Transportation Security Administration would happily check passenger manifests for him if the FBI asked. No court order necessary, the Bureau could simply tell the TSA it had added him to the Selectee list, a triumph of Orwellian naming. Another step in the long, slow death of privacy. Anyway, nothing for Wells to do but wait as the jet inched toward its gate. DFW was massive, with an awkward five-terminal design. Planes seemed to spend as much time taxiing as they did in the air.

At last, the cabin door swung open, and Wells strode out. No one was at the gate. He would have sprinted through the terminal, but these days airports were bad places to sprint. Or do anything that police might notice.

———

He reached the curb at 12:35, waited five more minutes for Shafer. "Cops made me move. They were going to arrest me. I showed them my CIA badge, and they literally laughed."

"Confidence-inspiring." Wells squeezed himself into the front seat of the RAV4.

"What you asked for, it's under the seat." Shafer eased into the airport traffic.

Wells reached down, found a 9-millimeter Sig Sauer. Not his favorite pistol, but sturdy enough.

"Loaded and everything."

"Where is he?"

556 | ALEX BERENSON

"Before we get to that, aren't you interested in the bombing investigation?"

"I'm not joking, Ellis."

"Neither am I. I'm trying to remind you this isn't just about you and Coyle."

The answer stopped Wells.

"Those FBI guys got some good stuff yesterday, even if they don't know why it's good. Short on imagination, but point them in the right direction and they swarm. God help anyone in their way. They're like locusts. **Robot** locusts. Do we have those yet? I'll bet we do."

"Please continue."

"They found this warehouse in South Dallas that I'm thinking was where our friends brought Ahmed Shakir to flip him. Metal desks, eyeball cameras in the corners. Looks like a hide for undercovers, which is what they would have wanted him to think. Two black SUVs that could have come out of an FBI garage. No cop lights in the grille, but our friends could have been smart enough to take 'em out before they bailed. Guess what? Someone cleaned their nav systems, too, so there's no record where they went."

"But the Feds haven't put it together?"

"Not a clue. They're just chasing what Duto told them to. They're not happy, but it's not like they can order the President to tell them the whole story. Maybe one day one of them will take another look at the interviews and realize what Jeanelle Pitts said. Hasn't happened yet."

"Once they hit Banamex—"

"Yeah, that'll change things. Duto might not mind if your friend Mendoz just took a runner. Or the Russians gave her a forever siesta. He's in a tough spot if she talks. I almost feel sorry for him on this one. All bad choices."

"Don't you worry about Vinny. Whatever happens, he'll protect himself." Wells flashed to Coyle, trying not to choke on his own blood. Trying not to die. The worst choice of all.

"Irony is, we're about to save his biggest political threat. He might not mind if we let Tom Miller take care of Birman."

"That would be cold, even for him." Though Wells wouldn't put much past Duto.

Ahead, signs pointed to Texas 114 and downtown Dallas. Shafer made a late turn, cutting off a pickup that responded with an angry honk. Shafer raised his right hand to offer a single-finger response. Wells pulled it down.

"Didn't you learn your lesson about Texas, Ellis? Don't need to piss off some guy with an open-carry permit."

"Yeah, yeah."

"Okay, I listened to you. Now, where is he?"

"In good time."

Wells wanted to reach over and throttle Shafer's skinny neck.

Shafer smirked. "At least now you know how Duto feels about you."

━━━━

Tom Miller stared at the digital clock on the cable box, willing it to roll from 1:00 to 1:01 . . . **There.** The witching hour had begun. He lay on the floor beside his Remington, checked the plaza where Paul Birman would speak. Hundreds of people were already there, with more coming every minute. But the flags and ropes were still limp, the wind quiet.

This would be the easiest shot yet.

━━━━

On Wednesday night, Allie had booked them a room at the W through a reservation site that took PayPal. **Don't think anyone's looking for us, but this keeps our names out of the system just in case,** Allie said. Miller didn't ask what system or how she knew.

They drove through the night on I-30, arrived in Dallas in darkness Thursday morning, found a motel where they could shower and sleep for a few hours so they wouldn't look homeless. By noon, they'd arrived at the American Airlines Center. Miller cruised the highways and surface roads around it. Not an ideal site. The blocks near the arena were more built up than he'd expected, lots of bulky mid-rises. He'd need to be above them to be sure he'd have a clean angle. The W itself was more than thirty stories high, a handsome building that loomed over the south side of the arena, but its glass-clad upper half was all condos. The hotel was stuck on the bottom fifteen floors. He hoped Allie had a plan to put them at the top of those.

Miller pulled up to the hotel, and a valet jogged up. "Checking in, sir?"

"Yes."

"Need help with your luggage?"

"I got it." Miller had hidden his rifle case in a green duffel bag, stuffed T-shirts and jeans around it. He didn't want anyone touching it. He hauled it and Allie's suitcase from the back seat of the Ram. The duffel looked a little unusual, but the W had lots of celebrity guests. The hotel staff would be used to unusual bags. Plus Allie was wearing a T-shirt so small it barely reached her belly button. No one was going to notice him.

The place looked pretty cool, to be honest. The lobby had huge chandeliers and bright silver-colored chairs and tables. Miller had never stayed anywhere this fancy before. Not even close. Truth was, he would have been too intimidated to hang out here by himself. These places weren't for guys like him. Even the bellboys were four inches taller than he was. But Allie walked right in like she owned the place. Miller followed. He hadn't seen this side of her before, the woman who could turn heads in a ritzy hotel. It didn't surprise him, though. The more time he spent with her, the more he realized he had no idea who she really was. But maybe all women were that way, and he just hadn't been close enough to any of them to know.

The check-in clerk, a skinny black guy with a diamond stud in his nose, looked over the reservation. "Just need a driver's license and a credit card for incidentals."

Miller would have been thrown, but Allie had told him what to expect. **Give them your license, that's fine, that's just to verify your identity. Your name stays in their system, even if someone's looking for us. No one will find it until later. But no credit card.**

"Can I give you cash instead of a card?"

"We require a four-hundred-dollar additional deposit per night . . . But, sure."

Miller handed over eight crisp hundred-dollar bills. Three weeks of disability. The clerk counted it, tucked it in a drawer.

"Great. I have a room for you, fourth floor."

Way too low. Miller felt Allie's hand on the small of his back: **Let me handle this.** He stepped aside. Allie gave the clerk her best smile, the one that had made Miller fall in love with her. He'd never seen her use it on anyone else. He was both jealous and pleased to see the way the clerk lit up.

"We'd really like a higher floor."

The guy pecked at his keyboard. "I can put you on eight."

"Nothing higher? I like to get as high as I can."

"I hear that." He grinned. "Okay, we have something on fourteen. I have to warn you, it's a suite, there's an upcharge."

"As long as it's on the west side of the hotel so we can watch the sunset."

"That's actually easier. Most people like the other side, they want to see downtown. Usually, it's an extra three hundred a night, but I think I can do it for a hundred with the override . . . Yes, there. Two hundred for two nights."

She kissed Miller lightly on the lips. "Can we, Tom?"

Miller handed over two more hundred-dollar bills, loving the feeling of being rich, handing out money like he'd always have more. Of having a beautiful woman beside him, a woman other men openly desired. For the next few hours, anyway, he would live like an athlete or a billionaire. A

baller. Whatever happened tomorrow, he planned to enjoy himself tonight.

===

He did, too. Room 1412 was positioned perfectly for the shot. It occupied the floor's southwest corner, with a clear view over the office building that sat between the W and Valor Place, where Birman would speak. The glass was thin, single-layer. He could break it easily just before he fired. The range was barely two hundred yards, and Birman wouldn't be moving as he spoke.

Even better, Birman's team would have to set up a stage, podium, speakers, and ropes to block off space for the crowd. Miller would know hours in advance exactly where Birman would be standing. Miller didn't know how much security Birman would have, but he doubted anyone would put a protective tent or cover over the podium and stage. Even if they did, they'd be too late. Miller would have locked in the shot. The car bomb had blown up slightly north of the arena's west entrance, so Miller figured that Birman would face that direction. Miller was shooting from the south, into the back of Birman's skull. The man would never know what had hit him.

"What do you think?" Allie said.

"No problem."

She stood beside him, wrapped an arm around him.

That night, she was sexier than she had ever been. She screamed so loudly, he worried someone might think he was hurting her. After the first go-round, they ordered room service: fries and burgers. He tried to ignore the gnawing fear that he'd traded the lives of two men for this pleasure.

Finally, they'd exhausted each other. They lay quietly on the bed, talking through the plan one more time. It was simple enough. After the shot, Miller would tear ass down the fire stairs, which were just outside the room. Allie would wait a block east, in an alley that didn't have any surveillance cameras. She'd have a car rented in her name, no way to connect it to him. He'd lie down in the back seat, and south they'd go. Three major interstates—I-30, I-35E, and I-45—were located within a mile of the hotel. The police couldn't possibly shut them in time to matter.

Once they were out of Dallas, Allie could stay on the interstate, or switch to the surface roads that crisscrossed the flat Texas prairie. She would drive to Eagle Pass, on the Mexican border, return the car. By then, the FBI would surely have connected Miller to the room. He'd be the most wanted man in the world. The hotel surveillance cameras would have caught Allie, too, but no one knew her name or anything about her. She'd dye her hair black, put on a shapeless dress. Give him a buzz cut, a cowboy hat, tight Mexican-style jeans and boots.

"You'll be surprised how different we look," she said now. "No one will recognize us. Especially once we get over the border. I'm trusting you on that part."

"I've been to Mexico once in my life."

"But you were a soldier, you can read a map. Walk south, find a hole in the fence, and cross the river, right? Everybody else is going the other way. Once we're over, we catch a bus to Mexico City, twenty million people who look like you." She stroked his chin. "I trust you, Tom. Trust me back, we'll be fine."

Miller wondered if they really had a chance to reach Mexico. If she'd even be waiting for him tomorrow in the alley. He knew he ought to care, but he didn't.

Way he figured, his soul had never been worth much. His dad had shown him that a long time back. He'd gotten full value for it already.

When he woke the next morning, Allie was gone. Renting the car, buying clothes and maps and a hammer to break the glass and everything else. Miller pulled the rifle case from the duffel, raised the privacy shade a few inches, set up. One advantage of the suite: It was big enough that he could stretch out on the floor with plenty of room to shoot.

The buildings west of the W were all low-rises, and the reflective glass made seeing into the room from below nearly impossible. Still, Miller planned to leave the shade down against the slim chance that a police or news helicopter buzzed close. He looked through the scope, saw a guy in a long-sleeved black shirt holding a rope line. **Already?** He stood, peeked at the plaza. Two guys stringing rope through stanchions. Two more grabbing speaker stands from the back of a truck. Seemed early to be setting up for a speech tonight, but maybe they expected a big crowd. Anyway, the rope would come in handy for giving him a sense of the wind, though the Weather Channel was forecasting a calm day, just a light southerly breeze off the plains. If the wind picked up, he would have to go for a body shot instead of the head. He hoped it wouldn't. He liked the idea of a head shot.

He peeked through the rifle once more, then called room service. Normally, the idea of spending forty bucks for eggs and orange juice and coffee would have drained his appetite. But he didn't have the chance to shoot a United States senator every day. Make his mom proud.

What would happen if he and Allie escaped today and she kept giving him targets? Would he get used to killing people this way? He didn't think of himself as a mass murderer, but he was. Five in Afghanistan, two more back home, and here he was about to add another to the list. With a head shot.

His right hand quivered. Excitement, fear, self-disgust—he couldn't tell anymore. He clenched his fingers in a fist, turned on the television to distract himself—

There. Paul Birman. Snazzy in a suit and tie. Telling the interviewer, a woman almost as pretty as Allie, he'd changed the time of his speech. "Two p.m. Hoping for a great crowd."

"And this is because—"

"I've just learned of an Intelligence Committee briefing tonight in Washington, urgent, I can't say anything else. But I look forward to seeing Dallas this afternoon. I'm going to offer specific new ways we can fight the War on Terror. We know President Duto doesn't have the answer—"

Miller snapped off the television. At least now he knew why they were setting up early. Changing the time of the speech? An urgent briefing? Could the FBI be onto him?

His mouth went dry as he realized how badly he wanted to kill Paul Birman. With his perfect teeth and his perfect chin and his perfect suit—

He heard footsteps in the hall, moving toward the suite. He slid to the door, pulled it open—

A brown-skinned man stood outside, holding a tray. "Room service, sir."

The rifle. Had he seen the rifle? Miller stepped into the hall.

"I can set it up inside for you—"

"Leave it."

"It's no trouble."

"Leave it." If the guy stayed much longer, Miller might lose his mind.

The man put down the tray and offered the bill without another word.

The rest of the morning ticked by agonizingly slowly. He had no way to reach Allie. Both their phones were off. He watched as the crew on the plaza put together a stage, set up a podium and chairs, hooked the speakers to a portable generator, finished setting the rope lines, tested the sound system, added a row of American flags. Around noon, the first television vans showed, the local stations. The audience started coming, too. Mostly men, mostly white. The Fox and CNN trucks arrived a few minutes later.

Then the cops, a dozen marked Dallas police sedans and at least three unmarked. The police spread themselves out, five on stage, several in the crowd, the rest at the edges. A police helicopter thrummed close, slowly circling the arena. The number of cops surprised Miller. He wondered again if they or the FBI knew about him. But, no, the cops just figured the speech might draw the same crazy **hajjis** who had hit the arena in the first place. If they'd really feared a sniper, they would have had tactical teams and undercover officers and their own snipers—big-time protection.

Still, Miller didn't mind the cops. They made the fight more fair. He'd only have one shot, for sure, and if he didn't get out of the hotel right away, they would be on him.

===

Then it was 1:01. He heard footsteps in the hall. A key card fit in the lock, the door swung open—

Allie's hair was jet-black under a Dallas Cowboys baseball cap, and she wore a baggy dress and a sweatshirt. Miller almost didn't recognize her. "Wow."

"Yeah, what a difference hair makes, right? I'd shave your head, but I don't want to leave any hair in the room." She grinned. "I took the stairs, no cameras. It's a circus down there. And they don't know it yet, but you're the star. You ready for this, babe?"

———

1:10 on the Toyota's dashboard clock. The streets around the arena were clogged with traffic, people driving in for the speech, walking over from downtown.

"He's popular, this guy," Shafer said. "Might give Duto a run. If we let him live."

"Funny," Wells said.

"Do I look like I'm joking." Shafer swung off Victory Park Lane into the garage behind the W, sped down a ramp past a sign that warned VALET PARKING ONLY—past the Mercedes sedans and BMW coupes, a bright yellow Porsche convertible—

And jammed on his brakes behind a black Dodge Ram. The pickup had a half-dozen bumper stickers on its tailgate and a white license plate, WASHINGTON in red.

Sometimes Shafer really did seem like a magician.

"First hotel I checked. Got the best sight lines

on the arena. Took me about five minutes. I slapped on a GPS in case they checked out early."

Wells stepped out, looked close at the Ram's tailgate, ran a finger over the LIVE FREE OR GET HIGH bumper sticker in the middle, touched the hole Miller had cut for his rifle. Wells understood the need for snipers, but he'd never liked them. They were both less and more than soldiers. In Afghanistan years before, he'd run across a particularly ugly practitioner. At least that one hadn't shot preachers for kicks.

Back in the SUV, he stuffed the Sig in the back of his jeans, pulled his sweatshirt over it. Not the best way to carry a pistol, but he'd be holding it soon enough. "Any ideas on finding the room?"

"As a matter of fact . . ."

———

They walked up to the valet station. "Afternoon," Shafer said.

"H-e-y—" The valet drawled out the word as if each letter were its own syllable. He had blue eyes, a perfect Roman nose, a granite chin. He should have been a model. The fact that he was parking cars for a living suggested he might not be the sharpest tool in the box. Wells hoped the deficit would work for them.

"Kind of a weird question, but you've got a

Ram pickup in the valet area," Shafer said. "Black. 1500 Quad Cab. I've been looking for that exact model for like six months. Can't find it anywhere."

"Huh."

"I'm thinking maybe I want to buy that one."

"That's cool."

Shafer looked at Wells. **I'd better break this into the smallest possible bites.** "So I need to talk to the guy who owns it."

"Sure, right."

Wells wondered if the valet was playing with them. But his eyes were as blue and empty as glacial melt.

"Give me his room number, I'll give you twenty bucks."

Greed and fear visibly struggled on the valet's face. **Twenty bucks! Not supposed to do that!**

"I'm just gonna knock on his door. If he's there, I'll ask him if it's for sale. If not, I'll leave a note."

"Twenty-five." As if he couldn't think of a larger sum.

Shafer handed him the money.

"What kinda car is it again?"

———

Sixty seconds later, Wells and Shafer were in the elevator, headed for the fourteenth floor.

"I don't think I knew what **too stupid to breathe** meant until now."

Wells pulled his pistol. "Focus."

The elevator door opened, and they stepped out, Wells leading. Room 1412 lay at the end of the hall on the right side. A room service tray sat by the door. Good. Wells could announce himself as room service, ask if Miller wanted the tray removed.

After he yelled and knocked for a few seconds, Miller would probably open up just to shoo him away. If not, Wells would go to Plan B. Plan B was shooting open the door.

———

Inside the room, Allie looked out over the plaza.

"I wish I could be here with you when you do it, Tom."

"I know." Though he didn't.

"Wait until he's a few minutes in, let him talk. I want him to be talking, thinking how wonderful he is." She leaned over, kissed him one more time, ran her hands down his back. Despite himself, he felt his skin tingle. "I can count on you, right?"

He nodded.

"I'll see you downstairs."

She kissed his cheek once lightly. Then she was gone.

The door to 1412 opened. Wells and Shafer were thirty feet down the hall. Wells lifted his pistol, expecting Miller. But a woman stepped out. Tall, black hair, in a long dress that tried, and failed, to hide her curves—

She turned to them as the room door locked behind her. Wells saw her blue eyes and knew who she was, who she had to be.

"Hello, sunshine!" Shafer yelled, the words meant to do nothing but confuse her. Slow her.

Wells sprinted, thirty feet, ten yards, not even a second and a half—

She reached into her purse, but too late, Wells was on her, two hundred ten pounds of muscle and bone. He slammed her against the wall so hard her head whipped like a shaken baby's. She groaned and dropped the purse. Wells kicked it to Shafer.

"Tom—" she yelled.

Her eyes opened wide, and she stopped herself as she realized the mistake she'd made. Wells knew, too. With his left hand, he covered her mouth. He put his body against hers and shoved her against the wall face-first, anyone watching might have seen brute sexuality. In truth, Wells wanted to be sure she didn't have a pistol hidden around her hips or strapped to her back, and pressing her was the fastest way to search her. He could smell the dye in her hair, feel her hips under her dress. She didn't shiver or try to fight him. She stayed still. Unafraid. Calculating.

She didn't have a weapon. It had been in the purse, he figured. He pulled her off the wall, turned her to face the door. Put his Sig to her head. "Be good."

Together, they waited for Miller to come for her.

Miller heard a scream.

"Allie?"

No answer. He ran for the door, pulled it open. A man he'd never seen, a big guy, a soldier, held Allie. A pistol to her head. Another man a few feet off.

Before Miller could say anything, the guy shoved Allie into the room. He followed her, kicked the door shut behind him so the second guy was stuck outside in the hall.

"Come on, Tom, sit, let's talk."

Outside, the police helicopter buzzed so close that the windows shook.

Miller had brought his pistol with him on this trip, of course. It was in the duffel. The duffel was at the base of the bed. The rifle was in the corner. He just had to keep thinking. He'd find a way to reach one or the other.

He sat on the edge of the bed. Allie stayed standing.

"Who are you?"

"Name's John Wells." The guy had a flat western accent. He was older than Miller had thought at first, but he had baseball bat forearms and the thick shoulders of a man who'd been winning fights his whole life.

"How do you know my name?"

"They sent him to kill us," Allie said.

"Hush," the man said. "You'll have a chance. Though if I were you, I'd keep my mouth shut." He looked at Miller. "You've done terrible things, Tom." Every word slow and low. "I don't know how she made you. I look at her, look at you, maybe I can guess."

A wave of shame, heavy and foul, washed over Miller.

"You don't know what you're talking about," Allie said.

"Allie. **Annalise.** Whatever your name really is. We're past that. I don't know what's going to happen to you, maybe the FSB has something to trade for you. But we know how this ends for him."

"He's crazy, Tom, don't listen to him—"

In one motion, fast, not even looking at her, the man brought up his left arm, backhanded Allie, a short, vicious swing—

The clap of knuckles on skin. Allie sprawled backward, banged into the silver couch in the center of the suite. She tripped over the arm but reached down, caught herself.

"Enough," the man said.

"I'll kill you," Allie said.

"I hope you try." He hadn't looked away from Miller. "Hurley, the Cardinal, Birman—you think it's a coincidence they all have anti-Islamic views? She used you to make folks angry at Muslims—"

"No," Miller said. He knew he ought to be furious with this man Wells for hitting Allie. Yet, somehow, Wells had acted with absolute authority, like he had no doubt Allie was guilty. And Allie hadn't questioned him, hadn't said, **Why did you do that?** She hadn't claimed innocence or begged for mercy. No, she'd threatened to kill him.

"You leave a spring gun in your trailer when you drove off to shoot Luke Hurley, Tom?"

Miller shook his head in confusion.

"Because there was one set when I got there last night. Shotgun wired to the front door. It killed the sheriff, Darby, the one who gave you the pickup. Tore up a Marine I know named

Winston Coyle, a good guy, three tours in Helmand. That's your girlfriend's friends."

With his left hand, Wells reached into his pocket for the ribbon. He held it like he was trying to hypnotize Miller, then let it flutter down. "Know what else I found, Tom? In the table by your bed. A picture. Of a dead Afghan kid. They leave that or was that yours?"

Miller had nothing to say.

———

Miller's silence was all the answer Wells needed. The Russians had seeded the apartment, but that pic had been Miller's. For a few seconds, none of them spoke. The thrum of the helicopter provided the only evidence that the world outside this room still existed. Poor Miller. With his scarred skin and his widow's peak. Fred Urquhart had been generous. Miller wasn't a five on a good day, he was a three. What had he thought when Allie came to him?

"I didn't kill him," Miller finally said. "The kid. But, yeah, it happened. It all happened."

The duffel bag was at Miller's feet, open. He reached for it.

Wells knew Miller must have a pistol in there. This was the moment to stop him, to tell him to lie facedown on the bed and to call the FBI.

"Don't touch it. Scoot back. I'll get the gun for you."

"Huh?"

"If I'd wanted to kill you, I would have already. Just do it."

Miller hesitated, moved back on the bed. "It's at the bottom, the end nearer you."

Wells reached into the duffel with his left hand, kept the Sig on Miller with his right. The pistol was where Miller had said. He pulled it. A 9-millimeter Glock, simple and professional.

"You ride with one in the chamber?"

Miller nodded. Wells released the magazine. It hit the floor, and he kicked it toward the door. Then he put the Glock on the end of the bed. It looked unloaded, but it had a round chambered, ready to fire.

Miller inched close, reached it, held it loose in his lap. He looked at Wells, his eyes defiant and lost at once, a trapped fox. Wells felt Allie behind him, edging toward the rifle in the corner. He let her. It was pointing the wrong way. And it was a single-shot bolt-action long gun. If she could reach it and bring it around and fire it before Wells dropped her, he deserved to get shot.

"One bullet. What'm I gonna do with that?"

"Whatever you like, Tom."

"So I can go for you and get smoked or just do it myself."

"Toss it down, I'll call the FBI, and we're done. Swear to you." Wells meant his promise. Though he didn't think he'd have to keep it. He didn't think Miller was going that way. Why he'd made sure Shafer was stuck outside.

Wells was taking a chance here, a hundred chances. What he was doing was illegal, maybe even immoral. He didn't care, he wanted to **break** Miller, and he didn't see another way.

"What do you do with her?" Miller looked at Allie.

"She'll be fine. My word. Soldier to soldier."

"Ever been in love, John? **Real** love? It's every-thing. I love her now, I'll always love her."

You poor lost soul.

===

Miller looked at the 9-millimeter in his lap. Sud-denly he flashed to the trailer, Allie holding this pistol in her hands, a perfect shooter's grip. Even then he'd known, hadn't he? The room shattered, and he was back in Afghanistan. He was six and waiting for his dad. He was in the Hyde Out, watching her watch him—

Allie sidled closer to the rifle, closer, only two steps away—

"Tom! Shoot him!" She broke for the rifle, picked it up, tried to turn—

Miller twisted the pistol in his lap and squeezed the trigger.

The blast echoed off the walls—

And the round caught Allie high in the back and spun her into the wall beside the window. Another perfect shot. She slid down the wall, leaving a bloody trail as she went, gasping, her eyes already vacant, and Miller knew he'd killed her.

———

Wells kept his Sig on Miller the whole time. Allie thumped down, gurgling, dying.

"John!" Shafer yelled from outside.

Wells ignored him.

Miller released the slide and pointed the pistol at Wells. He squeezed the trigger. The slide racked back and the pin popped into the naked chamber, the pistol as empty and useless as a paper cutout. **Click!**

"It's over, Tom." He felt the first stirrings of pity for this man, made himself push them down.

"Time for me to go." Miller released the slide, dry-fired again. **Click!**

"Not how it works."

"Nothing I can tell them. Spend the rest of my life trying to explain, it doesn't matter."

"Tell me."

"I was crazy for her. She said they'd raped her, all those men. I didn't want to know anything else. That's all there is—"

Click! Click!

"You know they're gonna lock me up until they put a needle in me, not asking you to cut me loose—" Miller closed his eyes. When he opened them again, they were clear and certain, the fear gone. "I'm sorry, John, truly I am."

Wells didn't know if this was mercy or justice, didn't know if it was his to grant. Only that he would. Over the thrum of the helicopter, he heard the ding of the elevator door, footsteps pounding down the hall.

"John!" Shafer yelled again.

Wells raised the Sig. Left it there. Giving Miller one last chance—

But Miller only nodded.

Wells pulled the trigger.

EPILOGUE

No one was happy with Wells.

Not the Dallas cops. Not the Feds. Not Shafer.

Wells could have lied, could have popped the mag back into Miller's Glock in the seconds before the police broke down the door. But he was done lying. At least today. Let someone else clean up the mess he'd made. Or make the mess he'd cleaned up.

"You gave him back his weapon?" the FBI special agent in charge of the Dallas office—a tall black man named Michael Jordan, and bald as his better-known namesake—said late that afternoon. They were in Jordan's office. No cameras. No recorders. No windows.

"Yes."

"With one round."

"Yes."

"Why?"

"I wanted him to have the choice."

"Why?"

The FBI guy sounded like Emmie now, a game she'd just learned to play. Every kid knew the rules. Keep asking **Why?** until you drive your parents nuts.

Because I hoped he'd draw on me. Because I hoped he wouldn't. Because I wanted it to be a fair fight. One I knew I'd win. Because he'd served, and I thought he'd do the right thing in the end. Whatever that might be. Because of Coyle. Because of Darby. Because . . . Because . . .

Wells shrugged.

"You think this is a game?"

I think I saved you a trial. I think Tom Miller told me all he knew, and Allie, a/k/a Annalise, a/k/a unknown female subject, wouldn't have said a word. She would have waited for the Kremlin to trade for her, waited her whole life, if necessary. She knew talking wouldn't have helped her. I think the only real question now is how far inside the Kremlin this plan went, and I doubt Allie, a/k/a Annalise, could have told us. I think we're way outside the realm of law enforcement, this is government-to-government business, and if you want justice, you're going to be waiting a while.

Wells shrugged again. Let Duto explain as he saw fit, conjure the perfect concoction of truth and lies to pour down the public's throat. With Allie dead, the only way the FBI could connect the original bombing to Miller was through Banamex. Wells figured Duto had already found a way to tell Mendoz **not** to make that connection for them. So the bombing would stand on its own. That investigation would stall in Quito. Hector Frietas wasn't around to answer questions, and his wife knew how to keep her mouth shut. The FBI would have a lot of smoke, and Russia might come up more than once. But no fire. They would ask Duto for more information from his mysterious source. Duto would say he'd pressed as hard as he could or national security interests prevented him from telling them more. Ultimately, the Bureau would be left with no way to prove the original source of the Banamex money or who had ordered the bombing.

Of course, Duto eventually would have to respond, to punish the FSB for what it had done. Wells wondered if Duto would invite him to the White House when that moment came. And what he'd say in answer.

"Mr. Wells, I'm talking to you. Do you think this is a game?"

Everything's a game.

———

By 10 p.m., the FBI had cut him loose. "I had my way, we'd be charging you," Jordan said.

Wells saluted him as the elevator doors closed. Shafer waited in the garage. "Prick."

"Takes one to know one."

"That wasn't your choice, John."

"Didn't see anybody else in the room."

Shafer stared at Wells with pop-eyed fury.

"I told him the truth, Ellis. If he'd tossed the pistol, I would have waited for the cavalry."

"Maybe. Or maybe you would have let her go for the rifle so you could shoot her."

"Maybe. Anything new about Coyle?"

"Last I heard, he was still stable, still on the ventilator. They were hoping to take him off tonight, but they decided to wait."

"That doesn't sound good." Wells wondered if he was betraying Coyle by going home. **No.** He had to see Anne.

"It's not."

———

They had predawn flights out of DFW, Shafer to Washington, Wells to Boston. Shafer had rented a room at the airport Hyatt so they could catch a few hours' sleep.

Neither Wells nor Shafer spoke again until they reached the fringes of the airport.

"Something else, John . . ."

Wells waited.

"It still doesn't make sense."

"**What** doesn't?"

"Paul Birman was setting up to be a giant pain for Vinny. Why kill him?"

"Come on. They wanted to make it look like a crazed wannabe convert is on the loose."

"They already had that. And she could have had Miller shoot fifty other guys who fit the anti-Islam profile. Why Birman? Why now? I'm telling you, something's missing."

"You're overthinking this, Ellis." Wells wished he felt as convinced as he sounded. Shafer's hunches had an unusual hit rate.

"You're **under**thinking it."

"I'm telling you that even in the unlikely event you're right, those two couldn't have helped us."

"We'll never know, will we? You go on home, John. Pat yourself on the back for a job well done."

The limousine carrying Paul and Eric had just pulled out of the Mansion on Turtle Creek for the fifteen-minute drive to the American Airlines Center when a fleet of black Chevy Yukons surrounded them. A dozen men in body armor jumped out.

"FBI! FBI!" In case giant white letters emblazoned on their black vests didn't give it away.

Eric knew before they'd said a word. A silly giggle rose in him. **How? How? How?** But he hardly needed to ask. Lucky Cousin Paul. Never bet against him.

Back in the Presidential Suite, the agent in charge explained.

A sniper at the W Hotel—unfortunately, he died at the scene before we could interview him—tentatively identified as a veteran named Tom Miller. Served in Afghanistan, two tours, suffered a traumatic brain injury . . . No ballistics match on the rifle as yet, but we have every reason to believe that this is the man responsible for the killings in St. Louis and Chicago.

Then the surprise:

A female was also in the room, she also died at the scene. She was white, late twenties. We

haven't identified her yet or her precise relationship with Miller . . . We'll show you pictures of both to see if you can identify them. Maybe you've seen them at other speeches . . .

Eric tried to parse what the agent wasn't saying. Not: **We killed him.** Not even: **We found him.** The FBI hadn't known Miller was in Dallas, much less that he was targeting Paul. Someone else had stumbled on Miller. Or chased him down.

We have to consider the risk that this is part of a larger plot. We recommend you return to Nashville until we know what you're facing, it's easiest to protect your home . . . The director's offered to fly out in the morning to brief you in person . . .

Any questions?

Paul shook his head. He'd kept himself together, but Eric knew he was terrified. Every few seconds, his eyes slid around the suite as if a monster might come through its walls.

Eric had a few questions of his own, but, unfortunately, he couldn't ask them: **A twenty-something white female**—had Adam Petersen called her from Maryland that morning? If he had, was she still holding the phone he'd called? What other evidence had she left? Most of all:

How did you find this guy, considering that forty-eight hours ago you didn't have a clue who he was?

"Thank you," Paul said. "I'd just like a few minutes to myself."

"Of course. I'll put men outside your door and on your terrace."

Paul nodded.

Then only Paul, Eric, and Paul's bodyguard, Jimmy Sanders, were left.

"I didn't get until now what it's like, Eric. What you went through all those years."

You still don't. No one actually shot at you, you fool. You didn't even know you were at risk until you weren't.

Paul's eyes flicked to Eric and then away. He looked to Eric like he needed a hug. Eric mustered thirty years of Army discipline and gave it to him. "I know. Awful. I'm sorry, cousin."

"I can't believe we moved up the speech—"

"That was your idea, wasn't it, Colonel?" Sanders said.

Eric looked at him. Sanders's face was flat. Neutral. He was stating a fact. Nothing more. Maybe.

"It was. I'm so, so sorry—"

"It's all right, cousin. You couldn't have known."

=====

The afternoon passed in slow motion. Eric arranged the flight to Nashville, put together a statement on what had happened, talked to the Dallas cops and the FBI. And every few minutes, he found himself reaching for his phone to call Petersen and ask for a one-way ride to Moscow.

But that night, when he closed his eyes, he hadn't.

The FBI, the CIA, all the rest, they didn't know. They weren't going to find out.

And he had to stay in Washington. He had work to do.

=====

Saturday, noon. Shafer landed at Reagan National to find a half-dozen calls waiting for him from Julie Tarnes. Each saying the same thing a little more urgently. **Call me.**

"Julie. What's up?"

"You know a guy named Jimmy Sanders?"

Shafer was surprised how happy hearing her brisk, no-nonsense voice made him. "I do not."

"Paul Birman's bodyguard. Ex-NYPD. Solid. Last night, he told the FBI that he wanted to talk personally to whoever found Miller. Pass along the Senator's congratulations, he said. They said no.

He said pretty please with sugar on top . . . And, by the way, you really want to piss Birman off right now? They got the message, kicked him to me. He has something to tell you. Says it's important."

"I just landed at National."

"Conveniently enough, so did he."

Sanders had flown from Nashville, left Birman not even twenty-four hours after the near miss?

"Guess it's important," Shafer said.

Tarnes stood just outside the security checkpoint, beside a forty-something guy. He was about her height and wore a dark blue suit and a tie a little too short. Shafer would have made him for an ex-cop even if Tarnes hadn't said so. Sanders had that relaxed awareness, the ability to pay attention without seeming to try.

Tarnes introduced them. Sanders stuck out a hand and looked at Shafer like he wasn't getting the joke.

"Nice job yesterday." The unspoken question: **You're the one who shot Tom Miller?**

"Thanks." Shafer wasn't going to explain, at least not until he knew what Sanders wanted. "What's so important that you broke Shabbat rules to come see me?"

"My rabbi said it was okay."

"Fair enough."

"Don't look so surprised. Might be Irish, but

I'm from New York." Sanders looked around, made sure no one was in earshot. "So, am I correct in assuming the FBI is less than fully informed on this? Based on the fact that if it had been up to them to find Tom Miller, we'd be making funeral arrangements for my boss."

"Possibly."

"They gonna find out?"

"There are obstacles."

"**Foreign** obstacles?"

"It's complicated."

Sanders gave Shafer a satisfied nod: **I figured.** "Nobody knows about this. Not even Paul. Maybe I should have told him, but, truth, I didn't know what he would do."

Shafer waited. They stood in a knot in the arrivals hall, passengers swirling by them, tugging roller bags and little kids, looking for carts and cousins. Sanders still couldn't seem to say what he'd come to say.

"Jimmy," Shafer said after a while. "I truly have no idea what you have. You want to play twenty questions or just spit it out like a grown-up?"

"It's Eric. Paul's cousin. You need to look at him."

Suddenly the last piece fit.

"I know it sounds crazy—"

"No," Shafer said. "It doesn't sound crazy at all."

New Hampshire, 1 p.m. Late winter now, the sun staying past 5, the snow crusty, melting during the day and freezing again each night. No flowers, no grass, no leaves, yet the cruelest days were unmistakably past.

Wells opened the front door to the farmhouse that was his and not his. Anne and Emmie were sitting, snugged on the rumpled couch, Anne's arm around Emmie, Emmie's hands high, telling a story so elaborate that for a moment she didn't see Wells step inside—

"Emmie," Anne said. Since Wells had last seen her, the pregnancy had taken over her middle.

"I'm **talking**, Mommy—"

"It's your dad."

Emmie jumped off the couch and ran at Wells, a cartoon of motion. "Daddy! Daddy! Daddy!" He scooped her, hugged her to him.

He had to quit. He couldn't quit.

He had to quit.

He couldn't quit.

"Hi, Em."

She stuck out her tongue to show him a pale green mint.

"She's discovered Altoids," Anne said.

Wells carried Emmie over to the couch, laid

her down, knelt beside Anne. She gave him a tiny smile that could have meant almost anything and then tapped her lips: **Kiss me.** "Gently. Unless you want me to throw up."

He did.

"How's the boy?"

Anne lifted her shirt. Wells watched as her belly rumbled, tiny earthquakes from the fists and feet inside.

"Just like his dad. Can't wait to get out."

ACKNOWLEDGMENTS

Wells is used to working alone, but I have plenty of partners. First and foremost, a shout-out to Neil Nyren, the editor of every Wells novel but **The Faithful Spy**. You may have noticed his name at the beginning of this book, and the dedication is well deserved. Thanks also to Ivan Held, Karen Fink, Alexis Sattler, and everyone else at Putnam.

Next up, a whole passel of lawyers: Robert Barnett and Deneen Howell for their advice and counsel; Dev Chatillon, who has kept me from getting into trouble more than once; and Mark Lanier, who practices what he preaches.

As always, Deirdre Silver and my brother, David, offered good advice on an early draft. Next time I'll take it. I promise. Mark Herron offered advice on sniping. Any errors are mine.

This goes without saying, but Jackie, Lucy, and Ezra have taught John (and me) what really matters.

And finally, thanks to all of you for keeping me and John honest. I can't wait to hear what you think! You know where to find me. (Just in case: alexberensonauthor@gmail.com or facebook.com/alexberensonauthor.)

Until next time.